BAD MEDICINE

BAD MEDICINE

———— ✕ ✕ ✕ ✕ ✕ ————

AIMÉE & DAVID THURLO

A Tom Doherty Associates Book
New York

This is a work of fiction. All of the characters and events portrayed in this novel are either fictitious or are used fictitiously.

BAD MEDICINE

Copyright © 1997 by Aimée and David Thurlo

This book is printed on acid-free paper.

A Forge Book
Published by Tom Doherty Associates, Inc.
175 Fifth Avenue
New York, NY 10010

Forge® is a registered trademark of Tom Doherty Associates, Inc.

Library of Congress Cataloging-in-Publication Data

Thurlo, Aimée.
    Bad medicine / Aimée & David Thurlo.—1st ed.
        p.   cm.
    "A Tom Doherty Associates book."
    ISBN 0-312-86328-4
    1. Navajo Indians—Fiction.   I. Thurlo, David.   II. Title.
PS3570.H82B34   1997
813'.54—dc21   97-23670
                                                                   CIP

First Edition: November 1997

Printed in the United States of America

0 9 8 7 6 5 4 3 2 1

To the following three people who helped make this series a success:

Melissa Singer, an extraordinary editor who supported us from the very beginning;

Cherry Weiner, who believed in us and gave us our start in the business;

Sue Stone, who has blurred all the lines as editor, friend, and agent.

ACKNOWLEDGMENTS

———✖ ✖ ✖———

With special thanks to Bill Hilburn, Jr., for his technical advice, and especially for his help in getting inside the heads and hearts of our cops. And to Mary Ann who stands beside him.

And to Walt Mestas of the Office of the Medical Investigator for all his help and for being there with the right answers when we needed him.

BAD MEDICINE

ONE

—— ✖ ✖ ✖ ——

Special Investigator Ella Clah glanced at the dark clouds that loomed over Beautiful Mountain as she drove down the highway. The sacred peak rose toward that brooding sky as if imploring rain from Water Sprinkler, the rain bringer of the gods. The old ones of her tribe said that the mountains were living beings and, in a way, she agreed with them. The four sacred mountains that bordered their land inspired a sense of history and permanency that was hard to explain, and impossible to deny. They were a part of her and the *Dineh*.

The smell of dry air and dust filled her nostrils. It was a parched, skin-drying sensation that spoke volumes to anyone who'd been raised on the reservation. Unless the summer rains came early this year, sheep would be hard-pressed to find forage, and crops would wither out in the fields.

Thunder echoed in the distance, resonating off the metal skin of her Jeep like the roll of a kettle drum. Despite the light show on the horizon, if today turned out like yesterday and the day before, there wouldn't be any rain. The clouds would dissipate over the mountains, and the sun would break through just before dusk to warm the evening.

Ella shifted in her seat, tugging at the seat belt and wondering why she couldn't shake that vague sense of uneasiness that was nagging at her. It was more than the possible 10-27, the homicide, she was on her way to investigate. Trouble was brewing on the reservation, as evidenced by an increasing level of bad news and violence creeping across the area. It wasn't just due to the sudden burst of warm weather after a long, dry winter either. It was much more than that. She could feel it as clearly as the blast of dry air blowing across her face through the gap in the window.

Some said that she had supernatural powers, a legacy handed down through her family. But that was only because they didn't understand how a cop developed special instincts, or how well-honed her training had made her subconscious observations. At times, such things could spell the difference between life and death but, at the moment, they tugged at her mental shirttail like a child trying to get a mother's attention.

Hearing the wind howling through the window, she gripped the wheel with one hand and cranked the glass down an inch more, easing the shriek to a dull roar. It was too cool right now for the air conditioner, but, inside the Jeep with the windows closed, it got stuffy and uncomfortable in a hurry, despite the open vents.

Miserable day, miserable mood, and now, on top of everything else, her skin was crawling. That was a feeling she'd learned not to ignore.

In deference to her FBI training, which had taught her to block out distractions and focus on the task at hand, Ella forced her thoughts back to the crime scene she was enroute to. From the initial report, she'd learned a Navajo man had been found beaten to death. The patrol officer sent to the area would secure the site until she and the crime-scene team arrived. On the Rez that task wouldn't be much of a problem. Usually, little effort was needed here to keep civilians from satisfying their morbid curiosity. Fear of the *chindi,* the evil in a man that stayed earthbound after death and caused problems for the living, was still strong here.

Distracted again by a sense of unease, Ella swept the area ahead with eagle-sharp eyes. All of her senses warned of danger drawing closer with each mile. She stared at the ragged cliffs that jutted up from the desert floor like enormous stone gods with their backs to a wall. The view looked the same as always, but something about Four Corners *felt* different today. Ella's hand went to the badger fetish that hung from a leather thong around her neck. Her brother had given it to her for protection and it comforted her now.

Ella's radio broke her musings with its crackle. Picking up the mike, she identified herself.

"SI Unit One, proceed along highway sixty-four west of Hogback to investigate a reported ten-forty-seven creating a traffic hazard," the dispatcher ordered. "We have no other units in the area free to respond."

"Negative, PD. I'm enroute to a 'twenty-seven south of Morgan Lake." She didn't have time to investigate a drunken driver complaint now. If by some miracle it did rain today, all the physical evidence would have to be gathered before moisture destroyed the integrity of the scene.

"Channel Six," came another voice, only a few seconds after she'd racked the mike.

Ella recognized the voice of Big Ed Atcitty, the police chief. She switched to the new frequency and picked up the mike again, guessing what he would say. "I'm enroute to the ten-twenty-seven, Big Ed."

"Take the ten-forty-seven, Shorty," the chief ordered, using the special nickname he'd given her, though Ella stood a head taller than he.

"But—"

"The victim will still be dead if you arrive ten minutes later. Get that driver off my highway first."

"Ten-four."

She replaced the mike, grumbling. They needed more cops on the Rez, but that wouldn't happen as long as the current budget crisis prevailed, especially with federal funds drying up and the tribe relying on its own resources. Passing the Morgan Lake turnoff, she continued west, away from the murder scene.

Ella was surprised when, instead of dissipating, her uneasiness increased though she was moving away from the crime scene. She tried to ignore the sensation, but the certainty that she was about to start down a dangerous path made her heart race.

Less than ten minutes later, as she drove toward Shiprock, she spotted a slow-moving vehicle ahead. The cherry red sedan, in mint condition, would have been enough to get her attention even if it hadn't been veering all over the road. Pickups and inexpensive sedans were common on the Rez, but not too many local folks drove flashy cars. Money was just too tight, and the roads were lousy.

Ella took note of the prestige plate that read ANGI then flashed the portable lights she'd affixed to the dashboard of her unmarked Jeep. The drunk driver in the car didn't slow down or show any sign that she was even aware of the signal. Ella tried the siren, but the driver seemed oblivious to that as well.

Moving over as if to pass, Ella pulled up in the left lane beside the red car to ID the driver and signal her to pull over. As she did, Ella saw that the woman was shaking, as if in the throes of a convulsion.

Ella quickly checked to see if the road was still clear ahead, then looking back at the driver, sighed with relief when she saw that the seizure, or whatever it was, had passed.

She kept her eyes on the young woman a moment longer, trying to assess the situation. Then, abruptly, "Angi" turned her head and looked directly at Ella. The girl's eyes were blank, glazed over as if she were stoned. There was no recognition, no sense of awareness.

Ella felt her skin grow cold. She took her foot off the accelerator, and fell back behind the red car, weighing her options. Should she pull ahead to warn oncoming traffic, or try to force the dangerous vehicle off the road? The narrow roadbed and sandy arroyos would make the latter option risky, not to mention the regularly spaced dump-truck loads of gravel left by the highway department crews upgrading the road.

Ella noted the long, wide curve of the asphalt ahead. After they made it around the corner, if the road was clear, she could pick a spot to force the driver off to the side. Until then, she had to make sure the driver wouldn't have a head-on with another vehicle.

She accelerated past the red sedan, sirens and flashers on again in case anyone was coming. As she completed the move, she checked the car in her rearview mirror. The red sedan had failed to negotiate the turn. All Ella could see was a cloud of dust where the vehicle had left the road.

Ella worked the brakes and turned the wheel hard, putting the Jeep into a controlled one-eighty with a screech. As she sped back, she called the accident in. Seconds later, she pulled to a stop by the side of the road, grabbed her hand-held radio, and looked down the slope. The red car had left the highway, nosed over into the shallow wash, then slid sideways and rolled down a steep embankment. It had come to a stop upside down, with the driver's compartment half buried in a mountain of gravel. It was impossible to tell anything about the condition of the woman inside.

As she slid down the incline on the seat of her pants, the notion that someone was watching her became a certainty in her mind. She tried to brush aside her uneasiness by telling herself that if someone *was* there, she hoped they would show themselves and help. She could use an extra pair of hands to dig out the driver.

Her forced optimism did little to ease the pitch and roll of her stomach. Her muscles were taut, and her hearing almost painfully sharp as she listened for sounds that didn't belong.

Focusing on the task that required her immediate attention, she began to scoop away the gravel by hand, trying to uncover the driver's door. She could hear the car radio playing an impassioned ad for a local auto dealership, and used that to guide her to the driver. As the smell of gasoline filled her nostrils, she slowed down. She had to avoid creating a spark. Gasoline was leaking through the gravel into the ground, staining the dry earth a reddish brown, like dried blood.

"Hang on. I'm going to get you out!" Ella yelled, hoping the driver was still conscious and able to understand her. The more she thought about it, though, the less likely that seemed. The woman hadn't appeared coherent before the accident. Whatever she had been on had definitely erased reality from her mind.

Ella carefully swept aside the gravel, blocking out her fear that the gas tank would explode taking the driver and her with it. Precious seconds turned into minutes as she worked, but at least the smell of gasoline didn't grow any stronger.

She stopped abruptly, her fingers scratched and raw, as she heard a woman's voice from inside the car. "Hello! Hang on!" Ella shouted, then listened intently. A moment later, she realized the voice she'd heard had just been the radio.

Finally she caught her first glimpse of the driver through the broken side window. The body, held upside down in the seat belt harness, was slumped in a peculiar rag-doll fashion against the deflated air bag. Blood matted the victim's long, dark hair.

Ella reached inside, avoiding the broken glass, and switched off the ignition. Then, taking a deep breath, she tugged at the door, struggling against the weight of the gravel and damaged hinges, until it opened halfway.

"Take it easy," Ella said quietly, though she strongly suspected the woman was beyond the reach of such assurances now. Fearing the worst, she reached for the pulse point at the victim's neck, and found none.

Ella sat back on her knees and looked the body over closely. Despite the numerous shallow cuts, there didn't seem to be any clear cause of death. The air bag had deployed, protecting the girl from impact with the steering wheel and windshield. Fortunately, determining the cause of death was not her job. That task would fall to Carolyn Roanhorse, the tribal M.E.

Ella stood up and moved away, aware of the smell of death that was already permeating the interior of the car. It was an odor distinct and separate from the acrid smell of gasoline and hot oil she'd detected outside the car. It wasn't decomposition either, it was death, pure and simple. Carolyn would have argued that it was Ella's imagination, but it was an argument that Ella would have never conceded. Death itself *had* a smell.

Ella crouched down and reached for the young woman's purse, which lay beside the dome light of the inverted vehicle.

She extracted the driver's license and, as she read the dead woman's name, her stomach tightened into a knot. "Angi" was Angelina Yellowhair. Now the fancy car and prestige plate suddenly made sense. State Senator James Yellowhair served on several powerful government committees. From what Ella had heard, the politician doted on his daughter. This news would hit him hard.

Ella knew she couldn't remove the body from the vehicle alone, so she climbed back up the embankment to get her evidence kit and camera. She'd photograph the scene while she waited for the emergency personnel she'd called to arrive. Everything here would have to be carefully documented. The victim's erratic driving and behavior was bound to raise questions nobody, especially a powerful politician running for re-election, would want to answer.

As she went to her Jeep, she heard the wail of a siren as a tribal police vehicle flew around the curve. Ella waited as the patrolman pulled up and climbed out.

Joseph Neskahi, recently promoted to sergeant, strode up to her. He was as he'd always been, Ella observed, a packet of compressed energy shaped like a safe—square and hard. "Sorry it took me so long," he said. "I was checking out a vandalized irrigation pump down by Waterflow and almost got stuck getting out of there. What have you got?" He looked down the embankment at the overturned car and shook his head in disgust.

She gave him a quick rundown while he wrote notes rapidly on a small notepad. As soon as she passed him the victim's driver's license, Neshaki looked up. "That's going to make things interesting around here."

"I didn't have a chance to photograph the scene yet, so make sure you cover the entire site. We'll need every detail. Also, tell the EMTs about the convulsions. I'm not sure if she was on something, or just ill, but they should take that into account when they handle that body. After you're finished here, try to locate the person who phoned in the report about the drunken driver. I have a feeling the senator's going to have a lot of questions, and I'd like someone else to corroborate what I saw prior to the accident."

"You're not sticking around?"

"I can't. I was enroute to a probable ten-twenty-seven south of Morgan. I'd like to get there as soon as possible."

Joseph Neskahi nodded. "I heard the patrolman's call earlier today." He looked around, gazing at the mesas thoughtfully. "You picking up any vibes about what happened over there at that crime scene?"

His tone and his worried expression made it unnecessary for him to elaborate. The problem the tribe had experienced with skinwalkers in the recent past was never far from anyone's mind. And almost everyone, including Neskahi, had heard about Ella's "intuition." Her hunches had a tendency to be disturbingly accurate.

She looked around again. The only vibes she had now were centered here. But she had nothing to base them on. Still, she was honor bound to do whatever she could to protect a fellow officer. "I'm not so worried about what I'll find at that other site as I am about what is here. This case is going to raise lots of questions. Be careful out here. Watch out for the scene . . . and for yourself. If you need me, you know where I'll be."

As she drove away, Ella felt her hands grow clammy. Trouble was brewing. She could feel it as clearly as the air blowing through her open window.

It took Ella twenty minutes to get to the scene of the murder: a small, steep arroyo running parallel to the Four Corners power plant access road and the largest open-pit coal mine in the west. By the time she arrived, the crime scene unit and the tribe's M.E., Dr. Carolyn Roanhorse, were already there. Unfortunately, so was Dwayne Blalock, the FBI agent assigned to this jurisdiction. Things had changed in the last few years, more of this kind of investigation was placed in the hands of the tribal police, but the FBI's presence remained. Murder on the Rez was still a federal crime.

Ella approached Detective Ute, the officer in charge of the scene, and stepped aside as Sergeant Tache, working with Blalock at his shoulder, photographed each piece of physical evidence in place. "What have you got?"

Ute held out the clipboard where he was writing a narrative description and showed her the name, "Stanley Bitah." "Have you heard of the victim?"

She nodded, respecting the tribal custom not to mention the deceased by name, particularly here where he'd met his death. "He's an activist in this area. I've seen him mentioned in a few newspaper stories. Who found the body?"

Detective Ute shrugged. "The helicopter pilot who inspects the power lines spotted the body as he flew over at noon." Ute gestured toward the steel towers standing in a row all the way to the horizon, like armless giants.

"What else can you tell me?" Ella continued.

"The deceased worked as a mechanic, helping maintain the heavy equipment at the mine. He was most likely beaten to death with some kind of club. I'll know more in a while."

Officer Justine Goodluck, Ella's petite young assistant, came out from behind a small stand of junipers. "We've really just started focusing on identifying and protecting the physical evidence. Even FB-Eyes over there is helping out." Justine nodded toward Blalock, who was placing small, wire and plastic flags beside footprints for Tache. The agent had received the nickname from Navajo officers because one of his eyes was blue, and the other brown.

"I can tell you a little more of what we've learned so far," Justine continued. "Okay, Harry?"

Ute nodded and looked back down at his narrative. Ella followed the youthful cop/lab tech toward an area filled with scuff marks, footprints, and droplets of blood. "Clearly, a struggle took place here."

Ella studied the ground. "From the spray patterns of blood on the ground, and the other signs, I'd say the murder also occurred here."

Justine nodded. "That's what Detective Ute and the others concluded, too." She crouched by Ella, and pointed. "Four people were present, and one—not the victim—ran away down the arroyo, escaping, maybe."

"Do you know where the others went?"

She shook her head. "I was just about to follow up on that when you arrived."

They followed three sets of tracks, which ended abruptly at the highway. Black tire marks indicated a vehicle had taken off in a hurry. "This is a bit of luck," Ella said. "These tracks are really clear. Ask Tache to take several shots and see if you can identify the type of vehicle they belong to. Blalock might be able to hazard a guess on the spot, so make sure you ask him. He told me recently that he was becoming an expert on tire patterns common to the area."

"I'll take care of it."

"I'm going to talk to Dr. Roanhorse," Ella said, glancing up and seeing that the medical examiner was working alone, as usual, talking into her tape recorder as she examined the body.

As Ella went up to her friend, she couldn't help but sympathize. Nobody ever hung around Carolyn for long. Fear of the *chindi*, of contamination by the dead, was always present among those of their tribe. Even the kids, who seemed to go out of their way to discount other traditional Navajo beliefs, stayed clear of the M.E.

As she approached, Carolyn switched off her tape recorder. "I was wondering when you'd get here."

"I had another emergency call on the way. I'll tell you about it in a little bit, since it's going to end up on your desk, too. But first, do you have an opinion on how this all went down?" Ella looked at the victim, and had to force herself not to cringe. The murder had been particularly brutal.

"In layman's terms, this man died as a result of several—four or five—heavy blows to the left side of the skull. The last three or four were probably unnecessary. The location and angle of the attack suggests the killer was right-handed, or had a wicked backhand for a lefty. The murder weapon was a blunt object, like a pipe, wooden club, or something of that nature. He's been dead less than eight hours, which would put the approximate time of death around dawn, plus or minus an hour or two. It's pretty straightforward from what I can see." Carolyn stood up slowly, and signalled for Ute to join her.

Ute, who always wore a glum expression, looked even more miserable now, as he put down his clipboard and walked toward them.

"You like to pick on poor Harry, don't you?" Ella whispered.

Carolyn smiled. "Don't begrudge me my little pleasures," she said, reaching for the body bag.

While Carolyn and Detective Ute loaded the victim's body into the M.E.'s van, Ella walked up to where Tache and Justine were working.

Blalock was nearby, placing blood-encrusted sand from individual droplets into separate plastic vials, labeling them as he worked.

"Hello Ella," Blalock nodded congenially, looking up from his work for a moment. "How's your family?"

"Doing real well. I'll tell them you asked." Ella knew that her mom and brother didn't care too much for Blalock, but at least they had acquired some grudging respect for the man. He was dealing with the *Dineh* with a lot more tact nowadays, especially since working with her the past two years. As ex-FBI herself, she had managed to instill in Blalock the need to pay more attention to their cultural differences if he wanted to get anywhere on a case.

Ella glanced at Tache, who had finished loading the camera. "Have you photographed the murder weapon?" she asked him.

"We haven't found it, at least not yet."

"Why would the killer or killers take it with them?" Ella mused. "They didn't try to hide the body, or obscure other evidence."

Justine joined them. "One of the three had enough presence of mind to balk at the thought of leaving a club full of fingerprints behind?"

"Maybe the blood tests will reveal that more than one person was cut up enough to bleed," Ella said. "That will help us later on in the investigation when we have a list of suspects. I have a feeling this crime is going to be far more complicated than it looks." Ella looked at Justine, then Tache. Wariness shone in their eyes. They knew about her hunches.

"It's time to get to that twenty-four/twenty-four rule," Ella continued. "The two most important things in an investigation are the last twenty-four hours of a victim's life and whatever we find within twenty-four hours after the body is discovered. Get me everything you can find on the deceased," she said, looking at Justine. "I want to know about his activities at the coal mine and his personal life. I want to know who he trusted, who he worked with, who he hung around with, and who his enemies were."

"I'll get right on that," Justine said, writing everything down in her notebook.

Ella looked at Tache. "I'd like the photos you've taken here developed as soon as you get back. Have them all on my desk before you go home tonight and make copies for Blalock, too."

Carolyn came up as Tache went back to help FB-Eyes, who was still collecting bloodstained sand. "You're really pushing on this one. How come?"

Ella looked at Carolyn, then Justine.

"I have things to do." Justine said, turning to leave.

Ella shook her head. "No, you might as well hear this now instead of at the station. I was detoured on my way over here answering a ten-forty-seven—a drunken driver—endangering traffic. But that's not what I found." She recounted what she'd seen, the convulsions, the unresponsive stare. "I have a feeling we're going to be getting a lot of heat on that one, and just at a time when we're going to need all our energy for this case."

"Why should that accident be different from any other drug- or alcohol-related death that happens on the Rez? Who was in the car?" Justine prodded.

"Senator Yellowhair's daughter." Ella saw Justine take one step back as if she'd been hit. She reached out to steady her assistant.

"Are you okay, cousin?"

"I went to school with her . . . " Justine muttered, her voice shaky. "Are you sure—"

Ella nodded. "I'm sorry."

"You said she was under the influence, or having some kind of attack?" Carolyn asked.

"I saw what appeared to be convulsions, but I can't even guess at a cause," Ella answered. "That's your department."

Carolyn expression was guarded. "You want toxicology?"

"I want you to establish the cause of death, like you always do. Unless I miss my guess, the *accident* didn't kill her."

"You'll most likely want a full autopsy then." Carolyn took a deep breath, then let it out again.

"Is there something wrong?" Ella looked at her friend curiously. She'd never seen Carolyn hesitate on anything pertaining to her job. Senator Yellowhair was bound to cause problems, it was certainly one of his major talents, but Carolyn had never been known to run from trouble.

"Let's just say I know how our senator operates," Carolyn answered with obvious distaste. "My findings are always substantiated by tests, so I can cover myself and my department. But he'll object to my doing tests or an autopsy on his daughter because he's going to want her buried quickly and without scandal. You can expect major-league trouble from him when I don't release the body right away. Cover yourself as best you can. He'll be after somebody's ass on this. Count on it."

Ella nodded. "Don't worry. I can handle whatever comes. I know what I saw."

"Which case do you want given priority?" Carolyn asked.

"This one, the homicide. Do the workup on it first. The faster we move, the better chance we have of not having it end up a real luncher."

"We won't have to eat this case," Justine answered flatly. "We'll solve it."

"Idealism of youth," Carolyn said, walking away.

Ella saw the spark of anger in Justine's eyes and laughed. "Relax, Justine. She just said that to annoy you. We'll do our jobs. And, speaking of our jobs, let's get back to work. There's a lot left for us to do here before we can release the scene."

TWO

Ella sat at her computer. She'd run a check on Bitah, and he was certainly no model citizen. From what she'd turned up, he'd been arrested for drunk and disorderly just two days before his death. He'd been in a fight with an Anglo by the name of Louis Truman, fellow employee of the mine, in a Farmington bar. The two of them had pretty much torn up the place. Truman, unlike Bitah, had no previous local arrest record.

Ella picked up the telephone and dialed Blalock's mobile number. She wanted to know more about Truman's background, and experience told her that the Bureau's files would be more comprehensive than her own. Though the Bureau was supposed to cooperate with tribal law enforcement, she hated asking for favors, and she knew that was exactly how Blalock would view her request.

Ella smiled as Blalock practically barked his name into the phone. "I see you're in Bureau mode," she said.

"Whatcha need?" he snapped. "I already spoke to your assistant earlier today. The vehicle tracks are too common to identify."

"Were you voted Mr. Congeniality in your graduating class at the Bureau?"

"First runner-up. How did you guess? Is there a point to this conversation?"

"I need you to check the Bureau's computer and see if you come up with anything on an Anglo by the name of Louis Truman. He lives in Farmington," she said, giving him the background and Truman's street address.

"I'll run it through, then meet you at the guy's house. I assume you'll want to question him ASAP."

"I can be there in forty minutes. How about you?"

"Same ETA. I'll see you there."

Ella picked up her jacket and stepped out of her tiny office. On her way down the hall she passed the lab. Justine was hard at work processing the trace evidence. Tache was nowhere to be seen, but the red darkroom light was on. Ella continued walking down the hall. Justine's talents were better used here for now than assisting at the upcoming questioning.

Ella drove out of the station parking lot, taking the highway east. As she approached the low-income housing area that bordered the road, she noticed fresh graffiti spray-painted on the cinder block walls. The reservation was changing, and it wasn't all for the better. Youth gangs, an ever-growing presence she'd thought she'd left behind in L.A., were now making their appearance here as well. Navajo kids, caught between cultures and needing something to identify with, were lured by the excitement gangs offered them. Passing the subdivision's main turnoff, Ella saw kids wearing baseball caps on backwards, baggy pants, and black pro-team jackets staring at her.

Drug use and juvenile crime were on the upswing, especially auto theft, and Jeeps were popular targets. She shook her head sadly. Though the tribe would survive this surge of lawlessness, as it had other dangers through the decades, anything that attacked their youth threatened the very existence of the *Dineh*. She wondered what toll this would take on the tribe, before harmony was restored again.

Ella continued her drive through the gap in the Hogback that had been worn by the San Juan River, passing the coal mine and power plant in the distance. It was here that Bitah had been employed, and here he had worked as a Navajo rights advocate on the side. She'd never agreed with the methods of most activists but, in this case, her sympathies were with them. It was hard to see Anglo companies making a profit from the few resources on tribal land. Though it was true that the companies that came in were required to hire a certain number of Navajos and pay the tribe a percentage of the profits, it saddened her to know that so much of the money from these resources left the reservation. But the *Dineh* needed jobs, and they hadn't had the expertise to manage the operations themselves. That's what had opened the doors to outsiders.

At least nowadays, Anglo companies were required to work with the land rather than ravage Mother Earth. Yet that was small consolation to those who'd had to relocate their homes and deal with contaminated water.

As Ella left the reservation, she brought her mind back to the case. The murder of a Navajo rights activist was bound to foster even more unrest within the tribe. The faster she cleared up the matter, the better off everyone would be.

Twenty minutes later, as she entered the city of Farmington, Ella weaved through the residential streets until she found the address she was searching for—a small wood-framed cottage in a rundown area among the cottonwoods which lined the river.

Ella pulled up next to the curb and saw a man in his midthirties sitting out on the porch in a folding chair. He was drinking something from a can, but from her vantage point she couldn't tell if it was a beer or a soft drink. She bet on beer. Blalock wasn't in sight yet but, to be fair, she'd made good time and was a few minutes early.

As she switched off the ignition, the man rose from his chair and headed her way. Ella noted he was weaving slightly as he approached, and the beer can she now could see clearly in his hand, confirmed his condition. Hating to deal with drunks, she decided to remain in her car until she could gauge his mood.

"Who the hell are *you?*" he demanded, coming out into the street and over to the driver's-side door.

"I'm Special Investigator Ella Clah, of the Navajo Tribal Police. If you are Louis Truman, I'd like to ask you a few questions."

The man's expression suddenly went sour, and he stepped back, throwing the can against her windshield. The container bounced off the glass without leaving a scratch, spraying beer everywhere.

He splashed himself as much as the car, and that only made him more angry. "I'm so sick of you Indians!" He crossed over to the toy-scattered lawn and picked up a kid's baseball bat. "Question this!" he yelled, swinging the bat down on the hood of the Jeep with a thump, leaving a groove in the sheet metal. "You've got no jurisdiction here." He stomped around the vehicle toward her door again.

Ella reached for the PR-24, the new standard-issue baton with a side handle, and pulled back from the window, as if terrified. The moment Truman drew close, she threw the door open hard, catching him in the chest. He stumbled back into the street, gasping for air. The bat flew across the asphalt, out of his reach.

Ella jumped out of the car and pushed Truman back toward the lawn using the tip of her baton. He tried to scramble to his feet so, with a quick lunge to the right, she hit him behind the knees. As Truman tumbled to the grass, she knelt on his back as she cuffed him. "Calm down," she snapped. "You're in enough trouble already."

She was lifting him to his feet when an approaching siren wailed in a short burst. She glanced up and saw Blalock's car screech to a halt behind her own.

"What's going on?" Blalock stepped casually out of his vehicle. "This Truman?"

Ella filled him in quickly. "Will you call Farmington PD and have him taken in? I'd also like that baseball bat bagged and tagged as evidence. The M.E. said Bitah was killed with a blunt object."

"I didn't kill nobody," Truman slurred. "You're just looking for some white man to put in jail."

Ella shoved him against the Jeep. "Pipe down," she snapped, then read Truman his rights.

"I'm going to ask for a search warrant while I'm at it, too," Blalock said, walking toward his car.

Ella held on to Truman, trying to shut out the tirade of obscenities while she waited for FPD to arrive. "I've heard all of those words before, buddy," she said, feigning boredom. "How about telling me something that may actually reduce your jail time?"

Truman sputtered, then tried to yank away. Ella pushed him back against the Jeep, forcing him to lean forward and stay off balance. "Your choice: You can stand here, or lay facedown on the ground."

Truman coughed, then made a gurgling noise. "I'm sick, let go."

Ella eased her hold and a second later, Truman threw up on the grass. He continued retching off and on for at least five minutes.

Ella rolled her eyes as Blalock and a Farmington cop finally approached. "He's all yours," she told the cop.

The cop glanced at the grass, then at Truman, and grimaced. "Thanks for making sure he was on empty before I loaded him into my car."

"We aim to please," Ella answered.

As the cop took away the prisoner, along with the bagged and tagged baseball bat, Blalock leaned back against Ella's Jeep, cellular phone in hand. "It shouldn't take us long to get that warrant. There's a judge I work with here. Under the circumstances, I think she'll do her best to cut through the red tape." He looked at the house. "Anybody else in there?"

"If there is, they haven't shown themselves. Does he have a family?"

"His wife's at work, and his kid's in school. As far as I know, nobody else lives there. But that doesn't mean he couldn't have company."

As the minutes ticked by, Ella kept her gaze on the windows of the house, searching for signs of a reclusive visitor. "Did you get anything on Truman?"

"He's an interesting piece of work. He was arrested once in

Utah for attacking some environmentalists and, although we can't prove it, we suspect that he's part of a radical militia group that's shown up lately in New Mexico: white supremacist, antigovernment, global conspiracy stuff. He was also hauled in a few years back on income tax evasion."

"What's a white racist doing working for the tribe?"

"Your guess is as good as mine, but it probably creates a little tension at the company picnic."

A half hour passed as they waited, and Blalock's patience was wearing thin. When, at last, another FPD patrol officer came up carrying the search warrant, he snatched it from the woman's hands. "About time."

"It wasn't *that* long. Damned fast, if you ask me," Ella commented, nodding to the officer, who simply rolled her eyes at Blalock and walked back toward her unit.

"Who's asking?" Blalock shot back.

"Right." Ella managed to keep her temper. What an incredible talent Blalock had for pissing people off. It was only recently, however, that she'd discovered it was his way of gaining the upper hand. Keeping a cool head when others around him were too angry at him to think straight, allowed him to emerge as the one in command every time. What annoyed her most was that it had taken her so long to figure him out.

Blalock strode up to the front door, pistol in hand. "FBI!" he shouted, then kicked back the partially open door as he flattened against the side wall.

As the door swung back on its hinges, Ella scarcely breathed. They waited, but no sounds came from inside.

Ella followed Blalock in and looked around, her pistol ready. Three tense minutes later, after it was obvious no one else was home, she holstered her weapon.

Blalock walked to the bookcase and stared at the contents with a grimace. "Will you take a look at this pile of crap? Hitler would have loved this guy. Books, tapes, everything for the well-read sociopath and his impressionable child."

"Interesting," Ella said, joining him and reading some of the titles. Racial hate books slightly outnumbered the how-to volumes geared for the amateur anarchist. "I'd like to be there when you question him. Any objections?"

"None. I'm going to let him sweat it out in jail and sober up first, though. How about if we meet at the Farmington PD around six this evening?"

Ella checked her watch. It was three now. "Sounds good to me. Do you mind if I have Justine pick up that bat and check it out? If she finds anything, Carolyn can run the necessary checks on her equipment and do a blood comparison."

"I have no problem with that, and I don't think the PD will either. I'll sign the release." He went through the house with her but, besides two legal semiautomatic weapons, gunsmithing tools and reloading gear, and over five hundred rounds of ammunition, found nothing out of the ordinary.

"This case is going to involve people on and off the reservation. Shall we keep it simple?" Blalock suggested. "You question all of the Navajos, including Bitah's coworkers. They're more likely to talk to you. I'll take the Anglos."

"All right."

"Something's bugging you, Ella." Blalock observed. "You usually argue more and take a few potshots. What are you holding back?"

"Just a feeling," she answered. "I'm not ready to talk about it yet."

Ella waited for Blalock to sign the protocol releasing the bat to her department before leaving. Since the evidence had already been taken in, she made arrangements for Justine to pick it up at the Farmington station.

As Ella drove back to the reservation, her stomach felt tied up in knots. Nothing was making a great deal of sense to her right now. First, the murder of a Navajo rights activist, and next, the same day and not ten miles away as the crow flies, a young woman had taken leave of her senses *and* the highway.

Now, to top everything else off, they'd taken in a suspect to the murder and learned he was a white supremacist who currently worked at the Navajo mine. The whole thing made her skin crawl.

As she sped down the highway toward the recently expanded Shiprock Medical Center, Ella found herself looking forward to seeing Carolyn Roanhorse and hearing someone start making sense of this situation.

She trusted Carolyn implicitly. In the beginning they'd been drawn together mostly because they were both outcasts. Carolyn had become a pariah because she was a Navajo working with the dead, and Ella was a woman in male-dominated law enforcement. It didn't help either that Ella had spent years off the rez in the FBI, and lost the trust of many she once knew.

Over the past year or so they'd become good friends, though they still usually saw each other mostly in the course of police business.

As her call sign came over the air, she picked up the mike. It was Justine.

"I'm on my way to Farmington now. What's your 'twenty'?" Justine asked, using the code for a location.

"I'm on my way to the morgue. Whatcha need?"

"We've been trying to notify the Yellowhair family. But with the state legislature not in session, the senator's not keeping office hours, and his wife's not home. Their neighbor suggested we talk to your mom."

"I don't get it. How come?"

"The senator and his wife are members of the church where your father used to preach, though he doesn't attend regularly."

Ella felt a cold hand squeezing her heart. More connections leading everywhere, yet nowhere. "I'll swing by my mother's home and see if she has any ideas before I meet the M.E. Anything new on the evidence processed from the crime scene?"

"Not yet. But by the time you come in, we may have something. And I'll go over that bat the minute I get it back to the lab."

"Good. Once the news is out about the accident, I'm going to be on the hot seat because of my report. If I have an open murder case on my hands at the same time, we're all going to be sweating, from the chief on down. Keep working."

"Ten-four."

Ella gazed at Ship Rock—standing like a distant sentinel

about a dozen miles southwest of the town named after it—thinking about her father. He had been dead eighteen months, and his killers had been caught and punished, but the memory of his loss still filled her with intense grief. Such a brutal, senseless death.

It was even worse for her mother. Ella could still hear her pacing the house at night, as if searching for the companion she'd known for a lifetime. Her heart twisted inside. So much pain, and so many dead because of beliefs as old as the *Dineh* themselves.

But right now Ella's focus had to be on the cases before her. She thought of Bitah, and then Angelina Yellowhair. Both those deaths had been just as senseless as her father's, in their own ways, and the questions about them needed to be answered.

Ella drove up the bumpy dirt track that led to her mother's home where Ella had lived ever since her return to the reservation. Her mother and she were both alone, both widowed, and living together had given each of them much needed companionship.

She parked near the side of the house and saw her mother, Rose, out back by the clothesline, hanging out laundry. Dog Two, or "Two" for short, lay nearby. Dog, her mother's old companion, had finally died of old age six months ago. Dog Two, another mutt, had wandered onto their porch one cold November evening, and had been around ever since.

Hearing the car, Rose turned her head and waved. Finishing with the laundry, she went to meet her daughter, Two at her side. "Is something wrong? You're home early."

"There was a car accident," Ella answered. "I was hoping you could tell me where to find Senator Yellowhair, or his wife."

"Their daughter?" Rose spoke in scarcely a whisper, avoiding the name.

Ella nodded. "She's dead. Just ran off the road."

Rose's eyes narrowed. "Was she drinking or something? Her aunt said she has been pretty wild nowadays."

"We're looking into that now, but we need to contact her parents. One of the neighbors suggested that you might be able to give us an idea of where to find them."

"Why? I used to see the senator's wife when she went to your father's church, but I don't go there anymore. Since your father's death, I haven't seen any of them except at the post office or grocery store. I could ask around, though. I heard someone mention at my weaver's association meeting that the family was going down to Fort Defiance to visit relatives, and that the senator would be stopping by Window Rock to give some speeches. But that was two weeks ago. They may be back, I don't know. Doesn't he have an office you can call?"

"Yes, but he's not keeping regular hours right now. But thanks for the suggestion, I'll check it out. Meanwhile, I better get back to work." As Ella headed back to the car, Rose called out to her.

"I just remembered something. Have you tried going to the church? I understand they've been getting some blankets and coats together to send out to the *Dineh* who live over by Mexican Hat. If the senator's family is back, his wife might be over there."

"Thanks, Mom. I'll have someone check it out."

As she drove back out onto the highway, Ella contacted Justine on the radio. She relayed what she'd learned then asked her to pay a call to the church and see if anyone had seen Mrs. Yellowhair. "If you need me, I'll be at Carolyn's." Her stomach growled, reminding her that she needed food, and soon. "I'll go ten-sixty-one there," she added, informing Justine she'd be stopping for something to eat.

"Ten-four."

As Ella stepped out of the hospital basement stairwell, she felt that peculiar coldness that was always present in the morgue and had nothing to do with the temperature. She wasn't sure how Carolyn stood it, though she knew that the reason her friend worked here was because this was where the tribe needed her most.

As she walked down the short hallway, she felt a shudder run up her spine. A sudden flashback to the day she'd come to see her father's body left her feeling weak at the knees. She took a deep breath, steeling herself, and touched the badger fetish around her neck. There was nothing she could do to change what had been. She had other duties now.

As she reached the outer office she could hear Carolyn's monotone voice as she spoke into a tape recorder inside the autopsy suite. Through the glass that separated them, Ella could see her friend's back and a corpse's foot and toe tag. Three stainless steel tables stood empty, but trays filled with surgical equipment surrounded the M.E.

The smell of disinfectant made Ella feel a little sick to her stomach. She leaned back against the wall for a moment. Suddenly a stocky young man wearing a blue vinyl apron over scrubs rushed out of the autopsy suite, looking pale in the bright lights.

"What are you doing here?" he demanded, after nearly running over her. As his gaze dropped down to her belt and he saw her badge, he gave her a thin smile. "Oops. Sorry. Dr. Roanhorse told me to expect a visit from the police."

"I haven't seen you here before. Who are you?" Ella asked, looking at the young Navajo with surprise.

"I'm Howard Lee, Dr. Roanhorse's assistant. I'm the med student assigned to work with her this semester."

Ella nodded. That explained it. Carolyn's job didn't attract volunteers. "Could you tell her I'm here?"

"I already know," Carolyn yelled out, reaching up to turn off the tape recorder's mike. "Come in."

"I'd rather not," Ella answered.

"Don't be such a wuss. You're a cop."

The barb stung, just as Carolyn had intended it to. Ella took a deep breath, then forced herself to enter the room. The body was half-covered with a sheet. Lines marking where the incisions would be made were clearly delineated on the skull and torso. Ella swallowed the bile rising at the back of her throat.

Carolyn turned around, bloody gloves held high and away from her body. "Hey, I was wondering when you'd come. You're just in the nick of time."

"For what?"

"Can you reach that drawer and get the peanut butter cup in there? I'm hungry, but I'll need you to feed it to me. I can't get it near the body or touch it with these gloves."

Ella did as she asked, wondering if this was legit or just one of Carolyn's pranks meant to make her squirm. Either way, she wouldn't balk.

Ella held the candy out as Carolyn leaned forward and took a bite. "How can you eat this now?" Ella said, forcing her voice to remain steady.

"Why not? It's not as if I have to share," she said, pointing to the body, "and I missed lunch."

Ella's gaze strayed past Carolyn to the face of the body on the table. It was Angelina Yellowhair. She fought the sinking sensation at the pit of her stomach. "What caused the convulsions? Was she ill?"

"I don't know yet, but I will soon. If you rule out drugs or poison, which of course I can't do until the tests are run, your description makes me think she may have had a stroke or a heart attack. But neither of those is consistent with the other evidence. People who are in the midst of a heart attack, or even a stroke, usually have enough presence of mind to slow down. Of course there are always exceptions, but the percentages bear me out."

Ella nodded. "Epilepsy?"

Carolyn took another bite of the candy bar, then swallowed. "There's no record of that in her medical history. I know her doctor. He's right upstairs. He said that she was in perfect health."

Carolyn was just finishing the last bite of candy when the med student came back into the room. He strode in confidently, and despite the fact that he was wearing a wide, gold wedding band, gave Ella a bold once over as if they were in a single's bar instead of a morgue. Then he turned to Carolyn. "Doctor, I've logged the blood samples and the other fluids." He looked at the body, trying to act casual, but his face turned a shade lighter.

Ella knew immediately that, despite his training, he was no seasoned morgue veteran. He was reacting to the body with the distaste most Navajos showed a corpse. When she glanced at Carolyn, and saw the gleam in her eyes, her heart went out to Howard Lee. If her guess was right, Carolyn was about to have some fun at the young man's expense.

Ella cleared her throat. "I was hoping to talk you into taking some time off and going out for lunch with me, upstairs, outside, anywhere but here." She needed to talk to her friend, but she wouldn't ask specifically. It wouldn't have been a fair request. What had allowed their friendship to blossom was their mutual understanding of each other. To both Carolyn and her, work always came first.

"Give me a few more minutes," Carolyn said. "Howard and I have a few more things to do here."

Ella braced herself when the high-pitched whine of a bone saw filled the room. Then she heard a sucking noise as the body was cut open. She would have run out of the room right there and then, but she was afraid that if she moved, her legs would buckle and she'd fall on her face. Ella leaned back against the cold wall, closed her eyes, and took a breath. The smell of death filled her nostrils, and she felt her empty stomach churning and bile rising again to the back of her throat.

Hearing a sound she could only describe as that of a runner wearing water-soaked shoes, she opened her eyes and saw Carolyn removing something large and reddish brown from the body. Ella rushed out of the room, knowing she'd have to put up with Carolyn calling her a wuss for the next several months.

"Hang on. We'll have lunch in a bit," Carolyn called out to her cheerily. "I just want to show my assistant one more thing."

Ella heard a drill, then a crunching sound that made her skin crawl. The next instant, she saw Howard Lee running from the room, one hand held over his mouth.

Carolyn looked up at Ella and smiled. "Oh good. You're still here. *Now*, we can leave. I have a valid reason for taking a break from the autopsy because my student's indisposed. He's an arrogant little twerp. He should be used to viewing autopsies by now. This certainly wasn't his first."

"The body is of a young Navajo woman. Could be it reminds him of his wife," Ella suggested. She knew how viewing a loved one here had affected her.

"I suppose. But he's been so annoying today, I couldn't resist pushing him a little. Ready for lunch?"

Ella stared at her friend. "You're positively amazing."

Carolyn peeled off her gloves and tossed them into the trash can used for biohazards. "Give me a second to wash up. Since you had to wait, I'll treat you to lunch upstairs. I hear the special in the cafeteria today is liver and onions."

Ella swallowed convulsively, recalling the reddish organ Carolyn had lifted from Angelina Yellowhair's body. She wouldn't break. Carolyn was goading her on purpose. That black sense of humor was one way Carolyn stayed sane. "If you can gag it down, Doc, so can I."

THREE

——— ✖ ✖ ✖ ———

Ella left the hospital still feeling queasy, despite the fact Carolyn had only been teasing about the liver and onions. Though, admittedly, Carolyn hadn't had much information to give her yet on either case, at least she'd spent time decompressing in the company of a good friend. Carolyn's macabre humor didn't endear her to many, but then again, nothing Carolyn could ever do was about to change her outcast status on the Rez.

Not that Ella herself was always welcomed with open arms. Acceptance was slow in coming, particularly within the department. Many still resented her for having been part of the FBI once. Among the *Dineh,* some saw her as too modern, a product more of the Anglo culture than of her own. Although there had been a time when she would have taken that as a compliment, Ella didn't feel that way anymore.

She drove toward the open pit coal mine, which was adjacent to the power plant it fed. As she'd been leaving the hospital, Blalock had called to ask her to meet him there. He'd been angry about something, though he hadn't been willing to specify what it was over the radio. Her curiosity was definitely up.

As she pulled into the parking lot adjacent to the operation, she caught a glimpse of Blalock a few feet ahead. His car was a maze of spray-painted graffiti. The paint would be impossible to get off.

"Look what they did to my car," he said, as she climbed out of her Jeep. "The punks. They're lucky I didn't catch them."

"The Bureau will pay for the repairs. Don't sweat it."

"Yeah, easy for you to say. You don't have to write the report." He shook his head. "This never used to happen here."

"Yeah, well, the outside is catching up to us." She glanced at several teenagers—who probably should have been in school—sitting in a highly polished old car, laughing and listening to rap music. Their clothing, and the way they wore it, suggested they were members of a gang. "Did you talk to them?"

"Yeah, but I got the usual smart mouth comments."

"You want me to give it a shot?"

He rolled his eyes. "You won't get anywhere either, Navajo or not. They might be Navajo by birth, but they're at war with everything, including their own people."

"They've lost sight of who they are, and grabbed onto the first and worst things they've seen of other cultures." She shrugged. "But tell me, what brought you here to the mine?"

"I wanted to know which Anglos Bitah had a problem with, or if there were any he considered friends."

"What did you find out?"

"Bitah wasn't big on Anglos, good or bad. There are a lot of racially motivated problems in this company, despite the line of corporate harmony the supervisors tried to shove down my throat."

"There has always been tension within the tribe about the role of mining companies on the reservation."

"My take on this is that the Navajo and Anglo workers are struggling against each other for power. Whichever faction wins will end up speaking for the workers as a whole, and will control the best jobs. There's some serious trouble brewing here, believe me, and the company knows it. They've been having a teacher from the college come over to teach the Anglo supervisors the Navajo language but, unless I miss my guess, that's not going to help much, especially since Navajo is so damn tough to learn."

"Who's doing the teaching?"

"Your old friend, Wilson Joe."

Wilson was one of the few people Ella trusted implicitly. He'd be able to tell her more about what was going on out here. She made a mental note to pay him a visit soon.

"I've got a feeling this case is going to involve more than just a labor relations issue before it's resolved," Blalock said softly.

As a cold breeze enveloped them, Ella felt a sense of foreboding that echoed his words. Forcing it aside, she looked toward the portable building that served as the mine's field office and first aid station. "Did you happen to find out if Bitah was close to anyone?"

"Jonathan Steele, his supervisor, said Bitah got along well with Billy Pete, another Navajo worker, and the only person he had major league problems with was Frank Smith."

"I know Billy. He'll talk to me without any problem. But who's Frank Smith?"

"An Anglo Bitah had it in for. According to Steele, he wouldn't hurt a fly. Smith comes in every day, does his job and leaves. Still, he and Bitah had a couple of go-arounds."

"About what?"

"From what I heard, Bitah started it, accused him of trying to stir up trouble among the Navajo workers."

"In what way?"

"Missing objects belonging to one Navajo would turn up in another Navajo's locker, that sort of thing."

"The most innocent-looking guy sometimes *is* the troublemaker, you know."

"Maybe. But I ran a check on him. This guy's a family man, and has never even had a traffic citation. I talked to several of the Anglos here, and they all said that Smith was an honest man. Churchgoer and all that. He belongs to the same denomination your father did."

Once again her skin prickled. "So do several million other people around the country."

He shrugged. "Yeah, well, I just thought it was an interesting coincidence."

"I'll go find Billy Pete," she said, heading for the office. "You coming?"

"No. I'd better get this car scrubbed and make arrangements to have it repainted. After that, I'll track down Frank Smith and have a talk with him."

Ella stepped inside the mine offices, and was told that Billy Pete had just punched his time card and left. Ella rushed back out to the parking lot and found him in the employees parking area at the far end. She jogged up to meet him.

"Wait up!" she called out, getting his attention.

Billy smiled, recognizing Ella, then grew somber. "It's been a long time. Are you here as a friend or as a cop?"

"Do they have to be mutually exclusive?" Ella countered.

Billy nodded slowly, pushing his Kansas City Chiefs cap up so he could look her in the eyes. "In this case, yes."

"Explain," Ella asked, leaning back against his car and looking over at the mountains of coal being formed by the drag line of an enormous crane over a mile away.

Billy's black eyes shone with wariness. "Are you still L.A. Woman, or are you truly one of the *Dineh* again?"

"L.A. Woman was always a Navajo."

"Maybe, but she was trying to forget that. Like them," he said, pursing his lips and pointing Navajo fashion at the gang now standing by their car, smoking cigarettes.

"No, never like that. They haven't a clue who they are or what they're doing." She paused, gathering her thoughts. "I won't take a Navajo's side if he's wrong, just because he's Navajo, if that's what you're really asking me. My job is to uphold the law, and that's what I intend to do by tracking down the murderer who took the life of your friend."

"It won't be easy, not the way things are around here."

"Do you have any idea who might have done it?"

Billy remained silent for several minutes, watching the gang members joking and strutting back and forth in front of the row of parked cars. Finally, he spoke. "There are many we fought with, but it's one thing to argue, and another to kill."

"Who's we?"

Billy started to answer, then clamped his mouth shut and shook his head. "I can't say anymore. You'll have to find your own answers."

"Didn't you say you wanted me to catch the killer? I need your help to do that."

"I have no knowledge of the killing. What I'm involved in is a matter of tribal rights and, more specifically, our rights as Navajo employees of the mine."

"Like your friend who was murdered?" she pushed.

"Whoever did that made a big mistake, and will pay a heavy price. But my concern now is for the living." He moved past her and slipped inside his car. "I've got to go."

"Where are you off to in such a hurry? It's not the end of your shift, is it?"

He looked up, but didn't answer her. A moment later, she watched his car disappear across the parking lot. The more she learned, the more her sense of disquiet grew. Something was happening here on the reservation, right under her nose. She couldn't shake the feeling that she was sitting on top of a powder keg with a burning fuse.

As she walked back to her vehicle, her pager went off. Identifying the caller, Ella jogged quickly back to the car, picked up the mobile phone, and dialed her assistant's number. "I'm here, Justine. What's going on?"

"I need to talk to you. Can we meet at the Totah Café?"

"I can be there in twenty."

"Good. I've made some progress, and I need to talk over the details with you."

Ella drove quickly, intrigued by the tone of Justine's voice. Her assistant hadn't attempted to discuss the matter on the cellular, or suggested the radio, so that meant something important was up. Eager for a fast break on the case, she hurried to Shiprock's Totah Café. As she entered, Justine waved to her from a booth at the back.

Ella walked across the almost empty diner. It was too late for the lunch crowd and too early for the dinner patrons: a perfect time for a meeting. She joined Justine and sat with her back to the wall so she'd have a clear look at anyone who came into the diner. It was a habit she'd developed after one particularly bad scene in an L.A. restaurant.

"We've got trouble. We finally located the senator after a tip was called into the station. He'd had one drink too many, and was with a blonde cutie at a motel in Farmington when his wife walked in. They were having a knock-down-drag-out when the cops arrived. The news shut them up real fast. About the only thing they're both in agreement on now is that they want their daughter's body released."

"Not until Carolyn finishes the autopsy," Ella shrugged. "We need a cause of death."

"That's the other thing. When the senator learned we were doing an autopsy, he went ballistic."

"Does he understand why one's necessary? Was he told about my report?"

"Yeah, and he's gunning for you. He thinks that you're either nuts, or negligent because you didn't pull her over immediately."

"I explained all that to Sergeant Neskahi. It's in his report." She shook her head. "The senator is just looking for someone to blame."

"I drove to the site and went over everything again with the sergeant. There were no skid marks anywhere or signs that she tried to hit the brakes. Until we get the toxicology report, we won't know for sure, but Angelina wasn't reputed to be a drinker. This isn't just another DWI accident, I'm certain of that."

"Carolyn is expecting trouble from the senator, so she'll get us answers as quickly as possible."

"I did examine Angelina's car at the impound. Except for crash damage, everything seemed normal, including the brakes. It's a new car, practically, and from what I found in the glove compartment, it had been serviced recently. I spoke to the mechanic at the station she uses, and he insisted there was nothing wrong with the car when he serviced it last time. I had him check it out again, and he agreed there were no new mechanical problems except those caused by the crash."

"Any reason to doubt the mechanic's skill?"

"No. Arnold Buck is as good as they come."

Ella's pager went off, and she glanced down at the number. "Blalock. I better get to a phone."

Ella returned to her cell phone in the car, preferring the privacy it would give her, and dialed the number. A moment later Blalock's voice came through clearly.

"We've got a problem," the agent snapped. "Truman's employee union got him an attorney. He's pushing for a hearing no later than tomorrow morning."

"Bail's going to be set high for assault on an officer. Will he have the resources?"

"There's no guarantee of a high bail, apparently. The lawyer's claiming you were in an unmarked car, and didn't identify yourself properly."

"That's a load of . . . manure."

"Yeah, well, it's par for the course. I think we should question Truman as soon as possible. He's going to get cocky now that he's got an attorney."

"How about meeting me over there now?" she suggested.

"Let's do it."

They entered the Farmington lock-up forty minutes later. Ella studied Blalock, who stood with his back to the wall while they waited for the prisoner to be brought in. He looked as fresh as if he'd just stepped out of the shower. She wasn't quite sure how he did that, particularly with the blowing sand that accompanied the afternoon winds.

She blew a strand of hair out of her eyes, noting the gray dust all over her boots. Maybe the FBI had developed a Teflon coating for agents since she'd resigned.

Moments later, an officer led Truman in. His shackled feet were connected by a chain to stout handcuffs so he was forced to take small, deliberate steps. Ella studied the man's openly hostile expression. His eyes were bloodshot and, if she'd had to bet, she would have laid odds he had one hell of a headache.

"I won't say another word until my lawyer gets here."

"We have you up on some serious charges," Blalock said. "Being uncooperative isn't going to get any of them reduced."

Truman glared at them, but said absolutely nothing. A minute later, a young, well-dressed attorney, wearing a western cut suit and a bolo tie, sauntered into the room, setting his expensive leather briefcase on the small table separating cops from accused.

"I'm Jeff Martinez, Mr. Truman's attorney. I hope you officers haven't been badgering my client. You know the rules as well as I do."

"We've only just arrived," Blalock said with obvious distaste.

"All right then. We can begin."

Ella glanced at Blalock, and saw his imperceptible nod. She took the lead. "After I identified myself as a police officer and stated my intention to ask you some questions, why did you attack me?"

"My client didn't hear you identify yourself as an officer— who was out of her jurisdiction, I might add." Martinez answered.

"Unless you're clairvoyant, counselor, I'd prefer if your client answered the questions," Ella said calmly.

"Tough," Martinez responded.

Ella looked directly at Truman. "You and I both know I identified myself quite clearly. You attacked me after you knew who I was."

"You might have a lot of power on the reservation, but here in Farmington, you're no better than anyone else. Don't try to intimidate me."

"I'm no better than anyone else, anywhere. And neither are you. Haven't you heard about the Bill of Rights?" Ella countered smoothly.

"You people are all the same," Truman spat out.

"Watch your mouth," Blalock growled.

"It's okay," Ella said quickly, then turned her attention back to Truman. "What people are you referring to? Cops? Navajos? Nonracists?"

"That's enough," the attorney said quickly.

"No, let me answer her," Truman said. "This isn't about any crime. This is about Indian cops hassling a white man just because he's white."

"Where in left field did that come from?" Ella narrowed her eyes and tried to keep her temper in check. There was something more going on here. Maybe that white supremacist junk had scrambled his brain.

"You run things on the reservation like it's your own private country. Why can't you act like real Americans for a change?"

Ella tried to make some sense of the man's ramblings. He wasn't drunk anymore. But she had no idea what he was talking about.

"Do you know Stanley Bitah?" Ella continued.

"Yeah, he worked at the mine. Pain in the butt trouble-maker—like you." Truman sneered.

"Just how much did you dislike Bitah? And where were you this morning just before sunrise?" Ella watched Truman's eyes carefully.

Just for an instant Truman glanced at his lawyer, then stared defiantly at Ella. "I was at home, in bed with my wife, if that's any of your business."

"It is, if you chose to settle your racist problems with violence. If you've laid a hand on anyone else like you tried with me today, plan on me finding out and sending you straight to jail."

"Then my brothers would even the score, count on it."

"Brothers? You have relatives in Farmington?"

"My spiritual brothers. The Brotherhood is strong, and—"

"That's it." The attorney stood up abruptly. "That's the end of this interview. If there are no further questions, then I suggest we all adjourn and get some work done."

Truman glanced over to his lawyer, then shrugged.

Ella studied Truman's expression. He'd enjoyed baiting her, but there was something about the way he was looking at her that gave her the creeps. The man knew something, and it was enough to make him feel superior. The possibilities made her uneasy.

As they stepped out into the hall and the attorney closed the door behind them, Blalock turned to Ella and smiled. "Well, that went really well."

"Stuff it. You wouldn't have fared any better."

"I certainly couldn't have done any worse."

She chose not to rise to the barb. "Did you get that about The Brotherhood?"

"Yes, but I have no idea what the hell he was talking about. Never heard of anything like that around here before."

"When a guy like this, a well-armed white supremacist, starts talking about his 'brothers,' I've got to tell you, we need to start paying close attention."

"What we need is to talk to someone who knows what's going on around that mine, someone who'll trust us," Blalock said. "Do you have any friends among the miners?"

"I know some of the guys, but not well. I do have one friend, however, who may be able to help."

"Who?"

"Wilson Joe."

"He's not a miner, he's a teacher."

"But if he's teaching the Anglos out there the Navajo language, he's talking to them. He's also working for the tribe, *and* in contact with power plant and mining management."

"Good thought, and I have to admit, the guy has got what it takes, too. He handled himself pretty well the other times our paths have crossed. While you're talking to Wilson, I'll keep trying to track down Frank Smith. He wasn't at home when I stopped by and the neighbors haven't seen him in a few days. I'll stay on it, though, and let you know if I learn anything from him or the other Anglo employees on my list."

Ella checked her watch as she drove back. It was too late to go anywhere except home now. She'd have dinner, and then maybe give Wilson a call.

Picking up her radio, she contacted Justine. "Channel six," Ella said, instructing her assistant to switch frequencies.

"You want a report, but I haven't got one," Justine said. "I just called the M.E. and she wasn't too thrilled with me for trying to hurry her along. She said if I kept calling to check, it would take longer—whether it did or not."

Ella laughed. "Don't bug her. It'll just make Carolyn dig in her heels. I've got something else I want you to do. Go over to the coal mine office. It's open twenty-four hours a day. Get a full employee list, current and former, for the past five years. If you see any name you recognize, any of our tribe you feel you know well, pay him a visit. I need some background on what's going on over there. We'll go through the official channels next, but in this case, an unofficial visit to a friend is probably going to get us further."

"I'll get on it. You taking a sixty-one?"

"Yeah, I'm going to have dinner at home. You can reach me there."

As she drove up the dirt track to her mother's house, she saw her brother Clifford's old truck parked there. Loretta, her sister-in-law was hovering near the living room window, watching her one-year-old, who was standing on the sofa, looking out.

Loretta waved as she approached. The young Navajo woman had managed to get her girlish figure back in record time. Ella studied her face and saw the contentment that shone there. Loretta was suited for motherhood. She practically glowed with happiness.

"Hi there!" Ella greeted, as she entered the house. She bent over and scooped the baby up from the sofa. "And how are *you* doing, short-stuff?" The baby squealed and laughed as she tickled him.

"Be careful now, Ella," Loretta cautioned. "If he gets too excited, he'll have an upset stomach when he eats dinner."

"Oh, come on. He'll be fine." There was an ongoing argument between Clifford and his wife concerning Loretta's overprotectiveness. Since the trouble with the skinwalkers right before Julian was born, and their attempts against the child at the hospital, Loretta refused to let the baby out of her sight for even a few minutes.

"I'm really glad you came by. Your mother was just complaining that she never has the family over here for dinner anymore. She says you're always working."

"Not always, but my job's never been eight to five," Ella agreed, leading the way into the den.

Clifford glanced up from his newspaper and smiled at his sister. "I'm glad to see you. You're going to stick around for a while?"

"That depends. I'm on a case, so if I get a call I'll have to go, but I'm glad you're here. I'd like to talk to you," Ella said, noting that Loretta had taken Julian on through to the kitchen.

Ella motioned Clifford into their father's former study. Nowadays the room had been converted into Ella's office. Her mother had hoped she'd do more of her work from home after that, but it hadn't worked out that way. As she'd tried to explain to her mother, field work couldn't be done from an office, and most paperwork had to remain at the station. Subsequently, she'd tried to get her mom to turn it into her knitting and weaving room, but there were still too many memories confined between these walls for her.

"What's going on?" Clifford asked the moment she closed the door.

"Have you . . . have you noticed anything unusual, you know, out of the ordinary, lately?"

"How so?" Clifford's eyes narrowed, and from the tightening there she knew her brother had guessed what was on her mind.

"I don't know. It's just a feeling," Ella said.

"Skinwalkers?"

She took a deep breath, puffed out her cheeks, and blew the air out slowly. "It's difficult to say *yes* or *no* to that. I don't sense anything specific. Well, no, that's not true. I sense . . . trouble. Something's brewing on the Rez, brother. And it's going to come to the surface soon. We may have a problem containing it."

"You're talking in the context of a police investigation, yet what worries you goes well beyond that."

She was always amazed at her brother's talents. He could read people better than anyone else she'd ever known. He had other gifts, too, some associated with his training as a *hataalii*. But some gifts he had surpassed his training, and those had always made her uneasy. Hers was an orderly mind, and anything she couldn't classify and explain disturbed her equanimity. She would have liked to explain away some of her brother's special abilities as trickery and illusion, much like a magician's. But, deep down, she knew it was far more involved than that.

"A police officer's instincts aren't always precise," she replied at length.

"But your intuitions are more than that, and you know it," he said, then raised his hand to stem her protests. "The problem with you is that you're too proud for your own good. You don't want to think that your intuitions are part of a gift, a special magic that you alone possess. You'd much rather think that it's simply an intellectual process going on in your subconscious because you're smart, and highly trained in law enforcement."

Ella forced herself not to cringe. There was truth in what he said, and that was why it stung so much. "I *am* smart, and I'm proud of my skills. I worked my hind end off to get them."

"But you should still acknowledge that you have an extra source of help within yourself that's made you successful."

"Yeah, well . . . " she shrugged.

"Pride," he said, shaking his head.

"Will you answer my question? It's important. I need your opinion." Ella watched her older brother as he sat down and regarded her thoughtfully.

"I can tell you that there's a restlessness among the people. I can feel that as well as you do, but I'm also not sure what's behind it. Conversations stop when I draw near, as if there's something happening The People want to keep from me. I haven't experienced anything like that since the time when our father was killed."

Ella nodded. "I had a very uncomfortable feeling out on the highway today when I was out investigating an accident. I felt I was being watched, but there was no one around. At least no one that I could see."

Clifford nodded. "Disturbing. I'll see what I can learn." He stood up slowly. "But now it's time for family, not business. Let's go, little sister."

As they joined the others, Ella couldn't shake the uneasiness that plagued her. She went through the motions, eating tasty mutton stew and fry bread with her family, trying not to take sides when Clifford and Loretta argued about the baby, but her mind was on the case. When the phone rang, her mother glanced at her.

"No doubt it's for you. It's just as well. You've been here physically, but your mind hasn't been with us all evening."

"I'm sorry, Mom. I didn't mean to be so distant." She walked into the living room and picked up the receiver. It was Justine.

"I just got a call from Billy Pete," her assistant said. "He told me that it's important he talk to you tonight."

"Where does he want to meet?"

"At the Totah Café."

She relaxed. At least that wasn't a likely place for an ambush. Not that she didn't trust Billy Pete, but people under stress did weird things. "Okay. What time?"

"Eight. Something else. Dr. Roanhorse released the body. She said she had all the tissue samples she needed. Rather than fight the senator, who showed up at the hospital with some honchos from the tribal council, she signed the papers."

"Did she give you a preliminary autopsy report yet?"

"No. She said she'd speak to you directly about that. She didn't want to bother you at home, so she asked me to tell you to call her anytime after nine tonight. She'll be in meetings at the hospital until then."

"All right. I'll take care of it. In the meantime, I'm going to go to the café. I'll talk to you later."

Ella reached back and checked her pistol, then put on her windbreaker. She was almost ready to go when Rose came into the room.

"You're leaving? You just got here."

"I won't be gone long."

"Don't you want any dessert?"

"I'll have some when I come back, okay?"

"When are you going to start taking some time for yourself? You haven't had your friends over in a long time. I can accept that you don't want to marry Wilson, though I just don't understand why. But how are you going to meet anyone if all you do is work and play with your computer?"

"I love Wilson, he's been a great friend. But I'm not in love with him; that's why we could never marry. And I'm not looking to meet anyone either," she said, kissing her mother on the cheek. "Not everyone's life's path is the same."

"You *will* want to marry again someday, daughter. I just hope it won't be too late by then for you to give me grandchildren."

Ella walked out the door, knowing from experience that this conversation was going nowhere. They'd had it a million times before. She'd fallen in love and been married once, and had found her identity as a wife, but she'd been young then, and more uncertain of who she was. But her husband had died. Since that time, she'd matured and found her own sense of purpose. She'd never again be able to adapt so easily to the needs and demands of married life, even if she did happen to fall in love again. Her priorities were different now, just as she was different from the girl she'd been then.

It had been an extremely long day, and Ella's thoughts drifted as she drove down the almost deserted highway. The moon was hidden behind a cloud, and the syrupy darkness of the unlit highway was by now so familiar to her it seemed routine. At night this stretch of highway was illuminated only by headlights, and the moon when a driver was lucky. But she knew every pothole and every curve by heart.

She listened to the silence around her. Even the two-way radio was still. Police work could be lonely at times, but she couldn't envision herself doing anything else.

Ella thought of Wilson Joe. Despite her mother's wishes, there could never have been a future between them. Although his devotion to teaching was as great as hers to police work, she didn't think he'd ever be able to put up with the long hours, and the pressure, and the nightmares that were all part of her work. Eventually, her career would have driven a wedge between them.

Ella was almost at the Totah Café when, along the outer edge of light cast by her headlights, she caught a glimpse of an elderly

Navajo woman wearing a canvas jacket and the usual colorful scarf over her head. With the assistance of a cane, she was walking back and forth beside a truck on the shoulder of the road, adjacent to what looked like a used pickup lot. Ella pulled in behind her and called dispatch, giving her '20.

The elderly woman approached Ella's vehicle, speaking fast in Navajo. Ella couldn't make out a word of it.

"Calm down," she said, hooking the mike back up and opening her door. "Do you speak English?"

Another stream of fast Navajo was her only reply. Ella got out and went over to look at the woman's truck. The minute she was clear of her Jeep, all the headlights came on from the parked trucks. Trapped by the row of bright lights, she couldn't see. Ella reached back for her gun with one hand, shielding her eyes with the other.

"This is only a warning," a surprisingly clear voice boomed out from behind the glare. She could tell from the rhythm of his speech that the man who spoke was Navajo, though she couldn't see his face.

"We could have killed you tonight—understand that. The danger to you doesn't come from us, but if you don't back off, we will not be held responsible for your safety. *We* will handle the problems at the mine, and restore harmony. Do not interfere."

"Who are you?" she demanded. "Why are you afraid to show yourselves?"

Instead of an answer, she heard engines start up. For a moment, she thought they were going to run her over.

FOUR

✖ ✖ ✖

Ella drew her pistol. If she went down, a few of them would go with her. She held her breath, but in a heartbeat, the trucks roared past her onto the highway.

Still shaking, Ella turned around, looking for the elderly woman who had lured her into the trap, but she, along with her broken-down truck, was gone.

Ella walked back to her Jeep, and called the incident in. A moment later, Justine was on the radio.

"Do you need backup?"

"No, it's over. I just wanted to alert any patrol units in the area to be on the lookout for five or six pickups traveling together, or meeting somewhere further up the highway."

"I'm near your location. I'll go look around."

"Watch yourself then. I'm going to see if Billy Pete is at the Totah Café, though I doubt it. I think that was part of the set-up."

Ella entered the Totah Café a few minutes later. The place was nearly empty except for one waitress, Betsy Bekis, who was sitting behind the empty counter. Ella had known Betsy since high school.

"Hi. Slow night?" Ella greeted.

"No more than usual," Betsy replied with a bored yawn.

"Have you seen Billy Pete in here tonight?"

She shook her head. "He comes in often for dinner since his wife left him, but he wasn't in today, at least on my shift."

"Do you have any idea where I might be able to find him?"

"You could ask Linda Begay. She goes out with him a lot. Do you know where she lives?"

After getting directions from Betsy, Ella drove directly to Linda Begay's trailer home, parked in an open lot north of the café, up on the mesa. She studied the surroundings for a moment, noting the absence of a hogan or any other sign that a traditionalist lived here. An old pickup with a starboard list stood empty by the trailer, where she could see the muted light of a TV flashing just beyond the curtains, and a half-dozen beer cans overflowing a beat-up trash can by the front steps. Taking one last look around, Ella walked up to the door and knocked. Moments later, a half asleep, chunky-looking woman appeared, still fastening her pink, terry-cloth robe.

"What is it? It's past nine, and that's my bedtime. I have to be at work early."

"I was looking for Billy Pete," Ella said, flashing her badge. "Any idea where I might find him?"

"Try the hospital. He's been there since dinnertime, stoned out of his mind on morphine. He's got a problem with kidney stones."

A quick call on the cellular phone and Ella's suspicions were confirmed. Since Billy was in the hospital, unable to make phone calls, someone else had used Billy's name when they'd phoned Justine. She returned to the trailer door to question an even grumpier Linda Begay. "I spoke to Billy earlier today, and I know he was very disturbed about what was going on at the mine," Ella said, using a technique she'd found effective. When she led people to believe she knew more than she actually did, she usually ended up getting good information.

"He and the others can handle it over there. Nobody's going to get away with anything. Those troublemakers that started it—" she stopped abruptly. "I shouldn't be talking about this."

"It's okay. All I'm trying to do is keep Billy from getting hurt."

Linda's eyes became cold and wary. "Billy can take care of

himself. He's only doing what has to be done to restore harmony. Your brother is a Singer. Maybe he can do an Enemy Way Sing at the mine."

"Why? An Enemy Way is for purifying those who have come in contact with the enemy."

"Or those who are ill because of contact with the whites. They've caused a death. Isn't that enough?"

"It isn't the same thing and, besides, an Enemy Way should be done in the summer."

"It will be summer in another two months."

"Our Way isn't like some kind of glue, where you put a little ritual here and a little blessing there to hold things together."

"Oh yeah, and you know all about it, L.A. Woman."

"What I don't know, at least I respect. My brother is a great teacher, but I'm not an expert in anything except law enforcement. From my police training I know that there's a situation brewing here that needs my attention. Yours, too, if you care at all for Billy Pete."

"I care enough to let him do things his own way, whether or not I agree with him. And that means not answering your questions."

Before Ella could say anything else, the door was slammed in her face. Ella shrugged, then walked back to her Jeep, wishing she'd had the energy to be a little more tactful and patient with the woman. It was time to call it a night.

By the time she arrived home, Ella felt an intense weariness stealing over her. The house was dark and the absence of her brother's truck told her that he and his family had gone home. Her mother was undoubtedly in bed. The problem was, Ella was too wound up to get any sleep.

Ella walked to the small PC in the corner of her room. With her hectic schedule, the only semblance of a social life she had these days was on the Internet. She liked getting E-mail and chatting with people from all over the world, though she rarely let anyone know she was a cop. If they inquired, she normally said she worked for the tribe.

As she entered the electronic service she subscribed to, she

saw her mailbox icon was blinking. As usual, Wilson Joe had
written her a short note. If it hadn't been for E-Mail, she might
have lost touch with him completely. Yet, by exchanging posts,
they'd grown closer. Funny how you could open up to someone
and say things on a computer that you'd never actually say in
person.

She smiled as she read about his day, then sent a reply telling
him bits and pieces of her own. She also promised to visit him in
person soon, though she didn't mention the business that would
bring her there. That was something better done eye-to-eye.

She also sent a short note to Carolyn, knowing she'd check her
mail before going to bed, and again before work. It was too late
to call her now about the preliminary autopsy report, but in her
post she assured Carolyn they'd meet the following day.

Once her posts were mailed, she visited the gardening forum
and, finally, a virtual museum in Copenhagen she was fond of
browsing. Downloading the art and viewing it right there in her
room was like taking a mini vacation without ever leaving home.
After a while, the thought occurred to her that she might be able
to find out a little more background about Senator Yellowhair on
one of the Internet databases. Using one of the search engines,
she typed in "Yellowhair" and "Navajo," and waited while electronic fingers searched computer files nationwide for any links
to her query.

Soon a list of possible links appeared at the bottom of the
screen. Scrolling down a few political and biographical articles
on James Yellowhair, Ella was surprised to find a corporate data-
base reference to Angelina.

After quickly establishing the hookup, realizing that she was
going to be paying a handsome surcharge for this business link,
Ella read that Angelina Yellowhair was the owner of a company
called Four Corners Trust, Inc.

Searching for other links to that corporation, Ella learned that
Four Corners Trust held thousands of shares in the Regional
Power plant and coal mining company. Angelina was—or had
been, a wealthy young woman.

Ella realized almost immediately that the shares must have

been purchased by the senator in his daughter's name, through a dummy corporation. The senator had wanted to hide his investments from the public, obviously. This certainly put a new slant on Angelina's death. Just what direction that slant might take, Ella had no idea. But she was going to start looking into it tomorrow when she'd be able to take advantage of whatever she found.

Still not ready for bed, Ella logged off the Net and started up her never-ending game of computer solitaire. After several minutes of that, her eyelids began to grow heavy.

Ella saved the game and crawled into bed. As the gray clouds slowly closed in over her thoughts and exhaustion won its nightly victory, she heard the cry of a coyote in the far distance. Too weary to fight her way back to alertness, she sighed and settled into her pillow, continuing her passage into oblivion.

Ella woke up slowly as the sun peered through a foot-wide gap in the curtains. Tossing the covers back, she checked the clock on her nightstand. It was just after 6:00 A.M. She walked to the window, ready to close the drapes, and saw her mother offering pollen to the dawn. Morning prayers. It was the sameness of things that afforded Ella the greatest comfort. She was glad she'd returned to live on the reservation. There was no other place quite like it.

Ella showered and dressed, then walked to the kitchen. Her mother was there before her, fixing breakfast. "I made you some hot cereal," Rose said.

"Thanks." It wasn't that she was hungry, but breakfast with her mother was sometimes the only time they had to talk and be together. Of course it was a ritual that was far more important to her mother, since Rose spent most of her time alone nowadays.

"You have to find other interests beside your computer and your work. It's not right. You're young. You should be enjoying your youth."

"I am. I love my life right now."

"You're not building something that will sustain you when you become old like me."

"What sustains *you*, Mom?"

"You do, and Clifford and his wife, and my grandson. He's a bright child with a future that's yet to be determined. I'm needed here."

Ella covered her mother's hand with her own, gazing down thoughtfully. Her hand was simply a younger version of the one she now touched. Sometimes the similarities between them amazed her. Her heart often whispered that what her mother was she would someday be, when the wheel of fate completed one full turn. "We're alike in a lot of ways. A sense of duty drives us."

"We are alike, and that's why I worry about you. I don't want you to wake up someday and feel that somehow you've missed the most important part of being a woman. Don't tell me you don't think about having a child, what it would be like, and how quickly the time is passing for you."

"Yes, it's true that I think about that sometimes, but I also know that the way I've chosen to live my life is right for me. There was a time when being a wife defined and satisfied me, but after my husband died, I found a new direction for myself. The life's walk we choose determines our options. I answer a need in law enforcement, and that's how I fulfill myself. I'm happy being who I am now."

Rose shook her head. "My heart aches for you, daughter. I'm afraid that one day you will want what you've turned away from now. And when that day comes, you may find that it's too late."

"It's a risk I have to take." Ella stood up and went to the sink. "I'll do the dishes if you want to work in your herb garden."

"It's mid April and weeds are already starting to show up," Rose said with a sigh. "But the weeding will wait a little bit longer. This morning I need to talk to you." She paused for a long time, but Ella didn't rush her. "I've heard about the murder of that mechanic at the mine, and I've seen the look on people's faces and heard the talk. There is division among the tribe. There are traditionalists who, like me, still cling to the old ways and see that as the only way to survive as a people. Then there are the modernists like Justine and Carolyn. And then, there are many who are lost in between, like those kids who say they're members of nothing except for the gangs they join. Our tribe is under attack and most of our people don't even realize it."

"I know, Mom, but the *Dineh* will get through it as we have other hard times."

"The outcome, I'm afraid, will depend on those who, like you, have not chosen sides yet. They'll ultimately give one side or the other the numbers to make the changes needed. But those decisions must be made soon, otherwise events will take their own course and decide our future. It's not fashionable these days to believe in evil, but it exists. There are those who use it, and those who are used by it. Guard yourself not only against those who create the incidents, but against the ones who stand by and try to use them to their own advantage."

Her mother hadn't mentioned skinwalkers, but Ella thought that was what was going through her mind. Whether one believed in the magical powers attributed to them, or not, didn't make them any less formidable as opponents. They knew how to manipulate people and how to confuse and frighten. They were enemies both of her clan and of the tribe.

Ella accompanied her mother out the back door to the herb garden. "Of course this trouble may just be the product of criminal activity here on the reservation. We may be reading much more into it than there is."

Rose smiled slowly. "You don't believe that any more than I do, so please be careful, daughter. Our family has enemies that will take any opportunity to destroy us. But they're cowards. They won't fight us as a family, they'll try to take us down one by one."

"If anyone threatens you or if you're ever afraid, just tell me," Ella said. Their family had come under attack in the past. She hadn't sat by idly then, and she wouldn't now.

"Always the fighter. You want to meet every threat with guns and bullets. But there are other ways to fight."

"That depends on what you're fighting," Ella said, leaning over to kiss her mother. "I've got to go back inside and get ready for work."

Ella left home shortly after seven and drove directly to the police station. As she walked into what had once been Peterson Yazzie's office and was now her own, she felt a shudder travel up her spine. On the reservation, crime sometimes had a different identity. Her adversaries were too often faceless and hidden behind superstitions that were as old as the tribe itself.

She forced such thoughts from her mind. This wasn't the time to indulge in fantasy. She had a very real murder to investigate. Ella tried calling Carolyn at the hospital, but only got her voice mail. After leaving a message, she began her daily paperwork. A few minutes later, Ella heard footsteps and glanced up to see Justine at the office door.

"May I have some time off this morning, or will you need me?" she asked.

"How much time do you need?" Ella asked.

"A few hours. I want to go to Angelina's funeral."

"They've already made arrangements?"

"It was in this morning's paper. I think the senator pulled out all the stops to get it in there. The service is going to take place in about an hour."

Ella regarded her for several seconds. "You know what? I'm going to go with you."

"You want to see who'll be there?"

"You bet. There's something about that accident that bothers me. I have a feeling that we're going to end up uncovering a real can of worms."

Justine nodded. "Why don't we go together then."

Ella was reaching for her jacket when the telephone rang. "Special Investigator's office," she said quickly.

"Have you heard that the memorial service for the senator's daughter will be today, this morning in fact," Rose asked.

"You're not thinking of going, are you?" Ella asked. Her mother was a traditionalist Navajo. The last thing Ella could imagine Rose doing was attending a function for the dead.

"Me? Absolutely not, but I thought you should know, particularly because it strikes me as so artificial."

"How so?"

"The senator's wife is active in your father's church, but the senator himself usually keeps his distance to avoid prejudicing traditional voters. It seems this time he's trying to cover himself with the traditionalists by saying that it's a memorial service, not a funeral, and the burial has already taken place. Of course he's not going to appease anyone. Traditionalists believe in the four-day mourning period where the name of the deceased isn't even mentioned so a memorial service within that time is, at best, ill-planned."

"Thanks for letting me know." Ella hung up, then hurried out to join Justine.

The ride to the church took almost half an hour. Ella stared at the structure, hating its presence because of the cost it had exacted from her family. "There are times when I wish this building would disappear off the face of the earth," Ella muttered. "Whenever I look at it I feel as if someone had dropped bricks on my chest."

"It's understandable," Justine said. "Why don't you let me go in alone? I can handle this."

"No. It's part of my job. I won't back away for personal reasons."

Justine nodded slowly. "I can understand. I wouldn't either if the situation was reversed."

"Let's get busy then."

As they stepped out of Ella's Jeep, Justine noticed the senator and his wife standing by the door, greeting the handful of people who'd showed up. "I'd like to talk to the family, if you don't mind."

"Go ahead. I'm going to focus on the others who've come. Later, we can compare notes."

As the mourners gathered and went inside, Ella chose a pew near the back. Five young women had shown up. Ella recognized Mary Tapahonso. Rose was a friend of Mary's mom, and Ella had heard about the wild crowd that Mary ran around with. Present, too, was Evelyn Todacheene. The girl had recently been brought in to the station after having been caught shoplifting.

Three other young women she didn't recognize were also

there. Ella suspected they were Angelina's classmates. One in particular didn't seem to fit with the rest. She wore her hair short, dyed a carrot-like red, and was clad in black clothes with what looked like underwear on the outside. The diamond-stud nose ring she wore was the focus of attention. Ella glanced over at Justine, then allowed her gaze to drift over the women, a question in her eyes. Justine nodded, understanding.

As the memorial service progressed, each of the girls stood up and tearfully shared memories of their friend. But it was the last young woman, Diamond Nose, who took them all by surprise. Her stance warned Ella even before she spoke a word.

"My name is Ruby Atso, and I've got to tell you all that Angelina would have hated this tear fest. She was a free spirit who refused to bow down to rules and ceremonies. Angelina was my friend and I loved her, but I think that we should cut this short and go remember her in the way she would have liked. If you ask me, she would have much preferred for us to get together with a six pack of long necks and talk about the good times. I'm sorry if what I'm saying offends you, but I know that somewhere Angelina is laughing right now."

Senator Yellowhair rose quickly to usher the girl away, but Ruby was already heading for the door along with a short, pudgy yet scholarly looking girl. Ella watched, struggling not to smile. Ruby's behavior had been undeniably rude, but it was an honest response and, as a cop, she'd learned to value honesty as the rare commodity it was.

The service ended shortly afterward and Ella met Justine by the Jeep. "Do you know who the girls were?"

Justine nodded. "Ruby, you just met. Chances are it'll be a long, long time before the senator forgets her, too."

Ella smiled. "Kinda strange, wasn't she?"

"That group of Angelina's is like that. They're all freshmen at the college. The short one who left with Ruby is Norma Frank. She's smart as a whip and, in my opinion, she's going to go far. She knows she can't rely on looks. Let's face it, contact lenses aren't going to help her much so she uses the assets she's got: her brains and personality. I've never met anyone who doesn't like her. Norma's really a nice kid and lives a few miles from my place. She was really quiet until last year when her mom died. I think she's sowing some wild oats now because she's never been able to before."

"That makes more sense now. She seemed out of place around the others. Let's get all we can on these kids, okay? I want a full background report on each of them. As soon as you finish one, put it on my desk."

"No problem."

They drove back to the office, Ella at the wheel of her Jeep. "I'm going to make a stop by the morgue for the autopsy reports. You don't mind a detour, do you?"

Justine hesitated noticeably before answering. "No, that's okay," she said finally.

"I know it's not the most cheerful place in the world, but it doesn't really bother you, does it?"

"Honestly?" As Ella nodded, Justine continued. "It gives me the creeps, but not because of the *chindi*. It's just a creepy place, with shattered bodies all over the room. I don't know how Dr. Roanhorse can stand working there."

"Neither do I," Ella admitted. "But it's a good thing she can. Without her, the tribe would probably have to do without an M.E., because the salary we can offer wouldn't be competitive. The tribe owes her a debt of gratitude. She should be treated with more dignity and respect."

"I don't think being such a loner bothers her," Justine said softly. "As a matter of fact, she really goes out of her way to keep people from getting too close to her, even though you'd think she'd want friends."

"She does want friends, I think. It's just that she's been so isolated because of her job for such a long time, she's built barriers around herself to keep it from hurting."

As Ella entered the hospital's parking lot, Justine looked, deep in thought, at an indeterminate spot across the way. "Do you mind if I stop by the cafeteria on the way downstairs? My sister-in-law works there, and I'd like to talk to her. She knew Angelina far better than I did. She would have been at the memorial service, too, but her supervisor wouldn't let her take off any more time. She used up all her leave when she got married last month."

"Let me know what you find out."

Ella parked near the side door, said good-bye to Justine, then went downstairs to the morgue. As usual the floor was quiet and, though fitting, the silence made her shudder. As she entered Carolyn's office, she heard the sounds of country western music coming from the autopsy suite.

Ella peered inside cautiously and saw Carolyn cleaning up. The acrid smell of disinfectant stung her nostrils.

Carolyn looked up. "I got your E-mail and the message you left on my voice mail. I've been expecting you. Come in, but be careful where you step."

Normally she would have asked Carolyn why she was cleaning up in the middle of the day but, at the moment, she didn't think she wanted to know. "What's up?"

"First of all, I have some info on the Bitah case. I found tiny slivers of French Walnut embedded in the victim's skull. The murder weapon was probably a leg from a chair or table."

"Great," grumbled Ella. "Now all I have to do is find somebody with a three-legged chair and haul them in."

"It's probably firewood by now." Carolyn shrugged. "I also found out that Bitah had traces of mescaline in his system, but not enough to have affected him at the time of his murder. He might have been a member of a church that uses peyote during their rituals, like the Native American Church."

Ella nodded. "What else did you find out?"

"The blood at the murder scene wasn't all Bitah's. Two of the smaller spots were type AB. Bitah was type O. The subject with AB probably suffered just a minor cut, or a nosebleed. I'd guess Bitah got in a punch or two. He might have even marked the killer or killers."

"What about the senator's daughter? Have you got anything on that yet?" Ella asked.

"I've got the report ready on the blood and fluid workup we did on her. It's interesting, to say the least, considering Bitah's tests. I found very high levels of mescaline in her system, which came from more than two partially digested, ground-up peyote buttons in her stomach. That drug would certainly account for her erratic behavior prior to the accident. It would have induced hallucinations."

"But the accident didn't kill her, did it? And I thought mescaline wasn't fatal."

"Correct on both points. What killed her was a lethal quantity of hyoscyamine, hyoscine, and atropine, as well as belladonna. All those, plus ground-up, partially undigested plant leaves, indicate that Angelina had ingested a fatal dose of jimsonweed."

"Were the peyote and jimsonweed ingested at the same time?"

Carolyn nodded. "I found traces of both plants in her stomach, and some of the jimsonweed was mixed in with a partial peyote button. I think the button had been hollowed out and filled with the jimsonweed. For the symptoms to appear, she must have taken the drugs forty to forty-five minutes prior to when you saw her. Her digestive juices were just starting to work on that plant matter."

"She could, I suppose, have been trying to commit suicide, but that seems highly unlikely. My guess is that she thought she was taking peyote only," Ella said thoughtfully. "Nobody would conceal a deadly herb like jimsonweed in peyote like that by accident, though, and that brings up an interesting question. If it was murder why would anyone want to kill her? Does this have something to do with the senator, or just with her?" Ella paused for a long moment. "It also seems too coincidental to have two deaths on the same day with peyote in the bodies of both victims. Those deaths are related somehow."

"You might look into the drug connection."

"Any idea where the drugs came from?"

"All I can tell you is that both jimsonweed and peyote can be obtained locally, more or less. Peyote is found in southern New Mexico and Texas and, as you know, the Native American Church uses it in their ceremonies. Jimsonweed grows wild here in New Mexico."

"That doesn't narrow the list of suppliers down very much, unfortunately. And I can't imagine Senator Yellowhair is going to take this news very well. I doubt he'll be helpful in tracking down the source of Angelina's drug connection, since that would mean admitting she had one."

"You can count on one thing," Carolyn said. "He's not going to thank you for what we've discovered. If anything, he'll fight our findings and deny everything. He's very protective of his image. If Angelina was in anything like the Native American Church, I doubt he knew about it."

"You sound as if you know him pretty well."

Carolyn shrugged. "He's a politician. What more is there to say?"

Ella watched her friend as she returned to work. There was more to it, she could tell that from Carolyn's voice. But she also knew the futility of pressing Carolyn for an answer she didn't want to give. "I better get back to the office. I'll see you later."

As Ella came out of the elevator on the first floor, she saw Justine in the lobby. "Did you find out anything useful?" Ella asked her assistant.

"I now know a little more about Angelina and her circle of friends. But my meeting had a down side. While my sister-in-law and I were talking about Angelina, Nelson Yellowhair came up. Do you know him?"

Ella shook her head.

"He's the senator's brother; he works here as an orderly. He started accusing you and me of turning his niece's accident into something ugly to smear his brother's name. Everyone was staring, but he never let up until I walked away. I've got to tell you, I was tempted to haul him in for being a public nuisance."

Ella laughed. "We would have had difficulty making that charge stick."

"Yeah, but it would have brought him down a peg or two."

"Don't worry. We'll be doing that soon enough. Seems my instincts were right. Carolyn's findings have confirmed that Angelina's death was caused by poisoning. Regardless of the senator's wishes, this is now a felony murder investigation."

FIVE

✖ ✖ ✖

Ella sat in her office staring at the stacks of report folders on her desk. Somewhere at the bottom, she knew, was the IN basket.

Desk work was the bane of any cop's existence. Justine helped, but there was still no way to escape the massive amounts of paperwork that were often required to cut through bureaucratic red tape, particularly in high-profile or cross-jurisdictional cases.

When the phone rang, Ella picked up the receiver, eager for an excuse to put off the inevitable paper shuffling a little longer.

"It's Billy," her caller said simply.

An ingrained caution made her tense up. "I can barely hear you."

"Can't be helped," he clipped, his voice still soft. "Do you recognize my voice, or do you want confirmation?"

She concentrated, trying to make out his words. "Considering recent events, confirmation would be nice."

"Remember our conversation at the mine? Like I said then, it's one thing to argue and another to kill, L.A. Woman."

Ella remembered his comment and although it was possible someone had overheard them it didn't seem likely. "Okay. What's up?"

"I may be able to help you."

"Why are you suddenly so cooperative?"

"I heard what happened to you. I don't like having my name used as bait, even if no one was hurt. I figure that this will even out the score."

She wasn't sure if he meant the score against his buddies, or if he was making up for what had happened to her. It didn't seem to matter at the moment. She needed a lead and it was worth a little risk to get one. "What have you got?"

"Talk to Colin Anderson. He lives in Kirtland."

"Who is he?"

"He's an Anglo who used to work for the mine."

"Do you think he had something to do with the murder?"

"That, I can't say, but I will tell you that there was bad blood between him and Bitah, and with reason."

She wanted to ask more but before she could, she heard the dial tone. She considered going to Billy and trying to squeeze more out of him, but that was bound to do more harm than good. Billy Pete had just become the closest thing to an informant she had on this case.

Ella buzzed Justine in the lab, then did a quick check on her computer, searching for Anderson's name. He had no criminal record. A moment later she located his DMV records, and had his address and photo.

Justine appeared at her door. "What's up?"

"Have you got that employee list from the mine?" Ella asked.

"I requested it, but they haven't gotten one to us yet," Justine answered.

"Keep on it. There's always been tension between the mine and the tribe, but if we don't break this case soon its likely to set things off in a way nobody's going to be able to control. And keep trying to find out where the drugs came from."

The tiny lines around Justine's eyes tightened and she nodded. "This isn't going to be an easy case to close."

"I've got one lead I'm going to follow up now," Ella said, then explained what she'd learned about Anderson, though she kept Billy Pete's name out of it. "In the meantime, get that employee list. See if there's anyone there who might talk to you candidly."

"You've got it."

Ella watched her assistant leave. Justine would get results because she would never back off until she got what she was after. That was a trait they shared.

Ella phoned Blalock and, after filling him in on the autopsy results and the drug link, arranged to meet him in Kirtland to pay Anderson a visit.

"Is he another white supremacist?"

"I don't know, but I have a feeling we're going to need to do this by the book. If he's involved in this, he'll eventually have an attorney who'll be looking for a reason to throw any case we make on him right out the window."

"I can meet you there in half an hour, give or take a few minutes. That suit you?"

"It'll do," she answered, then hung up the phone and strode out of the building.

Ella drove into Kirtland twenty minutes later. The town, a little closer to Farmington than Shiprock, was small and had its roots in agriculture, though oil and gas workers were plentiful. It didn't take long for her to find the small housing area where Anderson lived. Two rows of nearly identical frame houses lined narrow streets. Some of the dwellings had carefully groomed patches of lawn and tiny trees, others were bracketed with tumbleweeds that were waist high. She immediately had the feeling of déjà vu, recalling her attempted interview with Truman. This time, Ella made up her mind, things would be different. No trouble, just a worthwhile interview in her investigation.

As she drove up the street, named River's Edge, she saw a man fitting Anderson's description walk out of a pitched roof, stucco- and brick-facade house and go directly to his pickup. She slowed her Jeep and drove past, watching him for a moment, then decided to circle the block and follow him, hanging back.

Ella picked up her cellular phone and dialed Blalock, who she figured was en route, and updated him.

"Where are you now?" Blalock asked.

"We're heading west on the old highway, toward Fruitland. We just passed Kirtland High School. I think he has a precise location in mind, but he's not exactly breaking land speed records to get there."

"Has he made you?"

"No, no chance. I'm hanging way back."

"Okay. I'm going to head in your direction on sixty-four, then take the turnoff west of Flare Hill and try to intercept him."

As Ella hung up, she saw Anderson reach into the back of the cab of the truck and take a shotgun off the gun rack.

Toddlers were playing in one yard while a young woman was pulling weeds in a flower garden. Ella's blood turned to ice and her brain screamed a warning. She gunned the accelerator, knowing she had no authority to pull him over and that all hell was going to break loose when she did. But she couldn't let him drive on. There was no reason for him to reach for a shotgun, unless he planned to use it. She had just leaned forward slightly to switch on the siren, her intuition working overtime, when it happened.

Anderson suddenly pushed the barrel of the shotgun out the passenger's window and fired. The blast shattered the living-room window of the house next door to where the children were playing.

She heard the kids screaming with terror, frightened by the terrible noise, but they appeared unhurt. The woman ran over to her children as Ella called in for backup. Someone else would have to check the house for gunshot victims. She had to catch the lunatic behind the wheel before any more shots were fired.

Anderson spotted her as soon as she activated the emergency light and siren. He whipped his truck into a turn, holding it tight, and hurtled down a graveled side road, tires spewing dust and rocks in his wake.

Ella followed close behind, taking the corner at a terrifying speed and slant. When the Jeep didn't roll, she breathed again. She kept her eyes on the vehicle ahead, searching for a way to cut off his escape.

She knew that her souped-up engine would win a speed contest on an open road, but this was not an isolated highway on the Rez. Her quarry was maneuvering expertly down a well-traveled residential road, completely ignoring the twenty-five-mile-per-hour speed limit. She, on the other hand, was hampered by her concern for foot traffic and children on bicycles.

The road curved back toward the main highway and Ella spotted the roadblock ahead. Two police cruisers had parked back to front, blocking the pickup's access to the pavement. She had him now. Anderson suddenly slammed on the brakes, slid into a one-hundred-and-eighty-degree turn, then, throwing more gravel with his tires, surged forward, heading directly at her.

Ella braked expertly, crossing into the left lane and swinging her own vehicle to block the road. A shotgun blast shattered the rear window on the passenger side of her Jeep. Safety glass sprayed everywhere, some of it stinging her neck.

Anderson turned sharply to the right, going off the road and across an alfalfa field she could see led back toward the highway a little farther to the west.

Anderson was bouncing over the uneven ground as if he'd done this a million times before. Well, maybe he had, but so had she. Being raised on the Rez had a few advantages.

Then, unexpectedly, Anderson slowed down and drove off the field, disappearing behind a small apple orchard. She caught sight of him again as he eased his vehicle down into a tumbleweed-lined arroyo closer to the river.

Ella followed Anderson into the sandy wash, then pushed her Jeep for more speed. When Anderson saw she had discovered his hiding place, he slid to a stop and jumped out of his pickup with the shotgun, and ran down a smaller tributary too narrow for the Jeep.

Ella called in her position and raced after him. She saw him climb quickly out of the arroyo, scramble down into another even narrower channel, and disappear again from view.

She didn't relish the thought of following him there. It was cool enough for rattlers to be out. The reptiles gathered along the warm sand lining the arroyos at this time of year. Anderson presented a more lethal danger, however, if he intended to ambush her.

Dry brush scraped against her slacks as she wound her way through the twisting, claustrophobic wash, listening for her adversary. Only the cool breeze whistling mournfully through the ten-foot-deep maze answered her silent questions.

She stopped at a wide point and checked ahead. Narrower channels like the one she'd just been in branched off the main arroyo but led to nothing except abrupt dead ends full of caved-in sand and tumbleweeds. Despite the wind smoothing out the sand, she managed to track him until the trail ended abruptly as she rounded a bend and encountered a wall of tumbleweeds.

Instinctively, Ella flattened against the nearly vertical wall of the arroyo. "Give it up. I'm Investigator Clah with the Navajo Tribal Police, and I'm taking you into custody."

He didn't answer, but when she heard a minor avalanche of dirt and sand, she knew he was trying to scramble up the side of the arroyo to make his escape. Ella climbed up, too, using a narrow crack in the side like a chimney, pressing against both sides to gain a hold. She had done the same thing a hundred times as a child.

She reached the top and eased cautiously onto the ground. Staying low, she looked around and saw a pair of hands gripping the edge a little farther down. The rim kept crumbling, preventing him from getting a firm hold. Ella crouched behind a thick clump of sagebrush and remained silent, waiting. Several seconds later, her quarry threw one leg over and rolled onto the top.

Ella came out of cover, gun in hand. "Don't even think of moving," she said in a low, threatening voice. "Lock your hands behind your head."

"What's going on?" he asked, looking up from the ground as if bewildered. "You want my wallet? Is this a robbery?"

Ella smiled grimly. "Don't play stupid. It could get you killed. Where's the shotgun?"

"What? I'm not hunting. I just stopped to take a whiz. I really had to go."

"Weak excuse. I've been tailing you since you left your house, Anderson. I was a witness when you sent a shotgun blast through a home's front window less than fifteen minutes ago."

"It couldn't have been me. I'm not armed," he said.

"Yeah, so you ditched the gun. Don't worry. We'll find it," she snapped, handcuffing him. She noticed fresh scratches on his wrists.

"I don't even own a shotgun, Officer. You must have me mixed up with someone else."

Ella read Anderson his rights and helped him to his feet just as the sound of police sirens approached. "You can explain it to them," she said, turning to face the approaching cruisers.

Blalock was the first to reach her. "Good job."

"Threatening an unarmed man is a 'good job'? I bet this is the way you get your promotions, huh?" Anderson baited.

Blalock gave him a cold, hard stare. "Save it. You're lucky no one in that house was hit." His gaze traveled over Ella. "You okay?"

"Just scratches from flying glass and the tumbleweeds. No big deal."

As she turned Anderson over to the County Sheriff's Department deputy, Blalock glanced around. "Where's his weapon?"

"He ditched the shotgun, but it's got to be around here somewhere. His wrists were all scratched up. He must have jammed it into the brush."

As they started to look around for the weapon, Ella saw a familiar looking car on the dirt road not far away. She only caught a quick glimpse of the driver, but she didn't need more than that to know Justine had heard of her call for backup and had responded. News of an officer in trouble always traveled at warp speed.

"I have a feeling the shotgun is back in the arroyo," Ella said. "Let's go back and check it out after we get the people here organized."

Justine joined them as they walked back to Anderson's truck.

"How can I help?" she asked, looking carefully at Ella to assure herself her boss was okay.

"Go with one of the sheriff's deputies and start searching around for a shotgun. Anderson ditched his weapon somewhere."

"Who did he assault besides you?" Justine asked, looking toward the broken window on Ella's Jeep.

Ella glanced at Blalock as she reached into her vehicle for a pair of leather gloves. "Did you hear whose house that was? You said earlier that no one was hurt."

Blalock nodded. "Yes to the first question and no, nobody was hit, except for a lamp, apparently. You're going to love this part, though. Turns out the house is occupied by one of the Navajo supervisors at the mine, Jesse Woody. Do you know him?"

"I've heard of him, but I don't know him personally."

"I do," Justine said. "He's a friend of my brother's."

"Leave the search to us, then, Justine. Go talk to Woody. He's either at home or at the county lockup in Farmington by now, giving a statement. See if he'll talk to you."

They watched Ella's assistant drive away, then Blalock turned back to Ella. "Justine might be able to get more than the sheriff's deputy did. From what he said over the radio, Woody's a tight-lipped son-of-a-gun."

Ella led the way back to the arroyo where she'd chased Anderson, then scrambled down, Blalock behind her. "He ran this way, but I lost him for a while."

"Translation, the shotgun could be stashed anywhere in here," Blalock snapped.

"It twists and turns, but isn't really a very big area, and I didn't see it when I walked back along the top with the prisoner. There are a limited number of possibilities and he only had a few seconds." She gazed past the wall of tumbleweeds. "There. That's where I would have stashed it."

The breeze stirred the dry, prickly balls and they made a hissing sound as if alive. She glanced at Blalock, hoping he'd have the gentlemanly urge to spare her having to step into the bristly tangle. She wasn't about to mention she was allergic to tumble-weeds. It wasn't something a male cop would do. He'd razz her about being a wimp.

Typical for Blalock, he gave her a blank look. "No sense in both of us getting scratched up. You've got the gloves and are already halfway there. Since it's your arrest and your case, go for it."

So much for chivalry. Women cops were rarely that lucky. Ella began carefully lifting the balls and tossing them aside. The process was slow and painful. Despite her gloves, the needles stung her wrists between the gloves and her shirt cuffs, cutting into her skin and raising little welts. But the effort paid off. At the back of the pile, jammed down as far as it would go, she found the shotgun.

"Here it is. We need to bag it."

Blalock motioned for one of the deputies who'd been search-ing a nearby channel.

Ella's arms were sore and scratchy, and to make matters worse, unless she washed up soon, the small cuts would swell and hurt even more. FB-Eyes would have laughed himself stu-pid, had he known.

As two deputies eased the weapon into a pair of large grocery bags and wrapped the package with string, Ella felt the itching sensation around the scratches growing in intensity. She struggled not to touch them, knowing it would make things worse.

"Come on, Ella," Blalock said. "We better head back in." He took two steps back, lunged forward and, with a mighty leap, was at the surface again.

Ella scrambled up, surprised at Blalock's agility. "Fill me in on Anderson. I'm sure you ran a make on him when this chase started. I found nothing noteworthy on him, did you?"

"He has no criminal record, and he's not half as interesting as something Jesse Woody said, though he glossed over it. Woody alluded to an organization of Anglos at the mine who try to un-dermine the Navajo workers. You think that's The Brotherhood Truman mentioned?"

Ella shrugged. "Probably. I know that the mine has always been a center of controversy. Billy Pete said something about workers having problems there, but nothing specific.

"My gut tells me that the mine is at the center of what's happening, though," Ella continued. "For example, I recently found out that there's a company incorporated in Angelina Yellowhair's name—just a paper company without any employees—that owns shares in the corporation that runs the power plant and the coal mine operation."

Blalock raised his eyebrows. "That's some connection! You know the money for that had to have come from the senator."

"The more I learn, the more this case bothers me. Let's see what we can get from Anderson while my assistant talks to Woody. If anyone can get more information from him, she should be able to."

"Maybe Anderson will turn out to be Bitah's killer, and we can close at least one case right away," Blalock suggested.

Ella shook her head. "That's too simple. I never expect things to be easy, and I'm seldom disappointed."

A half hour later, Ella joined Blalock at the Farmington jail. She'd had a chance to wash up and her arms had stopped itching. The scratches still hurt, but it was a vast improvement. The shotgun was still being processed for prints, but tests run on Anderson substantiated that he had fired a weapon. Forensics could probably even confirm the gunpowder residue was from the same brand of shells found in the recovered shotgun.

As she walked down the hall to the room used for questioning, she saw Justine coming out of one of the offices. Her expression was one of frustration and anger.

"Did Woody give you anything at all?" Ella asked.

"He told me to go play cop with someone who hadn't been around when I was still in diapers."

"Don't sweat it. I'll give it a try."

Blalock nodded in agreement. "I'll grill Anderson while you talk to Woody."

Ella nodded. Considering what they were up against,

Blalock's chances of getting somewhere with Anderson would increase if she wasn't around. She didn't want to repeat the fiasco with Truman, and the situations were all too similar.

Ella strode into the office where Woody waited. The short, round-faced Navajo man stood by the window, staring at the parking lot outside. He turned his head to look at her then, pointedly ignoring her, turned away.

"I need to talk to you," Ella said, "and believe it or not, you need to talk to me."

"Don't speak for me. If you knew one thing about our ways, you would know it's not right."

"You want to talk about right and wrong?" she countered. "We've had two deaths on the reservation, all in less than a day. I have my hands full, and unless I get some leads on the miner's death soon, I won't be able to track down his killer. The person responsible will go free, and that serves no one's sense of justice."

Woody didn't respond. Ella sat down to wait. Long pauses were not uncommon among The People.

Finally Woody turned around. "I have no knowledge that can help you. I'm a supervisor," he said, measuring his words carefully. "To do my job I have to stay neutral and not get involved in controversies that interfere with business."

"If the lines at the mine are being drawn according to race, you'll be assigned a side whether or not you choose one."

He nodded slowly then pulled out a chair and sat down. "My division isn't plagued by troubles like some of the others have been, and it won't ever be. I can spot a troublemaker miles away, and as soon as I do, I have him transferred."

She watched Woody. It was evident in his features and the way he bit off each sentence that there was an internal struggle going on. "Was Anderson in your division?"

He nodded. "The *bilagáana,* Anglo if you prefer, spent only a few weeks working for me. I suggested he transfer to another section, and he took my advice. Then, a few weeks later, he quit. That surprised me, but I never asked why."

"Who are the other troublemakers?"

"There is a group of *bilagáana* workers who call themselves The Brotherhood. I don't know who they are and, in fact, the only reason I know they exist is because of their calling cards. Every time there's a dispute between an Anglo and a Navajo worker, the Navajo worker pays a price, whether or not the problem was his fault. Billy Pete, for one, got his truck vandalized. Did you know about that?"

She shook her head.

"The murdered man you spoke of, and others like him, are the counterpart to The Brotherhood. Anderson, judging from his actions and his talk, is part of The Brotherhood. They advocate violence to get their way. The Navajo group, formed by the man who was killed, kept the scales balanced."

"What will happen now that he's gone?"

"I don't know, but I've already seen more signs of trouble. Some of the men are restless and searching for answers on their own. They want revenge. And let me tell you, it's easy to pick a scapegoat when the lines are drawn by race."

"What exactly does The Brotherhood protest?"

"They oppose the hiring practices enforced on the reservation. They believe *we* are the ones who are racist."

"*Why?*"

He shrugged. "Outside the reservation, race can't be a factor influencing employment. Theoretically, Navajos compete with Anglos and vice versa without preference on either side. On our land, Navajos are given priority. Anderson and others like him have vowed to fight that policy. What they forget is that we mine the gift that comes from *our* land. But it isn't something that is renewable. When it is gone, the income it gives the tribe will be gone forever. When an Anglo man owns property and there is something of value in it, he can tell the company he authorizes to extract it to hire his relatives. It then becomes part of the deal the company accepts in exchange for the right to extract what is of value. The *Dineh* is doing the same thing with the resource we hold in common, acting as an extension of the small family units that exist on the outside."

Ella nodded. It was a concept that was hard for many outsiders to accept but it seemed clear and fair to her. "Is Truman part of The Brotherhood?"

Woody again said nothing for a long time. His gaze settled across the room, watching as the wind coming in from the open window pushed the blinds away from the wall, only to rattle back in place as each gust died down. "I believe he is, and so do others," he said at length.

"Are you part of the Navajo group that is trying to keep the scales balanced?" she asked.

"Yes. It's my way of protecting the mine and those who work there. I don't tolerate anything that fosters chaos."

"Is that what you feel The Brotherhood is doing?"

"They're bringing outside problems onto our land. We have precious few resources. This reservation was given to us, a land considered practically worthless by everyone else. Now that we find a few things of value on it, they want to dictate new terms." He shook his head. "We're bound by the old treaties. They should be bound by them also."

She nodded. "Does management at the mine acknowledge the existence of The Brotherhood?"

"If you're asking me whether they know about it, the answer is yes. On the other hand, if you're asking if they acknowledge it officially, the answer is no. And they won't. Not in a million years. It's the wrong kind of publicity for the stockholders."

"Who else is a member of The Brotherhood?"

"I don't know."

Ella gave him an incredulous look.

"It's true," he said wearily. "We learn who stands with them only by accident most of the time. They don't exactly wear uniforms. Secrecy serves them far better than publicity. What makes them even harder to fight is that most of the Anglos at the mine aren't involved, so it's hard to pick out the guilty."

"If you find out the names of others in the Brotherhood, will you tell me?"

He considered it, then at last shook his head. "I think police involvement will only bring more unrest. This needs to be handled behind the scenes, and decisively."

"Then you also advocate violence?"

"Not murder, no, but a certain amount of retaliation is right and necessary. The *Dineh* must protect itself."

Ella placed her card on the table before him. "If you change your mind, or if you need help, day or night, call me."

SIX

Blalock was waiting in the hall when she emerged from the room. "How did it go?" he asked.

"Better than I expected," she said, filling him in.

"You're not sure where your sympathies lie, are you, Clah?" Blalock observed.

She took a deep breath, giving herself time to think. "Where my sympathies lie is not the point. I don't condone murder," she answered. "How did you fare with Anderson?"

"He's one tough buzzard," Blalock spat out. "He claims he didn't fire into Jesse Woody's home, though the powder residue test came out positive."

"Did he happen to say why he doesn't work at the mine anymore?"

"He claims he quit for personal reasons. That would be easy enough to check, so I think he's telling the truth."

"Woody didn't fire him," Ella said. "But for Anderson to blaze away at the man's home with a shotgun in broad daylight implies a lot more is going on there."

"Keep digging from your end," Blalock said. "And I'll do the same."

"Did Anderson say anything about The Brotherhood?"

Blalock smirked. "He asked me if that was some kind of civil rights organization. After that, he refused to answer any more questions until he had an attorney."

"Well, that scarcely comes as a surprise."

"I'm getting a search warrant delivered and I've going to go over every inch of Anderson's home. You want to come along?

"You bet." Ella found Justine waiting for her by the damaged Jeep and asked her to come along to Anderson's house. If by chance they got lucky, either Justine or she could follow up immediately on any name they turned up, while the other continued the search.

They went through the house methodically, working with the precision only years of training could bring. Ella sat with a large photo album she'd found stashed on the bookshelf, searching through it for anything that would lead her to other members of The Brotherhood, or the opposing faction made up of Navajos that Jesse Woody had mentioned.

Blalock came back into the room. "Unless you find something there, we'll be leaving empty handed."

Ella showed him the page she was looking at. "All these are candid shots of mostly Navajo company employees, and none are looking at the camera. They either didn't care, or else didn't know they were being photographed. The page before is loaded with snapshots taken during official group functions, but most were obviously posed." Ella stood and walked to the shelf where three cameras had been placed side by side. "Look at these. They're all high quality, and the fast telephoto lens on the one on the left is worth some serious money."

"Like surveillance cameras?" Blalock glanced down at the open page of the photo album. "These remind me of the photos our guys take at funerals and parties when we're tracking criminal activities. Except in this case, Navajos seemed to have been singled out."

"Exactly what I was thinking. I'd like to make a note of all the Navajos pictured in there. Any objections to my tagging it and taking it to our lab? We can make copies there of any interesting-looking photographs, then return them to you."

"Go for it, but I'll need it all back ASAP."

Ella handed the album to Justine. "Give it top priority. Go."

Blalock's face was grim. "When will you have the final paperwork on Bitah's death?"

"I'm not sure, but I can call our M.E. and find out."

He handed her his cellular.

Ella dialed, then waited. She spoke to Carolyn briefly, then handed the phone back to Blalock. "She has it ready now."

"Have her fax me a copy as soon as possible. If we don't clear this case right away, the Bureau is going to send someone to *help* us. With all the press hate groups like this have been getting, it's a very touchy subject in the Bureau. The higher-ups won't want another front-page story. Get my drift?"

"Yeah, unfortunately." She knew from experience that having two agencies involved in one case only made it murkier.

"I'll see if the local narcotics teams or the DEA have anything on peyote dealers that would help us out. The Yellowhair girl was getting her stuff from someone around here, I'll wager. Maybe from one of the gangs, or else one of those churches that uses peyote in their rituals. You might check out whether she was a member," Blalock suggested.

Ella gave him a steely look. "Already on it."

Ella drove back to the reservation, her mind filled with speculation. If only she could rid herself of the certainty that the worst was yet to come. As the sun slipped below the horizon, she could feel the power of the night. It was as if something was holding its breath out there, the darkness resonating with a pulse of its own.

Ella raced along the nearly deserted highway, taking comfort from traveling at high speed. It forced her to concentrate on the road and helped her forget her troubles. Funny how danger could soothe her at times.

By the time she reached the hospital, she felt focused and ready to work the case again. As usual, the elevator going down to the basement was infernally slow, making Ella wish she hadn't taken the lazy route and had opted for the stairs instead. Waiting was always the hard part for her.

As the door slid open, she saw Howard Lee talking to someone down the hall. Automatically, she noted the orderly's name tag. What was Nelson Yellowhair doing down here, talking to Carolyn's student assistant? As soon as Yellowhair spotted her, he stepped into the stairwell, disappearing from her view.

Ella felt her skin prickle with a coldness different from that familiar to the basement. Brushing the sensation aside, along with her usual distaste for the morgue, she forced herself to look confident and waved at Howard. "Wait up."

Howard looked reluctant, but did as she asked. As she drew near he glanced at a clock on the wall. "I'm in a terrible rush. If I'm late one more time, Dr. Roanhorse is going to have my hide."

"Let's go, then," Ella said, quickening her steps. "We can talk while we walk. What was Nelson Yellowhair doing down here?"

Howard shrugged. "Not much. He was on break and came down to talk."

Ella watched Lee, certain the man was lying but not knowing why. "How long have you been friends with Yellowhair?"

"Friends?" Lee shook his head. "I wouldn't call us friends exactly. We're coworkers. He comes down here every once in a while because his supervisor wouldn't be caught de . . . well, he can take a break here without anyone bugging him."

Carolyn came out of the autopsy suite just as Howard and Ella arrived. "You're late," she said, glancing at Lee. "I'm not going to stand for this nonsense."

"Doctor, the detective needed—"

"Save it. Get the tissue samples I left for you and prepare those slides. Let me know when you finish."

"Right away, Doctor."

Ella watched Howard Lee scurry away like a dog who'd been caught up on the master's favorite chair. "I didn't hold him up."

"Yeah, I figured that. This guy isn't going to make it through med school unless he gets his act together." Reaching into the top drawer of her desk, she pulled out the autopsy reports on both

Bitah and Angelina Yellowhair. "Everything's pretty much the way I reported in my preliminary. Sorry there's not much new to add," Carolyn said, then reached into her pocket. "Oh, Justine just called. Here's her message."

Ella glanced at the note. "Interesting. According to Justine, Bitah was a member of a splinter group of the Native American Church called the Native Justice Church. The Native American Church is very pacifistic while the Navajo Justice Church is militant in the extreme. They don't operate under the same strictures, but they're able to use peyote legally for religious purposes under the same legal umbrella that protects the NAC.

"Unfortunately, that doesn't explain where Angelina Yellowhair got her peyote," Ella continued. "She didn't attend either church, or any other according to what Justine has been able to find out."

Ella leaned back against the desk. "By the way, have you heard anyone, patients or staff, talking about a pro-Anglo organization called The Brotherhood?"

Carolyn's eyebrows furrowed. "No, I can't say I have. You want me to keep my ears open?"

"If you could."

"By the way, there is one thing that may help you. I found out Bitah had a girlfriend on staff here. Her name's Judy Lujan."

"Thanks. I appreciate the tip."

"How are things going with you and FB-Eyes?" Carolyn asked, offering her a cup of coffee.

Ella took a sip. "It's hard to say. Sometimes I think we're working well as a team, but I still have trouble thinking of him as someone who's on the same side I am."

"Ingrained interagency competitiveness, you think?"

"That's part of it, sure. I hate relying on the Bureau. The tribe hired *me* to produce results because of my added training, and I want to be able to deliver the goods without calling in outside help. Big Ed, in particular, has taken a lot of flak on my account. I'd like to justify the trust he's placed in me."

"When someone shows faith in either of us we tend to go

overboard repaying them. That says a lot about us, you know, though I'm not always sure if that's good or just pathetic."

"I'll pass on that question."

Reports in hand, Ella went back upstairs to try to find Judy Lujan. It took awhile to track the woman down. Ella finally found her sitting alone in the staff lunchroom, nursing a cup of coffee.

As Ella introduced herself, the round-faced, high-cheeked woman in her mid thirties looked wearily at her. "I've been expecting you to come by," she said without inflection. "But I wish it hadn't been today. I just lost a patient. Tuberculosis—that strain that nobody can do anything about because it's resistant to antibiotic therapy. Medicine has come very far, but sometimes it just loops and takes us back to where we started."

"I need your help. I wouldn't bother you if it could be avoided, but we have to find your friend's killer," she said, avoiding mentioning the dead man by name in case Lujan found it offensive.

"I know." She stared down into the coffee cup as if searching for answers in the thick blackness. "I dated him, but there never was anything serious between us. I think he liked me because I never asked him any questions he couldn't answer easily."

"Were you aware of his activities outside work?"

She nodded. "I know he was fighting The Brotherhood, but not the particulars about it."

Ella held her breath. This was an unexpected break. "Do you know who any members of The Brotherhood are?"

"No, but neither did anyone else. That's what my friend and his friends were working to uncover. They needed to find out who their opponents were before they could handle the problem." Judy held up her hand. "And, before you ask, no, I never asked how they planned to take care of the problem." She leaned back in her chair. "I can tell you this, though. My friend helped form his new church because he believed in using violence to fight violence. That attitude was the major reason our relationship was at a standstill. I told him I had no intention of becoming the widow of a crusader."

"You believed his work would jeopardize his life?"

"When people use violence as a means to an end, they often end up its victim. In my opinion, that's exactly why he's dead now."

"Who was your friend close to?"

"That's easy to answer. Billy Pete and Kevin Tolino."

"I know Billy," Ella said smoothly, "but what can you tell me about Kevin?"

"Kevin is a Navajo rights advocate and an attorney for the tribe. He handles all cases pertaining to discrimination on and off the reservation on behalf of tribal members."

"Thanks. I'll talk to him."

"One more thing?"

Ella stopped near the door and glanced back. "Yes?"

"Don't tell anyone that I helped you. I don't need any more problems. I've got enough of my own."

"Are you afraid of our own people?" Ella asked, surprised.

Judy seemed to consider the question. "Let's just say that I'm not sure if I *should* be afraid of them or not."

Ella's mind was spinning with speculations as she walked out to the parking lot. If the *Dineh* were afraid of the Navajo activists, as well as leery of The Brotherhood, then the problem was even bigger than she'd realized.

She had almost reached the Jeep when she heard her name being called. Turning her head, she saw Carolyn rushing toward her.

Ella turned back to meet her. "What's going on?"

"I just saw the evening paper. Have you?"

"No, I haven't had a chance."

"Here. Take my copy. I think you'll find it interesting." Pressing the paper into Ella hands, Carolyn glanced back. "I better get back before that student of mine screws up every slide."

"See you."

As Carolyn jogged back, Ella opened the Navajo newspaper, grateful as always that it was written in English. Her Navajo was as rusty as an old horseshoe nail left in an arroyo for a decade or two.

As she unfolded it, three headlines competed for her attention. Bitah's murder was one, the other two were about the Yellowhair family. The final story described how Senator Yellowhair had been in a motel with his aide, a bosomy young woman half his age, when the police had found him and delivered news of his daughter's death.

Her call sign on the radio interrupted Ella's reading. She picked up the mike and identified herself.

"I've got IDs on some of the Navajos in the shots," Justine informed her. "It's a pretty mixed bag. Even that medical student of Carolyn's, Howard Lee, is in one photo. Apparently Lee works one shift a week in the First Aid Center at the mine for college credit. I've already tried to talk to the regular mine workers I know who were in the pictures, and I'll get to all the others. Not everyone has been cooperative, especially because many didn't know they'd been photographed in the first place. I did learn that Anderson liked taking photos as a form of harassment. It would be annoying to have someone taking photos of you if there was nothing you could do about it without starting a fight."

"I have a lead or two of my own. Meet me for breakfast tomorrow morning at seven at my mother's house. Mom will fix your favorite: fry bread with honey, and eggs."

"I'll be there. I wouldn't miss your mother's fry bread for the world."

Ella folded up the newspaper and decided to head for home. It had been a long day. She'd read the rest of the paper there later, along with the full autopsy reports on Bitah and Angelina Yellowhair. Things just weren't adding up right. A kid experimenting with drugs would have done that in the company of others, not alone in a car. Finding out Bitah had also had peyote in his system certainly had given rise to many questions, but fewer answers than Ella had hoped. Bitah had been twice Angelina's age and a member of a church where peyote was part of the sacrament. It seemed unlikely that he would have associated with Angelina unless she had attended his splinter church which, according to Justine's research, hadn't happened.

As Ella sped down the highway she decided to take a detour.

Maybe it was time to have a talk with her brother. Though the NAC was based on different beliefs and came from different roots, they both emphasized the spiritual. As a *hataalii,* Clifford might know more about it than the cops did.

Ella turned off onto the road to her brother's new home. After the trouble with the skinwalkers, and the threat to their baby, Loretta had insisted on a new start. Her brother had spent months building this new house on high ground, a few miles from her mother's, but in a nearly inaccessible area bordered on three sides by dry arroyos, and rock outcroppings.

As she approached, Ella stared at the gray stucco house. To her it would always look like a bunker she'd once seen in a photo of the Maginot Line, but Loretta was happy here and the baby, well, he would be happy anywhere as long as his family was with him.

She moved closer slowly, putting the vehicle in low gear and hoping that the headlights would help her spot anything on the unpaved road that could damage her vehicle.

Light flowed from inside the house, bathing the porch in a soft glow. Ella passed the house and parked by the sturdy log hogan beside it. The blanket that covered the east facing door billowed as a breeze blew against it. She caught the flicker of firelight inside.

Ella switched off the engine and waited. A minute later her brother came to the entrance, pulled the blanket aside, and waved an invitation for her.

"What brings you here so late? Is Mom all right?" he asked quickly.

"As far as I know. I came here to pick your brain, big brother."

"Ah." He walked back in and sat down on a sheepskin on the left, or southern side, of the center where a warm fire was going in the fire pit.

Ella entered, but according to tradition, went to the right, across from him and the fire, and on the north side.

As she retrieved another sheepskin from the ones folded and stacked on a low wooden table, she glanced around. The peeled pine logs above her had been carefully arranged at angles to form the strong-looking roof, and the joints between the logs had been carefully sealed with mud. Out of respect for the Holy People who had built the first hogans, Clifford had placed small pieces of abalone, turquoise, and obsidian in several places along the walls.

Ella sat down and turned to her brother. "What have you heard about that new splinter group of the Native American Church, the one they call the Navajo Justice Church?"

"What is it you want to know? I have very little to do with them or the NAC, as I'm sure you realize. I follow the Navajo Way."

"Can you tell me what part peyote plays in their rituals?"

"In the NAC, peyote is considered a sacrament. They claim the white man has the Bible to learn about God, and they have peyote, which induces visions to help them grow in wisdom. The church stresses family values, harmony and peace, and the avoidance of alcohol. I've heard the splinter group, the Navajo Justice Church, is radically different. They embrace the use of violence and use peyote to induce visions that may show them how to defeat their enemies."

"And jimsonweed?"

"*Nobody* experiments with that. Jimsonweed, the many-flowered four-o'clock, is like most of the poisonous plants. It has a counterpart that restores health if used in time. Without the antidote used by our people for generations, you'd get very sick, and could very likely end up dead. But why are you asking me these things?"

"Confidentially?" She saw him nod, then continued. "The senator's daughter had ingested peyote buttons and a lethal dose of ground-up jimsonweed before her accident. The M.E. also discovered traces of peyote in the dead miner's body. He's a member of the splinter church, but the senator's daughter is not, as far as we can tell. I'm looking for possible connections."

He appeared to weigh the matter. "What doesn't make sense is why anyone would deliberately swallow jimsonweed. Many of our people have been taught which herbs are dangerous and know enough to avoid them. But you said that jimsonweed was ground up before it was eaten by the senator's daughter?"

Ella nodded. "There are only two options: suicide or murder. And suicide doesn't fit in with the facts we have so far."

Clifford walked to a line of jars near the west wall, reached inside, and filled a small beaded pouch. "This is the antidote to jimsonweed, should you ever need it. And be careful what you eat or drink. The signs of jimsonweed poisoning range from headaches and thirst to drowsiness and convulsions. Eventually you go into a coma."

Ella nodded, taking the pouch and placing it carefully in her jacket pocket. "Thanks, brother."

"Once a person starts showing major symptoms of jimsonweed poisoning, it's probably too late. The best time to take the antidote is as soon after ingesting the poison as possible." He sat down again and regarded her thoughtfully for a long time. "We're starting another cycle of sorrows and, as usual, our enemies are staying well behind the scenes."

"As a cop, it's my job to find the ones responsible for creating trouble. I'll put things back on track soon. Count on it."

There'll still be problems, ones you won't be able to fix." He shook his head. "The *Dineh*'s children are caught between cultures: searching for an identity and looking everywhere except in the right direction. The gangs are getting stronger with each passing day. They, too, use drugs, but without reason and without regard to others or themselves."

"One step at a time, big brother. First, I have to find whoever is behind the two deaths we already have. That's what the tribe pays me to do. The unrest at the mine is an additional concern and may be connected to the murders. I don't know yet. That company's presence on our land has always caused trouble, only the form it takes changes. And as far as the gangs go, that's a problem that may be here to stay. We have to accept that some kids may turn away from our ways forever."

"They are our future."

"It's their right to follow a path of their own choosing."

"Sometimes I look at my son and wonder what legacy he'll inherit."

"The *Dineh* won't disappear, and neither will our ways. We've endured too long and come too far for that."

"I hope you're right." He leaned forward. "Do you still wear the fetish I gave you?"

Ella pulled out the leather cord, bringing the stone badger out from inside her shirt.

He smiled and nodded. "I'm glad. It may be the only protection you can count on."

Ella felt a chill seeping through her skin, and piercing her bones.

"I can say a blessing over you, if you'd like."

Ella nodded.

Clifford took a pinch of pollen from a pouch at his waist, touched the tip of his tongue, the top of his head, and Ella's, then threw it toward the heavens, invoking the gods.

"Keep your wits about you," he said, at last. "And don't forget that there is more to life than what you see with your eyes. When you discount everything you don't understand by labeling it as superstition, you stop being aware of an enemy who can destroy you."

Ella left her brother's hogan more disturbed than ever. Once again, she felt torn between the old ways and the new. She envied the way Clifford's staunch beliefs helped him face dangers with assuredness.

Ella then felt the weight of her pistol and the bulge in her back pocket where she kept her badge when it wasn't displayed. These were the things that defined her and gave her purpose. The old ways had power, she wouldn't discount them, but neither could she adhere solely to them. The truth was, she was a blend of the old and the new, and that was where her strength lay.

By the time she arrived at her mother's house it was very late. The house was encased in darkness. Ella went inside quietly, left a note informing her mother that Justine would be joining them for breakfast, and went to her room. Only Two, lying in the hall outside her mother's door, acknowledged Ella's presence.

Tired, but too keyed up to sleep, she began her nightly ritual, answering the few posts she'd received on E-Mail, then switching over to her never-ending game of solitaire. Maybe someday those cards would align right, but then again, that victory would only mean the start of another round.

SEVEN

✖ ✖ ✖

Ella was at the breakfast table, reading the last of the article on Senator Yellowhair. Justine read the story over her shoulder while taking bites out of a piece of fry bread she'd loaded with honey and butter. Ella could hear her chewing, and the irritating sound was getting on her nerves. "The way you eat, you should weigh about nine hundred pounds," Ella said through clenched teeth.

"I'm on a special diet," Justine said. "I eat only what tastes good. But then I jog until I'm ready to drop."

Ella remembered a time when she'd done the same thing. Lately, she hadn't done much jogging, and her favorite slacks were feeling as if they'd shrunk. She took a deep breath then let it out. Maybe it was time to diet. Then she saw the plate filled with fresh tortillas and eggs with chile that her mother was bringing over. The diet would wait until lunch.

"I can't believe the senator. He blames everyone but his own seedy self," Justine said.

Rose glanced at the article after setting the plates down. "That public apology of his doesn't amount to much. He says he met with the elders of his clan in his uncle's hogan and has promised to address his problems with his wife. Well, if he really did do that, you can bet it was only because he thought it would sound good to the tribe. And I don't believe his claim that his wife has forgiven him and harmony has been restored in his household. That statement has enough fertilizer in it to feed my herb garden for ten years."

"My guess is he got his wife to agree to that statement so he could save his own butt," Ella answered, wolfing down the still-warm tortilla. She glanced at Justine. "What we need to find out is how our people finally managed to find him. Who gave us the tip? And how did his wife find out where he was? I have a feeling those answers will give us more information than anything written here."

Rose studied the two women as they ate then shook her head sadly. "I'm going outside to work on my garden. I'll leave you two to discuss crime fighting."

Justine smiled as Rose walked out slowly. "I don't think she'll ever understand why we love police work."

"I think on some level she does, but since it's not the road she would have chosen for me, she rails against it, hoping somehow I'll change my mind," Ella said.

Justine nodded. "My mother is like that, too, at times. But she has plenty of grandchildren so it's not quite the same thing."

"Continuity and family have always been part of everything the *Dineh* are. At least my mother has Julian now, though. Having a grandchild is important to her."

Ella stood up and rinsed off her plate. "But enough of that. I've got another lead we need to look into: Kevin Tolino. He was a good friend of Bitah's. I want a complete background check on him."

"I know Kevin. Like you, he left the Rez for several years. But now he's back, working for the tribe. If anyone finds out I'm checking up on him, though, the fur's gonna fly. He's from the Towering House clan, the same as our tribal president."

"Go for it anyway, Justine. We need to get an inside track into the activities of the Navajos involved with the problems at the mine. I also want you to find out all you can about this splinter group of the NAC that Bitah founded. Maybe Tolino, being a friend of Bitah's, knows something about that."

"I could go undercover. With luck, I might even be able to join the church."

"No. I don't want you undercover. Any cover story we could concoct wouldn't be enough, not with these guys. Remember how they set me up to issue their warning? Be careful and watch yourself at all times."

"Late yesterday I finally received that complete list of employees from the mine. There are a few more names I recognized. I can follow up on those. And the report on Frank Smith also came in. He's the Anglo that Bitah had problems with," she reminded Ella.

"Yes, the man Bitah suspected of trying to stir up trouble among the Navajo workers. What did you find out?"

"Not much. I spoke to several people about Smith. Everyone knew about the problems Bitah claimed Smith had engineered, but nobody had any proof. Nobody trusted Smith, but I've got the feeling it was mostly innuendo that condemned him."

She thought of the distrust she and Carolyn faced every day. "It's easy to condemn when you don't have to prove your allegations."

Ella walked outside with Justine and waited on the porch as her assistant waved to Rose, then drove away. She'd done the right thing sending Justine to talk to the miners. Had she gone herself, it would have been an uphill battle to win people's trust and get the answers she needed. Among the Navajos there were many who still considered her an outsider and would not open up to her.

Ella said good-bye to Rose then drove to her office. The problem was her actions spoke for her. She was a cop and, to her, breaking the law demanded the same penalty from a Navajo as it would an Anglo. She was as likely to arrest a member of the tribe for fighting The Brotherhood and breaking the law, as she was to arrest one of the members of The Brotherhood. That fact would not gain the sympathy of any member of either faction or persuade anyone to become her informant. Justine had a more disarming personality and had not acquired that hard edge that Ella possessed after years with the Bureau.

Ella arrived at her office, resigned to working there for a while. She didn't like the tedium of paperwork, but there was no choice. She needed to plough through the reports to get the facts she needed. First, she assessed the report that had just come in on Frank Smith. The man had been honorably discharged from the navy after serving on a construction battalion as a heavy equipment operator. He had no criminal record. Bitah's allegations didn't fit in with the hard-working, churchgoer profile they had on this man, but stranger things had happened.

Just as Ella stood up to get some coffee, her intercom buzzed and she was summoned to see Big Ed. Trying not to feel like a kid being called to the principal's office, she went down the hall, knocked on the open door, then walked in.

"I got a call from Senator Yellowhair," he said. "He's accusing you of trying to ruin his reputation. He said you're looking into his personal files and violating his daughter's privacy, searching for a way to embarrass him."

"He's getting worried because what I'm finding is a good enough reason to keep digging." She recounted what she'd discovered about the peyote and jimsonweed that had killed Angelina, and Bitah's connection to the offshoot of the NAC that used peyote in its rituals. She also told him about the shares of the mine she'd found were controlled by the company listed under Angelina's name.

"Does the senator know that you have all this?"

"Not yet. I have an appointment to talk to him about the case this morning in the hope that I can get him to back off and let us do our job. But I plan to hold back any mention of the power plant and mining shares for now. Revealing that might cause him to clam up and send in a raiding party of lawyers. Holding a few things back now will give us an edge later on.

"Sounds like a good plan, but tread carefully. I don't want to have to spend the next week defending you and the department while there's important work to be done."

Ella left the building and headed out to the senator's house. She wasn't sure exactly how to approach the situation in order to get the best results. Her goal was simple enough, however.

First, she needed to learn everything she could about Angelina, then try to uncover whether any connection existed between the girl and Bitah.

When she arrived, several sedans and at least four new pickups were parked around the house, a large stucco building with a pitched roof. The residence was surrounded by a very un-Navajo-like block wall and an expensively manicured lawn. Ella waited in her car. Though she knew the senator wasn't a traditionalist, the gesture would show respect and might help set him at ease.

After a few minutes, Ella saw the senator's wife come to the porch and wave an invitation. Ella walked through the gate and greeted the tall, slender Navajo woman who was dressed in a black business suit. She wasn't wearing any jewelry except for a large diamond wedding ring, and Ella noticed that the skillfully applied makeup failed to hide the strain on her middle-aged face. Ella expressed her condolences for the loss of their daughter.

The senator stood up as they entered the formal living room. His eyes were as wary as an animal who knew it was being hunted.

"How can I help you, Investigator?" He gestured for Ella to take a seat in a high-backed wooden chair, then Yellowhair sat down across from her on a leather sofa.

Abigail Yellowhair chose an uncomfortable-looking armchair near the passageway into a formal dining room where, from the sounds of low conversation, Ella assumed guests of the family were gathered.

Ella noticed that the senator and his wife avoided looking at each other. Despite the senator's statement, it was clear that tension between the couple remained high. Their body language alone told her the senator's wife had not forgiven him, despite the public statement Yellowhair had made. If she had to venture a guess, she would have said that they were in agreement only about one thing—the way they regarded her visit. Their eyes were stone cold as they rested on her. Ella tried to soften her tone so she would sound less like a cop interviewing a witness.

"I need your help in my investigation of your daughter's death. Can you tell me more about Angelina? In your opinion, had she been moody or irritable recently?"

"My Angelina was not like that," Abigail Yellowhair said in a curious monotone. "She was always busy, doing things, seeing people. She loved her life at the college, and her friends there. To her, nothing was impossible. Her world was one filled with possibilities and dreams. She wasn't the kind to mope about worrying about things that didn't go right. She'd just move on to something else."

Senator Yellowhair held his body rigid and sat very still, his arms crossed over his chest. His face remained as expressive as one carved of stone. "Why do you ask?"

"I'll explain, Sir, if you'll just answer a few more questions first. Could you tell me where she and her friends hung out?" Ella sensed the wariness in his voice, yet tried to remain sympathetic in her own speech.

Mrs. Yellowhair gave her a perplexed look. "I suppose the college, but she was always rushing from one place to another. I couldn't have possibly kept up with her, and Angelina was no little girl who needed constant supervision."

"Did you know of any medical reason why your daughter might have become disoriented enough to cause her to drive erratically?" Ella's voice softened, knowing this was a tough question.

Mrs. Yellowhair's eyes grew wide and she gave her husband a sharp look.

Senator Yellowhair didn't move at all. His gaze was fixed on Ella. "Neither of us have any idea what may have caused the accident. Perhaps there was an animal in the road and she swerved to avoid running over it. Do you intend to tell us why you're asking these questions or should I end the interview right now and return to our guests?"

Ella bristled, but kept her voice and temper in check. "Senator, your daughter had been taking peyote, but that's not what killed her. We have reason to believe that shortly before she died, your daughter took peyote laced with a fatal dose of jimson-weed. Her death was no accident."

James Yellowhair bolted to his feet so quickly the sofa rocked. "Are you saying that my daughter was involved with drugs? That's not only preposterous, it's libel. If you continue with this investigation and those false claims become public, I'll sue you and your department. Count on it."

"The evidence of poisoning is clear, however there are many explanations possible. If she was a member of the Native American Church, or the new splinter group known as the Navajo Justice Church, peyote rituals are part of the religious practices. Jimsonweed, however, is not. It is my belief that your daughter was poisoned by whoever gave her the peyote."

Mrs. Yellowhair looked ashen. She was gripping the sides of the leather-and-wood chair with such force that her knuckles were white under the strain.

Senator Yellowhair returned to the sofa, sat down slowly, and regarded Ella as if she were a peculiarly disgusting insect. "What I believe is that your so called evidence is a result of bungled tests and a faulty investigation."

"I could show you the M.E.'s report, Senator. I assure you, the test results confirm my statement."

"Test results can be manipulated, or created. You know that as well as I do."

Ella wasn't sure what he was insinuating, but she clamped her mouth shut and tried to squelch the obvious retort: that data was often manipulated or created in politics, but not everyone was quite that willing to bend the truth. "The facts stand, Senator, and they're corroborated by independent witnesses."

"Explain," he clipped.

"The department found your daughter after we received a call from a citizen notifying us that someone was driving erratically near the eastern edge of the Rez. I was the first to arrive, and saw your daughter weaving in and out of the oncoming traffic lane. She appeared to be quite ill and incapable of driving safely. That's why I was trying to pull her over."

"If you had succeeded in doing your job, she might still be alive," the senator snapped.

"No, Senator. Later tests reveal she had already received a fatal dose of poison. It was already too late when I found her. But this is why it's very important that I find out who she was with that day. Where did Angelina go the morning she died?" Ella looked at Mrs. Yellowhair, directing the question to her.

"She didn't have classes that day so she was most likely coming back from Farmington after shopping, headed for the library. She often went there when she had studying to do."

Frustration corkscrewed through Ella, making her muscles tense up so tightly they hurt. It was clear that Angelina didn't confide much in her parents. All she had done by coming here was to rile up a potentially dangerous adversary.

"My daughter did not use drugs. She had an accident," the senator said, his voice too controlled to pass as natural. "Stop trying to make this into something it isn't. It's ridiculous to think anyone would have murdered her. I understand how a big case might boost your career, but I want you to know that I will not allow you to turn this into a media circus just so you can get your name in the headlines."

"I'm afraid you have confused police officers with politicians." The words slipped out before she could catch them. Ella mentally blasted herself for allowing him to get to her.

Instead of meeting her response with anger, he smiled slowly. His reaction made her skin crawl. It was clear to her that in his mind, he'd won that round. Unfortunately, she had to admit that he had.

"Senator, if your daughter was given these drugs, there is danger here to the rest of the tribe. We need to track down the person or people who supplied her. Other children could be in danger from whoever is passing off this poison. For the sake of the others, will you answer at least one more question? Your constituents would expect you to cooperate with us, if only on the slim chance that it could save another young person's life."

Mrs. Yellowhair now stared at her husband, urging him

silently to answer. She could see the hesitation in the senator's eyes, but she also knew that she'd pushed the right buttons. She'd backed him into a corner and although he wouldn't forget it, he would have to help her out now.

"I don't know who she was with earlier that day, but I do know the girls in her circle of friends. None of those kids use drugs of any kind. They may have a few beers off the Navajo Nation in Farmington every once in a while, but that's the extent of their involvement with anything like that."

"Has she made any new friends lately?" Ella asked, pushing for more information. If Angelina had only recently become involved with drugs, her supplier was probably not someone in her usual circle of friends.

"My daughter was friendly and outgoing. She made friends all the time," the senator answered, rising from the sofa and urging Ella toward the door as he spoke. "But she also had a good head on her shoulders. We raised her right and knew we could trust her." He opened the front door and held it open. "Make no mistake, Investigator Clah, if you try to ruin our family's reputation, I will fight you with everything I've got, and that's a considerable arsenal. I will not allow my enemies to use our daughter's death against us."

Ella turned around to walk out and practically ran into Justine, almost upending the covered dish she had in her hands. "What's going on?"

"I was driving by and I wanted to drop off this casserole my mom made." Justine handed it to Abigail Yellowhair. "Is there anything you need?" she asked the woman.

James Yellowhair glared at Ella. "Your subordinate knows more about showing respect for a family in mourning than you do. You should take a few lessons from her."

Ella strode off to the Jeep without looking back. She had tried to remain civil, but the senator was difficult to fake out. As she placed the vehicle in reverse, Justine jogged up. "Sorry about that. I hope I didn't mess things up."

"Don't worry about it."

"I need to talk to you a little more privately. Can you meet me at the end of the road, away from the house after I pay my respects?" Justine asked.

Ella nodded. "I'll wait for you on the shoulder of the road next to the highway."

Several minutes later Justine came up, parked behind her on the incline that bordered the road, and left her vehicle. Ella walked out to meet her.

"I've been looking into how our people found the senator to notify him of Angelina's death, and it's impossible to track. We got an anonymous tip. Even the voice was disguised. We can't tell from the tape of incoming calls at the station if it's male or female. I understand that's how his wife found him, too. My mom spoke to their cousins and then told me."

"Interesting. That means the anonymous caller knew about Angelina's death. But, then again, the emergency techs knew, so did the hospital staff, and anyone within gossip range. It doesn't narrow the field much. Anything else?"

"I found out that Ruby Atso's father works at the mine. I met her out there this morning. She'd dropped by to bring him lunch. I struck up a conversation with her and learned that Angelina had no respect for her father. She was always hostile whenever she spoke about him, but since she never told her friends why she hated him, everyone attributed it to different reasons."

Out of habit, Ella led Justine farther away from the road to a more protected area down the incline. "I wonder if she knew her father played around on her mother," Ella said.

"Or it could have been just the normal conflict between parent and child. Angelina was spoiled rotten. She may have resented the senator's busy schedule, since it left less time for him to share with her."

"That's possible, too."

"From the conversations I've had with the other girls, however, I can tell you this much: There's no way that Angelina ingested peyote to gain enlightenment or to make herself part of the NAC, or the splinter church. That kid couldn't commit to anything for long. Her most serious goal was trying to find ways to annoy her father."

"There's another possibility. She might have been looking into the skinwalker ways."

Justine shrugged. "It's possible. She may have thought that was a surefire way to drive her parents crazy."

"You know, we're making progress," Ella commented, thoughtfully. "But we're making powerful enemies along the way."

Justine nodded. "The miners really resent our involvement in this case. It's hard to get them to answer even the simplest of questions."

They had just reached the road when a van coming slowly up the highway suddenly left its lane and veered toward them.

"Jump!" Ella yelled.

Justine hesitated at the edge of the incline. In a heartbeat, Ella knocked her assistant's knees out from under her and shoved Justine over the edge of the steep hill. With one last glance at the oncoming vehicle, she slid down behind her.

EIGHT

Ella sat up slowly, rubbing her back. She felt as if every rock embedded in the sand and dirt of the incline had left a permanent imprint on her. "Cousin, are you okay?" she asked quickly, looking around for Justine.

Ella heard a yelp of pain and looked toward the sound. Justine had landed on a thicket of tumbleweeds. Ella winced, still remembering how her own skin had itched and swelled just the other day.

"I'm okay, but my ankle . . . " Justine crawled free of the thicket, pulling tumbleweed spikes from her hands. "I think I sprained it. But I shouldn't complain. I could have been spread flatter than a tortilla on that highway."

"I wish I'd managed to get a better look at the vehicle before I jumped clear." Ella glanced at the incline they'd have to climb, then back at Justine. "You stay here. I'm going to call the paramedics."

"Oh please, don't. A sprained ankle sounds like the type of injury a wimpy heroine gets in a bad movie so the hero can bail her out. The guys at the station would never let me hear the end of it. Give me a break, okay?"

"You may already have one," she said, glancing down at Justine's ankle. Unfortunately, she also knew exactly how the guys in the department could be. Seeing the pleading look in Justine's eyes, she relented. "Okay, come on. They'll still know, you won't be able to hide this, but at least you'll be able to say you took care of it yourself." Ella picked up a sturdy cottonwood branch and handed it to Justine to use as a cane.

Working together, they went up slowly, but finally made it to the top. As Ella guided Justine toward the Jeep she noticed a note tucked under the windshield wiper.

"Someone gave you a ticket?" Justine blurted.

"No, I don't think that's what it is. Hang on." She helped Justine inside, then snatched the note.

An icy chill gripped Ella as she recognized the writing and read the message. "Reach into the glove compartment and hand me an evidence bag," she told Justine.

"What is it?" Justine said, doing as Ella asked.

"The note reads, 'Looking forward to seeing you again, daughter-in-law.' It's signed, 'Randall.'" Ella suppressed the shudder that started at the base of her spine. It made no sense to let Justine see how much this unnerved her.

Justine's eyebrows knitted together as she frowned. "Your father-in-law, our former, very crooked police chief, is dead. You know it's a forgery."

"I'd like you to check out the handwriting anyway when you can. It'll let us know how skillful a forger the person who wrote this is."

"You did kill him, right?"

"I led the assault against him and the other Navajo witches who killed my dad and kidnapped my brother's wife. Several people witnessed his death." She glanced at Justine and saw her face contort in pain as she tried to shift into a more comfortable position. "I'll get you to the hospital right now. The note will wait."

"No, we can't go yet. We'll lose whatever evidence is here."

"Are you sure you can stand to wait a little bit?"

"Yes. Actually, my ankle is kinda numb right now."

"I don't know if that's a good or bad sign," Ella said.

"It doesn't matter. I'll hate myself if you don't follow through on this because of me."

Ella nodded, reaching behind her to the back seat. "I'll only be a few moments." Ella studied the ground. Beside her own boot prints and Justine's, were two, light, featureless padlike marks, the type moccasins would leave behind. Near them, she found two small, circular marks about the size of a quarter, but she had no idea what could have made those. She then studied the road for tire marks, but there was nothing there to record.

As Ella glanced around the area her skin prickled. There was danger here. She could feel an imbalance, as if something had suddenly been added to the equation, but not in her favor.

She hurried back to the Jeep and saw Justine's face covered with perspiration. "You don't look like someone whose injury is numb," Ella said quickly.

"I lied. You don't happen to have any aspirin, do you?"

Ella switched on the sirens and started the Jeep. "Hang on. We'll be at the hospital soon."

Ella dropped Justine off at the ER, then went downstairs to talk to Carolyn. The note preyed on her mind, leaving her feeling as if she were tottering at the edge of a cliff.

Carolyn was at her desk when Ella walked in, but as soon as she met Ella's gaze she immediately came to put an arm around her shoulder, leading her to the back room. "You look like hell. What happened?"

Ella stared at the bookshelves and the cot Carolyn slept in more nights than she spent at home. "It's been crazy," Ella said, and filled her friend in on the note. "I know it's a trick, but it threw me."

"Not surprising. But when you calm down it'll just make you spitting mad. I know you," Carolyn chided gently.

Ella smiled. "You're right. I don't like having someone jerking my chain."

Carolyn chuckled. "Nah, really? I figure—" She stopped as she heard a male voice boom out her first name. "What the—"

"Carolyn Roanhorse! I want to talk to you *now!*"

Carolyn smirked. "That almost sounds like a royal command, but I don't remember the Rez as a monarchy, do you? Hang on. I'll be right back." She reached into the top drawer of her desk and placed what she retrieved in her pocket before she strode out.

Ella recognized Senator Yellowhair's voice, saw the hard set on Carolyn's face, and knew the politician was about to get an earful. If there was one thing she knew about her friend, it was that nobody pushed her around. A minute later she heard Carolyn's voice.

"What do you think you're doing bursting in here and bellowing for me like I'm either your watch dog, or horror of horrors, some moron who is stupid enough to vote for you."

"You always had a mouth on you. Not that I mind, of course, the more enemies you make, the easier it will be to topple you."

"You're full of it," Carolyn snapped. "Now tell me what you want. I don't like the stench you bring into a room."

"This from a woman who works with the dead."

"A rotting corpse smells sweeter than a crooked politician."

Ella leaned closer to the door. Her theory that there was a history between Carolyn and the senator had just been confirmed.

"You're trying to ruin me with your phoney medical reports," the senator said. "But this form of revenge is beneath even you. How can you turn the death of my beautiful little girl into a scandal? She had a car accident, that's all there was to it and you know it. You've faked the tests and mutilated her body with your autopsy just so you can destroy me. It's all because I publicly stated that I don't believe our tribe should have an M.E. because of our beliefs."

"Don't flatter yourself. This has nothing to do with you or the irresponsible stand you took," Carolyn said, her voice soft. "My job is too important to me to throw it away over the likes of you. I know your grief is genuine and I'm very sorry about your daughter's death, but don't let grief cloud your thinking completely. When your daughter was brought here, the autopsy was necessary because there was no clear cause of death and, legally, one has to be established. The officer at the scene saw your daughter's car weaving all over the road, and she wasn't the only witness who can attest to that. The reason the police were called in at all was because someone else saw what your daughter was doing."

"I heard all that already. I understand the legal need to establish a cause of death, but my daughter didn't take peyote or any other drugs. And to claim that someone poisoned her is ridiculous. That was just your way of making sure my life went under scrutiny."

"This isn't about you or me. The tests were all properly conducted. The results are incontrovertible. Are you so worried about your reputation and political career that you're willing to let the person responsible for your daughter's death escape unpunished?"

"There was no killer, and there were no drugs," he said flatly. "You fabricated that. You told me once that you'd find the time and place to exact your revenge. You warned me that you wouldn't do it in anger, because you wouldn't allow that to interfere with what would otherwise be a perfect plan."

"I did say that," Carolyn admitted slowly. "I meant it at the time, too, but that was many, many years ago. I won't lie to you, James. You're not my favorite person. As a matter of fact, I believe you're crooked to the bone. But I wouldn't use my position as M.E. to bring you down. You'll hang yourself, probably with your own rope, too."

"If you cost me the election I'll find a way to bring you to your knees."

"You'll lose this election inch by inch all by yourself. It'll happen each time you open that mouth of yours or pull some fool stunt. And, I must admit, you're off to a great start with that tryst at the motel."

"I can contain the damage that caused. But I won't tolerate your games. I know you, Carolyn, and I know precisely how to destroy you."

"This conversation is pointless. My findings are all documented and the tests were properly conducted. There's nothing more for me to say."

"Remember my warning. I'm a better hardball player than you'll ever be."

Ella heard the senator's footsteps as he walked out. She waited, then stepped out of the back room. Carolyn was leaning against the wall, her face flushed.

"You okay?" Ella asked.

"Yeah." Carolyn pulled the miniature tape recorder she used during autopsies from her lab coat, clicking off the record button. "Good thing I thought of getting this out. I have a feeling I may need a record of this conversation sometime." She popped out the tape and handed it to Ella. "Hang on to it for me."

"May I make a suggestion?" Ella saw Carolyn nod, and continued. "Detail all the test results on the police reports. Then lock up all the tissue samples taken from Angelina at the autopsy. Those should be protected in case the senator pressures you to confirm your findings or brings in an outside consultant."

"Yes, you're right. He's out for my blood now."

"Yes, but what started it all? You still haven't told me."

"That's right. I haven't." Her voice was colder than Ella had ever heard it before. "It has nothing to do with Angelina's death, and it's strictly my business."

Ella clamped her jaw. Carolyn was as stubborn as a mule sometimes. It would do no good to press her now. She'd talk when she was ready.

Ella glanced up at Howard Lee as he came in. "I'm sorry I'm late, Doctor, but I had duties upstairs. I was helping Dr. Martinez."

"You're assigned to me, and I expect you to be on time," Carolyn snapped.

"Well, yes, I'm sorry, but—"

"Spare me the excuses. Now go get the tissue samples we froze from the Yellowhair autopsy."

As Howard turned and went into the next room, Carolyn glanced at Ella. "This boy is laid-back about almost everything. It makes me crazy sometimes."

Howard came into the room just as Carolyn finished, his face downcast. "Oh, Doctor, you're not going to like this at all."

"What's wrong?" she asked quickly.

"I can't find the tissue samples. They should have been in the freezer, but I don't see them anywhere in there."

"You did put them there after the autopsy, right?"

"Of course. They were on the top shelf, right-hand side, but they're not there now."

"Let me go take a look," she said, glancing back at Ella. "I'll be right back."

Ella watched her friend go. She had a real bad feeling about this. When Carolyn returned her expression said it all.

"They've been mixed up with samples from other autopsies," she said. "Some of the labels apparently came loose and were reattached, but very obviously to the wrong containers."

"Who had access to those samples?"

"Howard, myself, and anyone else on the staff who might wander in during the day. Of course, anyone who knows the layout down here could have just as easily found them. It wouldn't take a genius to know the samples have to be frozen, and there's only one freezer unit down here."

Ella gave Howard a long, speculative look, searching him for signs that he was responsible. He never blinked.

"I may not pay too much attention to time clocks," Howard snapped at last, "but I'm not sloppy when it comes to my work."

"Have you discussed this case with anyone?" Ella asked him, remembering having seen him with Nelson Yellowhair.

"Only Dr. Roanhorse. The type of work done in a morgue isn't exactly a popular topic of conversation."

She stared back at him for several more seconds, but he never flinched.

"Unlike you two, work isn't my driving passion, but I'm not careless," Lee added. "I hate to point out the obvious, but somebody has tampered with our samples."

Carolyn gave Howard a hard look. "This has cost us crucial evidence. I don't want any mention of what has happened to go outside this room. Is that clear?" Her gaze bored holes through him.

"Yes, Doctor, perfectly."

"Good. Get to work, then. I need transcripts of all the autopsy tapes. They're cutting back staff upstairs so we have to do it." She glanced at Ella. "Senator Yellowhair has been pushing to cut back operations at this center for months now. He wants some of our personnel relocated to Window Rock, so he fights by not allocating us sufficient funds."

"I hate to bring this up," Ella said as Lee left the room, "but if the senator pushes on those findings, we're going to be in major trouble. No physical evidence that has been compromised will hold up in court."

"Don't worry. We can weather this." Carolyn took Ella into the autopsy suite and gave her a determined, half smile. "It's all right," she said, keeping her voice low. "I can't say I expected this to happen, but I did feel I should cover myself at every turn. That's why I have a backup set of tissue and fluid samples from Angelina's autopsy labeled under a separate code number and stored in another lab."

"Good going." A heavy weight lifted off Ella's chest. "Now nobody can question the autopsy report."

"I generally take duplicate samples in case something goes wrong, but this time, I took the precaution of hiding my dupes. It was my intention all along to send them to an independent lab so my findings could be substantiated. When I learned the name of the deceased, I realized we couldn't afford there being any question about the validity of my results."

"Can I make a suggestion? Let me have Sergeant Neskahi hand deliver those samples to the lab we use in Santa Fe. I trust that man implicitly."

"All right. I'll sign them over to him. Make sure he comes after four in the afternoon though. I don't think my med student needs to know about this."

"You've got it. And keep an eye on that guy, will you? I found out he also works at the first-aid station at the coal mine. He could be involved in the trouble there."

Carolyn laughed. "Him? Howard is only interested in Howard."

"Just be careful, huh?" Ella walked to the door. "I better go check on Justine."

Ella left the morgue feeling more disturbed than when she'd arrived. She didn't think Howard Lee had purposely done anything to those samples. It would have been too incriminating, and he appeared to be too smart for that. But someone was certainly trying to cause trouble for Carolyn.

Ella was almost at the elevator when she saw Nelson Yellowhair coming down the hall, rolling a supply cart before him. Ella turned away from the elevator and headed for the stairs, making a point of passing him in the hall.

"Hello," she greeted. "You're down here quite often, aren't you." He certainly had a motive and the opportunity to sabotage the autopsy samples.

"It's my job. I bring supplies down. If you have any objections talk to my supervisor. I do as I'm told and collect my paycheck," he snapped.

"You wouldn't have a more personal agenda, would you?" Ella asked, hoping to goad the man into some unguarded admission.

"No, that's more up your alley," he said, then pushed the cart past her and continued down the hall.

Ella watched him for several more moments. Who better than the senator's brother to sabotage Carolyn's work or, at the very least, spy on her? Unfortunately, she had no proof of either.

Ella went upstairs, and as she reached the ER, saw Justine hobbling out of an examination room on crutches. Her foot was bandaged, but not in a cast.

"A sprain?"

Justine nodded. "It's not bad. I can still work, though I'm supposed to be keeping my leg up as much as I can."

"You could take some time off."

She shook her head. "No way. I want to get started analyzing the writing on that note, and then check out the photos you took back at the site where I got injured."

"It's four o'clock now. Neither of us had any lunch, so you might as well go home, have an early dinner, and go to bed. You can start working on the note in the morning. I can drop you off."

"I'm not tired, really. What I am is eager to find out who tried to turn us into roadkill. That just pisses me off."

Ella laughed. "Okay, I'll drop you off at the station. Have one of the patrols take you home when you're ready to call it a day."

A short time later, after helping Justine to her office and making arrangements to have her assistant's vehicle brought in from where they'd left it parked, Ella settled down in her office. She was trying to decide which of the overdue reports to tackle first when her intercom buzzer sounded.

"Get in here, Shorty."

"Will do, Chief." Ella stared at the stacks of files, grateful for the interruption, but depressed to realize they'd still be there when she returned.

As Ella passed the soft drink machine in the hall she spotted Sergeant Neskahi. She went up to him quickly. "I've got to meet Big Ed right now, but can you come see me tomorrow morning? I need to talk to you."

"No problem. I have to meet with a suspect's lawyer tomorrow at nine anyway, so I'll be around."

"My office at eight?"

"Sure."

"One more thing. After four this afternoon, go down to the morgue and pick up a set of tissue samples from Dr. Roanhorse. I want you to hand deliver them to the state lab today, so arrange for a flight out of Farmington. These samples are from the Yellowhair case and you are not to discuss what you're doing with anyone not working with my office."

"Understood. I'll call to make sure the lab people will have someone there to meet me. It'll be after hours."

"Good thinking, Sergeant. I'll see you tomorrow then."

Neskahi nodded, then walked away to make the arrangements.

Ella hurried down the hall and, knocking on Big Ed's open door, went inside. Concern was mirrored on his features as he glanced up, a muscle beat at the corner of his mouth, echoing his heartbeat. A big barrel of a man—about a head shorter than Ella who was tall for a Navajo woman—he delighted in calling *her* Shorty.

She sat down on the chair nearest his desk. "You heard about Justine?"

He nodded. "And I'll be reading all about it soon in your report, correct?"

That hadn't been a request and she knew it. "It'll be on your desk tomorrow, but I can fill you in right now if you'd like." Seeing him nod, she gave him a full report, detailing everything she'd learned to date.

"That explains why the senator's aide came to pay me a visit earlier. He was pressuring me to drop the case."

Ella started to answer when a loud knock sounded behind her. Senator James Yellowhair paused in the doorway, then made his grand entrance, sauntering to the front of Big Ed's desk and leaning vulturelike over it.

"Chief Atcitty, I insist that you remove Inspector Clah from my daughter's accident investigation," he said, treating Ella as if she weren't in the room.

Big Ed stood up slowly. "This is *my* department, Senator, not the merry roundhouse in Santa Fe. Nobody tells me how to assign my people."

"Your investigator is biased because of her friendship with Dr. Roanhorse, the Medical Examiner. I believe that the doctor falsified the autopsy results but, until I can prove it, I want someone on the case who'll conduct the investigation quickly and honestly."

"I can take care of that." Big Ed looked at Ella. "I want you to be honest and efficient, Investigator Clah. Understood?"

Ella almost burst out laughing, but managed to stifle the urge. "I'll do just that, Chief Atcitty."

Senator Yellowhair looked at Ella, then back to Big Ed. "You're treating this as a joke. Both of you." He dropped his voice to a fierce, frigid whisper. "If you continue to cross paths with me on this, you'll find I can be a bad enemy. You'll learn the hard way what kind of pressure I can bring down on your department, Chief." Anger locked his jaws. His dark eyes, always intense, shone with rage. "In politics we learn to get what we want."

Ella watched the senator storm out. "Political retaliation can be nasty business, Chief. He controls a lot of bureaucrats. Maybe you should have let him have his way."

"I'm in charge of this department, not him." His gaze locked with hers. "Go out there and get answers for me. Recruit an extra person into your division if need be, but don't let me down."

Ella squared her shoulders. "I won't. You can count on it."

NINE
✖ ✖ ✖

Ella sat in the window seat inside her darkened bedroom staring outside at the mesa illuminated by a rising moon. Even her nightly game of solitaire had failed to calm her tonight. Big Ed had taken quite a chance, probably placing both their careers in her hands.

She'd certainly come a long way in the department, yet the threat of political retaliation was not something to be taken lightly. The most vulnerable area was the department's already strained budget. Then came the more obvious focus of attack. As police chief, Big Ed got credit for successes, but failures weighed heavily on him, too. She would not let him down.

Ella heard a light knock on her door. "Come in."

Rose walked into the room, making use of the moonlight that streamed from outside instead of turning on the lights. "I thought you were still up." She sat on the edge of the bed. "What's disturbing you, Daughter?"

"The cases I'm working on right now. People I care about are involved and the answers I find, or don't find, will directly affect them and their jobs. That scares me," Ella admitted.

"You're expected to do your best, that's all."

"People have placed a lot of faith in me, Mom. I have to live up to it." She told Rose about Big Ed.

"He was standing up for himself as much as he was for you. The senator left him no other choice."

"The senator's been making some pretty wild accusations against Carolyn. This is going to be a tough time for her. She's not likely to have many allies to stand with her throughout all that lies ahead."

"She's more alone than most Navajos, it's true, but that was her choice. Her abrasive attitude doesn't do much to help her, either. The woman is argumentative, overly independent, and just outright rude sometimes. And that's with people she likes. She treats her enemies even worse."

Ella smiled. "Yes. But she's my friend."

"Naturally," Rose answered. "You've always been on the side of the underdog."

"It's more than that, Mom. Carolyn has a lot of courage, and she's doing a thankless but vital job. In many ways, she and I are alike. We're both driven to do the jobs we've chosen and we both need to feel that what we're doing makes a difference. We take pride in our work and it cuts deep when someone like the senator attacks our professionalism or our competency."

"Yes, I imagine so. Lies can hurt, but eventually, truth shatters them. And the truth always comes out, often when you least expect it."

"I hope I can find answers soon." Ella watched a rabbit foraging in the garden outside. Two was snoring noisily in the hall, obviously uninterested in hunting tonight. "It's so quiet and peaceful right now." A coyote howled in the distance and Ella shuddered. "But there's always that undercurrent of danger out there, wandering around, even in the stillness of the night."

"There's something else bothering you, Daughter."

"It's nothing."

"It must be more than that if it makes you this tense," she said, glancing down at Ella's hands which were curled into tight fists.

Ella exhaled softly. "I got a note today from my former father-in-law."

Rose inhaled sharply. "Impossible."

"Yes, I agree. But someone's playing mind games with me and I don't like it. There's something nasty brewing out there, Mom, I can feel it."

"Then trust your instincts, Daughter, like I do mine. You and I are right far more often than we're wrong."

"When I was at the accident site, the place where the senator's daughter died, I felt danger all around me. I could feel someone was out there, watching me, but I couldn't see anyone."

"Then it's starting again," Rose said sadly. "The problem is that we've never really defeated all of our enemies. We've won battles, but the war continues, and will probably go on as long as the *Dineh* exist. It's by understanding the role darkness must play that we find harmony."

"Finding the pattern, then walking in beauty," Ella said thoughtfully.

Rose stood. "Get some sleep. You'll need it to work with a clear mind tomorrow."

As Rose left Ella lingered by the window seat. The sounds of the night filled the room, making her uneasiness more pronounced. She kept her fear at bay by assuring herself that there was no logic in her response; there was no immediate threat here, except for the cost her insomnia might have on her the following day.

Ella crawled into bed and closed her eyes. Slowly her thoughts receded and blended into gray, brooding landscapes woven by the pattern of her dreams.

Ella went out to her car shortly after seven the following morning. Her mother was already in her herb garden weeding and watering the parched ground, while Two searched around for the elusive rabbit. If only the much delayed rains would come. Hard times would be upon them soon unless the drought conditions eased.

When Ella arrived at the police station Justine was already there. Justine hit the vending machine with her crutch, trying to get it to relinquish its booty, and almost fell.

Ella caught Justine just in time and steadied her. "You

shouldn't waste your time with this bandit. It has never worked quite right."

"No kidding."

"Why do you put money in it when you know it malfunctions?"

"It has always delivered for me. Will you hit it again, right above the dent where everybody else hits it?"

Ella complied.

A second later the candy bar dropped. "See? It's just slow sometimes," Justine said. "We just have to prod it along a bit."

Ella walked with Justine down the hall. "Anything new?"

"I have the photos you took of the area after the van almost ran us down."

"Anything interesting?"

"Interesting, yes, but I have no answers. Those quarter-sized imprints with that strange center are unusual. I haven't been able to determine what they are."

"Did you get anything from the handwriting comparison?"

"You're not going to like the answer," Justine warned. "I can't prove it's a forgery. The handwriting is that close."

Ella felt a shudder travel over her. Justine was right. She didn't like this one bit. "We know my father-in-law is dead, so that means whoever wrote that must have known the chief well. He must have handwriting samples to mimic, too."

"That doesn't narrow it down much."

"Not yet, but it's a start."

Sergeant Neskahi was waiting in Ella's office by the time she walked in. "Good morning," she greeted. "How did your delivery to Santa Fe go last night?"

"No hitches. I signed everything over to their senior tech. The paperwork was all completed according to procedure."

"Great. Now let's hope we get the results back before the turn of the century," Ella smiled.

"I better be on my way," Justine said.

"No, stay," Ella said. "This will concern you as well."

Justine hobbled to the nearest chair and dropped down heavily.

Ella crossed over to her desk and sat down in the tall-backed swivel chair. "I'd like to have you on my team again, Sergeant. How do you feel about that?"

"Will it be a permanent assignment?"

"No. Would you like it to be?"

Neskahi considered it. "I don't know. I'd have to give that some thought. But for now a temporary assignment is fine with me."

Ella knew from talking to Neskahi before that he loved being out on the Rez, with its endless vistas and lonely roads. But he had always sought out more responsibility. He was a good cop and he knew it without being proud: an admirable trait for any Navajo. She pointed to the cork bulletin board on the wall above her desk. "The employees on that list that don't have a red tack next to their name need to be checked out. Also, do you have any contacts at the mine?"

"I have a cousin who works there. He doesn't talk much, but if you need something specific I think I can persuade him to co-operate."

"We need a good, solid lead on Bitah's death. The mine is in a state of siege and we need an inside source. See what you can do."

Neskahi stood up. "I'll get started."

As he walked out Ella glanced at Justine. "I'm going to talk to Frank Smith this morning. Bitah and a lot of other Navajos didn't like him, but the Anglos claim he was a good worker known for minding his own business. I want to get a handle on him myself. In the meantime, I want you to continue the back-ground reports and get anything else you can on Bitah or his associates."

Ella finished the reports she'd promised Big Ed, then after ver-ifying Smith's whereabouts, left the building. Knowing Smith would be working today, she'd obtained permission to talk with the man during an early coffee break.

Then she phoned Blalock and asked him to meet her at the small lunchroom attached to the metal field office and first-aid station.

Ella arrived at the visitor's parking area of the mine an hour later. Blalock's car was just ahead of her as she pulled into an unoccupied slot.

"Well, for once you didn't beat me here," he said with a rueful smile. "I've already done a background check on this guy and I know you've done some homework on your own. There's nothing there to justify this visit. So what are you hoping to find out?"

"I'm not sure. But he had problems with Bitah, and until I catch the killer everyone who did is a suspect. Even if they're not very good ones."

"So we play the cards we're dealt. To add to my personal joy in this case, Senator Yellowhair has been talking to my supervisors and making lots of noise in Washington. They're really leaning on me to get results."

Ella shrugged and said, "Welcome to the club."

They walked up to the gray, metal portable building and Blalock opened the door below the blue painted sign identifying the lunchroom. A tall, dark-haired man wearing a denim jacket and jeans was seated alone at a wooden picnic-style table. In his hand was a half-eaten glazed doughnut. A wall of vending machines and two more tables were all that occupied the rest of the brightly lit room.

"You're here to talk to me about the murder, right?" the man asked. "This explains why I got my coffee break early today."

"Your first name is Frank?" The man nodded, and Blalock flashed his ID. "We've got a few questions for you, Frank," he said, sitting in the bench opposite Smith.

Smith looked at Ella and she took out her badge. She had jurisdiction here, too.

"This is about Bitah, right?" Smith asked.

Blalock nodded. "We understand that you had a lot of trouble with the man."

"He hated Anglos, pure and simple. Then he got it into his miserable bigoted head that I was out to get him. I wasn't. He never quite understood that I'm not interested in anything involving him or this mine if it isn't work related. I'm only here to punch in, work my shift, punch out, and collect a paycheck."

"That makes you a real exception nowadays around here, I understand. How do you stay so focused?" Blalock snapped.

Smith shrugged. "You can believe me or not. I don't care. But that's the truth."

"What exactly was the problem between you and Bitah?" Ella asked.

"It started one afternoon when I went to my locker and found some gear in it that belonged to Billy Pete. I didn't put it there, and it wasn't mine, so I tried to return it. Pete wasn't around so I dropped it in front of his locker. Just then Bitah came up. He figured I'd broken into Pete's locker and was trying to make off with his stuff. There were cameras installed after that, but I'm not sure whose idea that was."

"Have you ever heard of The Brotherhood?" Ella asked.

"Was that the movie about all those crooked lawyers?"

She gave him an incredulous look. "Try again."

He shrugged, his eyes focused near the top of her head. "Like I said, I do my work and come home. I have no idea what you're talking about."

"Any idea who might?" Ella prodded.

"Talk to the Navajos who work here. They're the ones with an organization. I think it's called *Hashké Nein*, or something like that?"

Ella blinked. "*Hashké* means fierce, or someone who is angry. The other word . . . could you mean, *neiniihii?*"

"That's the one."

"It means one who metes out anger. Where did you hear that?"

"Around work. The group is Navajos only."

Ella stared at Smith. "You say these Fierce Ones are the counterpart to The Brotherhood?"

"I never heard of The Brotherhood, so I couldn't say."

Ella started to ask him more, when her pager went off. She glanced down. "I need to use my cell phone," Ella said, leaving Smith to Blalock.

Stepping outside to her Jeep, she dialed quickly and got Justine on the line. "What's up?"

"Big trouble. A Navajo worker, Noah Charley, has disappeared. He didn't report to work today and nobody can find him anywhere."

"That's not necessarily a sign of trouble. There are many possible explanations."

"I thought so, too, at first, but Neskahi's cousin told him some of the workers believed Charley was being paid off by The Brotherhood as an informant. His aunt also came by the mine, asking if anyone had seen him. Nobody had. She's really worried because he hadn't stopped by her home to pick up some food she'd baked for him."

"Where does Noah Charley live?" What followed were the type of directions common only in rural areas across the country. Ella was to drive south on the highway toward Gallup until she reached the historical marker for Shiprock. On the opposite side of the road was a dirt track. She was to follow that track to the old watering tank, not the new one, then left along the fence line to a big gully. Noah Charley's house could be seen in a field just west of where the road crossed the gully. He had a new GMC pickup, either green or blue.

"You got all that?" Justine finally asked.

"Yeah, I'll be there. Get a warrant to search the place if you can't contact the aunt to get permission. He's connected to this case, if only as a witness."

"Okay. Sergeant Neskahi and I will join you there."

Ella went back inside the lunchroom and took Blalock aside to bring him up to date. "You want to ride along on this?"

"Sorry. I've got to interview a witness on another case I'm working on. I'm also scheduled to talk to a DEA agent about anyone who might be dealing peyote in the area. Fill me in later. Smith hasn't given me anything else, by the way."

"Okay."

Ella returned to the table with Blalock and focused her gaze on Smith who was drinking coffee from a foam cup. "Noah Charley has disappeared. Do you know who he is?"

"Sure I do," Smith said with a shrug.

"Any idea where we might be able to find him?"

"If he's not at work try at home, wherever that is."

Ella regarded him for a moment. "Let me ask you this. If there was a Brotherhood, who do you think their leader would be?"

He smiled slowly. "*If* there was an organization like that, only members would have that information. It wouldn't pay to advertise, if you get my meaning."

"Thanks for your help," Ella said.

"I *didn't* help you," he said emphatically.

Ella nodded slowly. "All right."

It took over an hour for Ella to find Noah Charley's home. It was in a low area west of the Hogback oil field occupied by a few head of cattle competing for the meager forage. The stucco house was simple and had few amenities. Electricity came from a generator, and not much of one at that. A well had been drilled, but water had to be carried inside from the old hand pump. Still, the man was better off than many Navajos Ella had visited.

No GMC pickup, or any vehicle, for that matter, was in sight. Justine's car appeared not long after Ella arrived, with Neskahi at the wheel and Justine playing passenger because of her injured ankle. Ella decided to search the place since it looked like nobody was home and Justine had managed to get oral permission from the aunt to look inside for clues to her nephew's whereabouts. Typically, the house wasn't locked.

Justine hobbled into the bedroom to look around while Neskahi searched the living room. "All his clothes are gone," Justine called out to Ella, "except for one shoe sticking out from under the bed. But this doesn't make much sense. If he had planned to go off, why wouldn't he have picked up his paycheck? He earned it, and it's been waiting for him since yesterday."

Neskahi spoke up from the other room. "It looks like he decided to leave in a hurry. But so far, I haven't managed to find anything that lets us know where he went."

Ella came out of the kitchen and took the shoe Justine had found. "Does this shoe size correspond to any of the tracks we found at the scene of Bitah's murder? The vehicle tracks Blalock identified were too common to help us out. Maybe we'll get lucky with this."

"We might. I don't remember any of the sizes, though. I'd have to check," Justine responded.

"Bag it, then check it out as soon as you get back to the office."

They helped Justine finish searching the bedroom as Ella filled her and Neskahi in on the *Hashké* group. "Did your cousin say anything about that?" Ella asked Neskahi.

"No he didn't, but just getting the few answers I did was like pulling up an elm. He made it clear that he didn't want anyone to see him talking to a cop, even if the cop is his cousin."

Ella frowned. "Do you realize what's going on here? We have people who are afraid to talk to us. They're being intimidated into silence, and that means big trouble for us and everyone who could end up a victim."

Ella glanced at a discarded newspaper on the floor next to an empty fried chicken bucket. A photo of Senator Yellowhair was on the page, but someone had drawn a black circle over one eye and darkened every other tooth. She picked the paper up and stared at it, lost in thought. "It's time for me to find out if The Brotherhood has anything against Senator Yellowhair."

"You're thinking they might have killed his daughter in retaliation for something he did or should have done?" Neskahi asked.

"The Brotherhood advocates violence, so why not? It would be a beautiful frame. If they knew Bitah was part of that splinter religious group they might have used the jimsonweed-laced peyote as a way to throw suspicion on Bitah. That will discredit him *and* the Fierce Ones and throw suspicions off of themselves. It's worth checking out, anyway." Ella was abruptly interrupted as her hand-held crackled and her call sign came over the air, along with a general alert.

"We have a ten-thirty-nine at the mine. Any available units please respond."

Ella acknowledged the code for a disturbance. "Ten-four."

Ella glanced at Neskahi. "Justine and I will respond to this call. I want you to stay out of this. One of us will need to remain low profile in order to work this case from behind the scenes. Everyone knows you're a cop, but not everyone knows you're part of this case." She glanced at Justine. "You can ride with me in the Jeep. Neskahi can drive back in your vehicle."

"Is there anything specific you want me to do here before I go?" Neskahi asked.

"Take one last look around. Make sure we didn't miss anything. Then go back to your cousin and pressure him to work with us."

"I suppose I could threaten to become his shadow, following him everywhere."

"Whatever it takes." Ella walked outside and headed for the Jeep with Justine, who was still using a crutch. Switching on her sirens, Ella hurried back to the highway as fast as the road would allow.

When she finally reached the parking lot of the mine, she saw a group of Navajo and Anglo workers standing outside the buildings. From their gestures she could tell they weren't discussing the weather. At least it appeared none of the anger had resulted in any violence, so far. No other units had arrived on the scene yet, and the few security guards were standing by the doors, protecting property rather than personnel.

Ella squealed to a stop and reached for her PR-24. The baton could give her the edge she needed.

Ella threw open her door and strode forward. She was as tall as most of the men here, but they outweighed her by a considerable margin, not to mention far outnumbering her and Justine.

Despite that, everyone took a step back, and the men exchanging insults stopped speaking abruptly. Ella started to congratulate herself on her intimidation skills when she realized they weren't looking at her. She glanced back quickly and saw Justine leaning casually against the side of the Jeep, shotgun cradled in her arms, gaze leveled on the crowd.

TEN

Ella had to fight back the urge to smile. Though she knew that Justine had no intention of using deadly force unless it was in self-defense, her tactic had worked, helping diffuse the situation.

Ella focused her eagle-sharp gaze on the closest man to her. She recognized Jeremiah Franklin, having gone to high school with him. "What's the problem here, Jeremiah?"

"There's no problem."

"Then there's no reason for everyone to continue standing around out here, is there?" I suggest you all go home. How come you're out here instead of working, anyway? You guys can all afford to lose your jobs?"

Billy Pete came forward, edging around two Anglos. "The company has just decided to change almost everyone's shifts. Most of the Anglos get straight days, eight to four, the rest of us get night and graveyard shifts."

"Did they give a reason for this?"

"They wanted to cut down on possible confrontations between the Anglo workers and the tribe, but what they're going to get is exactly the opposite. The few Anglos with vital jobs skills that have to continue working at night with us feel pretty isolated now. And everyone hates being put on shifts that force them to completely rearrange their family schedules."

"The Anglos working with us should be nervous," Jeremiah said, "if they've been causing trouble."

"This is not the time for such talk!" Raymond Nez snapped.

Jeremiah shrugged and walked away.

Ella looked at Raymond. His jaw was set and there was defiance in his eyes. She could see why Jeremiah had backed down. This guy was trouble waiting to happen.

"You were out here earlier this morning asking questions, wanting to find out what's going on," Raymond said. "And you've learned a few things. I give you credit for intelligence and skill and, most of all, for persistence. But you don't know the whole story. It would be far better for everyone if you'd let the workers here settle their differences without interference from the police."

"I know about the 'Fierce Ones who carry out vengeance'," she said, translating the Navajo group's name while watching Raymond carefully.

He smiled slowly. "I have no idea what you're talking about." He glanced around at the crowd. "And I doubt anyone else here does either."

The other men were trying hard not to look at her. In the Navajo culture it was considered impolite to look someone directly in the eyes, but Ella's gut told her that their avoidance had little to do with that. There was fear and mistrust here, two emotions that were almost guaranteed to create trouble.

Ella saw an Anglo worker separate himself from the other group and approach. She braced herself for more trouble. He was a tall, brown-haired, blue-eyed man with the look of authority. "I'm Randy Watson, Officer. I'm a supervisor here. How can I help?"

"I need information and answers."

He smiled. "I'll see what I can do."

"Let's talk inside. Could you find us a place?" Seeing him nod, Ella took Justine aside. "Call in and tell dispatch that things are under control here for the moment. Tempers appear to have cooled. I'd like you to stay outside and see what you can do to get us some information." Knowing her assistant, it was quite possible she'd get far more from the lingering workers than Ella herself would. Justine's approach mingled genuine sweetness with a core of steel, and her Navajo was a lot better than Ella's.

Ella strode inside the building, following Watson to one of the empty conference rooms. "This place is becoming a war zone. If trouble escalates, everyone loses. Do you agree?"

He nodded. "Of course."

"Then tell me what you know about The Brotherhood."

"I could say that I've never heard of them, but I won't insult your intelligence." Watson leaned back in the chair and stretched out his legs in front of him. "I've heard of the group, but I'm not a member. Personally, I don't think it's much of an organization. To my mind, if they counted any significant number of the Anglo workers as followers, they would have flexed their muscles more. That type of organization is by nature made up of racist bullies and there's nothing they like better than exercising their power."

"You may have a point, but it only takes a few to stir things up and create a crisis situation."

"I'm keeping a tight watch on the men under my supervision. If I find any of them deliberately creating division between the miners, they'll be fired on the spot."

"But you can't be everywhere at once."

"There are other supervisors who, like me, are keeping their eyes open."

Ella sensed the man was being honest with her. "If you discover who the members of The Brotherhood or the Navajo group are, will you call me?"

"I'll fire them, *then* I'll call you. I have a job to do here, too."

"Fair enough."

Ella stood up. "One more thing. Does anyone here, Anglo or Navajo, have any grievance against state senator Yellowhair?"

"James Yellowhair?" he asked, surprised. "No, quite the opposite. He's always supported the mine. Admittedly, he's trying to get the company to train more Navajos to take over key positions but, hell, he's an elected official whose funding for re-election comes mostly from the tribe. You'd expect him to take that stand."

"Do you think that gives The Brotherhood a gripe against him?"

He considered. "Maybe, but it's like resenting a porcupine for having quills. It's the nature of the beast. I really don't see what other position they could expect him to take."

She offered Watson her hand. Though like many Navajos she disliked touching strangers, she was making a concession she felt certain this man would appreciate.

He shook her hand firmly and gave her a nod. "We'll weed out the troublemakers. Just give us time."

Ella left the building, once again feeling that her help was not wanted and wishing it wasn't needed. As she joined Justine she saw most of the workers had left, but Raymond Nez was still there. His expression was no longer openly hostile, but Justine was still holding the shotgun.

As Ella approached she saw Nez's face grow taut. Justine turned, exchanged a few quick words with Nez, then hobbled over to the Jeep, stowing the shotgun.

"That's one *interesting* man," Justine said as they got underway.

Ella, alerted by her tone, glanced at her assistant. "Don't tell me you're attracted to him."

Justine shrugged. "He's good-looking and has a certain charisma, I suppose, but I'm not about to forget he's a suspect in our investigation. It's strange how he comes on really strong about Navajo rights, but is not fanatical in any way. He's loyal to the tribe and, as a supervisor, he claims he's trying to look out for the men under him. I think he's just trying to make sure our people get the breaks they deserve."

"You're basing all that on a ten-minute conversation?"

"I've met men like him before. You're going to have to trust my instincts on this one."

Ella wanted to tell Justine that it wasn't her instincts she was worried about. No matter how much Justine wanted to gloss over it, her experience in the field was limited. Inexperience, coupled with hormones, could color gut instincts. "You're thinking you can turn this guy into an informant?"

"It's worth a shot."

"It could also be trouble."

"I know I screwed up once before when our elders were being killed, but believe me, I learned my lesson."

Ella considered her reply silently for several moments. She didn't want to undermine her assistant's confidence, but neither did she want to see her in a situation that was beyond her capabilities to handle. "I think that Nez is a very smart cookie. If he's part of the Fierce Ones, and I tend to think that's a real good bet, chances are he's learned to cover himself far better than you think. I'm not sure how dangerous he is. You'd have to be *very* careful."

"I won't lower my guard around him. I admit it was a mistake getting involved with the wrong man in those killings last year, but I seldom make the same mistake twice."

"Make sure you don't then. I don't want to worry about you," Ella admitted at last.

"I'll treat him just like I do my brother's new stallion," Justine said with a tiny grin. "I won't be fooled into thinking he's harmless just because he takes food from my hand when it's offered."

Ella smiled. "All right. See what you can do." She had no right to hold her assistant back. Experience was gained in only one way. Hoping she was making the right decision, Ella headed the Jeep back toward Shiprock.

They walked inside the station a short time later. At once, Ella could feel the tension in the air. People were speaking in hushed voices, and phones were ringing continually.

Justine glanced at Ella. "Something is not right," she mumbled. "There are usually two or three uniforms hanging around, bringing in reports or suspects, but everyone is on the phone. It feels weird in here."

"I know."

Big Ed leaned out of his office doorway and motioned to them. "I need to talk to you both. We've got a situation."

Ella followed with Justine. When they stepped inside Big Ed's office, he uncharacteristically asked them to close the door and sit down. "There's been an outbreak of meningitis in the Newcomb area south of here. It started with one child believed to have the flu, but the child got sicker and by the time they brought him up to the hospital and the diagnosis was made, it was too late. There was no real alarm until it was discovered that the child had been staying at a daycare center because it was sheep shearing time. Now other children from the center have shown up with symptoms after they returned to their homes, some in Shiprock and eastern Arizona. We need to hold vaccination clinics for the entire New Mexico area of the Rez. Arizona officials will be dealing with everyone on their side of the state line."

"It's going to be a tough job getting everyone to come in. A lot of the rural families are traditionalists who would be more comfortable calling in a *hataalii* than working with a doctor," Ella said.

"No kidding," Big Ed snapped. "That's why I need you to go visit the hospital and see what kind of support we can give them. Talk to Dr. Natoni. He's in charge of this. I've already got units lined up to help transfer medical supplies to the Chapter Houses, but there may be more we can do. Maybe your brother can offer some advice, too."

"My brother is a *hataalii*. He believes in the old ways. I can't ask him to sanction vaccinations he doesn't believe in."

"Do your best. Maybe he can at least tell people what to look for in symptoms."

"I'm working two major cases already, Chief," Ella protested.

"Consider this your third one," Big Ed shot back. "We'll try to keep Justine out of this one, if possible, though." He looked over at Justine, who nodded.

Ella saw the determined look on his face and realized that no arguments, however logical, would be accepted. "I'll go over to the hospital now."

As they left Big Ed's office, Justine remained quiet.

"What's on your mind?" Ella asked.

"I'd like to do more background research on Raymond Nez," Justine said.

"All right, but stay focused and work fast. Big Ed will be on our backs in a hurry if we don't crack these cases soon."

Ella drove to the hospital. The chill spreading through her had nothing to do with the dry breeze that poured in through the window. She couldn't shake the feeling that events were hurtling her toward an explosive confrontation, but against who or what? The Fierce Ones were no friends of hers, neither was The Brotherhood. Then there was the senator. Her enemies were numerous and powerful.

Ella parked near the side of the hospital and walked in through the double doors. After asking directions, she found Dr. Natoni. To her surprise, two of the three medical teams assigned to the crisis had already left. Only one remained, having been organized at the last minute.

"How can I help you, Doctor?" Ella asked.

"I'm not sure you can," Dr. Natoni said. "But if you could persuade your brother to encourage families to come to the Chapter Houses, that would help."

"I'll tell him what's going on, but it's up to him to decide what kind of help, if any, he's willing to give. Can the department help you somehow?"

"You can have units go out and spread the word about how dangerous the disease is if left untreated. Encourage everyone to come and be screened for symptoms, and to get their shots. And have all your officers stop by here for immediate vaccinations."

"Consider it done."

"You might also want to catch Dr. Roanhorse before she leaves. She'll be heading the last team. Share any insights you might have on the traditionalists with her. I'd be willing to bet it's been a while since she dealt with any of them."

"I'll do that, but if you know that about her why did you choose her to go out into the field?"

He exhaled softly. "We're short of doctors and we need to

keep our trauma team and some GPs here. What I'm counting on is that people further away from Shiprock won't know anything about her duties as M.E."

Ella went downstairs quickly. Carolyn placed the telephone receiver down and looked up as Ella came into her office.

"I don't have time to chat," Carolyn said, "but I'll vaccinate you now. Dr. Natoni told me to catch you before you leave. We've got the supplies already loaded into the medical van and we'll be ready to roll in a few minutes."

Ella looked at her friend then began to roll up her sleeve. As the only pathologist the tribe had, Carolyn's workload had always been more than sufficient to keep her at the hospital long hours. This extra duty was not going to make things easier for her. She only wished they'd heard something on the tissue samples that had gone to Santa Fe. Carolyn needed to be vindicated, and the sooner the better. "How on earth are you going to tackle this extra responsibility? There are only twenty-four hours in a day."

"It wasn't my idea. I haven't practiced field medicine in years. I was recruited." She gave Ella a relatively painless injection, then lowered her voice. "If you want my opinion, I think the senator is behind this. There are other doctors who could have gone out into the outlying regions."

"Why would the senator be involved? That doesn't make any sense. He wants to prove you're a liar, not make you seem indispensable." Ella took the plastic bandage Carolyn handed her and placed it over the puncture mark.

"It's a strategy designed to overwork me. I'll soon be exhausted and start making mistakes. Then he'll either push for my resignation, or have me fired."

Howard Lee came into the room. "We need more syringes, Doctor, but our supply is almost depleted."

"Borrow some from any department in this hospital that has them. This emergency takes priority."

Carolyn shifted her attention back to Ella. "I have another cross to bear. I've got to take Howard with me as part of my team, and that promises to be a real pain in the neck. I gave him a very poor grade on his lab work and he's not at all happy. He's getting his revenge by making me spell everything out when I give him a job to do."

"Howard you can handle. But have you considered how to handle the traditionalists you're going to be dealing with? They don't trust modern medicine." Ella remembered to bring up Dr. Natoni's concerns.

"There's always someone who is suspicious of doctors and nurses, and our people are no different than them. I did my residency in Gallup, and got used to taking it slow with people. I found that a smile and a good simple explanation are your best allies in dealing with skeptics. I'll manage," Carolyn assured her.

"So do you suppose going into the field will attract you to working in general practice again?" Ella asked.

Carolyn considered it, then shook her head. "I doubt it. I used to love dealing with patients one-to-one. But that's no longer my job, and it's not where I'm needed the most. I can't go back to it so I don't relish the thought of reminding myself of things that might have been." She picked up her medical bag. "Time for me to go."

Ella watched Carolyn leave, then walked back to the stairwell. They had both paid a high price for their choice to serve the tribe, a price reflected in the solitary lives they now led.

As Ella walked to the Jeep bits and pieces of a conversation between two women on the hospital staff reached her. They were discussing their plans for the weekend. As she listened it became clear that they lived for their days off. Their work was simply something that had to be endured.

Ella took a deep breath. No, she had made the right decision. To find little or no satisfaction in work, the activity that took most of an adult's time, would weigh anyone down. Better to have a job that one loved than the kind that just marked time and an endless procession of days.

As she approached the Jeep, she saw a piece of paper stuck beneath the wiper blade. Ella fought a feeling of suffocation, guessing what it was before reading it. She opened the folded note with trembling hands, holding it by the edges in hopes of obtaining a fingerprint later. As she'd sensed, it was from the person calling himself Randall Clah.

"This sickness among our people is a demonstration. It's proof that my reach extends beyond the grave. More will die so that you may see clearly that the power of a skinwalker is greater than anything you imagined. Our battle continues, but this time, neither you nor your family will escape."

Ella began to tremble violently. She slipped behind the wheel, needing to shield herself from any curious onlookers. She placed the note in an evidence pouch and willed herself to calm down. Her father-in-law was dead. The evidence had been incontrovertible. She would not allow this crude attempt to unnerve her to succeed.

Ella drove back to the station. The wind had come up, stirring the dry sand and blasting it against her vehicle. The parched smell of the desert filled her nostrils. It was the smell of hopelessness. Without rain, more sorrow would visit the Navajo Nation.

Ella tried to block out the heaviness that settled over her. It was like having a pillow pressed to her face. She was suddenly certain things were only going to get worse.

She shook her head and pressed down harder on the accelerator. Speed gave the illusion of control, and as she hurtled down the highway, Ella found herself hoping that, for once, her instincts would be wrong.

After advising Big Ed of the plan to vaccinate all the police officers and hours of reading and writing reports, Ella suddenly remembered "Randall's" note. Clearing her desk, Ella locked her office and went to her lab to find Justine. It was disturbing to think of her young assistant tackling a hard case like Raymond Nez. She hoped Justine would learn what was needed without getting hurt in the process.

"How's it going?" Ella inquired, as Justine glanced up from her desk.

"Still trying to sort through the background reports we have on the employees at the mine. I split them with Neskahi, but it's going slow."

Ella handed her the pouch with the letter. "Check this for fingerprints. I would have brought it by earlier, but I got sidetracked."

Justine used two large forceps to open the note, spreading it out expertly on the desk. "It looks like the same kind of paper that he used before. That won't help us much. It's a cheap brand you can find anywhere. The writing in the other was done with a forty-nine-cent ballpoint. Not much help there either."

"Maybe this time he will have left us an inadvertent print."

"If it's there, I'll find it."

Ella leaned back against the wall and rubbed her eyes. "You know what? I'm going to call it a day. I'm just too tired to think straight."

"I'll check out this note, then call you at home later?"

"I'd appreciate it. Have you heard anything new from Sergeant Neskahi?"

"No. I know he went out an hour or so ago to talk to his cousin. That's the last time I saw him. He may be tracking some new lead by now. He's not at home because I tried calling there awhile ago to ask him a question about a file."

Ella nodded, and had just started down the corridor when Justine hobbled out and called her back. "Just a thought," she said. "This note threatens your family. Do you want to assign someone to guard them? There are half a dozen officers who'd volunteer their time."

Ella considered the possibility then shook her head. "Not yet. I'll warn them myself. The danger the writer of that note refers to is more esoteric, not the type of thing that a cop can guard them against. If things change, though, I'll get Big Ed's okay and have a guard posted near my home, and my brother's."

"What about Wilson Joe? He's almost like family to you and helped you fight the skinwalkers before."

"I'll talk to him, you're right. He should be told about this."

Ella left the station, the uneasiness plaguing her increasing.

Something was urging her to get home quickly and it wasn't just her weariness. The feeling grew so strong that she called home. Her mother picked up the phone.

"Is everything all right?" she asked.

"It's quiet here. Are you expecting trouble?"

"No, not really. It's just this feeling. . . . Are you alone?"

"Your brother will be stopping by shortly, and Wilson Joe, too."

"Why is my friend visiting so unexpectedly? He's welcome, of course, but he hasn't done that in a long time."

"His aunt is not feeling well. He wants to pick up some herbs from your brother, and our home was the middle ground for both of them."

"Not feeling well?" Ella's skin crawled and prickled as if she were being attacked by wasps. Wilson's aunt lived in the section of the Rez where the meningitis outbreak had taken place. "What's wrong?"

"Female trouble."

"Are they sure?" Ella's hand gripped the steering wheel hard.

" 'They'?" Rose asked, surprised. "Our friend's aunt is a traditionalist. There is no 'they.' But your brother has helped her before. Menopause is difficult for some women, Daughter. She has periods of sadness, and aches and pains she needs help with. But why are you so worried?"

"There's been an outbreak of meningitis between here and Gallup." Silence was her only answer. "Did you hear me?"

"I have to go. Two is barking at something, and he's not the kind of dog who barks without a reason."

"Don't go outside! Lock yourself in the house and wait for me." Two wouldn't have barked at Clifford or Wilson Joe. Ella switched on her sirens and called for backup. She'd been wrong not to assign her mother a bodyguard. Now all she could do was hope it wouldn't become a mistake she'd regret for the rest of her life.

ELEVEN

✖ ✖ ✖

Ella pulled up in front of her house, her heart drumming against her sides as she saw the kitchen light on and the front door leading into the darkened living room ajar. Ella cursed the blackness, and looked around quickly for signs of her mother. Finding none, she took a flashlight from the glove compartment, left the vehicle, and began to search the area.

Ella heard a soft whimper and felt her blood turn to ice. "Mom?" Pistol in hand, she walked in the direction of the sound.

"I'm here, with Two," Rose answered, her voice trembling.

Ella rushed forward. Seeing her mother unhurt, relief spilled over her. "Why did you leave the house? I told you to stay inside!"

"I saw an intruder standing by the twin pines. Two went after him and ran whoever it was off. But when the dog came back he was injured. I've given him something for the pain, but we need to move him inside."

Ella knelt next to the big, scruffy-looking mutt. Whatever herb her mother had used seemed to be slowly easing the animal's discomfort. His breathing was becoming less labored. "I'll get something to slide him onto then we'll carry him inside. He's just too big to carry and, besides, it might further injure him if he's broken a rib."

Ella returned quickly with a piece of three-quarter-inch plywood leftover from the time they'd added a pantry.

Ella looked down at the dog and saw he was sound asleep. Working together, they scooted him gently onto the flat surface, then maneuvered him inside.

They'd just set him down on the kitchen floor when Clifford walked in.

Rose looked at her eldest child. "The animal needs your medicine. I've done what I can for the pain."

Ella forced herself not to suggest that what the dog needed was a vet. She'd once seen her brother heal his own nearly fatal bullet wound almost overnight.

Clifford knelt beside the animal, placing his hand gently on Two's ribcage. "Leave us."

Ella heard her brother begin a song as she walked with her mother back to the living room. Ella went to close the door before turning on the room lights. "You scared me half to death, Mom. Don't ever go outside when you see an intruder."

Just then, red and blue lights from an arriving patrol unit flashed through the window, making a pattern on the wall. Ella went outside and saw Phillip Cloud, the son of a longtime friend of her family's, stepping out of his unit, shotgun in hand. "What's the situation?"

"Everything seems to be clear now, but I'm going to need to you to keep watch in this area tonight. I've received a threat against my family, and my mother discovered an intruder over by those pines about thirty minutes ago. I'll be here until morning, but I can use an extra pair of eyes."

"You've got it. I'm patrolling this sector on my shift anyway so I'll make sure it's covered. I can also call my brother, Michael. He's got the graveyard shift. He won't mind driving by your mother's place and checking on the *hataalii* from time to time."

Ella nodded. "Thanks, I'd appreciate that."

When Ella walked back inside the house, Two had already

stood up and walked over to his water dish. His middle had been bandaged and he was moving stiffly, but he *was* moving. "His ribs are bruised but nothing's broken. He'll need a few days to recover but he'll be fine. What happened?" Clifford asked.

Ella looked at the dog and felt a twinge of jealousy for her brother's knowledge and power. Quickly focusing on what she did best, she told him about the notes from Randall she'd received. Her brother's eyes narrowed and his expression became guarded.

"I'm going for a walk over by the pines to take a look around," she said.

"Be careful," he warned. "If our old enemies are back again, this is just the beginning."

The words were quiet and spoken without a trace of emotion, but they struck a chord that vibrated down to her bones. "We'll see it through. What other choice do we have?"

"None," he said, and went back to the living room.

Ella went outside, flashlight in hand, and walked carefully to the spot her mother had indicated. She kept the beam of the flashlight firmly in front of her. If there were tracks, she didn't want to cover them up with her own.

When she reached the area around the twin pines, she stopped and surveyed the entire area with her flashlight. Besides Two's tracks there were faint imprints on the ground, like the soft moccasinlike tracks at the site near where she and Justine had encountered the van.

Ella moved farther uphill and saw the same quarter-sized indentations on the ground. She followed the marks to a place where the ground leveled off, and they disappeared. After studying them for a long time, and unable to come up with anything except speculation, she made her way back to the house.

By the time she reached the door, Wilson Joe had arrived and Ella couldn't help but smile at him. There were few things rarer and more valuable in life than a friend who seldom asked for more than she could give.

"Your brother filled me in." Wilson's eyes narrowed. "Will someone be around to keep an eye on your mother?"

"Tonight, I'll be here, and Philip Cloud will be patrolling in the area. Later, his brother Michael will be coming by from time to time."

"Rose won't like all the attention."

"I know, but there's nothing I can do about that."

He didn't argue the point. "Could the threatening note be coming from another skinwalker, a friend of your father-in-law's that we failed to identify?"

"Maybe."

As Ella entered the living room she saw her brother sprinkle the corners of the room, then their mom, with corn pollen. Finally, he turned and bestowed a similar blessing on her.

"That was for strength," Clifford said when finished. "Being prepared spiritually is half the battle." He gave his sister a long look. "Don't repeat past mistakes. Don't discount the power of what you don't understand."

"I won't," she answered, reaching down to touch the badger fetish at her neck. There was one thing she was certain about. Belief could make a weak man strong, and a strong man weak. In it lay the survival and destruction of many civilizations. Adhering to a philosophy or not adhering to it did not lessen the power it gave to the ones she was fighting. They would use fear and, in fact, were already using it against her and anyone else who stood in their way.

After Rose had retired for the night, Clifford, Wilson Joe, and Ella met in the study. Ella filled them in on the outbreak of meningitis, cautioning them both to be on the alert for symptoms that might be mistaken for the flu. Clifford, as a medicine man, did not feel he could recommend modern medicine directly, but promised to make his patients aware of the danger. He also refused police protection despite skinwalker threats, but Ella wasn't surprised.

Finally Clifford stood. "I've done all I can here for tonight. It's time for me to tend to my family."

As Clifford left, Wilson Joe lingered behind. "There's something I want to tell you."

There was something in his expression that made her heart shrink. "What's wrong?"

"There's nothing wrong," he answered softly, "but there's something I wanted you to hear from me first. I'm getting married."

Ella felt as if someone had taken all the oxygen out of the air. She held her body perfectly rigid. "To whom?"

"Lisa Aspass. I don't believe you know her, but she's a teacher at the college. She started last semester with an introductory Navajo language class. I've been seeing her a lot, and I think this is the right move for me."

Ella noted his eyes were searching hers, but she wasn't sure what he expected her to say. She knew that their friendship would cease to be the ever present comfort it had always been once he had a wife and other responsibilities and priorities. Although she hadn't expected him to remain single all his life, the news hit her hard. "I wish you only the best," she managed with a weak smile.

"I'd like to say that it won't make any difference to our friendship, but I think we both know better," he said softly.

"Yes."

Wilson kissed her on the cheek then drew back. "I have to go now. Lisa and I are hoping to catch a late movie in Farmington."

Ella watched him leave, a tear falling down her face. She supposed it was inevitable that their paths would diverge like this. He was handsome, intelligent, and very well liked by everyone who knew him. And he was marrying someone in his profession, someone who would share the worries and daily ups and downs of his chosen field.

Ella walked back into her room and turned on her computer. For the first time in months, there was no E-mail message from Wilson Joe. Ella switched screens to the game of solitaire.

Ella left the house shortly after seven without saying good-bye to her mother, who was out in her garden with Two. The dog, almost fully recovered, was sunning himself as she watered the young plants. Still distressed by the previous night's revelations, Ella wanted to avoid her mother's eagle sharp gaze for a few more hours. Her heart felt leaden inside her chest, and her mother would not be likely to miss her mood. Ella tried telling herself over and over again that she was being selfish, but she had so few really close friends. Knowing that the camaraderie she'd shared with Wilson would dwindle left her with a flatness of feeling that was as wrenching as it was unyielding.

She drove slowly down the highway, noting the small corrals just off the road where sheep were being penned in preparation for shearing. The rhythms of the spring rituals she'd once found comforting because of their sameness now left her feeling worn down and old.

Ella arrived at the station and went to her office without encountering another person. Files covered the top of her desk, having no doubt reproduced themselves during the night. At least this would never change. Ella checked her voice mail, and there was finally one cheerful message. It was an invitation from Carolyn at the hospital to join her for breakfast. Realizing she was hungry and that company would do her good, she quickly checked the incoming reports for anything critical. The Santa Fe lab had still not completed the Yellowhair autopsy tests. The rest would wait a bit longer.

Before Ella had reached the door, Justine came in, minus the crutch, her injured foot almost back to normal. "You're walking a lot better," Ella observed.

"Your brother recommended a few herbs to me after the accident, but I've been too lazy to prepare the poultice. I started to use it last night, and you see the results. I only wish I'd done it sooner. The swelling is nearly gone and my ankle doesn't hurt."

Ella nodded, not surprised at Clifford's ability to get results. "What's on your agenda today?"

"I'm going to go over my portion of the mine's employee list one final time, checking it for anything that might lead us to a suspect. Then this afternoon I'm going to meet Raymond Nez before he goes to work. He called me earlier, and I think he's been thinking about what I suggested."

"Which was?"

"If he doesn't help us the crisis at the mine will eventually reach the boiling point. If that happens, jobs will be on the line and more violence will erupt, maybe costing lives on both sides. The best way to keep our level of necessary intervention low is to make sure trouble doesn't get the upper hand. Cooperating with us now is the best way to insure that."

"And he agreed? Just like that?" Ella shook her head. "Something doesn't smell right."

Justine nodded. "I agree, that's why I intend to be very careful."

"Go wired for sound. Neskahi and I will be your backup."

"I'd rather handle this solo."

"You will, but with help nearby. I have a bad feeling about this, Cousin. I just don't trust the guy."

Justine's eyes widened, but she said nothing. Ella realized again that few of her fellow cops argued with her gut feelings.

"Shall I contact Neskahi, then, and tell him to stand by for this afternoon?" Justine asked.

"Yes. And tell him I want a full report on his activities. I figure he's probably busy working behind the scenes, but we're a team. I want to be kept current on everything he's doing." As the words left her mouth she realized that she sounded just like Big Ed. Now there was a sobering thought. With her role in the department changing, and people under her command, she had new responsibilities that went well beyond keeping her own butt safe.

"I'm going over to the hospital, Justine. You can reach me there."

On the way to the hospital Ella contacted Blalock on the cellular to update him and find out about his own progress.

"I've been interviewing the Anglo workers, but so far I've got zip. Something big is in the works, though. They're just too squirrely when I talk to them."

"I've been getting the same vibes from my own people."

"Then we both better dig deeper."

Ella hung up, wondering if she should have told him about the meeting between Justine and her contact. At this stage it seemed premature at best. After all, she wasn't sure they'd get anywhere, and the more people who knew about it, the more likely it was that the operation would fall flat. Deciding she'd made the right decision by not saying anything, she pressed on toward the hospital.

When Ella arrived at the morgue she saw Carolyn packing cartons of medicines into protective foam containers. "You must have had a short day yesterday. Are you guys going to go back out this morning?"

"We had a real low turnout, so we came back around dark and dropped by the police station. We inoculated everyone there, and set up a schedule to get the rest. Word is slowly getting out, and we're booked the rest of the week. Unfortunately, two more confirmed cases of meningitis were reported during the night."

"Breakfast is off, then?" Ella asked, disappointed, but understanding.

"Not at all. We won't be leaving for a few more hours and I've got to eat something. I haven't had a bite since late afternoon yesterday."

"Me neither." Ella smiled ruefully. "Cripes, what a pair we make."

Carolyn led the way upstairs to the cafeteria. "I've got to tell you, going out onto the Rez has not been without it's pluses. They don't know me in the rural areas, or even about me, so I'm merely treated with the same contempt they'd show any other M.D."

Ella chuckled. "That's an improvement?"

"I've grown used to being shunned. But, out there, it's more a matter of just not being wanted. Do you understand the distinction I'm making?"

"You're pushed away, but without revulsion?"

"Exactly. Kind of strange when being soundly rejected is actually making progress, huh?"

"Sometimes I wonder whether either of us would have chosen the path we now follow, had we known the full cost."

"That's a question everyone asks themselves from time to time, not just us." Carolyn regarded her thoughtfully. "But what's really eating at you?"

"Did you know Wilson Joe is getting married to another professor at the college?"

Carolyn's eyebrows rose. "Don't tell me that *now* you've discovered you're in love with him."

"No, that's not it. What he has always been to me was a friend I could count on. It's terribly selfish of me not to want him to get married, but there it is."

"It is selfish, but also understandable. At our age, when you're single and career driven, friendships are hard to maintain. Making new friends is almost as difficult because we've become so set in our ways its hard to adapt to someone else's interests and needs. When a male friend gets married, it's often hard for the wife to accept another woman who is close to her husband, so the friendship is bound to suffer."

She smiled ruefully. "When you put it that way, I've got a helluva good reason to feel sorry for myself."

When they reached the cashier at the end of the cafeteria line, Ella had two apple fritters on her plate and two cartons of milk. Carolyn's tray was still empty.

"Hey, I thought you were hungry."

"I am, but I get a few perks 'cause I'm staff," she said, giving Ella a wink. "They baked pecan pies for lunch yesterday. I knew they'd all be gone by this morning so I asked them to set aside a jumbo slice for me." Carolyn waved at an elderly Navajo woman inside the kitchen.

"I've got your pie in the walk-in, Doctor. Just a minute."

Ella paid for her breakfast, then walked to a table next to the big window that looked west out onto the desert. Her favorite parts of the reservation were the huge areas that were undeveloped. The wide open country appealed to her, often soothing her spirit when nothing else would.

Carolyn joined her a moment later with her pie and a big mug of coffee. "I've been looking forward to my slice of pie all morning."

"Is that what you're going to have for breakfast?"

Carolyn nodded, then with a sheepish grin, added a packet of noncaloric sweetener to her coffee. "There are enough calories in this humongous slice to fill my quota for the week, so it makes me feel less guilty if I don't have anything else."

"Hey, far be it from me to counsel a doctor on the risks of poor eating habits, but since there's a health crisis where you're going, don't you think some fruit and cereal might be better, even if it is in addition to the pie?"

"Yeah, sure. But we all need to be bad sometime, and I don't smoke or drink." Carolyn took a huge bite, and smiled. "Ah. This is decadent." She held out a forkful to Ella.

"No, I'll pass. I feel badly enough about getting two apple fritters."

"Oh please. Like you have to diet?" Carolyn scoffed, then looked down at her own expanding girth. "I have a rule of thumb. When my waist gets close to my hip measurement, it's time to worry. I'm not quite there yet, and since my hips grow faster than any other portion of my body, it may be a while."

Ella laughed. "Oh, I love these rules you set up for yourself."

Carolyn continued devouring her pie. "We all have our own self-imposed limits."

Ella looked down at the remaining fritter. She didn't have any right to talk. In the past year, she'd put on close to ten pounds. She planned to lose it, but she hadn't quite got around to that yet.

Carolyn coughed then reached for her glass of water. She took another deep swallow, then began to cough again.

Ella looked up and saw Carolyn gasping for air. "You're choking!" She jumped to her feet to help Carolyn, but Carolyn pushed her away.

"No—not choking!" she managed, still coughing.

"How can I help?" Ella looked around for a doctor among the cafeteria patrons. People had noticed Carolyn's predicament and some were starting to rise from their seats.

Carolyn shook her head, struggling to gain control.

An Anglo doctor who'd been nearby rushed up to their table,

signalling for one of the nurses to come and assist. "Try to tell us your symptoms, Doctor," he said calmly.

"I—" Carolyn blinked several times. "Mouth, burning." She coughed then gasped for air. "Throat, tingling." She squinted with pain as she looked at Ella through watery eyes. "Poison," she added, then pointed at the pie.

"Jimsonweed?" Ella asked quickly, feeling in her pocket for the pouch Clifford had given her.

The doctor was trying to take Carolyn's vital signs, the nurse assisting him. "Stay calm, Doctor. What poison do you suspect?"

"Monkshood," Carolyn whispered, her voice weaker.

"What makes you so sure?" the doctor prodded.

Carolyn just gave him a look.

"Take her word for it, Doc," Ella said, and quickly picked up the plate containing what remained of the pie.

As Carolyn was placed in a wheelchair and hurried out of the cafeteria, Ella reached for her cell phone and dialed Justine. She needed her team here, now!

"Is Neskahi at the station?" Ella asked.

"Yes. He's working on his report now. I told him what you'd said," Justine answered.

"Good. I need you both here right away." Ella filled her in. "Get moving."

Plate in hand, Ella strode up to the counter and found the elderly woman who'd handed Carolyn the pie. Her face was ashen, as were those of all the cafeteria staff. "What happened?" the woman asked, her eyes wide.

"The doctor was poisoned. I think it was the pie."

The woman took one step back. "You don't think I—"

"I don't know anything at this point." Ella glanced at the woman's name tag. Vera Mae Francisco. "What I need to know is who, besides you, had access to that slice of pecan pie?"

"Everyone here," the woman blurted, waving her hand around the kitchen. "We all come and go out of the walk-in refrigerator."

Ella looked at the nodding faces. One tall, young woman

came and put her arm around the elderly kitchen worker. "Stop upsetting Vera. She didn't do anything wrong. She put the piece of pie into the refrigerator yesterday just like she always does."

Ella read the name tag. Barbara Tsosie was very protective of the older woman. Then again, judging from the expressions of support on the faces of the others, Vera Mae was a favorite of the staff's.

"I'm not accusing anybody at the moment, not until I make a full investigation. You should all start thinking about who had both the opportunity and a motive to poison Dr. Roanhorse."

"Then we are all suspects?" Barbara asked.

"And anyone else who might have come into the kitchen since yesterday, yes," Ella answered. "Who knew the jumbo piece was for Dr. Roanhorse?"

"We all did," Linda Buck answered. "Dr. Roanhorse always has us set a big slice aside whenever we bake pecan pies."

"Do other staff members ask for similar favors?" Ella asked.

"Dr. Natoni likes us to separate a slice of fresh peach pie when we bake them, and a couple of the nurses have us set aside apple fritters, but that's about it."

"So it would have been assumed that a large slice of pecan pie was for Dr. Roanhorse."

"Yes," Vera Mae said.

Ella was about to ask them more when Justine and Sergeant Neskahi arrived.

Ella took her two team members aside and filled them in. "Speak to them separately, and try to find out who besides cafeteria staff might have come into the kitchen. Someone knows something. I'd bet on it, even if they don't remember it right now."

"Do you suspect any of them?" Justine asked.

"Honestly? No. But we'll have to check them all out. And if any of them is related to Senator Yellowhair, I want to know right away."

"We're on it," Neskahi said, then, as Justine moved away, dropped his voice and added, "I'm sorry I didn't call in. My cousin still refuses to talk to me. I spent quite a bit of time following him, hoping to get him to change his mind."

"Did he?"

Neskahi shook his head. "He's too stubborn. He's also going on vacation, visiting in-laws at Zuni, so he won't be any good to us from now on."

"Focus on the situation here then and see if you can find out who poisoned the M.E.," Ella ordered.

Leaving them to work, Ella went down the corridor to the emergency room and asked the nurse about Carolyn.

"Dr. Roanhorse will be fine. It appears her identification of the poison was right on the money. We pumped out her stomach in time, and the contents have been sent to toxicology already. She's on oxygen to help her breathe right now, but that's not unusual at this point. Dr. Natoni has had her admitted and wants her hospitalized for at least a day."

Ella had a feeling Carolyn wouldn't be too pleased about that. "When can I see her?"

"She's in Room One-oh-four. I'm sure it'll be okay if you stop by. Just don't stay too long."

Ella went to her friend's room. Carolyn looked up at her from the bed, tired and weak, but the gleam in her eye told Ella that nothing had dampened her fighting spirit.

"If I catch the s.o.b. who did this, he'll end up on one of my stainless steel couches," Carolyn whispered.

"I'll track him or her down," Ella assured her friend. "Tell me, who knew you'd ordered that slice of pecan pie?"

"I do it every time they bake pecan pies. Everybody around here knows that. I ordered this particular piece when we were in the cafeteria yesterday, just before leaving for the Chapter House. I was treating the entire team to coffee and juice. Several orderlies who'd helped us load up were also there. And that list doesn't include whoever was on break, or visitors who had come to check on a patient. The cafeteria is open to the public, not just staff."

"You're not helping much."

Carolyn smirked. "I just ruled out everyone else in the world who wasn't here. I'm just lucky whoever did this did a sloppy job. They should have realized I'd know it wasn't a heart attack."

"That doesn't mean you would recognize the poison. How were you able to diagnose it so quickly?"

"I did a lot of research on native plants and herbs when I was looking into Angelina's death. I wanted to make sure that my report meshed with the toxicologist's, so I got volumes of toxicology books. They're still there in my office."

"Who normally has access to those books?"

"The entire hospital, practically. Dr. Charlie is our toxicologist and she makes most of her books available to any doctor who needs them."

"I'll see what I can do to unearth the scumbag who did this. In the meantime, take care of yourself. You really scared me, you know. I thought I was about to lose another friend."

She smiled. "No way. I'm too stubborn to die."

Ella walked down the corridor, her fear now giving way to cold anger. Someone had tried to kill her best friend. One way or another she was going to find that person.

Howard Lee met her coming the other way. "I just heard! Is Dr. Roanhorse okay?"

She gave him a long look. "She'll be fine."

"That's great news!" he said, visibly relieved.

"I thought you two were having your differences."

"That's true," he said, without hesitation. "But believe me, I had nothing to do with this. I need her well. If she doesn't give me a passing grade, my medical career is going to be stalled for a whole semester. Since she's our only M.E., the only way I have to get my grade up is to work with her until the end of the semester and convince her that I can do the job. If anything were to happen to her, at best, I'd get an incomplete. Or if the professors weren't sympathetic, they'd let my current grade stand."

Ella had hoped for a fleeting moment that she'd had her man, but logic now dictated she look elsewhere. Lee was laid-back, as her conversations with Carolyn had revealed, and killing his teacher for getting a low grade wasn't too credible a motive. He was the type to travel down the easiest path and, for that, he needed Carolyn.

"Do you have any idea who might have done this?"

"What poison was used?" he asked logically. "Something from the pharmacy?"

"It was monkshood, they believe."

"I could research it for you and see where it grows and where it might be available. But right off the bat, I can tell you that the people who know the most about the use of herbs are those who run health food stores, or our own medicine men."

She looked at him directly, uncertain whether he was intimating that her brother had been involved somehow. "There aren't any health food stores in the area I'm familiar with. What do you know about our local medicine men?"

"Some older *hataaliis* who live in the regions where we were giving the inoculations are not too happy with Dr. Roanhorse. In fact, our team had a bit of a problem with one of them yesterday."

"Who?"

"John Tso. Do you know him?"

She nodded. John had to be in his early nineties. He was a formidable man and a born leader, even now. She was also certain, however, that he was incapable of harming anyone. Most important of all, he wouldn't have had the opportunity, unless he'd come to the hospital for some unfathomable reason.

"How could he have contaminated the pie?"

"One of his patients was brought in. He made quite a ruckus about it, too, saying *we* were responsible for what happened."

"How so?"

"The man got sick just a few hours after he was inoculated. It didn't appear to be a reaction to the shot, either. It's some kind of bacterial infection. Tso is up on the third floor, watching over old man Todacheene, if you want to track him down."

"Thanks."

She didn't like it, but she was too good a cop to knowingly ignore any lead. Yet off hand, she couldn't think of anything that would cause a bigger stir than the police questioning a respected *hataalii* about a murder.

She entered the cafeteria and saw Neskahi writing something down on his pad. Noticing Ella, he went to meet her.

"You want it in a nutshell?" Seeing Ella nod, Neskahi continued. "Anyone could have walked into the kitchen. They have a meeting every morning and the doors to the kitchen stay unlocked. They had a heated discussion over budget cuts this morning so nobody heard anything."

"I want you to ask specifically if anyone saw John Tso in the cafeteria this morning."

"The *hataalii?* Why? He's practically a hermit nowadays. He lives down by Big Water Spring—" He saw the expression on her face. "He's not one of the meningitis victims, is he?"

"No, but he's here with Frank Todacheene. I'm going to go talk to him now."

As Neskahi moved off, Justine came up to Ella. "I keep thinking about the note you found where Randall Clah threatened your family. Maybe this is an offshoot of that. Everyone knows you and Dr. Roanhorse are friends."

"Randall Clah is dead," Ella said firmly, but she couldn't suppress the shudder that traveled up her spine. Memories sometimes were more powerful than the death of those responsible for creating them, and someone was using that against her.

TWELVE

—— ✖ ✖ ✖ ——

Ella went to the third floor and found John Tso sitting by the silk flowers in the waiting area. His long gray hair was kept in place with a red bandanna, and his deeply wrinkled face was tanned saddle-leather dark from decades of New Mexico sunshine.

Ella approached and sat beside him on the well-worn sofa. She waited, not interrupting his thoughts.

After several minutes he spoke. His voice was deep and his words were spoken slowly, with a slight hesitation between phrases. It wasn't his English that was at fault, but rather his age. "The medicines they bring to us don't cure. They just create new problems. Your brother would know this. Do you?"

"Your patient's illness has nothing to do with the vaccine."

"That's what they say, but he's still sick and he wasn't before they came. So what have they accomplished?"

Ella said nothing, and allowed the silence to stretch out.

"I heard about your friend the doctor," Tso commented. "She says she wants to protect us, but she doesn't even know how to take care of herself."

"She was poisoned with an herb."

The old man smiled slowly and mirthlessly. "Do you come to

me for advice or with accusations?" He shook his head. "I am not The People's enemy."

As a nurse approached, Tso stood up. "What is wrong?"

"I'm so very sorry, Uncle," she said, using the term out of respect, not to denote kinship, "but your friend has died."

John Tso fell back down heavily onto the sofa with a deep sigh. The nurse immediately bent down and, taking his wrist, tried to take his pulse.

He pulled away. "No. I am all right. I protect myself in the old way." He shot Ella a stern glance. "You and many others have grown up thinking the new is better than the old. But look clearly at what happened here today. We've lost neighbors before, but when they died, they did so with dignity, in their hogans. What dignity is there in dying in a place like this, surrounded by strangers, with tubes sticking into your body? Even the air they give you comes from a machine."

Ella watched helplessly as Tso stood and walked away slowly. She started to go after him, but the nurse grabbed her arm gently.

"Your questions can wait a little bit longer. He needs time alone to grieve for his friend. Give him that."

Ella felt her heart sinking with sorrow. "How long has he been here?"

The young woman shook her head slowly. "I know what you're getting at, but there's no way he could have been responsible for poisoning Dr. Roanhorse. He hasn't left this floor since his patient was brought in. He's so old, all the shift nurses have been keeping an eye on him, too. We've brought him food and something to drink, and made sure he was okay."

As Ella went downstairs she considered what she'd learned. It was possible that the nurses were covering for him. John Tso was not only well liked, he was also a very respected member of the tribe. Her gut was telling her to look elsewhere, though. A *hataalii* pledged his life to one of gentle healings and teaching, not death. It would have been totally out of character for him to harm anyone.

Ella returned to the cafeteria as Justine finished the last of the interviews.

"I've got zip," Justine said. "But it's time for me to go meet Raymond Nez. Maybe I'll find out something there. Would you like me to go alone so you can continue here?"

Ella shook her head. "No. We'll proceed as planned. Where were you supposed to meet him?"

"It's a hogan in the middle of nowhere, northeast of Beclabito, about halfway between there and the river. He says that's the only place he's reasonably sure nobody can follow him without being seen, and a place where we can talk without either of us endangering the other one."

"He's right, but it's going to be tough for us to do anything except listen in. If you get in trouble, it'll be awhile before we can reach you."

"I won't get in trouble," she assured. "I think he's glad to have someone to talk to. He's a leader, and sometimes it can get lonely for people in those positions."

Ella smiled. "People in leadership positions often are nothing more than experts at manipulating others."

"He's a potential informant. I can handle this."

Ella sighed. Young officers were always so tremendously confident, often with nothing substantial to base it on except for their boundless enthusiasm. "Tell Neskahi to get you some gear and find us a lookout point. I'll pick him up at the station. We'll set out twenty minutes after you and stay as close as we can, but we'll have to hang back and go in on foot in case he's got a lookout."

"Okay."

As Justine hurried down the hallway, Ella stopped by Carolyn's room one last time. Carolyn seemed to be breathing easier now. "Hey, you're looking better by the minute."

"I'm improving," she admitted, though her voice was still shaky. "Come up with anything?"

"I'm considering an interesting theory. Maybe the person who poisoned you was the same one who wrote the Randall Clah note threatening my family. You're almost family, you know. It's obvious that person wants revenge, and by hurting you they would be striking out at me."

"You're reaching. This is connected to Yellowhair. I'm sure of it, though he wouldn't be stupid enough to do it himself."

"Or it may not be linked to him at all," Ella answered, palms upward. "I'll see you soon. I've got to get back to work."

Ella went to the parking lot, then, after switching on the sirens, made record time to the station.

Neskahi was making one final check of the listening equipment as Ella entered the lab. The wire had been taped to Justine's skin and was hidden by her shirt. "You'll be okay, but don't fidget so much. You'll give yourself away."

"It's uncomfortable."

"It's not leisure wear."

"Right." Justine glanced at Ella. "I'll do my best to get some answers."

"I know you will, but watch yourself." Ella went with her cousin as far as the door, then watched Justine drive away.

"Do you think she really can handle this?" she asked the sergeant.

"I'm not sure. Nez is one smart cookie. I think she's underestimating him, and that does concern me. I've got a good location picked out for us, though. It's just on the other side of a ridge east of the hogan. We'll be shielded, but should be able to pick up the transmission."

It took over an hour for them to get in place. Though they were on time for Justine's meeting, Ella felt uncomfortable cutting it so close. Neskahi adjusted the receiver and the static disappeared. Justine's voice came through clearly.

"For a while I wasn't sure I could find this place," the young officer said clearly.

"It's out of the way but, like I said, that's what makes it safe." Nez's voice was easy to recognize.

"Are you afraid for yourself? Are you in danger?"

Nez laughed. "We're all in danger at the mine, but your boss is only making things worse. You've got to find a way to get Clah to back off. Every time she comes around things get even more tense. People are afraid she'll be arresting them for murder. Or worse."

"I can talk to her about that *if* you give me something to work with. Tell me what's happening there. Who are the members of The Brotherhood? Are the Fierce Ones the bad guys or the good guys?"

"In my opinion, neither side is completely right. But if I have to side with someone, I'll side with our own people. How about you?"

"Why don't you tell me more first?"

"None of us know who is part of The Brotherhood, but we do know that they've got paid informants among The People. That's the real danger. Distrust breeds violence more often than not."

"That's precisely why my boss insists on keeping a close watch on the mine."

"The more she stirs things up, the worse it gets for those who, like me, are trying to keep trouble from escalating."

"We keep coming back to the same thing. If you want the department to stay away you have to help us."

"How? I have no answers to give you. I have my hands full making sure I keep everyone's tempers in check during my shift."

"Who leads the Fierce Ones?"

"I truly don't know—wait, you didn't think it was me, did you?" He started laughing. "Oh, little one, you're even younger than you look if you believed that!"

"Why couldn't it have been you? Don't you think of yourself as a leader?"

Ella looked over at Neskahi. "That's a score for Justine."

Neskahi nodded.

"To lead, you have to believe in what you're doing. To be truthful, I'm not sure the Fierce Ones aren't responsible for Bitah's death. Maybe they wanted to get rid of him for their own reasons. The Fierce Ones are cut from the same mold as The Brotherhood, though they have opposing philosophies. Both groups advocate violence as a justifiable method to effect change. I can't condone that."

"Then help us. Find out who the members of the Fierce Ones are, and who is in The Brotherhood."

"No. I won't do that."

"Because you're afraid?"

"Yes, but not for the reasons you think. I won't get involved in anything that furthers division among the miners. That will bring the mine down. It may end up closing for good if the company running it bails out. My job is to keep things from reaching that point."

"But if you helped us—"

"I am, but not in the way of your choosing. I strongly suggest you make sure my message gets through loud and clear to your boss. If she chooses to disregard it and continues to interfere with what we're doing behind the scenes, there will be a price to pay."

"By who?"

There was silence for several long moments. Finally, Justine's voice came over the transmitter. "Nez has walked off, and I still have no answers."

Ella smiled, wishing she could communicate with Justine but knowing it was impossible at the moment. "She does have answers. Nez talked about what 'we're' doing behind the scenes. I'd bet my last dime he's a member of the Fierce Ones, and that the warning was a veiled threat from them."

"Nez is a strong-willed man. I wouldn't assume it's a bluff."

"I'm not. We have enemies on all sides, and they're gaining power quickly. Our job is to break that hold, but to be honest, I'm not sure how."

As they returned to her vehicle, the cry of a single coyote rose high in the air. Ella kept her eyes on the path ahead, refusing to give in to fears she couldn't support with logic. Coyotes were not to be trusted, according to traditional beliefs that linked them with Navajo witches and bad luck. She saw Neskahi look around, but keep walking.

It was a coyote, nothing more, nothing less. Ignoring the way her skin prickled, Ella strode quickly to the Jeep with Sergeant Neskahi.

. . .

Ella met with Justine back at the office. She could see from Justine's expression that her assistant was disappointed with the results of her meeting. "You did well," she said, explaining what she'd surmised. "You don't threaten him, so he may contact you again with some information."

"That's not quite what I'd hoped for. I wanted answers now."

"Patience."

Neskahi came in, a triumphant look on his face. "I've got news. I've been following up on the caller who first made the report of the drunken driver, the one who led us to Angelina." He glanced first at one of them, then the other. "I played a hunch and contacted all the gas station attendants between Shiprock and Farmington. Nothing happened for a while, but I just hit pay dirt. I got a call from the man who owns the Last Stop on the road to Farmington. He admitted he had made the call when he saw the girl driving erratically. He said he'd known it was the senator's daughter from her fancy red car, so he'd decided not to leave his name."

"Now we have another witness. Good job," Ella said.

"Maybe we can talk to her parents and learn who she may have met in Farmington, or between there and Shiprock. She wasn't gone that long, judging by the time the accident occurred, so we can narrow down the places she may have been," Neskahi suggested.

"Do you want me to go?" Justine asked. "The senator may talk to me more willingly than he would with you."

"No. It's important he know that I'm going to stay on this case until I get answers—whatever those might be." Ella replied.

"Speaking of answers, I've decided on one myself," Neskahi said, smiling. "If you can use another permanent member of your team, or even if it's only part-time, I'm your man."

"That's great news, Sergeant. I promise to keep you busy no matter how many hours the chief can spare you. And speaking of busy, it's about time I visit the senator again." Ella stood up from her desk and followed Justine and Sergeant Neskahi out the door.

Ella drove to the senator's home, a less-than-half-hour journey. Abigail Yellowhair was sitting alone on the porch weaving a blanket. She smiled thinly as Ella parked in the driveway, then waved for her to approach. "My husband is not here. Is there something I can help you with?"

"I certainly hope so. Can you tell me who your daughter might have visited in Farmington, or maybe between there and Shiprock? Did she perhaps have a boyfriend in that area?"

"Not that I know of, but she really loved to go shopping in Farmington. There's a little shop in the mall on the west side that she particularly liked. They carry very nice country western clothing. Do you know it?"

Ella nodded. She'd been in there herself more than once.

"If she was in Farmington she probably went there." Abigail Yellowhair stared at the blanket she was weaving and sighed. "I used to be able to weave, but somewhere along the way, I've lost my skill."

Ella saw that the design was uneven, but refrained from commenting.

"I thought that if I did some of the things that had given me pleasure as a young woman, it would stop hurting so much in here," Abigail said, pointing to her heart. "But nothing helps." A tear rolled down her face.

Ella heard a vehicle approaching. She turned her head and saw the senator climbing out of a late model brown pickup. He strode toward Ella, anger flashing in his eyes.

"What are you doing here bothering my wife? She's upset enough, or can't you tell?" He helped his wife up from the porch where she'd been seated in front of the giant loom. "Stay here. I'll be back," he said, escorting his wife inside the house.

Ella waited. A few minutes later the senator returned.

"My wife said you wanted to know about my daughter's shopping habits. Don't tell me you're finding fault with that, too."

"It's not a matter of finding fault," she repeated patiently. "I need to reconstruct what happened the day she died, Senator. It's my job, and one that ultimately will be a benefit to your family and our people. I'm sure that what you want is the truth."

"I know the truth. It's your fabrications I have problems with. My daughter went shopping, got sleepy after a hectic morning, and lost control of the car. Why not leave it at that?"

"The medical and eyewitness evidence doesn't support that conclusion," she said simply.

"Then take another look at where the evidence comes from." Ella kept silent this time about the presence of drugs in Angelina's system. Mentioning that would end the conversation. "Have any young men come by to pay their respects?" Ella asked, searching for a lead to Angelina's boyfriend.

"No, but that's to be expected. Our tribe isn't big on funerals or funeral sentiments."

Ella considered that. She hadn't really expected Angelina's mysterious boyfriend to come out of the woodwork, but it had been worth asking.

"Now I'm asking you to leave. You're upsetting my wife and I won't tolerate that."

Ella drove home deep in thought. The senator's attitude disturbed her deeply. He was either really convinced that Carolyn had manufactured her findings or was willing to deny anything to save his political career: This was not just a case of a man unable to accept the lifestyle of a daughter who was now dead.

Ella trusted Carolyn. She was not the type of person who would have falsified documents and reports. Regardless of the senator's beliefs, Carolyn lying was not part of the equation.

She was getting near the turnoff to her mother's home when she noticed a truck following her. The truck stayed well behind but kept the distance between them consistent, speeding up and slowing down when she did.

Ella picked up the mike and called in for backup. Neskahi responded almost instantly. "I can be at your 'twenty in five minutes. I was just about to make a swing by your mother's home anyway."

She hesitated, reluctant to take him away from that errand. "Is there anyone else in that area?"

"Your brother's pickup was parked at Rose's house an hour ago."

"Okay. I'm going to play this out. Stay on high ground and keep an eye out for any signs of an ambush or diversion."

"Ten-four."

Ella slowed down as she reached the road that paralleled the one leading to her mother's home, then turned abruptly, going across country. She knew this stretch like the back of her hand, and Neskahi would be able to keep her in visual contact without any problem.

She was halfway down the dirt track that led to some sheep pens when the truck behind her closed in. Ella stepped on the brakes, spinning her vehicle across the road. Using the Jeep as cover, she drew her weapon and steadied her aim by resting her arm on the hood.

The truck drew near, stopped, and a moment later Billy Pete emerged. "It's me, relax."

"What the hell do you think you're doing? I could have shot you!"

"You said you needed help. That's why I'm here." He sauntered toward her. "I have some information about Noah Charley you may find interesting. We believe he was an informant for The Brotherhood."

"Who's 'we' and what led you to believe that?" Ella secured her weapon.

"I spoke to a member of the Fierce Ones. They'd been watching Noah and discovered he was having clandestine meetings with Truman."

"Maybe they were friends," Ella countered, not really believing it but still annoyed.

"It's up to you to check that out. You said you could keep things from getting worse at the mine if you got some help, so that's what I'm giving you."

"Tell me this: Can you think of a reason why The Brotherhood would try to hurt Senator Yellowhair's daughter? Does The Brotherhood have any hold on him?"

Billy Pete's eyes grew wide. "I really doubt that. But if they'd killed his daughter, I assure you he wouldn't let it pass. If he hadn't been their enemy before that he would have been afterwards. He's not the kind to back away from any fight."

"I realize I may be reaching, but that's because there are so few solid leads."

"I can tell you this much. What the mine officials are doing to make things better isn't working. If anything, things are worse. Do you know Randy Watson, the Anglo supervisor? I heard he talked to you the night we all found out about the shift changes."

Ella nodded, remembering the Anglo who'd first spoken to her at the mine. "What about him?"

"He was in a bad accident. His pickup rolled three times. The seat belt saved him, but he's at home now with a bad back."

"You think the Fierce Ones caused it?"

"No, I don't think it had anything to do with our people. I think that if anyone was responsible, it was the Anglos. Some were angry that he'd spoken to you. Like the rest of us, they want to handle this without the police."

"Thanks for the tips on Watson and Charley. I'll check them out."

"There's something I'd like you to do for me."

"What is it?"

"Don't write me up in any of your reports and don't talk about our meetings to anyone. I'd like my head to remain attached to my shoulders."

"That's standard operating procedure. Your name never appears, just a code designation."

"Okay then. Just keep it that way."

As Billy drove away Ella headed home. It wasn't late, but there were matters to take care of there.

Ella arrived at the house and found Neskahi waiting. "What was that all about?"

"You never saw anything. Is that clear?"

He smiled. "So we have an informant, finally."

Ella said nothing, just looked at him.

"Okay, I get the drift." He glanced back toward the house. "I think you're going to have to do some explaining when you go in. Your mother doesn't want anyone watching her or the house."

"So what's new?" she asked with a sigh.

Ella scribbled down the name of the store Angelina frequented in Farmington. "Go talk to the store manager. Take a photo of Angelina and see if anyone remembers her coming in the day she died, and whether she ever came with a boyfriend. Report back to me first thing tomorrow."

"Got it."

Ella walked inside and saw her brother and mother waiting. Rose's expression was one of undisguised annoyance. "You could have told me that I was going to be watched."

"It isn't a permanent thing, Mom. Officers were just passing by more than usual. I just wasn't sure you'd be safe after that intruder." Ella glanced at Two who was walking around normally now, though his bandage was still in place.

"Guards won't be necessary," Rose said flatly. "It was a measure taken to frighten us, and if we let them know that it worked we've lost a major battle."

"Fear and caution are two separate things," Ella protested.

Clifford sat down and regarded her thoughtfully. "I've never liked having our mother alone, but I respect her right to do whatever she wants. There's no need to have policemen passing by so often."

"Oh, and you two have decided this, have you?" Ella snapped.

Clifford shook his head. "She won't be alone, not anymore."

"You're planning to stay here?"

"No. But a friend of mine, who like you went to make a living outside the reservation, has returned for good now. He will be building his home nearby, on this side of the mesa by the dry arroyo. He'll be just a short distance away."

"What friend?"

"Do you remember Kevin Tolino?"

Ella felt a rush of adrenaline surging through her. Judy Lujan, Bitah's girlfriend, had said he had been an associate of the murdered man.

"He serves the tribe as an attorney. He's a good man, little sister. You don't have to be concerned."

Ella struggled between the need to keep police business confidential and the need to protect her family. "He was also a friend of the miner who was killed," she said at last.

"I know," Clifford answered. "He told me. But when the miner left the Native American Church that my friend belongs to, their friendship cooled considerably. The only time they ever met was on business, since my friend was handling some legal matters for him."

Ella shook her head. "I don't know about this. . . . It sounds too pat."

"Talk to him yourself. If there is more to it than he's saying, you'll know," Clifford said.

Rose placed her hand on her daughter's arm. "This man is not an enemy. I've spoken to him. He is a very private person who will not interfere with us unless he's asked."

Ella knew her mother's intuitions were as accurate as her own. "Okay, but I'm still going to talk to him myself."

Clifford smiled. "You may find he's as curious about you as you are about him. Distrust of others is a quality you share."

Ella said nothing.

"Either way, you'll remove the watcher, right?" Rose insisted. "I can't believe those men aren't needed elsewhere right now."

"They'll go for now, Mom. That's the only promise I can make to you."

Ella met with her team the following morning.

"So far, I've got zip on Noah Charley," Justine said.

"What about you?" Ella glanced at Neskahi. "What did you learn in Farmington?"

"I found out that Angelina purchased an expensive man's belt the day she was killed. It couldn't have been for herself since it was way too large, a size forty-two. I checked the accident report and I found out that there was no belt in the car when she was found."

"So that means she met the man after she went shopping, and before her accident," Ella said, sitting forward. "Did the clerk remember anything else?"

"Only that the senator's daughter was alone and acting just fine when he sold her the belt. The salesman claims she was flirting with him and insisted on buying the most expensive belt there. I got a copy of the receipt and put it in her file."

"Good. Now if we find the man she gave the belt to, then we may also find her killer. Did you get a description of the belt?"

"Silver buckle and brown braided leather. And I checked to make sure she hadn't given it to her father or another male relative for a present."

"Don't expect to find anyone wearing it, but keep your eyes open whenever we question suspects. I want updated reports on my desk by noon tomorrow. I need to make a report for Big Ed, and I want to add yours to it."

As her two assistants left her office Ella leaned back in the chair. They were getting closer to finding answers, she could feel it.

Ella dialed Blalock's number and filled him in on what she'd heard about Randy Watson. "Can you go interview him and check out the accident report on his truck? He seemed really open with me when I spoke to him."

When Blalock agreed, Ella left her office and drove out to see Kevin Tolino. The morning was already hotter than it had been in months. The dry air and heat made her roll up the windows and switch on the air conditioner, all the while cursing herself for going soft.

When she finally arrived at the half-completed wood-framed dwelling, surrounded by low piñons and junipers, she found Tolino stripped to the waist, cutting through a piece of two-by-six across a work bench with a hand-held power saw. A portable generator provided the electricity.

His body was lean and muscular, and he was tall for a Navajo, at least six two. The sheen of perspiration that covered his chest made his bronzed skin gleam in the strong light.

Ella climbed out of the Jeep, deliberately keeping her expression neutral. She was surprised to see the same guarded look mirrored on the face looking back at her. "Hi," she greeted. "I heard you were building here and thought I'd stop by and introduce myself."

"No introduction is necessary. I know who you are, just as you know who I am. I believe your assistant, Justine Goodluck, has been looking into my background."

She smiled. "I'm sure you realize that this is a difficult time for everyone on the reservation." Seeing him nod, she continued. "My family has many enemies and you've chosen to build your home fairly close to ours. That makes me want to be very cautious."

Tolino nodded slowly. "I'd do the same if our situations were reversed." He took a deep breath, then let it out again. "But I'm at least five miles away from your mother's and your home. It's close only in the relative terms used here on the reservation."

"True enough, but your choice of locale still raises questions in my mind."

"This land was set aside for my grandparents long ago, even before your father built his home."

"Why claim it now?"

"I have returned to the reservation to live and this land is part of my family's legacy. I want to connect myself to that again." His voice was deep and persuasive.

"You'll be doing the construction work here yourself?"

"Most of it. It'll take time, but I have plenty. In the meantime, I have an office and a small apartment in Shiprock." He leaned the cut piece of two-by-six against what was obviously the beginning of a door frame among the wall studs. "Your brother has asked me to keep an eye out for any strangers. Is that what you want, considering that you don't really trust me?"

"You're right, I'm not sure I do trust you. You were the murdered miner's friend, so I'm not exactly sure where, if any place, you fit in with his death," she said directly. With some people it was better to be blunt, and she had a feeling Tolino was one of them.

He picked out two cans of soda from the ice-filled cooler near his feet. "I knew Stanley and we were friends at one time. He was a member of the Native American Church for a while, too, but then he started crossing too many lines." He offered her one of the soft drinks.

Ella opened the lift tab, glad for something cool to moisten her dry throat. "What do you mean, 'crossing lines'?"

"The Native American Church holds to certain tenets. Stanley no longer felt he could adhere to them," Tolino said with a shrug.

"Counselor, I could use a little more help," she prodded.

"Yes, but nothing I can tell you can be substantiated."

"I'd still like to know."

"Stanley Bitah was a strange man. When he first joined the NAC he wasn't like that. But then he began to change. He told the others that the enlightenment he received during our peyote rituals dictated he stand up for the rights of the Navajos in whatever way got results."

"Meaning confrontations and violence?"

Tolino nodded. "When he finally left us for the Navajo Justice Church he created, none of us were sorry to see him go."

"Did you see him after that?"

"From time to time, but not often. I handled a lawsuit that stemmed from a car accident he had, but our meetings were strictly business."

"Do you know much about the Navajo Justice Church?"

"Only that their philosophy is very different from ours, and dangerous. As I see it, the only link we have in common is a peyote ritual." He regarded her thoughtfully. "Does that ease your fears?"

"Meaning do I trust you any more now?" Ella paused, measuring her words. "Your answers make sense, but I'd like to check them out. If you learn anything that could help solve the crimes that have been committed, will you let me know?"

He said nothing for several long moments. Finally he nodded. "I will not go in search of answers for you, but if they cross my path I'll pass on what I feel you might find useful."

"That's got more qualifications than a politician's promise," she commented.

"It's the best I can do."

As Ella drove away she felt glad that she'd spoken to Kevin. A man who was used to lying wouldn't have qualified his statements so much. She sensed he was basically honest, but his loyalties were divided. Whether he'd be any help to her still remained to be seen.

Ella had reached the highway when Blalock called to ask for a meeting in Farmington. She agreed to rendezvous at the diner at the east end of the shopping mall on Twentieth in half an hour.

It was closer to thirty-five minutes later when Ella found herself sitting across the table from FB-Eyes. Blalock, sipping a glass of iced tea, was the first to bring up business. "I spoke to Watson. He insists that he swerved to avoid an old lady with a cane standing in the road, and lost control. Nothing in the police report contradicts that, though the officers who checked out the accident scene couldn't find any old lady. Watson swears that no one came after him and that his accident has nothing to do with The Brotherhood."

"Do you believe him?"

"I'm not sure. He sounded convincing enough, but he's a proud man and likes handling things on his own terms. That fact came across very clearly. What have you uncovered?"

Ella filled Blalock in on everything, except Billy Pete. "Next I'm going to try to find out more about the Navajo Justice Church."

"Good idea. I'm going to follow up on Truman. I've been questioning his neighbors, showing photos around, and trying to find out who he has met with during the past few months. I'm hoping to get a lead to The Brotherhood that way."

Ella returned to her vehicle. As she reached for her keys she glanced down at the driver's-side door. The exterior of the Jeep had been vandalized. Someone had taken a metal object, perhaps a key or pocket knife, and etched the word "traitor" into the paint.

THIRTEEN

—✖ ✖ ✖—

Ella went to the passenger's side and unlocked the back carefully. With her investigative kit in hand, she worked over the surface, trying to find fingerprints. After ten minutes she gave up. Everything that had shown up was too smudged to be of much use. Not that she'd really expected to find anything. One didn't leave many fingerprints when using a sharp metal object to vandalize a car. Still, it had been worth a try.

Ella drove back to Shiprock, anger clouding her thinking. She'd been labeled worse than a traitor before, but this particular incident had come from out of left field.

When Ella entered the station a short time later, Justine was just coming out of the lab.

Justine's eyes widened. "Wow. You sure look angry. What happened?"

"Someone keyed my vehicle, and from what they wrote, it wasn't just vandalism. I know I'm being followed." Ella filled her in on the way to the office.

"Who do you think it was?"

"I was asking Kevin Tolino questions about the Native American Church and the Navajo Justice Church earlier, so common sense would suggest a Navajo, perhaps one of the Fierce Ones.

But this happened in Farmington, outside the Rez, so it could have been an Anglo miner trying to set me against others of our tribe. I'd like to think I would have spotted anyone following me, but it's possible I missed something. Or maybe they'd been tailing Blalock, but that doesn't seem very likely either."

"Do you want me to see what I can do about expediting a repair?" Justine asked.

"No, we can get to that later. Right now, you and I are going over to the college. We'll track down Angelina's friends and grill them separately about this mystery man."

"They don't intimidate," Justine warned. "We've tried pressing them before."

"We'll see."

Ella grabbed a vehicle incident report form on her way out, then drove to the college with Justine. Out of stubbornness she'd refused to use Justine's vehicle, opting for her own despite its vandalized appearance.

Justine, sensing Ella's mood, kept quiet as they continued down the highway. After ten minutes she broke the silence. "Dr. Roanhorse is back at work. She called you earlier, and I talked to her briefly."

"Did she leave a message?"

"No, she said she'd catch up to you later. She was on her way to an inoculation clinic at Burnham. She sounded pretty chipper."

"I figured nothing would ever keep her down for too long. She's a fighter," Ella commented with a tiny smile.

"So are you."

"We have a lot in common, that's true enough. What helps us remain friends is that we both know there are boundaries neither of us is welcome to cross. Our work always takes priority."

Ella parked in the visitors lot near the large, octagonal building where Wilson Joe taught. "I'll see if Wilson is in his office. You go to administration and get the schedules for the girls who were at the funeral."

Ella went directly to Wilson's office. He was alone, grading papers, and greeted her with a distracted smile. "What brings you here, Ella? Police business?"

She nodded. "Yes, I'm afraid so. Did you know Angelina Yellowhair, and if so, was she especially close to anyone?"

"Yes, she was a student of mine. Ruby Atso was her best friend, I think, but she's not going to help you much. She's really tougher than nails for a woman so young. Your best bet would be to talk to Norma Frank. She's a sweet, mannered young lady. I know she and Angelina spent a lot of time together between classes. Not that Angelina spent that much time *in* class, mind you. She cut more than she attended."

"Do you happen to have any idea where I could find Norma now?"

"Yes, as a matter of fact. I saw her a little while ago when I was coming back from a late lunch. She was studying under the cottonwood. She might still be there."

"Thanks, I appreciate it."

"No problem. It's always good to see you."

She smiled, but didn't answer. Once he was married, their closeness would fade. She didn't need to look into his eyes to see that knowledge mirrored there. "I better go find Norma before she leaves."

Ella stepped outside and found Norma Frank exactly where Wilson had told her to look. Norma was so engrossed in a book she didn't notice when Ella sat down beside her. Ella cleared her throat.

"Oh, I'm sorry, Officer. I was trying to finish this chapter and I assumed you were just another student looking for a shady spot."

"I need to ask you some questions, Norma, but we don't have to talk here, if you'd rather it wasn't so public."

"I don't mind, but I'm not sure I can help you."

"Angelina's boyfriend. What do you know about him."

"A boyfriend?" Norma's eyes grew wide. "I don't know who you mean."

"I think you do."

"No, you're wrong. Angelina wasn't committed to anyone or anything, except having fun. If you'd hung around with her you would have known that. She flirted with practically every guy she met."

Ella knew Norma was keeping something back. The girl shifted nervously as if she were sitting on a bed of ants. "You're not helping anyone if you don't tell me what you know."

"I *did* tell you." She opened the book again, refusing to look at Ella. "Now if you don't mind, I've got to get some studying done."

Justine was coming up the sidewalk as Ella stood. Glancing down at Norma, who had almost literally buried her face in the book, and realizing she wasn't going to get anything else from her, Ella walked over to meet Justine.

"I saw Ruby Atso and Mary Tapahonso. Ruby wouldn't tell me anything—at all. She started singing to herself when I asked a question. Mary looked like I was trying to lynch her. But even though she talked to me, I got very little that was new from her, either. According to Mary, Angelina wasn't committed to anyone or anything, except having fun. They went out in groups and—"

"Angelina flirted with practically every guy they met?" Ella cut in.

"Yes, how'd you know?" Justine's eyebrows rose.

"I got almost exactly the same words from Norma." Ella nodded her head. "Looks like the girls rehearsed their stories a little too well."

"Which means they're covering up for some reason," Justine added excitedly. "This is classic interview stuff right out of the lectures at the police academy."

"Seems the tribe's getting a little payback on our training. But go back to what you were saying about Mary." Ella was encouraged.

Justine nodded. "Mary said they liked to go to the Roundup, a country western bar between Farmington and Bloomfield. It's far enough from the Rez that they could cut loose without meeting people who might carry tales back to Shiprock. According to Mary, half the fun was seeing who was there and who would hit on them."

"Tonight you and I will go to that bar—with photos—and see if anyone remembers Angelina. It's possible she met her boyfriend there."

As they returned to the car Ella glanced at Justine. "I'm going to drop you off at the station. I want you to keep digging into the Navajo Justice Church. While you're doing that, I'm going to pay another visit to Bitah's ex-girlfriend, Judy Lujan."

Ella's thoughts raced as she drove back toward the station. She could feel the heat of the chase intensifying with every beat of her heart.

"Why are they protecting Angelina's boyfriend? That's what I can't figure out," Justine mused. "Can you?"

"No. None of those girls comes across as particularly noble. They're young and self-serving. That means they're keeping quiet for personal reasons as well, not just to protect Angelina or some man."

"What are you hoping to get from Judy Lujan?"

"She's my link to Bitah, and I intend to find out all I can about his involvement with the Navajo Justice sect."

"They're one heckuva rough group."

"You've heard about them?"

"Sure, from local gossip. But the only people who know for sure what goes on in that church are their members."

Ella kept the Jeep above seventy until traffic thickened. "We have a special file on all kinds of reactionary groups. Access that and see if we have anything on the NJC. Talk to Blalock, too. He says the FBI knows more about us than we do. Let's give him a chance to prove it," she added with a smirk.

By the time they arrived at the station, Ella was eager to get started. She went directly to her office and pulled up everything she could find on Judy Lujan. After verifying that she was not on duty, and getting her home address, Ella left the office.

Judy's trailer home was bordered by wild grasses and sage, and a low mesa lay about a quarter mile to the north. From her Jeep, Ella could see two large dogs barking furiously in wire pens in the backyard. A small horse enclosure stood to the east of the trailer home.

Ella stepped out of her vehicle and, as she looked around, Judy came around the trailer from the back. Her hair was pulled into a ponytail and she was holding a saddle in both hands. "What brings you here?" she asked.

"I hate to intrude on your time off, but I have to talk to you."

"I've told you all I know. Really."

"I have some new questions," Ella insisted.

Judy sighed, then cocked her head toward the trailer. "Okay. Come inside."

Ella watched as Judy dropped the saddle onto a wooden stand, then continued into the small kitchen. "Nice place," Ella commented, noting how everything in the tiny trailer had been carefully selected for matching color and design. She didn't care for lavender and blue, at least not in every room, but it was obvious Judy was fond of those shades.

Judy dropped down into a chair and motioned for Ella to sit. "Okay, this is my day off and I've got tons to do. You're not here to chitchat, so tell me what's on your mind."

"Your friend belonged to the Native American Church, then he quit to join the Navajo Justice Church."

Judy made a face. "That's not much of a church, more of a legal dodge to allow activists to use peyote without being put in jail."

"Tell me about your friend," Ella said, avoiding the name. She wouldn't have categorized Judy as a traditionalist, but she had noted that Judy never mentioned Bitah by name either. Some habits were too ingrained in the *Dineh* no matter what their views on Navajo tradition were.

"He said he could no longer follow the teachings of the Native American Church, so he left. He was, after all, an activist who believed in the rights of the Navajo."

"Was he happier being a part of the Navajo Justice Church?"

"Yes, he often told me he felt needed among his allies. He helped lead the rituals."

"What did he do?"

"I only went to two of their *meetings* and what he did there was pass out the peyote buttons. It was his responsibility alone. I went with him a few times when he drove down to southern New Mexico and Texas to gather the buttons for their rituals."

"The peyote is something they take right there in church, right?"

"Oh yes. The people in both churches—the Native American Church and the Navajo Justice Church—share the belief that the peyote doesn't work outside the meetings."

"Could someone steal some of the peyote buttons and use them later?"

"I don't see how. It's a ritual that usually takes all night. It's held in a member's hogan and, as I understand it, they take turns as to whose hogan will be used. The rituals begin at sundown around a ritual fire in the center of the hogan. There is no altar, only crossed spears to represent their will to fight for the *Dineh*. There are songs at first, and cedar smoke to purify the peyote buttons. Then, during cycles of songs, prayers, and personal contemplation, each member consumes a total of four peyote buttons. In each contemplation cycle, peyote is said to talk to the person, inspiring and instructing them on the ways of dealing with their lives, and the ways of protecting and serving the *Dineh* against enemies."

Ella nodded thoughtfully, figuring that during the peyote phases, it would be impossible for the members to know exactly who had eaten what.

"It isn't disorganized or chaotic at all, even as the evening progresses. It's a very peaceful ritual, and only Navajo adults are allowed to participate. Nobody is alone, you're sitting next to each other around the fire. There's not a lot of room—in the hogan I was in, at least. Then everyone goes outside for a feast. That's when people get more vocal, discussing their revelations and debating while they eat."

Ella thought of her brother and how different the Navajo Way he taught was. But The People had always adapted to other cultures. The Peyote Road rituals had reached the tribe in the early 1920s, when Southern Ute medicine men had treated Navajo patients. The cult had taken hold slowly, and now more militant versions were surfacing.

"After the peyote buttons are gathered, before the rituals, where are they kept?"

"Under lock and key, literally, at least when my friend was in charge. They don't want to be accused of distributing drugs to minors or those outside the church."

Ella stared across the room, trying to figure out a connection to Angelina. "Did your friend know the senator's daughter?"

"I don't believe so, and I think he would have told me. He liked knowing people he considered important. He was always mentioning his friend, the tribal attorney. He liked knowing someone who was a member of the same clan our tribal president belongs to. He said he could feel their power."

There were no obvious connections, yet Angelina had managed to get peyote, and she and Bitah had died on the same day. She had just opened her mouth to speak again when she saw a flash of light playing against the flowered blue wallpaper.

It took her only a moment to interpret it. "We're being watched," Ella said, tearing off a sheet of paper from her pocket notebook and writing down a number. "Don't turn around," she added immediately. "The person is using binoculars, and that's what's sending flashes of reflected light against the wall." There was also the possibility of a rifle scope, but for some reason she didn't think that would be the case. The instincts that always warned her of immediate danger were silent now.

"What do you want to do?"

"I'm going to duck out your back door and see if I can spot the watcher. Use the phone and call the number I've jotted down on this paper. Tell the person who answers that I need backup, and give them your address. Then come back to your chair and pretend that you're still talking to me. I'll be back."

Ella stepped away from the window then ducked out the back door, moving behind the juniper hedge that bordered the trailer. Hiding in the shadows, she crept away, heading toward the mesa across from Judy's home.

Ella caught repeated glimpses of the flashing light, and barely managed to make out a figure crouching near the top. Moving quickly and as noiselessly as possible, she climbed the flat-topped hill.

She had almost reached the top when a cloud of foul-smelling white smoke nearly engulfed her. Ella choked on the acrid fumes and pulled out her handkerchief, trying to cover her mouth and nose. She blinked hard, her eyes burning as if they were on fire. When her sight finally cleared a bit, the ground appeared tilted. Dizzy, Ella stopped, unable to figure out where she was. Every possible step she could take would send her tumbling down a steep incline.

She remained still, breathing deeply and telling herself it was only a drug-induced illusion. Still, her senses were impaired and she didn't dare risk a wrong step that would send her toppling off the mesa because she had guessed wrong.

Ella wasn't sure how long she'd stood there, when she heard Justine calling out to her from somewhere in the distance.

"Here."

Ella saw Justine coming toward her, as if in a dream. It looked as if she were walking in midair at times.

"Hey, Boss, what happened?" Justine grasped her arm.

Ella forced herself to focus her thoughts. What she was seeing was not real. "Illusion. A skinwalker's trick. Like I'm on a cliff. Help me down."

Justine nodded. "Don't worry. I'm here."

Ella followed blindly where Justine led, focusing away from the ground as they made their way downhill.

Judy rushed up as Justine led her toward the trailer. "You look awful. What happened?"

Ella forced the cobwebs back. "I don't know. There was this foul cloud of white smoke, then everything went crazy."

"Did you see the person?"

"No." Ella blinked, and was grateful to see that the earth was no longer angled away from where she stood. She turned to Justine. "Go back up and check for footprints and other evidence. But stay sharp."

"Are you going to be okay?"

"Yeah. I've been exposed to this type of thing before. It never lasts long. It's already starting to clear. Go."

Judy led Ella back inside. "Here," she said, placing a glass of iced tea in front of her. "Just relax."

Ella took several swallows, easing her parched throat. "Thanks."

"Do you think that the person watching us is gone for good?"

"For *now*, is more likely. But he or she could have done a lot more damage had they wanted to harm either of us. If you'd like, though, I can see about putting you in protective custody."

Judy considered it, then shook her head. "No, I've got my two dogs and my horse. The horse whinnies whenever anyone gets close, and the dogs will bark their fool heads off. I'll have advance warning."

"They may be up against what happened to me on that hill."

"I'll keep the dogs inside with me, then. Either way, I've done nothing wrong and I can't see that I'm a threat to anyone. The information I have, others also know. If they come after me they'll still have a long list of others to deal with."

"You were the murdered man's friend. They may think you know far more than you do."

"If that were the case they would have made their move before now. In my opinion, they were here because of you. They certainly weren't close enough to eavesdrop."

"If they've been staking out your house, my being here to spot them was only luck on your part."

"I'm *not* going anywhere."

"Can you get someone else to come and stay with you?"

"I'm an adult. I don't need a baby-sitter."

"Even cops need backup every once in a while."

Judy thought about that for a while then said, "How about if I ask my cousin to stay here? He's visiting my aunt and it's crowded over at their house anyway."

"Good."

As Justine came back inside, Ella stood up. Her thoughts were clear again and her dizziness was gone. "You need any more help up on the mesa?" she asked.

"I've already got what evidence there was. But will you be able to drive when you're done here?"

"I'm fine and I'm done out here for now."

Ella said good-bye to Judy Lujan, then walked out with Justine, asking "What did you find?"

"Boot tracks, size eight, leading down the back of the hill. No one was in sight. By the imprint, I can tell you that it was someone of average weight. That's all. I photographed the prints for comparison, and then I searched for something that would have accounted for the smoke that disoriented you. I couldn't find anything. Your brother might know what to look for, but my guess is that the smoke came from something the person burned. What you were dealing with was some kind of homemade psychedelic flash-bang."

Ella got into her Jeep. Justine looked worried. "I'm really okay. But you can follow me back to the station to make sure. I want to talk to Big Ed there anyway, then this evening you and I are heading over to the Roundup. We have to follow up on Angelina's boyfriend."

"Are you sure—"

"Yeah, let's get going."

Ella met with Big Ed and made her report. His face was clouded with worry and he kept looking at Ella for adverse effects from the smoke.

"My predecessor had a lot of those tricks up his sleeve," he said. "I heard the stories."

Ella nodded. "He's dead. The person writing the notes knows his handwriting well enough to make some skillful forgeries, that's all. The smoke I encountered on the mesa is something else though, requiring special knowledge only a few people have. There are a million herbs and combinations that can be used to confuse. I've encountered them before."

"But the man on the mesa obviously had that special knowledge, and that worries me. Are we dealing with skinwalkers again?"

"The person used a skinwalker trick, that's for sure, but that doesn't necessarily mean he's a skinwalker." The coolness of the breeze from the oscillating fan on Big Ed's cabinet felt good on her skin. "I think the key to cracking Angelina's murder is finding her boyfriend. I have a real good shot at doing that tonight. Believe me, I'll be fine."

Big Ed looked her over carefully one more time then nodded. "Good hunting."

FOURTEEN

✖ ✖ ✖

Ella met Justine in the lab around seven that night, having finally cleared her own desk of backlogged paperwork and leaving a message for Clifford asking about the smoke-drug she'd encountered. "You ready to go?"

Together, they set out for the bar in Ella's Jeep. "I made some inquiries about this place," Justine said. "It's rougher than most, but that's because the people who frequent it are usually just over the minimum drinking age."

"I think we can handle it," Ella said. "We can pass for young."

"No doubt. But what was a kid like Angelina, who could afford the classy bars and restaurants, doing in a dive like that?"

"Mingling. If there's something that's emerged from her profile, it's that she seldom did what was expected." Ella glanced at Justine, then back at the road. "Keep your eyes open tonight, and watch your back. Asking questions about Angelina has become a risky proposition."

They arrived around eight. As expected, the dark, smoke-filled place was crowded with young people wearing denim, western hats, and holding beer bottles. Tiny, circular tables were crowded into the room around a spacious dance floor. A room-length bar was at one end, and served as a roost for boot-clad fellows surveying the room for dance partners.

Ella tried to shut out the sound of the country western band, which was substituting loud for good, as far as she could judge. She located a waitress wearing the lounge's tight uniform T-shirt, smoking a cigarette at one of the side tables. "I'm going to talk to her," Ella shouted to Justine, who was barely three feet away. "See what you can do."

"Break time?" Ella said, giving the woman a pleasant smile.

"Got that right. If you need a beer, ask one of the other girls," the skinny blonde answered, shouting to be heard above the music.

Ella settled into the chair across from her. "Nah, I'm looking for some people, that's all. Do you happen to know a pretty young Navajo girl named Angelina? She's a regular."

"Haven't you heard? She was killed. Wrecked that cute little sports car."

"Yeah, I know, but I was looking for her boyfriend."

"You don't have the lawyer look. You a tribal cop?"

"Got that right." Ella smiled. "Tell me, do you remember Angelina's boyfriend?"

"No, but there were always lots of men hanging around her and her girlfriends. Try them," she said, pointing to a small group near the band. "They may be willing to help you, or not. They're really a pain in the butt. They do anything to get attention."

She looked at the group the waitress pointed out and recognized Mary Tapahonso from the funeral, but none of the other Navajo girls at her table. When the band took a break, she approached.

Mary's face became guarded as soon as she recognized Ella. "What are you doing here?"

"Why don't you introduce me to your friends?" Ella asked smoothly.

Mary looked as if she would have rather been set on fire, but she complied. "This is Velma Nez," she said, gesturing to her right. "And this is Gail Manuelito," she said, turning to her left. "This is Investigator Clah."

Gail rolled her eyes. "Oh please! You want to talk *here?*"

"Why not? It's as good a place as any. I'm trying to track down Angelina's boyfriend. Anyone know where I can find him?"

Velma glanced at the others. "She had a boyfriend?"

Mary stared at the beer mug by her hand, but refused to meet anyone's gaze.

"I never hung around with Angelina, I just came with Velma tonight," Gail said quickly. "Sorry, I can't help you."

"But *you* can, can't you, Mary?" Ella said, watching the girl squirm. The danger of attracting the *chindi* made most Navajos reluctant to speak of the dead, and Ella wondered if that was part of the problem. But then she discounted the idea. Mary was no traditionalist. She was scared, but not of the dead. Ella allowed the silence at their table to stretch.

"You want us to catch her killer, don't you?" Ella insisted.

"I thought she died in the accident."

"It was her death that *caused* the accident. She was poisoned by someone she was with just *before* she got into the car. I need to find out who that was."

"Why would that matter? It won't bring her back." Mary looked up. "Why don't you just go away?"

"I could, but the situation won't. If you know something, tell me. In a case like this, you risk your own life by keeping the truth to yourself."

Mary's eyes grew wide. "You don't know what you're talking about."

"You're wrong, I do. I've been a cop a long time. Trust me. You're far better off talking to me, than trying to protect someone else by keeping quiet in a situation like this."

Mary opened her mouth as if to speak, but then shook her head. "You're slick, but forget it. For your information, Angelina didn't have a boyfriend. She hated being pinned down to anything or anyone."

"You forgot 'she flirted with practically every boy she met.' Wasn't that the next line?" Ella stood up, noting the wide-eyed look on Mary's face. "If you change your mind you know where to reach me." She placed her card on the table. Mary made no move to pick it up.

Ella went out the side door, indicating to Justine with a nod where she'd be. As she stood outside in the cool evening air, she replayed the encounter in her mind. She was certain that the other two girls did not know anything, but why were the ones in Angelina's inner circle keeping the identity of their friend's boyfriend such a secret? Was he someone in a powerful position, or a man who, for one reason or another, had a hold over them all?

"Hey, baby, you ready to party now?" A tall, lanky blond cowboy sauntered up to her. He smelled of beer and cigarette smoke, which was not surprising.

Ella looked at him and shook her head politely. "Not interested, cowboy. Try inside the bar."

"Now, baby, this is no time to develop a negative attitude."

"Give it a rest, will you?" she said firmly.

Justine came out just then and saw what was going on. "You ready to go?" she asked Ella, pointedly ignoring the cowboy.

A second cowboy came out right behind Justine and walked up, putting his arm around his buddy's shoulder as he leered at the women. "It's a done deal, ladies. We're all going to *party* tonight."

Justine turned to confront him, her body taut. "You guys have had a six-pack over the limit, I think. Go back inside, buy yourselves some coffee, then go home."

The tall one, whose glazed eyes had never left Ella's face, reached out and grabbed her arm. "Come on, beautiful—"

Before he could complete what he was saying, Ella broke his hold and pushed him back. "Back off, now."

He laughed. "You like it rough, do you, baby?" He moved forward again, but this time, Ella sidestepped him and with a little push, sent him sprawling to the ground.

Justine stepped around the other man who was laughing hilariously at his friend's predicament. "You want to call a local cop to haul these guys in?"

"No, it'll take too much time. Let's just leave."

The cowboy on the ground scrambled to his feet with the help of the second one. "Hey, ladies, quit playing around. You're ticking me off. We've already paid out cash money for your services. Now let's cut the crap and go to my truck, okay?"

Ella walked back toward them. "What?"

The cowboys laughed. "You were hoping we'd pay twice? No deal. We spoke to your 'manager' inside, and he sold us your services for the entire night. You better start earning your money before we change our minds."

"What manager? Point him out," Justine asked, moving to the side door and peering inside.

"Your pimp, little darling. Said his name was Dan. Now let's stop playing these games. My truck's not far. Time to go."

He placed his arm around Justine's shoulders and tried to urge her along. She twisted free easily and kicked him in the shin.

Ella moved toward her assistant to help, but the tall cowboy grabbed her by the hair. Blocking the pain, she threw herself back against him, then smashed her elbow into his midsection. He doubled up in pain, cussing loudly.

"We're police officers," Ella clipped, moving back around him and bringing out her handcuffs, "and you boys are headed for an unscheduled visit with the sheriff's department."

At the sight of the cuffs, both men clambered over the bed of the pickup, hurtled a chain-link fence, and took off down the road.

Ella and Justine went after them, skirting the fence rather than trying to leap over it. They were halfway across the highway when an eighteen-wheeled tank truck came flying around the corner. Ella whirled and pulled Justine back, out of the path of the speeding vehicle. They both fell down hard onto the graveled road shoulder.

"You okay?" Ella gasped, rubbing her back and brushing away oily pebbles as she sat up.

"Yeah," Justine managed. "I landed on my butt. Not very dignified, but there's nothing there that can't afford a bruise or two."

Ella stood, then helped Justine up. "Let's go back inside the bar and find our 'pimp.' I'd love to have a little chat with Dan."

"You think Angelina's boyfriend was there all the time, watching us?"

"There's no telling. The entire bar is dark and smokey, and with those hats over their eyes, you wouldn't recognize your own brother except up close. But I'm going back to try to make somebody nervous."

Justine and Ella divided the room. Forty minutes later, and nearly hoarse from shouting over the dismal sounds of the country western band, Ella returned to the waitress she'd spoken to earlier.

"Someone was having fun at your expense," the skinny blonde explained, glancing over at the Navajo girls. "I told you they were obnoxious."

"I need a name for this Dan character. Can you give me any idea who the guy was that set us up?"

She shook her head. "No, but I did catch some gossip while I was serving customers. People don't seem to care what a waitress hears. I found out that Angelina sometimes came with a good-looking Navajo guy. But the guy was jealous, never letting her out of his sight to dance with one of the cowboys. It would make her nuts."

Ella tipped the waitress for the drink she hadn't bought, then waited a while before going up to Mary Tapahonso. Ella spoke low enough so the other girls at the table couldn't hear her. "You're playing a very dangerous game. You're either covering for a murderer, which makes you an accessory, or else putting an innocent man on the hot seat by drawing this out. If I find out who he is before you tell me—and he's guilty—you'll be up on charges yourself. And if I don't arrest him soon, you may be his next victim. Anyone who can connect him to Angelina is a potential witness against him, and he's still running around loose. Think about that, and start locking your door at night," Ella said, then turned and walked away.

She didn't have to look back to know that she'd rattled Mary. The story would carry to the others, too, and hopefully make at least one of them nervous enough to come forward.

"That was a waste of time," Justine said, joining Ella in the Jeep. "Nobody knew who our *pimp* was, I'm sorry to say."

"We may have lost that battle, but we scored a victory on another front."

The next morning Ella was in the lab comparing notes with Justine, when her cellular rang. When she picked it up, she recognized Billy Pete's voice right away.

"I need to meet with you. It's important," he said.

"When?"

"In an hour? I can meet you on the south side of the mesa behind your home."

That would be near the place where Kevin Tolino was building his home. It would work out just fine. Afterwards, she'd stop by Kevin's property and talk to him, if he was there today. He moved in higher tribal circles than her. Maybe he knew something about the senator or his daughter that could prove helpful.

"Expect me."

"Will you be needing me this afternoon?" Justine asked. "There's something I want to follow up on."

"What is it?"

"Raymond Nez."

"That's a lost cause."

"Not to me. I know I can get him to help us, I just feel it."

Ella doubted it, but she didn't want to dampen Justine's enthusiasm for the case. "The most you'll get from him is information he considers unimportant. But even bits and pieces could come in useful in the long run. Just make sure you have backup when you meet him."

When Ella left to meet with Billy, it was only mid-morning, but the wind was already starting to gust. It had been breezy when she awoke just around dawn, but now it was worse. Sand blasted the side of the car, pushing it toward the center line. She compensated automatically, used to driving in crosswinds.

As she drove off the highway and headed down the dusty track, visibility quickly fell to only a quarter mile or less. Walls of sand traveled across the desert floor, one after the other, repeating endlessly. Ella eventually reached the designated spot, parked her vehicle and, covering her nose and face with a handkerchief, made her way forward against the force of the wind.

"You're here." Billy Pete came out from behind a cluster of boulders at the base of the mesa.

Sand stung her eyes as Ella turned around. She'd never heard him approaching above the howl of the wind. The knowledge that had he been an enemy, she might have been dead, sobered her.

"What have you got for me?" she yelled above the incessant whine.

"Our slain brother," he said, without mentioning Bitah by name, "had been following an Anglo by the name of Anderson. He believed that Anderson was the head of The Brotherhood. I'm not so sure of that, but considering his actions against Jesse Woody, shooting into the man's home like he did, it's a good bet he is involved. The Fierce Ones believe that Anderson gave the order to kill our friend because he believed our friend was the leader of the faction opposing him."

"I'll look into that."

"Will he be out on bail soon, too?"

"What do you mean 'too'?"

"Truman was released last night. I heard he came to work this morning claiming he was framed by the Navajo police. He wants to sue the tribe."

"That figures." Now Ella knew what had motivated Billy to come forward this morning. He was worried about what The Brotherhood would do next. As a gust of wind blew against them, Ella staggered, pushed by the sheer force of the wind. "We better get out of here," she said, blinking to clear the sand out of her eyes. When she looked around for his reaction, Billy Pete was gone.

Ella trudged back toward her vehicle, looking down to protect her eyes from blowing dust. She was on a low spot now, and everything in the air seemed to be coming her way. Forced to look up to make sure she was walking in the right direction, Ella spotted a particularly thick cloud of sand headed right for her. Her heart started pounding, as if she were just about to encounter an armed gunman rather than lung-clogging dust!

Trusting her instincts, Ella whirled around quickly, her palm resting on the butt of her pistol. Nothing but dust could be seen in any direction, the wind had whipped up so much earth that it was as if she was walking in a gritty cloud.

Her uneasiness intensified and Ella abruptly realized there was something unusual about that rapidly approaching dust cloud, a darker, inner core, like the heart of an evil thing. Instinct compelled her to try and avoid it. Ella started jogging toward the Jeep she knew she'd left somewhere just ahead.

Suddenly a black van emerged from the cloud, heading right for her. Pulling out her pistol, Ella hoped to be able to ward the driver off without taking out a tire or shooting him. That was assuming he could see her in the first place, and wouldn't attempt to run her down.

The driver must have noticed both her and her pistol, because he suddenly swerved away, creating another cloud of dust that swept across the desert like a tidal wave, enveloping her completely while it obscured her aim.

She started toward her Jeep again, this time running faster than before. This wasn't just a couple of kids out to give her a hard time. That van held danger.

The van appeared again out of the dust, this time between her and the Jeep. It had circled around, heading her off like a sheep dog trying to herd the flock in a particular direction.

Ella stopped, uncertain whether she should try to run the other way. If she did, she'd be further from safety, not closer, and the van could move faster than she could, though it couldn't change direction as fast. The van stopped, too, still between her and where she had left the Jeep.

Ella decided to take the direct approach and call their bluff. Pulling out her pistol again, she ran directly at the van. It was time to force the issue. As she got closer, the van started up again but instead of fleeing, it came right at her.

Ella stopped, assumed a combat stance, and leveled her sights at the driver's side windshield. The glass had been darkened, but she knew exactly where the driver had to be seated. Abruptly the van wheeled away to the left, shooting up another cloud of dust. Ella didn't fire. Reacting instantly, she made a frantic dash for her Jeep.

She was almost there when the van skidded around, cutting her off once more. Suddenly another vehicle appeared from the direction of the highway, a pickup. It turned toward her now, and Ella's heart sank. Perhaps the van's driver had managed to call in an ally to help run her down.

As the pickup got closer, Ella turned to face it, aiming her pistol toward the cab. That windshield wasn't tinted, and as the pickup drew near, she made out the face of the driver.

Ella lowered her pistol slightly, but not completely, as Kevin turned the pickup to block the van, and slid to an abrupt stop. "Jump in!" he yelled over the roar of the wind. "Come on, hurry!"

Ella dashed up to grab the door as Kevin threw it open. She jumped inside, her pistol still in hand.

"What the hell is going on?" Kevin's eyes were wide, focused on the gun, not Ella's face.

"That van is trying to run me down, I think. The threat of my pistol is all that's keeping them at bay." Ella looked around for the van, and noticed it was heading away rapidly. "Quick, don't let them get away."

"Right!" Kevin yelled, and hit the gas, turning the pickup around with spinning tires; the truck fishtailed as he accelerated. Ella reached down to her hip for her cellular phone, but remembered it was still in the Jeep. There was no way to call for backup, not without letting the van get out of sight.

"What were you doing out there in the open, on foot, in this dust storm?" Kevin shouted, trying to drive as fast as he could without losing control on the dirt track.

"Police work. Sorry, I can't tell you more." Ella noticed the van was pulling away and was nearly out of sight. "Can't you go any faster?"

"Not unless you want to risk me rolling this baby. This sand isn't the best place for racing, especially with me at the wheel. Those guys might be running for their life, but I'm not!" Kevin tried to smile, but Ella could see he wasn't used to living on the edge.

Just then, they hit a tremendous bump, and the truck flew up in the air, landing with a thump that sent them bouncing off their seats, cracking their heads on the top of the cab roof. The truck slid to a stop in a particularly sandy spot.

"Sorry. They didn't offer combat driving one-oh-one at the college I attended. You want to give it a try?" Kevin smiled weakly.

Ella looked out the side window. The van was long gone, probably to the highway by now. "No, I don't think it would be worth our time trying. Just take me back to my Jeep so I can call this in, okay?"

"I can do that. I was on my way home, but what about you? Are you sure you can't tell me what you're doing out here?" Kevin asked.

"I'm sure. But I do need a favor from you," Ella replied. "I'm trying to find a connection between the senator's daughter and those involved in the peyote cult. Do you know of one?"

"No, can't say I do."

"Will you keep your ears open for me?"

"I'm a defense attorney, not a police informant."

"I hope that doesn't mean you're not interested in justice. Will you do it anyway?" she insisted.

He smiled. "I'll see what I can do. And there's your Jeep. Want me to wait around until you start it up?"

"It might be a good idea, just in case the guy in the van did something to it. One more thing—may be related to what happened today. You've chosen to build in this area. That's your right, but that choice may end up costing you. I think you've already seen that you may be drawn into a conflict you never intended to make yours."

"I won't be drawn into anything I don't choose to get involved in. If I have to defend myself or a neighbor, I will. That's the extent of what you can expect from me. I'm not here to fight, but to build a life for myself."

Ella gazed into his eyes and found them to be unreadable black pools. "Your plans and the reality of what's around you are two separate things. You may yet find that fate makes its own rules."

FIFTEEN

✖ ✖ ✖

Ella met Blalock at the agent's favorite diner in west Farmington, at the mall. He was in his usual surly mood.

"I'm getting a lot of flak about this problem with Bitah and the mine. My bosses are demanding results. To make matters worse, Truman was released last night. I grilled him for over an hour before he got his walking papers, but I got nothing out of him. His wife maintains he was home with her from the time he got off work at midnight to around noon the following morning. That gives him an alibi for Bitah's time of death, though it isn't much of one."

"I have some new information. Anderson is still in jail, correct?"

"Yeah. The judge setting bail was half Navajo and didn't take it kindly when Anderson mouthed off. Bail's astronomical."

"Mouthed off to a judge? He's dumber than I thought. Or else he thinks he's safer in jail. Either way it works to our advantage. I have a lead. One of my sources told me that Bitah had been following Anderson," Ella said, and filled him in.

"So Anderson might be the leader of The Brotherhood after all? Now wouldn't that be convenient! But we still have to place him at the crime scene, and find evidence that he struck the fatal blows."

"Let's go see what we can get from him today."

Ella followed Blalock to the city jail where Anderson was being held. As they went inside to the cell block, Blalock glanced at her. "You want to take the lead?"

"No. Let's play bad cop—really bad cop. You be the lesser of the two evils. I'm almost certain I can make Anderson angry enough to say something stupid that we may be able to use."

Anderson, in chains and handcuffs, was escorted into the small room by a burly jailer. "I'm going to give you a break," Blalock said, taking the cuffs off Anderson but leaving the leg bracelets in place. "Don't make me regret it."

Anderson nodded once, scarcely looking at Ella. "I have nowhere to go, not dressed in prison orange and leg irons. What is it that you want? My attorney isn't available right now."

"Some new information has come to our attention about your involvement in The Brotherhood."

"Still never heard of it," he answered, a trace of a smile on his face.

"We've learned from witnesses that Bitah was following you prior to his death. In fact, he may have been following you the night he died. Did you lead him over to the power plant?"

Anderson stared at him, expressionless. "If you're suggesting what I think you are, you're being mislead." He glanced at Ella and gave her a look of utter contempt. "It's no secret that I have philosophical differences with the hiring practices of the tribe. But I did *not* murder anyone."

"I didn't think The Brotherhood cared whether things got violent or not." Ella kept her voice deceptively soft.

"I never heard of that organization. You can believe that or not. I don't care. But I'm no murderer. If I was, I'd have a solid alibi, with plenty of witnesses. I'm many things but I'm not stupid," he said, glaring at Ella.

"If you think I'm going to let this drop then you are very, very stupid," Ella baited. "I'm betting you killed Bitah, with a little help from your racist friends."

Anderson's eyes darkened and his expression became one of unbridled hatred. "Just what I expected from you, squaw. You want to hang an Anglo for this crime, whether he did it or not. It fits the theory about how oppressed your people are."

She would have loved to bring up specifics about the treatment the Indians had received at the hand of the white man, but now wasn't the time to get sidetracked. "I'm trying to find the truth," she answered coldly. "Something you've been hiding all along. If you know I'm after the wrong man, then show a little backbone and steer me in the right direction."

Anderson smiled, then leaned forward in his chair. "Then look among your own people. You'll find that there are plans to sabotage the mine and shut down the entire power plant."

"What do you mean? What plans?"

He leaned back, smug once again. "I'm not going to do your work for you. Do I look dumb enough to be a cop?"

Blalock leaned against the wall and watched him. "You're in a lot of trouble, Anderson, but maybe you're starting to see the light. If you have information to trade, now is the time, while we still can use your help. If we get this on our own, you won't have anything to bargain with."

"You've got nothing on me because there's nothing to find," he answered. "With an Indian judge, you might be able to get a conviction on that trumped-up shooting incident, but that's all you're going to get." He stood up. "That's it. From now on, we meet only when my attorney is present."

As an officer came to take Anderson back to his cell, Blalock stared at the wall, his face pensive.

"Shall we get out of here?" Ella asked, as soon as Anderson was handcuffed and led out.

"Yeah. I have an idea. I think I know a way to track down some of Anderson's cronies. Today's Saturday, though. Are you willing to put in a full day?"

She nodded. "I never take time off when I'm working on pressing case."

"Good. I'll fill you in on the way."

Ella watched Blalock as he signed up for the gun club's shooting competition. She had to admit this had been a great idea. The background report Blalock had run on Anderson had revealed that they both used the same private firing range.

"Okay, I'm registered and assigned to a relay. Joining the competition is going to tie me up, so you'll have to do the leg work."

"No problem. I think you're right about competing. That way, our real reason for being here won't be as obvious." Ella glanced around trying to find any faces she recognized from the mine. "Do you remember ever seeing Anderson at this range?"

He shook his head. "I shoot in black powder competition. That's a different bunch of people and a completely different mind set, too. Black powder appeals to history buffs, and to those who like shooting a weapon that's more of a challenge. Let's face it, with some modern guns equipped with laser sights, electronic triggers, and custom wraparound stocks, anybody can put a bullet in the black."

Ella watched the shooters warming up at the firing line. There were as many misses as hits. "Not everyone would agree with you." She gestured toward one of the men on the sidelines. "Look at Randy Watson. He's here with a back brace on. I didn't know he was even getting out of the house yet."

Blalock glanced at Watson. "Steve Chambers, the young-looking guy with him, is one of the miners, too. He tried to convince me that he was practically sainted. The other is Tony Prentiss. I interviewed all those men, but none were any help at all. Yet I'm sure that they're involved in whatever's happening. The way they went round and round but never answered my questions was so practiced—part of a predetermined strategy. It set off alarm bells something fierce."

She nodded. "You can sometimes learn a lot about a person from the way they don't tell you anything."

Tony Prentiss was a bulky man in his mid thirties. He sauntered over, his gaze faintly mocking. "I see you brought your girlfriend along as a guest."

Blalock glowered at Prentiss, but didn't speak.

Prentiss gave Ella a derisive smile. "I hear you tribal cops can't hit a sheep at ten paces. Smart move to stay out of this competition. Could be real embarrassing."

Ella met his gaze but remained silent.

"Maybe you just like to see how a real man handles his weapon," Prentiss goaded.

Blalock stepped in front of Ella. "I'm surprised you can even find yours, tubby."

Ella fought the urge to kick Blalock. She didn't need anyone to protect her. She was hoping Prentiss would get all wound up and say something he really hadn't intended to reveal.

"She's a law enforcement officer," Blalock growled. "Show some respect."

"You guys are up right now, I believe," Ella said, as the first relay of competitors was called to the firing line.

Blalock nodded, then checked his nine-millimeter service pistol. Following the rules, he opened the action and unloaded his weapon before approaching the firing line. Until the ready command was given and the shooting field was declared clear, no one would be allowed to load their weapons.

Ella watched Blalock outshoot everyone in the first round, knocking down all ten metal silhouettes at the twenty-five-yard range.

During the subsequent rounds, Ella walked behind the lines, watching, making careful note of the weapons used by the men from the mine. Although most were fairly competent with their handguns, they really weren't at the same skill level as a trained agent from the FBI or Treasury Department.

Leaving them to their contest, which had several categories based upon the type of firearm, and glad that Blalock had diverted them by joining the competition, she went to the parking area and wrote down the license plate codes and vehicle types. One never knew where a lead would turn up.

A beat-up old pickup at the end of a row of vehicles carried a tribal sticker from the power plant parking lot. She glanced inside the rolled-up window. A zippered rifle case had been laid on the seat. She saw the initials S.C. Later, she'd verify it was Steve Chambers, but at the moment she figured it was a good bet that Chambers shot different types of weapons.

By the time she returned, all rounds had been completed and Blalock still had the top score. His closest competitor was four points behind, and Prentiss had failed to place. Ella watched Blalock collect his pin and the small trophy.

Spotting her, Blalock came over as the competitors packed up their gear and began to leave. "What have you been up to?"

She gave him a quick rundown. "Your computer might be able to get us information on those plates faster than mine."

"Agreed. I'll handle it." He checked his handgun and left the action open. "Let me clean my pistol, then we'll get out of here."

As Blalock walked to his car, Ella stepped over to the firing line and saw that a set of targets remained up at the seventy-five-yard distance. The turkey silhouettes looked small against the earthen bullet trap behind them. She glanced around. Only Blalock was around, still by his car. Apparently the competition officials had left for another meet somewhere on the range. Feeling comfortable with no one else around, she pulled out her service pistol. Each of the ten targets fell, one shot for each. Finished, Ella smiled, proud of herself, and turned to wave to Blalock, assuring him that nothing was wrong.

As Ella stood at the firing stand reloading her weapon, she suddenly felt as if clammy fingers had been pressed to the back of her neck. She glanced around slowly, noting that Blalock had opened his trunk and was busy putting away his gear. Everything seemed normal. Just as she was about to relax, she noticed a flash of light coming from the rocky hillside to her left, Ella dove to the ground, rolling to the side just as the wooden pistol stand in front of her exploded. The distant report of a rifle shot echoed between the hills.

Ella crawled down the drop-off in front of the firing line, then waited behind cover in the low spot for several minutes. Nobody came and no second round followed. Moving parallel to the firing line in a crouch, and unable to discern any new threat, she climbed out of the target area and jogged over to what was left of the stand. The bullet had passed completely through the four-by-four post and lodged in the adjacent post, splitting it nearly in half lengthwise. She pulled the wood further apart with her hands and carefully lifted the metal jacket bullet out and wrapped it in her handkerchief.

Ella walked back to the parking area and found Blalock standing by his car, wiping down his pistol with a soft cloth.

"Is there a rifle competition today?" Ella asked.

He shook his head. "You heard the rifle shot, too? There's no scheduled competition, according to my monthly flier, but a member might be sighting in his weapon. We can use the range after the shoot is over. Members each have a key to the gate."

"I did more than hear that rifle shot. I had to dive for cover." She filled Blalock in and showed him the recovered bullet. They both agreed it was probably from a .308 rifle.

"I'm going to find Chambers," Ella continued. "He had a rifle case in his truck. Let's see what he has to say." Ella searched the area on foot, but the truck she suspected had been Chambers' was nowhere on the range. Blalock came to meet her as she stood, scanning the area one more time. "I'm ready to go. Why don't we run that truck's license and if it belongs to Chambers, we can have a talk with him."

Having confirmed Ella's tentative ID, and having secured Chambers' address, they set out in Blalock's car. Ella shifted in her seat, restless, yet at a loss to explain the sense of impending danger that would not leave her.

"You want to tear this guy apart, don't you?" Blalock observed, misinterpreting her reaction.

"If he is our man, I'd like to use *him* for target practice. I can't decide if he should be standing with the silhouette pigs or the turkeys."

"Can't say I blame you, but what do you think triggered the incident?"

"I'm not sure, unless he saw me writing down license plates. It's possible that during the times when other relays of competitors were shooting, he left the line to see what I was doing."

"Do you think the sniper meant to kill you?"

"No. It was close, but with a scoped rifle, he shouldn't have missed. My guess is that it was meant to rattle me. Of course I don't think he would have gone into mourning had he slipped up and hit me. He might have seen it as a win-win situation."

Blalock shook his head. "No, we're not dealing with total wackos. We've got people who think they're in the right and can't see past that. My guess is he knew he could hit the target he was aiming for, and he did."

As they pulled up into the expansive driveway of a large pueblo-style, adobe home, Ella glanced at Blalock. "This house didn't come from a miner's salary."

"No kidding." He glanced around. "I don't remember a discrepancy like this in any of the background reports I read on the Anglo workers, but I do remember reading that there was one miner who still lived with his parents. This may be the guy."

Ella walked up to the front and rang the doorbell. An elderly woman came to the door and looked at her curiously as she flashed her badge. "We're here to see Steven Chambers."

"My son is out in the back cleaning his guns," the woman said, without any trace of surprise. "I'll show you the way."

Ella glanced at Blalock. Most people she knew would have asked what the police wanted, or if there was trouble. Perhaps Mrs. Chambers had learned not to ask questions.

They found Steven sitting by a redwood table in the backyard, disassembling his Colt .45. A scope-equipped Remington Model 700 rifle was lying on a soft old blanket, the bolt removed.

Blalock glanced at Ella then back at Chambers. "Nice rifle. Seven millimeter, isn't it? Shoot it in competition?"

"Sometimes. And it's a three-oh-eight."

"There was no rifle competition today, was there?" Blalock asked casually, his tone showing Ella he was pleased to have confirmed the caliber of the weapon so easily.

"Nope." Chambers started running a patch through the barrel of the .45. "What brings you here? Are you looking for some shooting tips?"

Blalock's expression was as cold as winter wind. "My rifle training qualifies me as a sharpshooter. You probably have a bit to go before you reach that level."

"Well, then maybe you can teach me. I'm always anxious to improve my skills."

Ella watched Chambers. He was smooth. "Someone took a shot at me at the range today, someone with a rifle of that caliber."

He looked Ella up and down. "They must have missed." He picked up the rifle, inserted the bolt, and checked the action.

"I recovered the bullet. A full metal jacketed three-oh-eight bullet. I wonder if the rifling marks will match a round fired from your rifle."

"I doubt it," Chambers said confidently, opening the action again to check the magazine from above. "If I'd shot at you, I wouldn't be anywhere near the rifle I'd used."

"You didn't know we were coming here," Ella countered.

"I wouldn't have risked bringing it home, either way."

Ella knew from his answer that he'd probably fired the shot, and now was taunting her. There was no way to prove it without testing the weapon and they didn't have enough probable cause at the moment to confiscate the rifle he was holding. In an area where many people owned rifles, and there were no registration laws, finding the weapon used would be difficult.

Ella purposefully slid her hand slowly back toward her own handgun. She saw Chambers tense, and then place the rifle back down onto the blanket. She would have laid odds that he'd seen her skill with her pistol out at the range.

"I've got work to do. If you have something to say, then say it, but if not, then get out of my home."

Chambers focused on the .45 again, wiping the action with a cloth he'd sprayed with a silicon product. He refused to look at either of them. Ella realized this was one guy who would never crack.

"Thanks for your time," Ella said, then added, "We'll be talking to the next competitor on our list. It's strange how people tell you things, even when they're trying to keep cool. That's what led us here. Have a nice day."

Chambers stopped cleaning his pistol and met her gaze. "Who told you to come here?"

"He asked us to keep his name out of it, but thanks for your cooperation."

Blalock burst out laughing when they reached the car. "Now you're starting to think like me."

"Hopefully the con will make him nervous. Let's see what he does now."

They parked about a block down and kept an eye on Chambers place, but he never left.

"Too bad we don't have enough to get a court order and tap his phone," Ella commented.

"Yeah. He could have called half a dozen people by now." Blalock started the car again. "I'm going to take you back to your vehicle."

An hour later, she was on her way to the office. Clouds dotted the horizon and again the winds whipped the desert sand into a crazed frenzy.

Hearing her cellular's ring, Ella picked it up and identified herself.

Justine's voice sounded strained as she said, "There's something strange going on."

"That statement leaves a lot of room for interpretation."

"Joseph, Sergeant Neskahi, didn't come in to work today. At first I thought he'd gotten an early start and was off talking to that cousin of his, or interviewing miners, but nobody's seen him since yesterday."

Ella felt a chill travel over her. Now she understood the restlessness that had plagued her before. She'd sensed something wrong, though she'd been unable to define it. Not having heard from Neskahi must have stayed in her subconscious. Her family, however, would have explained it much differently.

Ella focused her thoughts. "Did you check his home?"

"He moved a week ago to a trailer, but he didn't report his

new address. At the moment we're trying to figure out where it's parked."

"Ask either Phillip or Michael Cloud. They might know. I'll be at the station in another ten minutes."

Ella felt a sense of urgency tugging at her. Neskahi was a good cop, he wouldn't have gone undercover without notifying them. To stay out of contact like this, particularly after she'd warned him against it, was not his style. There was only one explanation for his failure to report in. He was unable to do so. The possible explanations for that were endless, and all equally alarming.

By the time Ella arrived at the station her body felt as if a giant bolt of lightning had traveled through it. Her hair stood out as if electrified, and her skin felt as if a million ants were crawling over her. The sense of danger grew with every passing second.

She hurried toward the door and met Justine coming out. "Anything yet?"

"I was going to call you on the cellular once I was on my way. Phillip knew the location of the trailer." She handed Ella a map as they walked back out toward her Jeep.

Ella studied it for a second, then handed the map back to Justine. "Let's go. I'll drive. You can navigate if I get lost."

Ella turned on the sirens and hurried out of Shiprock. It was past dinnertime and most people were at home now. The kids would drive in and around the community, cruising, but there wasn't enough action to draw them out on the open road toward Gallup.

Her thoughts raced ahead to Neskahi. "Does he have any neighbors who could check on him?"

"No. Phillip said we were closer to him than just about anyone else, providing we were willing to travel cross country. Turn here."

"Right," Ella said, braking hard, then pulling off into a dry wash. The Jeep slid, but quickly straightened out in response to Ella's expert touch at the wheel. Frustrated by the uneven center that pulled the Jeep from side to side, Ella was forced to slow down. She was shifting down when they hit a bump and Ella heard a sharp crack. Taking her eyes off the ground ahead for a second, she saw Justine rubbing her head with one hand.

"You okay?"

"Yeah," she grumbled.

"Hang on."

It took another ten minutes for them to arrive. Ella glanced around. Besides Neskahi's trailer and pickup, there was not much else out here.

Ella knocked on the door and it swung open, hinges squealing. "Sergeant?"

There was something eerie about the silence flowing out from the interior. Ella drew her weapon, and saw Justine do the same. Moving quickly, Ella went in, keeping her back to the wall. Justine followed. There was no sign of a struggle. Ella moved down the hall, then, with Justine behind her, searched the bedroom.

The trailer was spartanly furnished, with only bare essentials. It was definitely a man's place, for a man who didn't spend much time at home.

Justine went into the last room, and Ella slipped past her, checking the bathroom.

"We need an ambulance," Ella yelled the second she stepped inside.

Neskahi, still in uniform, was curled up on the floor in front of the sink, his body jerking slightly from muscle spasms. But at least there was no sign of blood.

Ella crouched beside him and felt the pulse point at his neck. His heart was strong, but his breathing was labored. Remembering the rash of poisonings, her skin went cold. "He may have been poisoned," she called out. "Ask for permission to transport now."

Justine returned a moment later and handed her the phone. "The doctor wants to talk to you."

Ella described Neskahi's condition to Dr. Natoni, reminding him of the other poisonings. "Transport," Dr. Natoni said. "Do you suspect any particular toxin?"

"It could be jimsonweed, or monkshood or something else entirely, I just don't know." Remembering she still had the remedy for jimsonweed, Ella asked the doctor for permission to use it. "If it isn't jimsonweed, it won't hurt him. But if it is, it may help."

"All right, do it," Natoni agreed. "Just don't let him choke. Then get moving. The faster you get him here, the better chance he'll have."

"Understood." Ella closed the phone unit, then placed a pinch of the herb inside the sergeant's lips. Grabbing Neskahi under his arms, she motioned to Justine. "Let's go. Every second counts."

SIXTEEN
✖ ✖ ✖

Ella waited in the lobby as the emergency room team worked on Joseph Neskahi.

Justine's face looked drawn. "I can't believe that someone would try to kill him. He's part of our team, yes, but his death wouldn't have accomplished anything. We would have gone on with our investigation."

"It would have affected us, though, whether or not we admit it, and it would have sent a message to everyone we've been dealing with that we're unable to keep even our own people safe."

"Is it possible that Joseph stumbled onto something that made the killer nervous?"

"Sure, but we won't know about that until he can talk to us. While we're waiting, I want you to track down what he was doing before this happened. He may not have filed an official report yet, but Neskahi is methodical. Look at his notes, then check his computer at the station. See what you can turn up."

As Justine left, Ella went to the elevator. She'd stay in touch with the hospital, but for now, she had things to attend to. She intended to return to Neskahi's home and search it and his pickup from top to bottom. Perhaps there was a clue there.

As the elevator doors slid open, she heard her name being called. Dr. Natoni, the Chief of Emergency Medicine at the hospital, waved to her. Ella approached him, bracing herself for whatever news he might have.

"I think he's going to be okay," he said somberly.

Ella breathed, "That's great news! Why are you so glum?"

He smiled. "I'm sorry. It's the implications of this that bother me. The hospital is going to come under fire, and that's the last thing we need."

"Under fire? You've lost me."

"We were running out of time trying to identify the toxin that was killing the sergeant. Then one of our interns remembered a report downstairs this morning about a missing bottle of furosemide."

"Of what?"

"It's a drug used as a diuretic for patients with congestive heart failure, among other things. Our pharmacist discovered a bottle missing right after Dr. Roanhorse went in to get some allergy medications. They have several med students working down there, and the pharmacist was worried that it might have been mislabeled. Since some of Neskahi's symptoms matched an overdose of that drug, like bleeding under the skin, labored breathing, and muscle spasms, we added potassium through the IV while we checked. He began to improve even before we had confirmation that furosemide *was* the toxin in his system. We've checked. The sergeant wasn't on that drug as therapy. Neskahi's still got a long road ahead, but what caused his collapse was severe dehydration and electrolyte depletion. We're making sure he gets what his body needs most right now."

The mention of Carolyn's name in conjunction with the missing medication made Ella's stomach clench. She could see a new possibility emerging. What had happened to Neskahi wasn't just a poisoning, it was part of a frame-up, and she now needed to know how the drug had been administered.

"I should be able to release him in a few days," Dr. Natoni continued, "but he's going to have to take it easy for about a week or so. This is going to leave him feeling pretty weak."

"Thank you, Doctor." Thoughts racing, Ella watched Natoni

return to the ER. There was no need to go to Neskahi's trailer now. Her first stop would be the pharmacy downstairs.

Ella went directly there. The pharmacy was directly over the morgue, one story above. The proximity to the place where her friend worked would undoubtedly come into play. Carolyn would soon come under as vicious an attack as Neskahi. Ella could feel that in her bones.

The pharmacist, a middle-aged Anglo man, came out from behind a metal shelf stocked with medications. "Yes? Can I help you?"

Ella flashed her badge and saw him tense. "I need to ask you a few questions about the missing bottle of furosemide."

"They called the police? I assure you, we're tracking it down right now. It just takes time—"

She held up her hand. "It's more complicated than that. The emergency room just treated a man who almost died from furosemide poisoning."

The man's face slowly turned ashen. "Did he take the medication thinking it was something else because it had been mislabeled?"

"No."

He reached for the counter, bracing himself. "Then it *was* stolen from here."

Ella opened her arms, palms outward and shrugged. "You tell me. When did you discover it was missing?"

"This morning. It was a madhouse here. I've got two students working full-time, and we'd just received a shipment of drugs, all controlled substances. Those have to be catalogued and entered in separate databases. Unfortunately, at the same time, three medical teams were leaving for inoculation clinics and they needed orders filled quickly. Dr. Roanhorse, who'd come in for allergy pills, ended up helping us for a while, mostly typing up labels and the like, but then she had to leave. It wasn't until noon, when I was asked to send up some furosemide, that I realized an entire stock bottle of the liquid form of that drug was missing."

Ella tried to shake the sinking feeling in her stomach. "Did anyone else help out during that crisis?"

"Her med student, Dr. Natoni, and a couple of the orderlies."

"It was the Death Doctor," Nelson Yellowhair said, coming into the pharmacy, his gaze hard.

"I beg your pardon?" Ella challenged coldly.

"You *know* what happened, or you should. The sergeant, the one that was poisoned, was here earlier and had coffee with your friend, the Death Doctor. Did she forget to mention that?"

Ella kept her face expressionless. She would not give the orderly the satisfaction of knowing how the accusations worried her. "I haven't spoken to Dr. Roanhorse yet. Maybe you'd like to enlighten me."

"The sergeant had coffee with the Death Doctor, then was going to pick up a file he'd left at home before going to see you. I guess something in the coffee disagreed with him."

"How do you know so much about his plans?"

"I overhead them talking."

"Thanks for your cooperation," Ella clipped.

Ella went around him and walked down the flight of stairs to Carolyn's office. Things were starting to look really bad for her friend. Knowing the way gossip traveled on the Rez, and how nicknames stuck, she realized she had to work fast before irreparable harm was done. There was no doubt in her mind that Carolyn was the victim of a frame. Carolyn was incapable of harming anyone. Even in self-defense, she doubted Carolyn would ever use deadly force.

Carolyn glanced up as Ella came in. "Gads, you look like hell. What happened?"

Ella took a seat across the desk from Carolyn and filled her in. Carolyn's expression remained guarded throughout.

"Someone's trying to frame me," Carolyn said, when Ella finished.

"I know. But I'm going to have check your coffeepot as well as look around the rest of the morgue."

"I insist." Carolyn placed the coffeepot in a plastic bag and sealed it, then handed the bag to Ella. "Don't let it spill. You'll want the contents of the trash, too, including the thrown-out foam cups we use. Let's go to your vehicle together. That way you'll be able to testify that I didn't tamper with the scene while you were getting evidence pouches."

Ella and Carolyn returned a few minutes later. Wearing rubber gloves, Ella sifted through the hazardous materials disposal containers and the trash, searching everything from traces of the stock bottle to signs of spilled liquid. She recovered several foam coffee cups, some with lipstick smudges. After a thorough search of the morgue, Ella walked to the door. "I'm sorry I had to do this."

"It's your job."

Ella nodded. "I'll have Justine check the samples out. If we find anything, I'll be back."

Carolyn exhaled softly. "Someone is sure doing a number on me."

As Ella stepped out into the hall, she saw another trash bin. "I better go through that one, too," she said.

Carolyn followed, but stayed well back as Ella tilted the container so she could look inside. It was only a few seconds before Ella saw the nearly full bottle of furosemide nearly buried in the trash. Ella pushed it to the surface with the tip of her pen, then eased it into an evidence pouch.

"Would there be any reason for this bottle to have your prints on it?" Ella asked.

"None," Carolyn answered.

Ella motioned to Nelson Yellowhair, who was standing with Howard Lee down the hall, watching them. "Get me a big plastic trash bag. I'm taking the entire contents of this container with me."

"Yes, ma'am."

When Yellowhair brought her the bag, Ella fought the urge to wipe the smug look off his face with a clean blow to the bridge of his nose. Without ever uttering a word, he had "I told you so" written all over his face.

Carolyn accompanied Ella to the stairwell door, holding it open because Ella had to maneuver through without hands because of the bags she was carrying. "You realize that this can cost me my job, and my work is all I have." Her voice had dropped to a whisper, letting Ella know how seriously Carolyn was taking this new revelation.

"You'll be okay. You didn't do this."

"Reputations are usually ruined by innuendo, not fact."

"I know," she said. "I'll do everything I can to find the person who's doing this to you."

Ella walked toward her Jeep, her heart leaden. Her friend was being set up, and by doing her job she'd made things even worse for Carolyn. As she approached her vehicle, she saw Nelson Yellowhair walking in her direction from the hospital's side entrance. Ella braced herself for trouble.

"You didn't want to believe me about your friend, did you?" Yellowhair goaded as he arrived. "But you see now that I was right. I'm sorry the truth is so unpleasant for you to face."

"What truth is that?"

Nelson smiled. "Ah, my brother said you'd be difficult to convince, that you would side with your friend to the bitter end."

"I'm not siding with anyone. I just want to make sure I have all the facts, before I pass judgment. I suggest you do the same."

"You can't cover up for her, you know," he said smoothly. "The word is already out. Many believe that the Death Doctor is paying for ignoring our taboos, that the evil that follows her is a result of her work. Someone who works with the dead can't help but become contaminated by the *chindi.*"

"You don't believe that," Ella scoffed. She set the trash bag on the asphalt to free one hand for her keys.

"I believe that there's been a strong motive behind everything she's done lately. The doctor wants to destroy my brother. To her, falsifying my niece's test results was as easy as poisoning your sergeant. She only cares about herself. If you neglect your duties in order to protect her, you'll be guilty along with her."

"I don't need you telling me how to do my job. If you'll excuse me," she said, turning her back on him and unlocking the Jeep door, "I've got work to do."

· · ·

Ella walked over to her desk and sat down. She'd left the bags with Justine. After checking the bottle and foam cups for fingerprints, her assistant had been instructed to send the containers directly to the state crime lab. Ella needed to know if any of the cups contained furosemide along with the coffee. It was finally quiet, and she needed a moment to gather her thoughts. The moment she leaned back, the intercom sounded and Big Ed asked her to come to his office.

Ella rose slowly. She was tired, hungry, and ready to call it a day. But she couldn't very well put Big Ed off until tomorrow.

As she stepped into his office, she found him standing by the window, staring at the ever darkening horizon. "I'm looking forward to daylight savings time. Then, even when I put in a long day, I'm usually home in time to see the sun go down." Big Ed was tired, and not just from putting in a ten-hour day.

Ella eased into an armchair. At the moment, she would have rather seen her pillow and her bed. "I suppose you've heard the latest from the hospital."

"The news reached me, along with reports that you might not be the best choice to investigate this crime."

"I resent that, Chief. I've never given this department any reason to question my integrity, and I expect the department to back me up."

"There *is* a conflict of interest. You're investigating your friend—" A note of impatience appeared in his voice as he walked over to his desk.

"—who is getting buried with innuendo, but few facts," Ella added.

"Is it true, that a bottle of that drug was found right outside her office?"

"Carolyn is a very bright woman. If she had poisoned Neskahi, she would have covered her tracks better. This is a frame-up and a crude one at that."

"Prove it, or turn the case over to Justine."

"She's already handling all the evidence, but she doesn't have enough experience for the entire investigation. You know that."

"Until this problem with Dr. Roanhorse is cleared up, Justine *is* in charge of that investigation."

"I've done nothing to deserve this." Ella stood up, angry.

Big Ed brought his fist crashing down on the desk. "Do you think *I* like this? This entire department is under siege. The politicians work together like a pack of wolves running their prey into the ground through sheer exhaustion. Senator Yellowhair is relentless. When he complains, and it's been at least once every day, his call is followed within minutes by complaints from his colleagues. I can't ignore them all. I want you to stay on the Angelina Yellowhair investigation, but Neskahi's poisoning goes to Justine. You can supervise her progress and assist, but she calls the shots, at least on paper."

Ella nodded, weary and dejected. "All right."

"Go home and get some rest. You look as if you're ready to fall on your face." Big Ed's expression could almost be taken for a smile, except that he never smiled.

"I am. I'll check for messages, then go."

Ella stopped by her desk and glanced at the report on Neskahi that Justine had left for her. Justine had found nothing of value stored in Neskahi's computer. All he'd recorded in his unfinished report were speculations. Neskahi had been investigating a possible link between Angelina's poisoning and Carolyn's, so he'd gone to the hospital to question the doctor.

Ella turned off the lights, locked up, then walked out to the parking lot. As she approached her Jeep she saw a note held in place by the windshield wipers. She picked it up gingerly, knowing it would be signed just like the others.

"What do you have there?" Big Ed asked, approaching. "I was on my way to my car when I noticed what you were doing. Did somebody leave you a note?"

Ella shook her head. "If they did, they have quite a reach. It's another message from the person claiming to be my late father-in-law. This time he's taking credit for poisoning Neskahi. He says that I should think twice every time I take a swallow of coffee, or a bite of lunch."

"Process the note just like the rest. If Justine can't find anything, then pass it along to FB-Eyes. See what their lab can find out from it."

"All right. I'll go log it in."

Big Ed walked back inside the building with her, obviously not finished with his instructions. "Whoever poisoned Angelina Yellowhair and Dr. Roanhorse is working overtime to make us look bad. But make sure that you don't put Bitah's murder on the back burner either. We can't afford to ignore what's going on at the mine. Tension is getting higher by the moment over there. My neighbor's son drives one of the big coal-hauling trucks. He said that having Truman out on bail has polarized almost everyone."

"I'm not ignoring that case. I've been searching for leads, and right now Anderson looks promising as the main suspect. I've made some progress but, admittedly, not enough to arrest anyone."

"One miner is still missing, another dead. Clear the case before those numbers rise."

It was shortly after ten the following morning when Blalock came into her office. Ella looked up at him, surprised. "What brings you all the way to Shiprock unannounced?"

"We need to brainstorm on this case eyeball to eyeball. I've had half a dozen calls from Washington this morning alone. Senator Yellowhair and some of the other tribal officials are pulling all the right strings. I had to fight like crazy to buy myself some time and not have the Bureau send in a team to assist."

"That's the last thing we need here."

"Agreed, but we damned well better find some answers, and fast. I've made extensive background checks of all the members of the gun club, but there's nothing particularly noteworthy there. The handful who are members and also work at the mine have all-of-a-sudden gone very low profile, too. I asked around at the club, but nobody's seen that group at the range since the match. They usually go together to practice three times a week."

"I think our visit to Chambers so soon after the incident rattled them. I'm sure they all know, or at least suspect, he was responsible for shooting at me, but they don't want to take any heat for him. I have trouble believing that they sanctioned that incident as a group, on such short notice. I suspect Chambers decided to have himself a little bit of 'good ole boy' fun at my expense," she said.

"You might be right, but we still have zip on these guys, and that's got to change."

"Agreed."

"I tried to bring pressure on Truman, but he's playing it cool. He goes to work, and comes back home. That's it. I even tailed him back and forth. Nothing. What about that miner who disappeared, Noah Charley. Anything on him?"

"There's that rumor I haven't been able to substantiate that he was working as an informant for The Brotherhood. If that's true, then that explains his disappearance. He was last seen the evening Bitah was murdered. And he never picked up his paycheck. It looks like he got scared and bailed on everyone."

"You're thinking he was paid for delivering Bitah?"

"Yes, but I can't prove it. I've got people afraid to talk to the police, and others determined to solve it themselves."

"It just gets better and better, doesn't it," he snapped sarcastically.

Justine knocked on the open door and came in holding a newspaper. "I've got bad news."

"What's new?" Blalock muttered.

Justine dropped the newspaper, opened to the front page, onto Ella's desk.

Ella glanced down and, although it took some effort, managed not to cringe. Yellowhair's charges against Carolyn were the headline. In the article, Yellowhair claimed Carolyn had compromised the evidence on his daughter's autopsy. He also maintained that anyone else under the cloud of suspicion the M.E. was currently under, would have been asked to take leave, rather than continue working while under investigation. He accused the police department of being in league with the M.E. to conceal the truth. Yellowhair had wrapped up by saying that the only reason the M.E. hadn't been suspended was because Dr. Roanhorse's friend, Ella Clah, was in charge of the investigation and she was filtering the information being made available to the public.

Ella tossed the paper aside. "Carolyn could sue his butt, and win."

"I called the paper and told them *I* was investigating the M.E. I told them to get their facts straight." Justine gave Ella a tiny grin, then shrugged, adding, "So what if that happened after they printed the story?"

Ella chuckled softly. "At least Neshaki's poisoning has been kept out of the paper. For now."

"That brings me to another piece of news I have to share with you," Blalock said. "We're all about to become one big, happy family. I've been ordered to get involved in the Angelina Yellowhair investigation, too, by no less than the regional director. I'm to look into the M.E. role in the investigation, and go the whole nine yards."

"You realize that what they want is for you to declare that the M.E. compromised the evidence by using sloppy procedures. They're hoping you'll discover that she mislabeled everything, or mixed up the samples, thus making the autopsy report highly questionable. The senator wants this case closed, one way or another. Howard Lee, Carolyn's med student, could turn out to be a key player, too. Depending on which way the wind is blowing at the time, he might defend Carolyn or decide to destroy her."

Blalock shrugged. "Just like you and Chief Atcitty, I've got my orders."

Ella stood up. "If you're really going to be in on this, then let's go to Big Ed's office now. There are some things you have to know about."

Ella led the way down the hall, knocked on Big Ed's open door, then escorted FB-Eyes inside. "We have some interesting developments," she said, noting that the chief had already tossed today's newspaper into the trash.

Big Ed waved them to a chair and listened as Ella explained about Carolyn's second set of samples, the ones she'd given the police to be sent to the state lab to corroborate her own findings.

"I can guess what you want to do. You'd like to make it public that there were two sets of tissue and fluid samples, one of which has not been compromised. Correct?"

Blalock's eyebrows rose. "That's an interesting bit of news. It sure helps protect your case."

"I would have preferred to keep that second set of samples a secret for now," Ella admitted, "at least until we had the results of the test. But if we do that, Carolyn's going to have an additional, pointless battle to fight when she has more than enough trouble already." Ella glanced at Big Ed then at Blalock. "How do you two vote?"

"Look, I'm going to put my cards on the table," Blalock said. "I hate having someone jerk my chain, whether it's Washington or local politicians. I've been put on this case in hopes that I'll dance to Yellowhair's tune. The way I see it, you folks have a good grip on this case. I'll go through the motions, but as far as I'm concerned, this case is all yours. Handle it any way you want. When it's over, just let me read your report so I can make sure my own matches, Okay?"

"Let's see how Dr. Roanhorse feels. She's taking the heat over this. Give her a call." Big Ed handed Ella the phone.

In a few minutes, Ella had Carolyn on the line. "Hi. I'm at a meeting with Chief Atcitty and Agent Blalock, and I just told them about the second set of samples sent to the state lab. In light of the latest news stories, what do you think about releasing the news of this second set?"

"I'd like the department to keep those samples a secret, if my vote counts. I have a feeling we're going to need an edge before everything's said and done," Carolyn confirmed.

"I agree, and I'm glad you're willing to tough it out a little longer." Ella nodded to Blalock, who was now ready to leave. She said good-bye to Carolyn, then confirmed their strategy with Big Ed.

Ella spent the rest of the day in her office. Sometimes a paper trail was the best way to access leads. That's how she'd first discovered Angelina's shares in the power plant operation.

Ella made careful note of the senator's voting record. Senator

Yellowhair had always promoted coal mining interests, and she knew now that it was because of "Angelina's" interest in that company. But whether that made him an enemy of The Brotherhood, or a friend, remained unclear. The Brotherhood didn't appear to want to close the mine, but according to Anderson, there were Navajos willing to risk such a closure through sabotage. Or maybe Anderson had just been trying to confuse the issue.

Only one thing remained clear, Carolyn was being used as a scapegoat. The only things she hadn't been blamed of so far were the murders themselves.

Ella leaned back and rubbed her eyes. She was hitting a brick wall, no matter which direction she turned. Needing a break, she walked to the vending machines in the lunchroom and bought herself a bag of corn chips. She'd skipped lunch altogether, but she wasn't hungry, just frustrated and tired.

She sat near the window, staring outside. For the first time in about a week, the winds had not come up today. The sun was high in a cloudless sky, and it was deceptively peaceful. But, with each sunny day that passed, the more parched the land became.

Restless, Ella picked up her empty bag of chips and tossed it into the trash. As she approached the door, she heard a conversation taking place out in the hall.

"Who knows? With a job like that maybe the M.E. does have a hidden agenda, trying to stir up things," Ella heard a man say. "The evil ones thrive on chaos."

Anger corkscrewed through her, bubbling up, and practically choking the air from her lungs. She stepped out into the hall and stared at the young Navajo cop by the door and his buddies. "I will not have this department's M.E. being bad-mouthed. Dr. Roanhorse is a hard-working professional who, like most of us, is doing a thankless job. As a cop, you should sympathize with her struggle to stand up and do what has to be done, instead of chiming in with her enemies." Ella struggled to keep her hands from shaking, curling them into tight fists and shoving them inside her pockets.

The officer backed up a step. "Sorry, ma'am, we were just kidding around."

"Only a coward lashes out at a horse that's already tied up." Her voice shook, outrage filling her. She wanted a fight, something to vent her anger, but the officers, speechless and embarrassed, dispersed and fled.

When she turned around she saw Justine standing behind her, her eyes wide. Ella stared at her, still hot. "You've got a problem?"

"No, not at all." Justine smiled slowly. "Bet that felt good."

Ella glared at her for another moment, then smiled back. "Yeah. I was getting tired of not being able to do anything to help Carolyn. This, at least, was something I could act on right now."

Justine nodded. "It's a frustrating time. I wanted an informant inside the mine more than you can imagine, but it's not going to happen." Justine took a deep breath then let it out again. "You were right about Nez. He wants me to be *his* informant. Do you believe it? I've met with him twice now, both times very briefly and at night near my cousin's, so I wouldn't be alone, like you said."

"What happened?"

"It was apparent from his questions that his interest is in you, and what you're doing, not me."

"What do you mean in me? What kind of interest?"

"Professional," Justine said with a shrug. "He said he wants to work with you, but you'd have to agree to let him run things his own way."

"In a pig's eye," Ella spat out. "That's not working with the police. He wants to put himself in charge of the investigation. Convenient for him, but out of the question."

"In either case, I can't do anything with him. Maybe you can."

Ella shook her head. "No. First, he's been using you to get to me, and that's a bad sign. He wants to play games. My guess is that he's with the Fierce Ones, despite what he says. What I can't make up my mind about is whether he's one of the leaders."

"What makes you think there's more than one leader?"

"It's closer to our way to have councils rather than have one man making all the decisions. Of course, that's just a guess."

Ella picked up the file folders from her desk and locked them in the cabinet. "I'm going home for dinner. I need to get away from here, if only for a while. You want to come? Mom would love to see you."

"What kind of relaxing would you do with me along?" Justine shook her head. "No, I'll go take the last two notes you received over to Blalock. He wants to add them to a special shipment that's going to their FBI lab tonight."

"Okay. You leaving now?"

"Yeah."

"I'll walk out with you."

Justine stopped by the lab, picked up a sealed pouch, then went with Ella to the parking lot.

As Justine got into her unmarked vehicle, Ella continued across the parking lot toward her Jeep. It was on days like today that she wished she had managed to find a hobby, something besides E-Mail and computer solitaire. If she didn't find a way to relieve the stress, she was going to go crazy.

Ella opened the driver's door, then, with a sharp gasp, jumped back. Walking across the driver's seat were several scorpions.

SEVENTEEN

— ✖ ✖ ✖ —

There were at least five of the nasty creatures walking around on the front seat of the Jeep. Ella backed away and glanced around, searching for a stick or something to gather them up and remove them from the vehicle.

A moment later Justine drove up, parking beside her. "What's wrong? A bee get inside?"

"Worse, I think. Scorpions," she said, gesturing to the front seat.

While Justine peeked inside, Ella noticed a Russian olive branch that had fallen to the ground just off the pavement, and went to retrieve it. As she reached down to pick it up she saw some tracks in the sand that chilled her to the marrow. Four quarter-sized imprints marked the soft sand beside the asphalt, then disappeared into the pea-sized gravel that covered the ground farther away.

"Interesting," Justine muttered, joining Ella and looking over her shoulder.

Ella stepped around the marks and went back to her Jeep. "Let's get back to those in a minute. Right now I've got some unwelcome passengers to get rid of."

"How did they get in there? Was your window open?"

"The window was up and the doors locked."

Ella brushed the scorpions out onto the pavement and Justine started to step on them. Ella pushed her aside gently. "No. Don't kill anything that doesn't have to be killed." Scooping them up one or two at a time, she set them off the parking lot in some buffalo grass.

Justine hesitated briefly, but then, as if with a burst of courage, started to open the back door.

"No! Don't touch anything else. Look around for any other critters first, and check for a bomb," Ella said, remembering their encounters with skinwalkers in the past.

After several minutes of careful observations, Ella gave Justine the all-clear. Justine opened the back door and searched the rear of the vehicle while Ella checked the front and the engine compartment.

"I can't believe I'm looking around for bombs *and* scorpions," Justine muttered. "This is some job we're in!"

"We chose it. Keep reminding yourself." Ella searched every inch of the vehicle, including underneath and the glove compartment. "Okay. I'll concede now that we've found everything that's in here."

"You think they got in here on their own somehow?"

"No, not five, especially after seeing those odd tracks next to the Dumpster."

Justine crouched on the ground and studied the marks. "This is starting to get creepy. Every time we see these something crazy happens. You know, these marks remind me of something, if only I could remember what."

"Maybe skinwalkers are trying to unnerve me," Ella speculated.

"Or maybe the scorpions were a gift from Yellowhair's people. You're not on their most-favorite-people list. Of course your list of nonadmirers doesn't end there," she added cynically. "By defending Dr. Roanhorse, some of the *Dineh* are angry with you, too."

Ella drove home, leaving Justine to photograph the markings for the ever-growing case file. Pain stabbed her temple, shooting all the way across her head and down her spine. She stretched her neck from side to side, trying to relax her muscles. It didn't work. Tension kept her body rigid and her nerves on edge.

By the time she reached home even her stomach ached. As she pulled up next to her mother's house and parked, she saw another car coming up the dirt track. She left the Jeep and waited.

A moment later, she recognized Carolyn's beat-up maroon pickup. She took several deep breaths, and forced herself to relax. The pain eased.

Carolyn climbed out of her pickup and waved. "I tried to call you at the office, but Justine said you had already left for home. I hope you don't mind my dropping by."

"Since when do you need an invitation?" Ella smiled and led her inside. "What brings you by?"

"After reading the newspaper account again, I just wanted someone to talk to, someone I trust."

"Then you came to the right person. How are things going for you at the hospital?"

"I'm still working the inoculation clinics. To be honest, it's a real perk for me to go into the remote areas. I don't have to deal with the suspicion cast on me by Neskahi's poisoning, or with people who know I'm the M.E."

Rose stepped into the living room and smiled at both women. "I was going to go out to Mrs. Pioche's and help her dye some wool, but I'll stay now that you're both here and fix dinner for you."

"No, Mom, don't. Carolyn and I can fix something for ourselves."

"Well, there are some freshly made tortillas and some cheese and beans . . . "

"Great. We'll make burritos. Go on and have fun. Just be careful and check the pickup before you climb in."

Ella told her mother about the scorpions, then walked her out to the truck. In a few minutes she joined Carolyn back inside. "Mom needs to get out more. Heck, I do, too. I need a life."

"You and me both. But, you know, I can't see us spending afternoons dyeing wool."

"It's not so bad. It's interesting to see them prepare the dyes, but what I enjoy most is the actual spinning. I never got the hang of it, and nowadays Mom buys her wool from one of the other women, but I'd like to learn someday."

"I miss the companionship of other women, too. Loneliness itself becomes a companion after awhile, though. It becomes so much a part of life that I think I'd miss it if it wasn't there."

"Our family legacy is a bitch to live with. That legend about the young people from our line having to fight the evil that's part of our heritage makes things tough. Since it is said that the outcome is never certain, that sometimes evil will win over the good, many people prefer to stand back and give us a wide berth."

"I've heard about that legend, but not its origins."

Ella brought out the fixings for their burritos and told Carolyn what she knew as they worked. "It's something that's not often discussed with anyone outside the family, so I don't know how it became so generally known. I must have been sixteen before my mother ever said a word about it. But, in general terms, one of my ancestors broke our taboos and got pregnant by a man from her own clan. She was shunned, but Navajo witches sought her out and she learned their skills and magic. She became very powerful, then taught her daughter all she knew. In the end, my ancestor redeemed herself by using the powers skinwalkers had taught her to help others, not harm them.

"Her daughter, too, continued on the side of good, but the belief that the line couldn't escape the evils that were in their blood from the beginning still remained. Each generation's offspring would be endowed with certain powers, but what remained to be seen was whether they'd use them for good or evil. It was then decided that those of our clan would always have two children. If the darkness seduced one, then the other would be there to counter it."

"How do you feel personally about all that? I can't see you taking any of that to heart." Carolyn finished preparing the last burrito.

"I don't know," Ella said, sitting down to eat. "My thoughts on that subject change, depending on what's going on in my life. But the cost the legend exacts never changes. It's an invisible barrier that separates me from people. They're afraid, and I can't blame them. Son of a gun, it scares me, too, sometimes. It's a darkness just below my feet, waiting like quicksand beneath a layer of thinly packed earth."

"Is that why you haven't remarried?"

"No. I can't honestly say that, though admittedly it would be a dandy excuse. Sometimes I've even wondered if I wasn't using my job as a rationalization, but I honestly don't think so. My job takes everything out of me. By the end of the day, I don't have much left to give."

They were halfway through their meal when the cellular phone rang. Ella answered it, afraid it was more bad news. As usual, she was right.

She recognized Blalock's voice.

"I hate to bother you, Clah, but Senator Yellowhair filed a complaint with my home office stating that all the samples the M.E. used to base her findings were taken from a body other than his daughter's. He's demanding a separate autopsy be done."

"That body's been embalmed. It's too late," Ella said. "He probably knows that."

"Our experts say some tissue samples might still provide results, though toxicology is out. Also, our forensics experts can check for physical injuries that might have caused her death, as opposed to the drugs."

"What are you proposing? Exhumation?"

"Precisely."

"Oh, that's going to score a lot of points around here. You know how my tribe feels about bodies and the dead. Digging up a corpse is not going to make things easier for anyone. Does the senator know what you intend to do?"

"I think he believes we'll just throw up our hands and drop the case without exhuming the body. Personally, I'd rather call his bluff, even if we don't get squat."

Ella considered it. "I think you're right. He's hoping that his charge coupled with the fact the body's been embalmed will cause you to throw out the case. Well, let's throw him a curve ball. Get a court order and let's go and dig her up."

"I'm ahead of you—the order's already a done deal."

"When are you going to exhume?"

"Right away."

"Who do you want to bring in as the M.E.?" She saw Carolyn glance up.

"Dr. Michael Lavery," he answered. "He works for the Bureau on special occasions, and is the chief pathologist at the University teaching hospital. As a matter of fact, Dr. Lavery is in town now, and I'm calling you in transit. We should be at the gravesite shortly. I'm hoping you can get a crew there to dig up the body."

Ella laughed. "You're kidding, right? Navajos? In the evening?"

"Failing that, it falls to you and me."

"Oh, crap," Ella muttered. "I'll meet you at the gravesite, and bring some tools."

Carolyn went home, but Ella was there with two shovels and a pick by the time Blalock arrived. Since it was the church cemetery, Ella informed the minister. He was Navajo and wanted no part of the exhumation, but he made no attempt to interfere. Ella was relieved.

Ella and Blalock dug for twenty minutes. Finally, Ella took a breather, leaning on her shovel. Blalock's tie lay over the hood of his car, along with his jacket. He had rolled up his sleeves, but amazingly, his white shirt remained white, and not a bead of sweat dotted his forehead.

Ella wiped the perspiration from hers. "At least this sand is not hard-packed, though you'd think they would have pressed it down with one of those thumpers."

"Keep digging, Clah. Daylight's running out."

"Yeah, some time you picked. We're going to be here, carting off a body after dark."

"Dr. Lavery has limited free time. We're lucky he agreed to come at all."

It took some time, but finally the tip of her shovel touched something hard. "We're there."

Dr. Lavery stepped forward. "You don't have any heavy lifting equipment. You're going to have the devil of a time bringing up that casket," he said.

"Interesting choice of words, Doc," Ella said.

"I'll tell you what," Blalock suggested. "I'll open the casket down here, we'll put the body in a croaker sack, then transport."

"You have such a way with words," Ella said with a grimace.

"Mr. Diplomacy, that's me." Blalock gestured to the casket. "Get busy, Ella. We'll need to dig out around the casket a bit more so we can stand clear when we open the lid."

"Once you get it open, let me take photos and do a preliminary on site," Lavery instructed. "And Blalock, I expect to be reimbursed for overtime, *and* the working conditions."

Ella glanced at Blalock. "How the heck do you open a casket? There are no snaps or latches."

Blalock reached for the side, found the handle and began turning it. The lid lifted with a high-pitched squeal.

"If I didn't know better, I'd suspect you arranged that just for effect."

"Don't kid yourself. I find this as revolting as you do."

As the lid lifted, Ella pressed her back against the earthen sides of the grave. Her stomach contents came up and she forced them back down with a foul-tasting swallow. Then a smell reminiscent of strong perfume mixed with the odor of damp earth hit her. She coughed and scrambled out, gulping for air.

It took her a minute, but when she was relatively certain she wasn't going to vomit after all, she returned to the grave and jumped back into the hole, avoiding looking at Blalock and Dr. Lavery, who were intent on the body. The mutilated body stared at her accusingly, and memories of what had been done to her father assailed her. Ella staggered backwards and slammed into the earthen wall.

"The organs are missing," Dr. Lavery said, oblivious to what was going on. "Explain," he asked, glancing over at Ella.

Ella tried to regain her composure. "I'm sure the body didn't leave the morgue that way. Dr. Roanhorse uses the same protocols as every other M.E. in the state. She's told me the organs are returned to the body cavity once the autopsy is complete. This must have been done afterwards." She paused, then added, "No wonder the ground is still soft. This grave's been dug twice now."

Ella struggled to keep from shaking. She wouldn't come apart in front of the men. If they could handle it, so could she. She finally looked down at the body as Dr. Lavery took photographs. "That mutilation looks like—" her voice trembled and she stopped speaking abruptly.

"What was done to your father?" Blalock finished for her.

Ella nodded.

"You're losing me here, folks," Lavery said, setting his camera on the surface out of the way.

Ella looked directly at him. "In the eyes of someone not fully versed in our ways, this mutilation might have been viewed as part of the ritual intended for War Medicine. In olden times, when an enemy was defeated, the tendons of his legs, arms, and neck were taken, along with his scalp. These would then be used by a medicine man to make the victors' enemies weak, and their own warriors more powerful. But in this case it doesn't fit. Angelina couldn't have been much of an enemy."

"What about her father, the senator?" Blalock suggested.

"The symbolism might have worked—had her father known about it, or if they were counting on one of us telling him."

"But this body's mutilations go way past what you described," Dr. Lavery said. "Somebody wanted to make sure they removed every piece of the vital organs."

"You're saying that someone was making sure that duplicate samples couldn't be taken," Ella said.

"Yeah, that's exactly what I'm saying."

"So now we have to track down whoever did this," Blalock said, helping Dr. Lavery place the body in the bag.

Ella and Blalock helped Dr. Lavery bring the body up and load it into the back of Blalock's government van. "What can you possibly do with that body now, Doctor?" Ella asked.

"I can examine the muscles and skeletal system to determine if there was a physical injury or trauma that could have caused death. I'm also going to check and see if there are any minute sections of the organs still present. But if I were you, I wouldn't hold out any hope that I'll come up with a startling revelation."

As Blalock and Dr. Lavery drove away, Ella looked back at the grave—now covered with a piece of plywood so no one would fall in—lost in nightmarish thoughts. Then she turned and walked hurriedly to her Jeep.

As she drove back, vivid images of the corpse continued to flash through her mind. She wondered if whoever mutilated the body had more than one purpose. Maybe the person who did this was hoping it would be blamed on skinwalkers at the same time he was covering his tracks. Or it might have been one of the senator's men, acting under orders to sabotage any further investigation. But it also could have been a way to rattle her, to bring back old memories that would disrupt her thinking as well as the investigation.

Ella knew she could be dealing with someone who hated her and her family, as well as someone who was trying to protect the senator. Unfortunately, that didn't do much to narrow the suspect list.

It was shortly after noon the following day when Ella got a call from Blalock. "Despite the way the body was torn apart, Dr. Lavery was able to determine a few things. There were no broken bones or evidence of trauma severe enough to have caused Angelina Yellowhair's death. So, the case is still open."

"Have you told the senator?"

"Oh yeah. There was this silence at first, then he went ballistic. He claimed that Carolyn Roanhorse was responsible for desecrating his daughter's body, and insisted that the evidence points to her."

"What evidence?"

"Dr. Roanhorse would have known about Navajo lore. He claimed she'd tried to mislead us all, while wiping out evidence of her own incompetence."

"That's total garbage. We wouldn't have exhumed at all unless Yellowhair had pushed us into it," Ella argued.

"I pointed that out. I also checked on a few other things, including having Dr. Roanhorse view Lavery's photos. She was horrified. The body didn't leave her office torn up that way. She has photos of her own to prove that. It turns out, the mortician who took care of the body was from Farmington. He corroborates Dr. Roanhorse. The man said the body was intact when he placed it in the casket, and the organs had been placed back into the body cavity, which was then closed with those staples they use. So whoever took the organs removed them after the corpse left the funeral parlor. Problem is, the driver who took the body from the church to the graveyard left the casket for the burial detail. He didn't wait to see it done. It sat there in the cemetery alone for a couple of hours."

"Who took care of burying it?"

"The preacher and five Anglo men. I've already talked to them. They all vouch for one another."

Ella exhaled softly. "Those incisions were crude. I can't imagine it taking very long to gut an already embalmed body."

"I brought all of this up with the senator. I don't think he heard half of it. He's pretty steamed that we're not arresting Dr. Roanhorse, despite the evidence and a witness verifying her work."

"Yeah, well, then he's got two problems."

"What do you mean?"

"Getting steamed and getting over it." As she hung up the receiver, Justine walked in. "I just came back from the mine. There's been some trouble over there again, scuffles breaking out and that sort of thing. Big Ed ordered increased patrols in the area."

The telephone rang and Ella picked up.

"You recognize my voice?" a man asked.

It was Billy Pete. "Of course."

"Then meet me at Kevin Tolino's place."

"Why there?"

"He's away, working, and it's out of the way. Nobody hangs around his property, either. He's too well connected. Nobody will see us there."

Ella stood up. "I'm going out to meet a contact at the place where Kevin Tolino is building his home. In the meantime, see if you can find out how Neskahi is doing. If he can talk to us, find out if there's anything he can tell us about what happened, what he ate or drank, who had access to it, etcetera. And we're going to need someone to fill in for him. Ask the chief for a recommendation. Since he's the one who told me I could add to my team, he may be more inclined to give us the extra help. I don't think we have much of a chance of actually getting anyone, not with these increased patrols, but it won't hurt to ask."

Ella was well outside Shiprock when she spotted a van several hundred yards behind her on the all but deserted highway. It wasn't Billy Pete's vehicle: He drove a pickup. As Ella watched, the van matched her speed, staying with her whether she slowed down or sped up. Ella turned up a dirt road, then drove cross country, wanting to see if the van would follow. It stayed well back, but remained on her tail, the dust that rose up high into the air giving it away.

Ella picked up her cellular to contact Justine. Too many people nowadays had radio scanners. "I need backup," she said, giving her assistant a rundown. "I think my contact set me up. Where are you?"

"I was on my way to the medical center to talk to the sergeant, so I'm not too far behind you."

"Do you remember the long dirt track that leads into an open field about three miles west of the high school? It was going to be a housing development area, but it never happened."

"Yeah. I know exactly where you're talking about."

"That's where I'm at. There's a canyon just ahead that will give me a place of concealment to turn around and come straight back at this van. I'm going to turn the tables."

"I'll block the way out if the van decides to make a run for it."

Ella continued on, keeping one eye on the vehicle behind her. It was still hanging back, like someone experienced in surveillance tailing. She headed up the canyon, knowing Justine wouldn't be far behind. Ella pressed the Jeep for more speed the minute she hit the sandy soil that would give her the advantage. Once out of sight of the van, she skidded into a one-hundred-and-eighty-degree turn, and started back toward where she'd last seen the van.

"Do you have a visual on them?" Ella asked Justine when she emerged from the canyon without confronting the vehicle.

"I'm turning down the track now. I can see it ahead. But it's stationary. They never followed you into the canyon."

Ella frowned. It was smart of them not to follow blindly, but stopping didn't make any sense either. That could mean trouble. "Is anyone still inside the vehicle?"

"Not that I can see, but they have tinted windows. I'll go in on foot for a closer look."

Ella's chest tightened, dread filling her so completely it was as if her blood had suddenly frozen. "No! Hold your position."

"At least let me drive in closer."

"No. Consider that an order."

"All right. I'll just block the track and make it more difficult for them to try to take off."

Ella drew closer, parked sideways on the road, then took a pair of binoculars out of the glove compartment. She focused on the vehicle ahead, but the tinted windows made it impossible to see anything inside. She searched the surrounding terrain, but couldn't see where anyone could be hiding in ambush.

As a breeze blew against her, she felt a chill and realized her body was bathed in sweat. Something was wrong, very wrong. She tried to analyze everything. She could see no driver or passengers. It was possible they'd jumped out and were hiding in a nearby gully. With the dry, hard-packed ground, it would be difficult to track them, and there were thousands of places in the surrounding desert they could use to conceal an ambush. She glanced around, searching for anything that would give her some answers.

"We can't just sit around forever," Justine said, using the radio.

Ella picked up her mike. "I know. Give me a minute to put on my kevlar vest. You do the same. Then order them to come out with their hands up. If they don't respond, we'll move in. You'll cover me, but be alert to an ambush from behind cover."

She heard Justine blare the order. Five minutes later, there was still no sign of movement in or around the van. Gun in hand, Ella circled around, planning to approach from the rear. With no back facing windows, anyone inside could only use the outside mirrors to keep watch. Her skin felt as if electric currents were traveling over it, not painful, but pushing her nerves to the very edge of awareness. She listened and watched as she crept forward, but the van looked deserted.

Ella saw Justine come out from cover briefly, shotgun in hand, to protect her from anyone trying to exit the van. Ella continued, placing herself so she couldn't see either of the van's side mirrors. That meant they couldn't see her either. She was about ten yards away, when she decided to halt and wait for a moment. Suddenly the van blew apart, and a hot wall of air hurled her to the ground with a wicked thump. The air shrieked as bits of metal flew overhead in every direction.

Ella felt as if a wrecking ball had slammed against her. Struggling to catch her breath, she remained prone, turning onto her belly to search behind her for Justine.

Her assistant was rising to her knees slowly, looking around for her shotgun, slightly dazed. "Whoa. Never done that before."

"At least we're both in one piece," Ella said, moving toward Justine to verify she was unharmed.

"Yeah, but I hurt all over, and I can barely hear you. What a noise."

"Same here."

They walked around the burning van. Flames shot out the holes where the windows used to be. The back doors had been blown clean off, and one lay about ten feet from where Ella had been knocked off her feet. It was smoking like a hot coal.

"I'll call to get Sam Pete out here. I want an expert opinion on this explosion. He can search the scene for bomb parts and whatever clues are left." Sam Pete was a distant relation of Billy Pete's, and he was also their entire bomb squad. "I want you to work with him on this," Ella said.

"No problem." Justine reached for her notebook and saw her right sleeve dripping with blood. "Uh-oh. I sprung a leak."

Justine pulled her tattered sleeve, exposing several small wounds oozing blood. Cubical pieces of glass had peppered her upper arm like shotgun pellets. "It's nothing. I caught a little flying glass, that's all. Lots of little cuts, which hurt like hell, but I'll live."

Unclipping the two-way radio from her belt, Ella called in the incident and added a 10-83, an officer-needs-help call. After hearing that the medical team would be unable to reach them for at least a half hour, Ella motioned to her car. "Come on. I'm taking you in. We're only twenty minutes away from the Medical Center. Fifteen, the way I drive."

As Ella raced down the highway, she spoke with Sam Pete about the bombing and arranged for him, Tache, and Ute to secure the site. "I want to know what kind of explosives were used, where the bomber got them, and how they were detonated. And I want the information yesterday."

"So what's new?" Sam answered. "I'll do my best."

Ella parked by the ER doors, and hurried inside with her young assistant. Dr. Natoni met them and led Justine away. Before Justine was even out of the room, Ella's cellular began to ring. Ella opened it up, wondering when she was going to have time to take a deep breath.

"I got the news on the notes." Ella recognized Blalock's staccatostyle reporting. "Nothing conclusive. The notes could have been written by a skilled forger, or Randall himself. The ink is from an ordinary ballpoint you can buy anywhere, same with the paper. One thing is certain. Since it has to be a forgery, we know the person who wrote it must have studied Randall's handwriting for a long time. Also, it's clear the person knows you, too.

"Now for another tip," he continued. "I learned that Noah Charley spent the night in the Holbrook, Arizona, jail on a disorderly conduct charge, and was released the day after he was reported missing here. It just showed up on my computer. I've put out a request to all law enforcement agencies in that area to detain Charley if anyone sees him."

"Thanks. Now let me update you." Ella told him about the explosion.

"Any idea who's responsible?"

"It's too soon, but I've sent our people to look over the van. I'll let you know more as soon as they report in."

Ella saw Justine as she walked out of the examining room. Her arm had been bandaged. She looked pale, but okay. "Hey, you need a ride home?"

"Uh-uh," Justine shook her head. "If my mother sees you, there's going to be trouble."

"You think she'll blame me because you got hurt?"

"She blamed you for my sprained ankle," Justine said, with a sheepish smile. "When I come in with this bandage, she's going to hit the ceiling. Better if you're not around. I'll call one of my brothers to pick me up. I'll be at work tomorrow, but I'm taking the rest of today off. Okay with you?"

"Take whatever time you need."

"I had expected to go right back to work today. But I needed a couple of stitches and they gave me a painkiller. Now, my mind really feels fuzzy."

"Okay, then. I'll get back to the station and report this mess to Big Ed. He's going to want to know about this as quickly as possible."

"There's a report on your desk about that bottle of furosemide that you found in the trash downstairs. There were no prints on it whatsoever. It had been wiped clean."

"Thanks." That meant someone had added the poison to Neskahi's coffee at the hospital. She'd have to question Neskahi to find out who'd had the opportunity. Her cellular rang again. As she heard Big Ed's voice, Ella gave Justine a weary smile. "I'm on my way in right now, Chief."

Ella stopped by her office before going to see the boss. She hadn't had a minute to even gather her thoughts, and to make matters even worse, she hadn't made it to her meeting with Billy Pete either. There was no telling how he'd take that, or when he'd reschedule. She wanted to question him about setting her up, too.

As she dropped into her seat, she saw an envelope from the state crime lab on the desk. Ella opened it and found the test results on the second set of fluid and tissue samples Carolyn had taken from Angelina's body. The report confirmed that the senator's daughter had been under the influence of peyote, and that she'd died from jimsonweed poisoning. Carolyn's findings were completely supported.

Angelina's ability to maneuver the car safely while she was hallucinating or having seizures would have been minimal, at best. It was a wonder that she hadn't died from a wreck before the poison had taken full effect.

Ella suspected *that* had been the killer's intent all along. In New Mexico, if a person died in an automobile accident, and physical trauma was extensive, an autopsy was not usually performed. If no one had witnessed Angelina's erratic driving and if her injuries had been more pronounced, the murder would have probably gone down in the reports as just another highway fatality.

Ella took the report with her into Big Ed's office. He glanced up as she went in, then leaned back in his massive chair. "You're a disaster area when it comes to tribal vehicles, Shorty."

"My Jeep wasn't damaged this time," she protested, "though it still needs some paint touched up."

"Yeah, well, the van that blew up was a tribal vehicle that had been reported stolen two days ago."

"Anything on the source of the explosives?"

"Sam Pete recovered traces of packaging material and explosive residue that indicated it's the same type and brand of low explosives used by the mine—ammonium nitrate."

"I figured things would lead there, sooner or later."

"Have you got something for me, something tangible I can present to the politicians who are crawling all over this department?"

"Good news, and bad—I suppose." Ella told Big Ed about the state lab confirming Carolyn's autopsy results, but also had to point out the poison in Neskahi's coffee cup.

"But we still don't have evidence to tie to a particular suspect."

"I'm working on it, but I'm not going to insult your intelligence by making promises I can't keep. I'm one man short, and that's not making things any easier. Neskahi will be out for another week, at least. And I can't see him going back on this case and working long hours even after he reports back in."

"I can't spare any other officers right now. I've had to increase patrols around the mine, and I've got to keep my units as visible as possible."

"I know."

"And you haven't heard the worst of it." Big Ed rubbed his whiskerless chin. Like most Navajos, he didn't have to worry about five o'clock shadow. "The M.E. is under fire again."

She felt her heart sink. "What now?"

"It seems that people have begun getting sick in droves after visits from Dr. Roanhorse and her medical team. Word is spreading like wildfire that the doctor carries the *chindi*, and that evil follows her. That poison in the coffee cup isn't going to help change anybody's mind either."

EIGHTEEN

———— ✖ ✖ ✖ ————

Ella was on her way to the hospital to talk to Carolyn personally when her cellular telephone rang. Annoyed with its incessant tone, she sighed, then answered it.

"This is me. I heard what happened."

She recognized Billy Pete's voice. "I'm sorry I missed our meeting. When can we reschedule?"

"How about right now? Same place."

"I was on my way to the hospital, so I'm almost at the cutoff. I can be there in fifteen minutes. But it's past five. What if Kevin shows up?"

"He won't."

"How can you be so sure?"

"I checked."

Ella drove to the prearranged spot, watching carefully. She wasn't sure Billy hadn't set her up before so she was going to be extra cautious this time. She wanted to get whatever information Billy had for her if he really was being honest, but she was also eager to talk to Carolyn. Ella was determined to find out once and for all what was at the root of the problem between the senator and her friend. It was time to get tough with her friend.

Ella slowed down as she turned up the dirt track that led to

Tolino's. As she drove up, Billy Pete came out from cover and stood by Kevin's loafing shed, two cans in his hand.

She got out of the Jeep slowly, and glanced around. It didn't feel like a trap, but after all she'd been through, she decided a little caution could go a long ways.

"You were warned to stay out of it," Billy said, coming to join her. "Now you see why. Here, have a soft drink." He tossed her a can.

Ella caught it in midair. "What's going on, Billy? Blowing up that tribal vehicle makes no sense."

"Unless you'd gone up with it."

"Was that the intent? I wondered for a while if you had set me up, you know."

"Why would I do that?" He shook his head. "We heard rumors that The Brotherhood wanted you sidelined, but we also knew that they couldn't touch you. You've got ways of knowing things. Most Navajos around here have heard of your family's skills."

"In my case, it's called cop training."

He shrugged. "Doesn't matter what you call it, does it? You're okay, just like we knew you would be."

She pulled back the lift tab, and leaned against a boulder. "Okay. So you guys figured I didn't need a warning. What else is happening. Why *did* you call me?"

"We've got trouble. One of our Navajo drivers at the mine broke his leg working a green horse. That alone wouldn't have mattered much, except that they replaced him with an Anglo."

"Why not a Navajo? Surely they had plenty of applicants for that job."

"They did, but the mine people claim that Joe Bragg had his application on record for the longest time, and that he was qualified. They hired him. He's been on the job only two days, and is already creating a ton of trouble. He's siding with the Anglos, and holds to The Brotherhood's party line that the tribe shouldn't give preferential treatment based on race for reservation jobs."

Ella considered what he was saying. "You're saying that Joe

Bragg is a candidate for The Brotherhood, and our one lead to identifying the others?"

"Yes, *if* you can keep up with him. We've tried, but he's lost us every time. He's good, which makes us suspect he's got some kind of training. Maybe he was in Special Forces or something."

"I'll look into it."

Billy glanced around. "You know, you're lucky to have Tolino as a neighbor. Nobody will harm your place or your mom with him around."

"Why do you say that? You mentioned he was well connected. What exactly did you mean?"

Billy looked incredulously at her. "You know Tolino is from the same clan as our Tribal President. He's also one of the top defense attorneys our tribe has, maybe the best. Nobody wants him as an enemy. Who knows when we'll need him?"

"Is that all?" She had a feeling Billy was holding something back.

Billy frowned. "That's all I know for sure."

"Okay. What else do you suspect?"

He shook his head and walked to his truck. "Forget it, I've said enough. You don't speculate when you're talking about Kevin Tolino."

Ella wasn't sure what to make of Tolino now. Instinct told her that anything that would deter troublemakers was a plus. But the question Billy Pete had raised preyed on her mind.

As Billy Pete sped away, Ella stared at the trail of dust rising in the air. The air smelled of sand, not sagebrush or damp soil. They needed rain desperately, but the weather forecasts were still predicting more sun and heat.

Ella got back into her Jeep and headed to the hospital, certain Carolyn would still be there. Carolyn would be trying hard to find an answer to why so many people were getting sick.

When Ella entered the morgue, she found Carolyn studying some medicine vials. "Hello there."

Carolyn turned around, resignation in her eyes. "You here to arrest me?"

"Don't be a jerk."

"It's not so far-fetched. Tribal public health people, pressured by Yellowhair I'm sure, came in to test my supplies of medicines. They suspected I'd contaminated them somehow. They found nothing, of course, but random samples are being sent to the CDC in Atlanta for further examination."

The afternoon newspaper lay open on Carolyn's desk. Senator Yellowhair had gone on record saying that Dr. Roanhorse should be suspended, pending a full investigation.

"Remember I told you that I was welcome in the outlying regions?" She saw Ella nod, and continued. "Well, these mysterious illnesses have changed all that. I'm now the Death Doctor out there, too, particularly since the illnesses only crop up after inoculation clinics I head. The other teams haven't had this problem. Of course, our senator is using this crisis to blast me out of everything I love."

"Why does he hate you so much? This fight is really getting nasty. Your personal life is now part of the case, and I have to know."

Carolyn moved away from the cabinet and sat down wearily in her leather chair. "You're not going to give up on this, are you?" Seeing Ella shake her head, she continued. "I met James many, many years ago back in college. He was hot stuff back then, so charismatic and all. He sure could turn heads."

Ella stared at her friend. To think of Carolyn as a lovestruck girl was a stretch even her imagination had difficulty with.

"I liked him a lot at first, but I always sensed there was something wrong about him. When he asked me out, I turned him down. He didn't take no for an answer, even back then, so he didn't give up easily. But, finally, he decided I wasn't worth the aggravation. Then, through a twist of fate, we ended up running against each other in the college senate election. At first, he treated it like a joke, but when I won things got nasty. He took every opportunity to make my term absolute hell. He undermined everything I tried to do. I used his own dirty tactics against him and managed to make him look like a jerk in front of a real public meeting. He's never forgiven me for that. It wasn't until recently, however, when our paths crossed again, that the resentment was rekindled."

"Tell me more about this problem at the inoculation clinics."

"It's not the vaccinations, per se, or the classic reactions a few people always have. Those meds are clean. And after the clinics, the ones who get sick don't all come down with the same thing. Some have flu symptoms, at other times we've seen some really nasty bacterial infections, unexplained fevers, and the like."

"When do the illnesses start?"

"Usually a day or two after we leave. At first there were just a few cases, here and there. We had one nasty bacterial infection that resulted in a death a while back, too, but nobody connected it to me or my team. Well, almost nobody. John Tso, that elderly medicine man, always claimed that it had something to do with us."

Ella remembered. "How do you explain what's happening? Why are people getting sick?"

"I don't know. But I can tell you this: If people stop coming to the inoculation clinics, things are going to get a lot worse. I'm really worried, not for myself as much as I am for those members of the tribe who will stay away from the med teams out of fear. Meningitis is a really nasty, dangerous illness." Carolyn paused, staring down at the floor, lost in thought. "I need your help, and they need your help."

Ella nodded slowly. "There's got to be a way to make people understand what's at stake if they *don't* get the shots."

"I have to leave tomorrow first thing. I'll be at the Chapter House near Standing Rock. We have a batch of vaccines that are certified clean of any kind of contamination. Why don't you come by? My team will hopefully be too busy to keep an eye out for whatever's behind this trouble, but maybe you could spot something. But check your E-Mail before you set out. I have a feeling that I'm going to be taken off active duty any day now. I've heard rumors about that around the hospital."

"How can they do that? There's no real evidence against you."

"I could have weathered this, had it not been in conjunction with the mess surrounding Angelina's tissue samples and Neskahi's poisoning."

Ella told her about the test results with Neskahi's coffee cup. "Do you have any idea how the furosemide got into that cup?" she had to ask.

Carolyn shook her head slowly. "I poured the coffee for both of us, then he got the urge to buy some cookies from the vending machine outside the pharmacy. While we went upstairs, I went to the storeroom to get some more cups. We'd used the last two."

"Did he take his coffee with him?" Ella asked.

"No, I don't think so. I left my cup there, too, after taking a sip."

"And you knew it was your cup later, because of the lipstick marks."

Carolyn nodded. "And so did the person who added the poison. I bet that's when it was done."

"Was Howard Lee around or Nelson Yellowhair?"

"Probably, but I don't recall for sure. There were others here, too, passing through. It was the end of a shift, and the elevator was constantly opening and closing. I have no idea who could have done it."

"Don't worry. The truth will come out. Then you'll have the satisfaction of seeing certain people eat their words."

"I'll look forward to that."

Ella drove home slowly, for a change. It had been a long, long day, but she still wasn't finished. She turned off at the road leading to her brother's home, and shifted down, avoiding the major holes that dotted the dirt track like craters on the surface of the moon.

As she approached Ella saw her sister-in-law bringing in their small herd of sheep. She waved to Loretta and continued to the house, hoping to catch Clifford. As she parked by his old pickup, she saw him talking to Kevin Tolino.

The two men were both tall and lean. Each had his own brand

of charisma but were different in other ways. She met Kevin's gaze, acknowledging him with a nod as she approached.

"I'd better be walking back," Kevin said, holding his bandaged hand close to his side.

"Let me get you the herbs you need for that cut," Clifford said. "I'll be just a minute."

As Clifford disappeared inside the hogan he'd constructed beside his home, Ella studied Kevin. "I hope you're not leaving on my account."

He smiled slowly. "No," he said softly. "If anything, you tempt me to stay. But I have work to do."

Ella felt a stirring she scarcely recognized, but was impossible to mistake. She glanced away and suppressed it. "Yeah, I know all about work responsibilities."

"So I've heard. Your brother says you work way too hard."

The realization that Clifford had been speaking to this man about her made Ella nervous both personally and professionally. She wasn't sure about Kevin, and she certainly didn't want her brother giving away information.

Clifford appeared before she could answer and handed Kevin the herbs. "Soak them first, then apply them as a poultice, held in place with a clean bandage. It'll take care of the pain. By tomorrow, the cut should be well on its way to being healed."

"I thank you." Kevin nodded to Ella, then walked back in the direction of his home.

"What happened?"

"He was trying to work on his home in the dark and slipped with a chisel. He'll be okay. It wasn't a serious injury. What brings you by, little sister?"

"First, tell me. Did he ask you about me, or did you volunteer information?"

Clifford's eyebrows rose and he smiled. "You're interested in him?"

"It's not that."

Clifford continued to smile. "Yes, it is."

"Stuff it. Answer my question."

"Kevin asked about you. He wanted to know how you liked living on the reservation after being on the outside. That's what he's facing now, that transition."

"What did you say?"

"The truth. You bury yourself in work so you never have time to think."

"Is that really how you see me?"

"I see you're a beautiful woman who tries very much to hide her femininity. To you, wanting or needing another is a sure sign of weakness."

"No, that's not true. I keep to myself because I've made my choice of a life's path, and I want to honor it. Not every road is open to us."

"This is an old argument and not why you're here," Clifford answered, deliberately not conceding.

Ella swallowed back her irritation. "I have an idea, and a favor I need to ask of you."

He waved her inside the hogan. "We can talk there while I mix some herbs for another patient."

Ella followed him inside, then sat down on the ground while he worked. "You know my friend, the doctor." Normally, she didn't hesitate to use names but, in here, it seemed out of place.

He nodded. "She's in a great deal of trouble."

"It's not just her anymore. She's being used, but in the end it's going to hurt a lot of people." She explained about the rash of illnesses.

"I don't know very much about the medical sciences. I don't believe in that way of healing. It seems to me that their failures are as spectacular as their triumphs."

"I'm not asking you to change your views, and nobody's forcing people to go to the inoculation clinics. But they shouldn't stay away because they fear that Carolyn or the med teams will bring illnesses."

"The illnesses are there, though. You said so yourself."

"It's not the medication, that was checked, and the ones that will be taken to Standing Rock tomorrow have been checked very carefully. Something is going on, something that is a very real threat. If people are getting sick it's not just coincidence. I don't know how it's being done, but I do know Carolyn isn't responsible."

"You think someone else is causing those illnesses."

"Yes, but I don't know how. That's why I want you there. If there's a contaminant someone is bringing in, that person is not just an enemy of Carolyn's, he's an enemy of the tribe."

"Like a skinwalker?"

"Maybe. If so, you're needed. If not, if it's strictly a matter of criminal activity, I'll handle it. But I need you there with me. People who go to the inoculation clinics are ones who have elected not to practice the Navajo way exclusively. They are caught in the middle between the old and the new. It would be a shame if we both let them down."

Clifford stared pensively at the bowl he was using to prepare an herbal mixture. Ella didn't interrupt him. She knew what she'd asked would be difficult for him.

"I don't like what is being done to your friend. And I will stand against anyone who uses fear to control our people. I'll be there and Loretta will come with me. We'll bring food. I won't take part in anything to do with their medicines or medications, but my presence there will show our people that they shouldn't be afraid."

Ella stood up. "I really appreciate your help in this. Carolyn will, too, though she may not say anything."

Clifford smiled slowly. "I don't expect her to. She is a lot like you, too proud for her own good."

Around 9:00 A.M. Ella drove through Standing Rock, which was about halfway between Coyote Canyon and Crownpoint. She'd passed through once as a child when her father had been preaching at a revival near Crownpoint, and all she remembered about Standing Rock were the school buildings north of the main road. She'd been driving for almost two hours, but the scenery, with the Zuni Mountains to the south, was fantastic.

When she pulled up next to the Chapter House, the medical team's van was already there. Howard Lee and the nurse, Judy

Lujan, were unloading medical supplies. She spotted her brother's pickup, too, and not long after saw Loretta with Julian, looking at a wagon and its team of horses.

Ella went inside and noted that only a few Navajo families had shown up. Carolyn walked up to meet her.

"Not exactly a horde of people, but they've been trickling in steadily since eight," she said.

"News travels more slowly out here, but it still travels."

"Your brother's presence has helped a lot. People know and trust him. If he's not concerned, they figure they shouldn't be either. He doesn't exactly recommend the vaccination, but neither does he tell them not to get it. When he's pressed, he says that nothing here is meant to hurt them and that they should not let fear stop them from doing whatever they feel is right."

"That's as much of a recommendation as he can give."

"I know, and I really do appreciate it. I'm going to thank him just as soon as I get a chance."

Loretta came in from the back holding Julian and walked up to them. "We're going to set out some food for anyone who is hungry. Would you like to help us, Sister-in-law?"

"Sure," Ella answered.

As Ella went to the back, two elderly Navajos were brought in by a young woman. Had Ella ventured a guess, she would have said that the younger relatives had probably driven their pickup to a remote hogan to persuade the older ones to come on in for the vaccination. The elderly couple looked at Clifford, seemed to recognize him and were heartened by his presence.

As Ella set out food she kept a close watch on the medical team. Out of the corner of her eye, she saw Clifford keeping a sharp lookout on the shelves where the medications were being stored, searching for trouble.

Shortly after two, Carolyn received a call on her cellular. Transmission was poor, as it was in many places on the Rez, and she went outside hoping to clear it up. When she came back into the Chapter House, her face was somber. "Pack up, people. It's time to head back."

Ella gave her a surprised look, but Carolyn shook her head.

As Howard and the nurses were packing things up, Ella pulled Carolyn into a hallway. "It's still early to be calling it a day. People could still be coming in."

"I've been ordered to return to the hospital and bring the team in with me. Pending an investigation, I'm restricted to my job as an M.E. The theory is—I can't kill the dead."

As Carolyn and her medical team drove away, Clifford came to speak with Ella. "I saw nothing unusual, little sister, though I sensed there was danger near."

"Same here. Let's see if there's a rash of illnesses showing up in a few days. That's all we can do for now."

"Where did your friend go?"

"She's been ordered back to the hospital and won't be doing any more fieldwork."

Ella gave Julian a hug, then walked to her own vehicle. As she drove back, she heard something shuffling on the floor. The sound was annoying, and she finally pulled over.

As Ella leaned to search the floorboards for whatever was making the sound, she remembered what it must be. She'd picked up her rubber-banded stack of mail earlier at the station, and taken it with her to read later. It must have fallen off the seat.

Picking the packet of mail up, she looked through the stack quickly and found a letter she wished she'd seen earlier. It was stamped and canceled, with that bar code mark post offices were using nowadays. There was no return address, but that wasn't what stopped her heart. Her name and address were written in a handwriting style identical to Randall Clah's.

Carefully opening the envelope by the edges, she recognized a familiar signature. She read the note, careful not to handle it except on the edges in the hope that the person passing himself off as Randall had grown careless and left a print.

The message was brief:

> *The Death Doctor has evil secrets she keeps*
> *even from her best friend.*
>
> *Randall*

Ella's hands began to shake. The post date on the envelope said it had been mailed only yesterday. Knowing the implications would create even more problems for Carolyn, she placed the note and envelope into an evidence pouch, then locked it in the glove compartment. For now, it would stay there.

NINETEEN

✖ ✖ ✖

When Ella entered the police station later that afternoon, people were talking in hushed tones and hurrying about. Something had happened.

Justine called out to Ella as she went past the lab doorway.

Ella noted her assistant's sober expression. "What happened here?"

"There was more trouble at the mine. Billy Pete and Tony Prentiss started a fight. We had to send five units over there before we could restore order."

"Neither of those two guys is that physically imposing. Why didn't the miners or the supervisors separate them?"

"They tried. The way I heard it, people who came to split them apart would end up becoming part of the fight. It looked like a major league baseball game after a batter got hit with a pitch. Everybody was in a pile, rolling around on the ground."

"Were Pete and Prentiss hauled in?"

"No. After all that, the mine decided not to press charges. If everybody involved had been arrested, they'd have lost most of two shifts. They just docked everyone a day's pay and sent the ones whose shift had finished home. I went over there myself to see if I could help out and, I've got to tell you, things are getting out of hand."

"Did you find out what triggered the fight?"

"The fight, if you can believe Raymond Nez, was started by Prentiss. Billy apparently had been saying that the Navajo workers should get together and run out any Anglo who showed support for either The Brotherhood or their views. Prentiss accused Billy of trying to find excuses to get rid of all the Anglos."

"And that started the fight?"

"No. Then Senator Yellowhair showed up. He came to tour the power plant and get some cooperation from both sides for a change. He was obviously out to counter some of the bad publicity he'd been getting. Unfortunately for him, trouble broke out among the workers who'd gathered for a look at him. He was suggesting that both factions 'set up a constructive dialogue' when Prentiss made some comment to Billy. Before long, it was a free for all. The senator's aides spirited him away. They didn't want voters associating him with a disturbance like that."

"I'll bet you the senator finds a way to convince the press he's all but sainted."

"Good guess. He gave a speech just a short time ago at the hospital, drawing attention to another hot topic. Since the threat of meningitis still exists, he's calling for all tribal resources to be readied. He knows that many of the traditionalists will resist getting shots, so he's asking that *hataaliis* be compensated by the tribe for doing Sings to protect those in affected areas who choose the Navajo Way. He says he wants The People to be safeguarded regardless of which path they choose to follow."

"Smart cookie. He's covering all the bases."

"He also made some calls to the governor's office and got two medical teams on loan from the state. They'll be going out to assist the tribe with the inoculation clinics."

"It's a great idea; I just wish I could believe his motives were pure. What a man," Ella added sarcastically. Ella had barely entered her office before the phone started ringing. It was Carolyn and she sounded scared.

"They're going to search my home and those of my team members. I need your help."

Ella dropped down into her chair. "If the officers don't have a properly executed search warrant, you don't have to consent."

"There's no search warrant, and the searchers aren't police of-ficers, they're bureaucrats from the hospital. This is Yellowhair's doing. He put pressure on the hospital administrator, and now he's demanding that we consent to having our homes searched for contaminants or microbes that might be causing the illnesses at the sites. Everyone else in my team has already consented. If I say no, it's not going to help matters, but I have the awful feel-ing I'm being set up again."

"Insist that we both be present when they search your home."

"Okay. Will you come right away?"

"I'll meet you at your trailer. Don't allow them to go in until I'm there."

Ella hurried out of her office and went to see Big Ed. His eye-brows rose as she explained the situation.

"What are you going to do? You're no lawyer."

"No, but I can make sure that nothing is planted there while they're searching. I figure I can say it's a professional courtesy, since Carolyn is this department's M.E. Or I can say that I want to make sure no legal evidence is compromised in the search. Which do you prefer?"

"Neither. Let Justine go."

"I have to be there, too. Someone's playing games, not just the senator with his grandstanding." She told him about the latest note that had been mailed to her. "That conveniently arrived in my office just before this hit the fan. It screams of a setup, don't you see?"

He nodded slowly. "Did you turn the envelope and note in for the FBI to go over?"

"Not yet."

"Don't screw around with this. Cover yourself every step of the way. Unless you do, they'll take you down and you'll burn right along with Dr. Roanhorse."

"Is that what you think is going to happen to Carolyn?"

He steepled his fingers and regarded her with a pensive frown. "I think things are going to get a lot worse before they get better, I'll tell you that."

Ella stopped at Justine's office and asked that she follow her to Carolyn's using her own vehicle.

As Ella drove, her thoughts were racing. Someone was out to destroy Carolyn. Had this happened at another time, she would have done her best to concentrate exclusively on that case, but right now too many other things were demanding her attention—life or death issues. Manpower in the department was stretched to the limit. Torn between friendship and duty, she felt her heart breaking into pieces.

Ella headed north, past the graffiti-covered mesa the gang kids had spray-painted recently, then turned west onto the dirt track that led to Carolyn's home. The road rapidly became nothing more than a stretch of vehicle trodden sage and desert shrubs. Carolyn's small trailer was sheltered from the elements by a low, juniper-covered hill. It was a rocky, canyon-ridden location, beautiful but not hospitable enough to appeal to anyone interested in raising melons or sheep.

But here, Carolyn had privacy, and no one to make her feel badly about what she did for a living. Ella understood Carolyn's reason, though she would have given anything if she could have made things different for her friend.

Two hospital administrators were standing next to the trailer as she and Justine pulled up. Both Navajo men were dressed in western-cut slacks, boots, and bolo ties, with matching bellies protruding over their tooled leather belts. One wore a heavy, silver-inlaid bracelet containing his wristwatch; the other wore no jewelry except for a massive turquoise ring.

Carolyn was sitting in a chair in the shade cast by the green canvas awning of her trailer home, waiting. She stood up as Ella approached.

"Thanks for coming." She glanced at Justine, and nodded.

"My name is Andrew Slowman," the eldest of the two said, coming forward. "I'm the Medical Center's chief administrator. This is my associate, Lonnie Hoskie. I really fail to see why your presence was necessary. This is an informal search, not a police matter. We're simply acting on behalf of the hospital."

"We all know you're here because an influential official has suggested such a search could yield evidence of a criminal nature. That's why we're here," Justine said. "We want to make sure any evidence you find holds up. What are you searching for anyway?"

"Anything from the hospital that shouldn't be here. Medical equipment or supplies, hospital records, things like that. But we'll be conducting the search. You'll just be in our way," Hoskie said.

"Tough. If this really is an informal search, done with the consent of Dr. Roanhorse, you're not going to be making up any rules about how it's done. It will be done by the book and the police will be present because that's the way Dr. Roanhorse wants it," Ella said, nodding to Carolyn.

Ella followed the men inside. As she glanced around she felt her heart sink. Some of the things here were not going to endear Carolyn to traditional Navajos, or even more fundamental Christians. She saw Lonnie Hoskie pick up a Ouija board from a shelf and look at it with obvious distaste. Ella shut her eyes and opened them again. She knew that Carolyn had kept the board as a memento from her college days, but she doubted that Hoskie was into nostalgia.

Hoskie turned around and gave Carolyn a long look. "Interesting tastes, Doctor."

"Her tastes are her own," Ella said, in quiet warning. "You probably just flip a coin to make *your* decisions. Respect her privacy. You're not here to pass judgment on her recreational material, but to search for potential contaminants."

Hoskie's face hardened, and he moved off to search a desk.

Andrew Slowman entered the bedroom, Justine at his heels. Ella positioned herself between the two rooms, watching both men. If it had been her searching, she would have checked the refrigerator first for biological agents. These two were obviously just businessmen on a fishing expedition, not scientists or experienced investigators.

Slowman went to the nightstand and opened the drawer.

Nothing seemed to interest him there, so he went to the closet. He lowered several shoe boxes that cluttered the top shelf, and put them down on the bed.

As he opened each, Ella realized that Carolyn seemed to store everything but shoes inside the shoe boxes. Check registers, old photos, and product warranties occupied the boxes. One box, however, actually did contain a pair of white sneakers. Giving up, he moved to the small writing desk and began to search the top drawer. He pulled out a worn tarot deck, then held it up to Ella. "I don't think we'd find many of these on our land."

"I've never counted. Have you?"

He shrugged, then returned to the kitchen where he finally looked inside the refrigerator and cupboards. The man must have finally remembered what he was supposed to be looking for. Hoskie was in the living room searching the bookcase, removing books and shaking them out one by one. As he took a handful of medical texts down from the shelf, he uncovered a pack of syringes in the space behind them.

Hoskie stopped, books still in hand, and glanced back at Slowman, who had just entered the room.

Slowman came over and took the pack down from the shelf, examining them closely. "These medical supplies must have come from the hospital. It's a brand we purchase."

"You can also find them in any doctor's office for a thousand miles. But, for the record, I didn't put them there," Carolyn said. "There's also nothing around here to inject. Think about it and you'll see it makes no sense. If I had stolen the syringes, would I have gone to the trouble of hiding them? I didn't know you were planning to search my place today, and you arrived here the same time I did. Had I been worried in general terms about them being found, I'd have put them some place other than my home. I have eight years of medical school training beyond college. I'm not stupid."

Slowman nodded. "Yes, that all makes sense, but the fact is they're here. How *do* you explain it?"

"Besides the obvious, that someone's out to frame me?" she countered waspishly. "Face it. I don't have to steal syringes like those. I could have written myself a prescription. Do you think I can't afford it on my salary? It's no munificent sum, that's true, but look around, I don't have big expenses."

"That doesn't explain their presence here."

"Oh, for cripes sakes! I just told you that I can't explain their presence because I didn't bring them here. What part of 'I didn't do it' don't you understand?"

Ella stepped in front of her friend. When Carolyn got truly ticked off, there was no telling what would come out of her mouth. And Ella knew from experience that, under the circumstances, whatever did, would only make things worse.

"What do you want to do with those?" Justine challenged. "They're not evidence of anything you came here in search of, and legally they would be thrown out in a hearing. Those syringes are in sealed packets, so it's highly unlikely they could be contaminated."

"But they could be used to contaminate medications," Slowman said.

Carolyn rolled her eyes. "So could anything else, even a regular sewing needle, you nitwit! Use your brains. Surely you have some, after all you are the hospital administrator. Of course, it's possible you got your job by kissing butts. Your lips do look a little chapped."

Ella covered her face with one hand, took a deep breath, then diverted Slowman, who was giving Carolyn a venomous stare. "As the officer said, that's not the kind of evidence you came here to find. Your search has been unsuccessful. It's time for you to leave."

Andrew Slowman met Ella's gaze. "I wasn't aware that our tribal police department always fought so vehemently for the rights of suspects."

"She's not a suspect, not based on the information you have uncovered," Ella answered, in a deceptively calm voice. "And remember, this is *not* a police matter—your words."

"If she isn't currently the target of a police investigation, then maybe it is *she* who has friends open to persuasion," Slowman baited.

Ella stared back at him, willing herself not to react. "You're finished here, so it's time you went back and made your report." She gave him a puzzled look. "Which brings me to an interesting point. Who will you report to? Senator Yellowhair?"

Slowman's face clouded. "He's one of many."

"Yes, no doubt, at your actual level of authority. The higher your position, the fewer people you account to."

Carolyn chuckled.

Slowman took the syringes from the bookshelf and dropped them into a paper sack. "We'll be in touch, Dr. Roanhorse. Don't bother coming back to work. Until this matter is settled, you may consider yourself on suspension."

Ella and Justine walked outside with them and waited until the men drove away.

"I'm going back to the office now," Justine said when they were out of sight. "I'll let Big Ed know what went down here."

"Thanks."

Carolyn was putting books back on the shelf when Ella went back inside.

"You should have kept your mouth shut," Ella said.

"It wouldn't have made any difference. Once they found those syringes, I knew they would put me on suspension. Besides, Slowman's an ass."

"Maybe, but you really shouldn't go out of your way to antagonize people. You need some friends right now."

"I shouldn't have to suck up to people in the hope that they'll give me a fair shake. They won't, and besides, I'll hate myself afterward."

As Ella drove back into town she listened to the news on the radio. More cases of bacterial infections were popping up at all the sites Carolyn and her team had visited. Quarantines were being placed on affected areas.

Ella felt as though there was a hand squeezing her heart. Her best friend was being systematically destroyed, and there seemed to be nothing she could do to prevent it.

Then a thought dawned on her. Ella drove to the tribal newspaper's local office. If she could convince them to give Carolyn a fair shake, that would go a long way to helping her friend's image.

Ella walked inside and asked to see the editor-in-chief, Jaime Beyale. After a few minutes, Ella was invited to her office.

As Jaime saw Ella approach, she frowned instead of greeting Ella with her usual smile. "What are you doing here?"

"I was hoping we could talk," Ella said, wondering about her friend's uncharacteristic reaction. "What's the matter?"

"I don't want to be the piece of taffy the senator and you start pulling on."

"What's that mean? Is he pressuring you on something?"

"Of course. We're all under the gun here. Senator Yellowhair has control over the funds that support this paper. He put pressure on the tribal council, and they put pressure on us."

"The tribe is asking that you all take a position against Carolyn Roanhorse?"

"No, of course not. They'd never do that directly. But we will be running an article about the M.E. and the claims that are being made against her competency. It'll be fair, with criticism aimed at both sides. The piece will be out in tonight's edition, if you want to read it."

Ella studied her for a moment. "There's more, isn't there?"

Jaime sat back and gazed at Ella pensively. "I'm working on another article right now. It'll be out in a few days. I decided to look into the M.E.'s past, everything from her personal history to her professional record, and I've found some . . . shall we say, interesting things."

"Don't get coy. Give it to me straight," Ella snapped.

"Carolyn Roanhorse had a twin sister. The girl died in a fire caused by a faulty heater at their home. The children were alone when it happened, so only Carolyn knows why she was able to get her two brothers out—though their rooms were farther away—but not her sister."

"What exactly are you implying?" Ella asked, spitting out the words as if they were a rotted piñon nut.

"I'm not implying anything. I'm stating a fact."

"You know damn well what a story like that will do if you print it."

"Some people might, quite naturally, conclude that she's a skinwalker who paid the price. And that *is* a possibility, you know. The evidence against her so far—"

"Is circumstantial. There is not an ounce of actual, physical evidence." Ella spun Jaime's chair around, forcing the woman to look directly at her. "I'm not in the least bit impressed by innuendo, or the games the press likes to play with public figures. But Dr. Roanhorse is a private citizen, and I *will* make damn sure she knows she can sue you for libel if you step out of line. Clear?"

"Of course. But you realize that the way you're acting just supports the senator's allegations. Your friendship with Dr. Roanhorse clouds your judgment."

A choking anger almost engulfed Ella, but she managed to keep a lid on it. It was obvious that Jaime had already sold out to the senator. Wordlessly, she turned and went back out to her Jeep. Had she stayed, she knew she would have been far too tempted to do something that went along well with a charge of police brutality.

Ella drove down the highway, trying to gather her thoughts. Too many things were happening at once. Before she could figure out her next step, a call came over the radio.

"Chief Atcitty wants you to investigate a ten-thirty-eight at the Medical Center. What's your ETA?" the dispatcher asked.

The code for vandalism was clear enough, but what she couldn't figure out was why the chief had specifically wanted her to respond. "Thirty minutes. Enroute now."

"Ten-four."

When her cellular rang, she wasn't surprised to hear the chief's voice. "Tread carefully with this one, Shorty. Our M.E.'s personal car was vandalized at the center."

"What was she doing there? She's been suspended."

"Ask her."

"Count on it."

"The evening paper's out. Have you seen it?"

"No, but I was told that a story weighing the M.E.'s competency was coming out. I was assured it would be fair."

"Yeah, that story was quite objective, but the sidebar on the M.E.'s personal life wasn't. And it's only part one."

"That wasn't supposed to be appearing tonight—" Ella clamped her mouth shut. Jaime had obviously lied, suspecting that Ella had been in no mood to hear the truth. "The story about her brothers and sister. Is that there?"

"It tells briefly about a childhood fire that claimed the life of her twin, but not the circumstances. That is supposed to be revealed in tomorrow's edition."

"Thanks for letting me know, Chief."

Things were getting worse and worse. For the first time in a long time, she felt inadequate. Her best just wasn't enough. No matter how hard she tried, she wasn't uncovering the answers that so many were counting on her to find.

She brushed that thought aside firmly. This was no time to start feeling sorry for herself. If Ella knew one thing about herself it was that she always got results because she never gave up on a case. That, more than her intuition, was what had made her such a good investigator.

Ella arrived at the medical center and drove to the back lot where Carolyn usually parked. She saw her friend there, leaning against her pickup door.

Ella parked, then approached. Carolyn gestured to the flat tires and busted windshield. "Some farewell gift. Most people get a watch when they're forced out. I get this."

Ella studied the damage. There wasn't much in the way of obvious clues. "When did this happen, and what were you doing here at the hospital?"

"I came to get some personal things from my desk, you know, poison, voodoo dolls, and black candles. I went in, picked up my stuff, and when I came out this is what I found."

"I can make out a report, but there's not going to be much we can do about it. I'll have an officer check with security to see if anyone saw or heard the vandal."

"Thanks. I need this on the record so I can file a claim with my insurance."

Ella wrote it up and took some photographs as documentation. "Let me give you a ride home, then you can call a garage and have someone come over and fix the tires. You and I need to talk."

"You mean about the newspaper story?"

"You've seen it, then?"

She nodded. "When I walked into the morgue, Howard Lee was reading it aloud to Nelson Yellowhair."

"Who's going to take your place as M.E?"

"Nobody, as far as I know. But that's the tribe's problem now."

The weight of responsibility hung heavily on Ella's shoulders. "I'm going to find answers, but until I do you're in danger."

"Danger? Why? I've lost my job. I don't pose a threat to anyone now."

"Don't kid yourself. That newspaper article is going to make people think you're either a skinwalker, or have strong connections to them. You're going to be an easy scapegoat."

Carolyn leaned back against the headrest. "I hadn't thought of that, but you may be right. As I was walking down the hall at the hospital I heard my new nickname. I'm the *chindi* doctor now. Charming, don't you think?"

Ella heard the pain in her friend's voice, though the casual tone had been meant to disguise it. Sorrow wrapped itself around her. "I'm really sorry this is happening to you. I know how much your job means to you."

Carolyn covered her face with one hand, then stared out into the darkness. "It's a real mess, I'll say that."

"There's something that's bugging me . . . " Ella said.

"Why I didn't get my sister out?"

"No, of course not."

"Admit it, you're curious."

"I wondered about it, but I know you must have had a good reason."

"I did," she said quietly. "I was only fifteen, but I remember it like yesterday. I'd been sitting at the kitchen table having a late-night snack, waiting for my parents to return. They had gone to the trading post for groceries and were overdue. I saw smoke filling the hallway that led to the bedrooms. By the time I got out of my chair and started yelling, flames had erupted from the heater further down the hall. I got to the boys, since their room was on my side of the fire. But I was never able to reach Anna, who was sleeping in the back room. The flames were in my way and there was no window where she was."

Carolyn closed her eyes and said nothing for several long moments. "You know what they say about the bond between twins? It was that way for me and Anna. We were really close."

"I'm sorry, Carolyn, I really am."

Carolyn sat up and wiped a tear from her face. "It was a long time ago," she said, her voice firm. "What I resent is having people use it against me in this way."

"If I could have stopped it I would have."

"I know that."

"But there's something weird about the timing for this newspaper story," Ella said. "The latest note I got from the person claiming to be Randall Clah was a warning that you had many secrets. That was only a little more than a day before this story came out in the newspaper. My question is, who knew about your past?"

"It happened over twenty years ago, but everyone around knew back then. There are no secrets on the Rez. I'm just glad my brothers are in the military and not here. At least I don't have to worry that they'll be hurt by this."

"If the story was common knowledge, it couldn't have been easy for you as a kid growing up here."

"It wasn't. The same rumors flew around then. But we lived in an isolated area. We didn't have many neighbors and only rarely did we see other relatives and members of our clan."

Ella parked the Jeep next to Carolyn's trailer. "Did you go to the boarding school in Holbrook?"

"Yes. And as far as I was concerned it was a great place. Nobody knew me there." Carolyn pushed open the door. "Hey, why don't you come in and have something cold to drink with me?"

Ella might have said no with all the work she had to do, except that she sensed how badly her friend needed company. "Sounds good."

Ella walked inside. The room had been restored to order and a huge bouquet of flowers now adorned the desk at the far corner.

Carolyn smiled wryly. "I got them for myself. I needed a pick-me-up."

"I was wondering if Dr. Lavery had contacted you."

Carolyn smiled widely. "How *do* you do that?"

Ella chuckled. "So, he has been in touch. I thought you two might have met before, being M.E.s and all."

"Sometimes I wonder if you do have powers."

"You're evading."

Carolyn laughed. "Yeah, he called. He's been very nice and supportive, too. We met last year at a symposium."

"Maybe he just likes you."

"No, he's not interested in me in that way. But it feels good when there's someone else in my own field who I can discuss business with."

Ella stiffened suddenly, her skin prickling. "Do you hear it?"

"What?" Carolyn listened for a moment, then shrugged. "There's no one around here for miles."

Ella peered out the side of the curtain as Carolyn poured soft drinks into two glasses. "Someone's out there," Ella said.

She started toward the door, when the window behind her exploded inward, sending a shower of glass into the room. As she dove to the floor, a second window shattered, cascading down in a clangor of tingling glass. Ella looked up and saw a growing pool of flames from each of the broken bottles. The smell of kerosene was unmistakable.

Reacting instantly, Ella grabbed Carolyn's arm and ran to the door, shoving it open and jumping out of the trailer.

Carolyn sputtered, wiping blood from her arms where the broken glass had cut her. "My home! Everything I own!"

She started to run back in, but Ella tackled her. "Nothing there is worth your life."

"No, listen! We can still get in. It hasn't reached my bedroom, or the study. I can grab my papers, and I may be able to save part of my trailer."

Carolyn scrambled to her feet and ran toward her open bedroom window. Ella started to go after her, but then turned and ran to her Jeep. As she grabbed the vehicle's small fire extinguisher, she called in the emergency.

Assured of help she hurried into the trailer after Carolyn. The flames were still confined to the living room. Carolyn was battling the flames there, fire extinguisher in hand. Ella joined in.

"I have an extinguisher in each room. A leftover from my childhood. When yours runs out, go get the other one from the study. It's on the back of the door."

Ella and Carolyn worked together to beat back the flames, but, after a short while, it was clear they were fighting a losing battle. The small extinguishers didn't have the capacity to deal with the intensity of the flames fueled by the kerosene Molotov cocktails.

"Let's get out of here," Ella choked. "The flames are spreading and the air is getting dangerous."

"I'm not leaving! This is my home."

Ella threw her empty fire extinguisher down and forced Carolyn toward the door. "It *was* your home. Don't let it become your grave."

Carolyn resisted, pushing Ella away. In a lightning fast move, Ella jabbed Carolyn right in the nose, stunning her. Then she pushed her dazed friend out of the burning trailer.

TWENTY

———— ✖ ✖ ✖ ————

Carolyn hit the ground wheezing, with blood streaming out of her nose. She pinched it hard, trying to stop the flow. "Thand's a lot!"

"I didn't break it," Ella said, then added, "I didn't, did I?"

"No, but id hurths and ids a meth." She looked back at her trailer. Flames were visible in every window now and all the contents, papers and everything, were lost. "My thome!"

Ella wiped soot from her eyes. "You'll find a new one."

"Id won'd be thimple. People won't thell to me."

Ella's heart ached for her friend. "You can always buy in Kirkland or Farmington if that happens. But I think you'll be able to cut a deal here. Not everyone will believe the stories."

"How did you dow? Did you thee thomebody?" Carolyn demanded.

"I heard someone. My hearing's acute."

Carolyn stopped pinching her nose and breathed slowly through her mouth. "It stopped bleeding, at least." Carolyn stared at the flames that licked at what was left of her trailer. "Fire and I are old enemies. I wonder if whoever did this thought of that. And here's another cheery thought. Now that I don't have a job, I can't sleep in my office either."

"No problem. You'll come home with me."

Carolyn shook her head. "That wouldn't be fair. I might be placing you and your mother in danger."

"My mother is already in danger, just by virtue of who our family is, and what we stand for. Look at it this way. If you come with me, you'd be doing us all a favor. I could count on you to watch over Mom for me."

Carolyn nodded, conceding the point. "I can do that. I wouldn't let anyone touch her, rest assured. They'd have to kill me first."

"Of course. I know that. My invitation isn't magnanimous at all. It's really very self-serving."

Ella searched the ground around the smoking trailer as they talked. There were footprints leading to and from the trailer and, as she neared the spot where a vehicle had been parked, she saw the by now familiar quarter-sized imprints on the ground. They didn't go up to the vehicle, however. They disappeared into a twisting canyon, where hiding places were almost unlimited. A chill traveled through her.

Carolyn came up from behind her. "What's wrong?"

Ella pointed to the tracks by pursing her lips, Navajo style. "What do you make of those?"

"Someone on a pogo stick?"

Ella smirked. "Not likely."

"A crutch?"

Ella nodded slowly. "Maybe. A thin crutch, though. I've been tossing the idea around in my head that it is more like a walking stick, or cane."

"If it is a person with a bum leg, where are the footprints?"

"Moccasins don't leave much of an imprint." Ella pointed to a small, flat indention about the size of a foot.

"Maybe someone is pressing bottle tops into the dirt to drive you crazy. Little things like that do, you know. If I was trying to confuse you, that's what I'd do."

Ella glanced up at her in surprise. "It *is* making me crazy."

"See? I bet I'm not the only one who knows you well enough to push the right buttons."

"But it's an important clue. I can't just ignore it."

"Then factor it in along with the tread marks, footprints, and notes you've been getting."

Ella heard vehicles coming up the dirt track, and when she glanced down the road, saw the flashing police lights. "That's my crime scene team. They'll search the trailer and entire area as soon as the fire department guys extinguish the fire."

It was another hour before the fire was completely out and the police team could enter the ruined structure, but at least the fire truck in the district had not been on call, so they'd been able to respond fairly quickly. Had it been later in the summer, they might not have received any response at all. All available pumpers would have been busy elsewhere. In a drought year, fires had a tendency to spread and go out of control. Even though the vegetation in this area of the Rez was sparse, the plants were very dry, and flames could travel quickly when fanned by the wind.

Fortunately, Carolyn's propane tank had not exploded, so most of the shell of the trailer was relatively intact. When the captain of the four-man fire-fighting unit gave them the all-clear, Justine and Ute moved in. Ella helped them search through the ruins of the trailer and recover what was left of the Molotov cocktails. They were tagged and bagged for further information.

Ralph Tache stayed outside, photographing the tire tracks and the quarter-sized imprints.

When the search was finished, Justine reported to Ella, and offered her condolences to Carolyn.

"Do you think you'll be able to find whoever did this?" Carolyn asked Justine. "Were there any clues at all?"

Justine looked at Carolyn. "We'll do our best, Doctor, but to be honest, our department has their hands full right now. It'll be a while before we have the time and manpower to start checking up on the people you'd consider your enemies."

Carolyn nodded. "Yeah, and that's a list that's growing with each passing minute, isn't it."

Ella gave Justine a hard look then glanced sympathetically at Carolyn. "We may not be able to give this our undivided attention right now, but we're not going to let it drop either."

Justine nodded in agreement, then moved away to rejoin her team.

"The police would rather forget all about this, you know."

"It's true your trailer isn't a top priority, despite your personal loss. But the assault on your life—and mine—is. Don't judge Justine too harshly. We're all overworked and tired of hitting our heads against the wall. But don't mistake weariness and frustration for indifference. We'll see this case through."

"Thanks for saying that. I needed to hear it."

As Ella's team cleared out, Carolyn sat on her one possession that had survived, a metal and nylon lawn chair that had been outside the trailer all along. "It cost all of five bucks at the flea market, but now it's all I have. That and my trashed pickup."

"No. You've got yourself and your medical degree. With that, you can recoup what you've lost. You're your own most valuable commodity."

"Thanks for the pep talk, old pal, but maybe you should start thinking of distancing yourself from me."

"I'm not sure who that comment insults more, you or me," Ella said flatly.

"It's expediency, nothing more, nothing less. I need you to investigate what's happening. The more we're linked together, the more of a shadow people will cast on your ability to remain objective. I have enough problems without having you, my best hope for a fair investigation, taken off this case."

"Unless Senator Yellowhair becomes the next chief of police, that won't happen. Big Ed has a lot of pride. He will *not* allow anyone to tell him how his department should be run. He also knows that I'll turn over every rock on this reservation until I find the people behind these crimes. I won't let him down, anymore than I'll let you down."

"Is that your pride talking, or confidence in your skill?" Carolyn countered.

"A bit of both," Ella conceded. "But in the final analysis, it all amounts to the same thing. I *will* get answers."

Ella drove Carolyn to her mother's home. Throughout the drive, a curious silence hung between them. Ella wasn't at all sure what her mother would say, or think, about having Carolyn as a semipermanent guest. But Ella was sure Rose would not embarrass either her or Carolyn by turning away Ella's friend in need. That assurance, for the moment, was enough.

Rose came out to the Jeep as soon as Ella drove up. Her features were shrouded with concern. "I heard what happened. It was on the radio." She smiled sympathetically at Carolyn. "I know what it's like to lose the irreplaceable to a fire," Rose said, reminding them without further explanation of the fire that had gutted Ella's room about a year ago. "Yours was even worse than the problem we had here, if the reports are true."

"There's nothing left of the trailer except a shell," Ella said.

"Then Dr. Roanhorse will stay with us until she can find a new home," Rose said firmly. "And share our clothes until she can buy some of her own." She turned to lead the way inside the house.

"That wasn't an invitation. It was more along the lines of an order," Ella said with a smile.

"I noticed," Carolyn answered. "But don't worry, I won't wear out my welcome."

"*I* wasn't worried. *You* were."

Rose fixed Carolyn and Ella a simple meal of tortillas layered with meat, cheese, and chile. "You have to eat something. You've been through a great deal tonight, and it's just the beginning."

Ella glanced up quickly. Her mother sometimes knew things before they happened, and Ella knew that her predictions were seldom wrong. "What do you mean, Mom?" she asked, her voice taut.

"Carolyn will have a difficult time finding a place to live. She will also have to fight for her career and her reputation, and her enemies will gain power if she allows herself to grow weary of the battle."

Carolyn looked at Ella, then at Rose. "I *am* tired of fighting, but I won't give up. I can't. Everything I am, and everything I love about my life, is on the line."

"When you get discouraged, you must not let others see that." Rose said. "Like wolves, they'll zero in on weakness."

"But here, I'm among friends," Carolyn said with obvious relief.

Rose smiled and nodded. "Here, you don't have to keep up appearances. We'll guard one another. Isn't that what my daughter suggested?"

Ella glanced at Carolyn, who was already looking at her in surprise. "I may have said . . . "

Rose held up a hand. "Don't bother to deny it. You forget, I know my daughter." She stood up and went to the sink.

Carolyn looked at Ella and opened her hands in a gesture of helplessness. "I didn't say anything," she mouthed.

Ella sighed and shrugged. "Get used to it," she whispered. "She does this a lot."

"I have some other news," Rose said, turning from the sink. "I went to a weaver's guild meeting today. You know, it's funny how women reveal things during our work and practice sessions. Everyone talks so freely. I guess it's just relaxing to weave."

"What did you find out, Mom?" Ella prodded gently.

"It's about the senator's daughter. Did you know that she was running around with a married man?"

"You *know* who her boyfriend was?" Ella sat up abruptly. "I've been trying to find out his name for days."

"I don't have a name for you. All I learned was that he was a married man."

"Who told you? Maybe I can ask her . . . "

"She doesn't know his name. If she did she would have told me."

"Mom, this is a police matter. I've got to ask her myself, to find out what else she might know."

"No," Rose answered firmly. "What we say during the meetings is confidential. It's an unwritten rule. That's what fosters the closeness between us. To violate that trust would cost me dearly. I wouldn't be welcome again." She met her daughter's eyes. "I don't want to lose that, I've lost too much in my life already. I need the companionship these women offer, and their friendship. Do you understand?"

"You're putting me in a terrible position," Ella said, sympathizing with her mother, yet torn by duty. She knew that her mother's visits with the other women in the community represented her recent attempts to build a new life of her own. It was a step in the right direction for Rose, but Ella's duty compelled her to keep pressing. "Maybe I should talk to all of them, and reason with them."

"If you go to talk to the members of the guild about this, they will not confide in you. And, from that point on, they will never speak freely to me again."

Ella weighed her options. "Mom, I really need the name of the boyfriend. There's got to be a way for you to help me."

Rose said nothing for several long moments. "Come to my next Plant Watchers meeting. It's tomorrow afternoon. Many of the same women will be there. Listen more than you speak and tread carefully with your questions and maybe they'll help you." Rose took the dishes away. "Why don't you get some sheets and a pillow from the hall closet, and then decide where you want your friend to sleep."

"Okay." Ella led Carolyn down the hall. "You can have my room."

"Absolutely not. You're doing enough putting me up. Tell me where you would have slept had I accepted, and I'll sleep there."

"I was going to sleep in my father's old study. It's now my office," she said, taking some bedding from the linen closet. "There's a sofa bed in there but, I warn you, it's lumpy and only slightly more comfortable than sleeping on the ground."

"That's my spot, then. You have a full day at work tomorrow."

"Normally I'd at least try to pretend I'm a good hostess and argue with you, but I'm too beat. And I know you're too stubborn to concede." She handed Carolyn the bedding. "Make yourself at home."

Ella woke up to the shrill ringing of the phone. She reached over to the nightstand and accidentally knocked the receiver to the floor. Grumbling, she pulled it up to the bed by the cord.

"Yes? Hello?"

"Wake up Shorty. We have a situation."

Ella sat up. She knew Big Ed well enough to know that a "situation" meant all hell was breaking loose. "What's the trouble, Chief?"

"The miners were finishing their shift, when half of them decided to tear the other half apart again. We have a few units there, but the fight keeps moving to other areas of the parking lot. All my available cops, on or off duty, are being ordered to respond."

"On my way."

"Watson, the Anglo supervisor who spoke to you, has been injured again, by the way."

"Where's he now?"

"In the infirmary. The mine has a full-time RN in addition to the part-time help from the Medical Center. Go talk to Watson as soon as you can. When people have a gripe they generally become more talkative."

"On my way," she said, pulling up her jeans as she cradled the receiver between her head and shoulder. "Who's in charge at the scene?"

"Sergeant Hobson."

Ella hung up. Arnold Hobson was a cop's cop. He was in his mid fifties, and came from a long line of law enforcement officials. Quite imposing, he resembled the trunk of an old cottonwood, gnarled, rough, and totally immovable. She couldn't think of anyone better to handle a civil disturbance.

Ella rushed out to her Jeep, checked her riot gear, then sped away. Carolyn and her mom were still sleeping. There seemed little point in waking them. They'd know she was out on duty once they saw the Jeep was gone.

Once on the main road, Ella flipped on the sirens, and sped toward the mine. She was completely alert, but she still wished she could have had at least one cup of coffee. Her mouth tasted like the bottom of a bird cage, which probably meant terminal halitosis. If anyone gave her any crap, she'd breathe on them.

She pulled to a stop behind the line of patrol cars. Four uniformed cops were trying to pull apart a group of at least twenty-five men. A breeze was blowing, and that made it difficult to use pepper gas. The apparent plan was to grab a combatant, handcuff him, then go back for another, but with two cops per man, it was difficult keeping up. Fists were flying and angry shouts filled the air. As she stepped out of the Jeep and hurried to put on her gear, she saw Justine pulling up.

When one of the Navajo men turned to attack an officer who already had his hands full, Ella jumped in, poking the man in the stomach and chest with the end of the baton, forcing him back.

Justine soon followed, fighting beside Ella. "Back off!" she snapped as a tall Anglo almost twice her weight approached. The man limped back, grabbing his knee where it had been struck sharply with the baton.

Ella moved to back Justine up, but before she could, Justine had the man on the ground, cuffed, and was looking around for another troublemaker.

Ella worked her baton overtime, separating the men one at a time, then cuffing them with tough nylon strips designed for that purpose and included in their riot gear. Soon her arms were aching and tired, and her body sore from all the buffeting and deflected blows she'd taken. At least now there were more men on the ground than standing up.

Like her, Justine remained on her feet. Sergeant Hobson was following Ella's lead with the temporary cuffs, then hauling troublemakers away, two at a time, and tossing them into the back of the police van.

"You're in fine form," Hobson said, as he slammed the doors of the van shut. "Glad to see I don't have to baby-sit you out here."

Ella glared at him. He was part of the old school, and this type of harassment wasn't uncommon. "Stuff it, Grandpa."

He grinned. "Good. You have a sense of humor instead of a chip on your shoulder."

Ella stared at him wordlessly, her hand gripping the baton tightly while she told herself that she would not use it against a fellow officer—no matter how well deserved.

"What triggered all this, Sergeant?" she snapped.

"Near as I can figure, one of the Anglo workers found someone had poured sugar into the gas tank of his truck. He blamed
one of the Navajo miners, and threw a punch. Everyone else
jumped in, and the free-for-all was too much for the two security
guards on duty."

Justine joined her. "Between the guards, who are really ticked
off I might add, and the rest of our guys, this situation is under
control now. Shall I help you question those in the infirmary?"

She nodded. "Let's go."

Ella waited for Howard Lee to check the bandage on Randy Watson's head. The infirmary was crammed, with some bandaged
miners sitting on the floor. Lee greeted her quickly, too busy to
do more than nod. As soon as he examined Watson, he moved
away. Watson stood, caught Ella's eye, and headed for the door.
Ella went with him, matching his strides down the hall. The calm,
logical man she'd spoken to before was now angry, struggling to
keep the lid screwed tight on his temper.

"The tribal police can't keep the peace here, that's painfully
clear. And the Anglos are having the worst of it. We have no protection of any kind. We're outnumbered, and on your ground, so
you've got the advantage. We're being discriminated against because we're white, even though we work for the tribe."

"Discrimination?" she shook her head. "It's more complicated than that. A pickup that belonged to an Anglo was ruined,
that's true, but a Navajo, maybe two, lost their lives a few days
ago. Right now, you're angry because you've got a bad back and
now someone whacked your skull, but I saw several Navajos in
the infirmary with injuries, too."

"I don't see the tribal police doing anything to protect anyone, except show up after the fact to arrest people. It's particularly bad for the Anglos. We're all being targeted. Vandalism is
rampant. The other day a half-dozen men had the sides of their
cars keyed or their headlights smashed. I had bags full of ashes
spread all over my brand new truck, inside and out. It was hell
to clean."

Ella was shocked. In the Navajo way, the power was never in

the item itself, but in what it represented. Spreading ashes during the day was said to be an insult to Sun, and left a trail for Poverty. It had been meant, in this case, as a curse. What bothered her most was that it was a stunt a skinwalker would have pulled. She was relieved when Watson didn't ask her any questions about it, and dismissed it as an act of vandalism.

"Ashes? When did that happen?"

"After daybreak yesterday. I was just back at work the first day since my accident, putting in some overtime to make up for the time when I was laid up. The purpose of all this, of course, is to force us to quit, because we can't afford to keep fixing what's broken or having their vehicles repaired constantly. You see that, don't you?"

"Have many Anglos quit?"

"Only a few have, but I'll tell you this. The rest of us who are still here won't quit. We have families to support, and we're too damn stubborn to allow anyone to run us out. Confrontations like the one outside today will happen more often because neither side will back down."

"Tell me who you think the members of The Brotherhood are."

"I don't know who they are, but even if I did, I wouldn't tell you now. As far as I'm concerned, the Anglo workers have to stand together. You take your allies as they come, you don't always choose them."

Ella questioned several other injured miners, but none of the interviews with them disturbed her as much as the one with Watson. Afterward, she met with Justine out by the front.

Justine's frown tipped off Ella long before she had said a word.

"Let's not talk here," Ella cautioned, aware that two office workers from the mine were standing near the windows.

Ella led Justine to where they'd left their vehicles. "Okay, now we can speak freely. What did you find out?"

Justine flexed her hand. Her knuckles were bruised and raw, a souvenir from the riot. "I think someone's manipulating the situation here, hoping to turn the miners against each other. I learned of one incident that sounded just plain crazy. One of the

Navajo workers was seen talking to an Anglo, just talking, mind you. That night several trucks came to his home, aimed their headlights into his windows, and he was warned to stay loyal to his own or face the consequences."

"Who was it?"

"I don't know. I couldn't get that name from anyone, though the incident was obviously common knowledge." Justine shook her head. "In a way, it sounds like the kind of rumor that is spread to enhance fear, rather than something that actually happened. But that's just my feeling."

"I think you're probably right on target with this." She recounted the incident with the ashes.

"You think it's a skinwalker playing tricks?" she asked in a whisper-soft voice.

"I think maybe someone is taking advantage of the problems that already exist here to divert us."

"Makes sense," Justine said. "I'm going back to the station to see if I can turn up anything from the remnants of the Molotov cocktails that started the fire at the M.E.'s trailer. Or is there something else you'd rather I worked on next?"

"No, go on with your plans. I'm going to stop by home, shower and eat breakfast, then I'll meet you at the office."

Ella headed home. Driving often helped her lose the edginess that went hand in hand with a tough case. This time, however, it wasn't helping. There was a cold, tight knot in the pit of her stomach. Life was becoming a lot more complicated on the reservation. Separate realities were intertwining. A world filled with facts and logic surrounded her at work. But there was another level, too. That one was fed by beliefs as old as the *Dineh* themselves. It was there that the skinwalkers thrived and preyed on fear. The threat she was facing proved just how cunning and lethal her adversaries were.

As Ella drove up to her mother's home, she saw her brother's truck parked there along with another she didn't recognize. Ella left her Jeep cautiously, but relaxed when she saw her mother casually picking herbs in her garden, accompanied by Clifford.

Ella went inside the house and found Sergeant Neskahi in the kitchen finishing one of her mother's breakfast burritos. "Well, hi there! What are you doing here? Should you even be up?"

"I'm not ready for active duty, but when I heard what happened to the M.E., I came over here with a proposition. Let me stick around the area and keep a watch on your home. If I just lay in bed I'm going to go crazy."

Ella smiled. She could understand the way he felt and his need to remain useful. "Okay. Where do you plan to set up your surveillance?"

"I figured I'd take my binoculars and keep watch from the top of the mesa out back. Once I see you're home for the night, I'll go."

"Deal. But it's going to get pretty hot out there. Are you sure you're up to it?"

"I'll take plenty of water. Don't give it another thought," Neskahi said, grabbing a slice of bread from the table and heading out the door.

Ella looked out the window and saw her mother and brother heading back inside. Seeing their somber expressions, she met them at the kitchen door. "What's going on?"

"My wife and son are ill. At first I didn't worry too much, but it started the night of the inoculation clinic."

"But they weren't immunized, were they?" Ella felt instantly guilty, knowing she'd pressured her brother into going.

Carolyn came into the kitchen. "Are you talking about the last vaccination clinic *I* was at?" She saw Clifford nod, and looked at Ella. "Neither your sister-in-law or her son were given any shots, or medication. I can assure you of that. I would have known."

"She's right," Clifford said. "That's why I wasn't concerned. But then my wife's fever went up, and my son got sick to his stomach. I will be doing a Sing over them. Now I have the herbs I need."

"Why not do all that, and also take them to the hospital?"

"They couldn't have anything that came from contaminated medication, but they could end up catching something at the Anglo hospital," Clifford said.

"My medications *weren't* contaminated," Carolyn replied firmly.

"It's possible someone switched just a few of the vials," Clifford said with a shrug.

"But they didn't come into contact with any of the vials—or anything else. And we were all watching for that type of thing, you and your sister included. It simply wasn't possible," Carolyn said.

"Unfortunately, it's something that would only take a second to accomplish. Just because we didn't catch anyone, doesn't mean it wasn't done. Let me see if I can demonstrate." He glanced around, opened the refrigerator, and pulled out two plums. "These are roughly the same size as your vials?"

Carolyn nodded. "More or less."

He marked one with a pen, set it down on the table, then walked away. "Keep in mind it wasn't this quiet at the clinic." He stopped and turned his head. "Oh, I forgot to tell you, little sister, our new neighbor came around and asked about you. He's heard of the trouble the police are having because of the pressure our senator is putting on your department. He said that he's got some pull of his own, and would help you if you needed it."

Clifford went back into the room and walked past the table on the way to the window. "I think that's him coming now."

Ella joined him. "Where?"

"Good trick," Carolyn said, pointing to the unmarked plum, which had replaced the other one at the table. "I was watching, but I never saw it happen."

Ella forced herself not to cringe. Kevin was nowhere in sight. He'd deliberately diverted her, using Tolino. "Smooth, big brother. Real smooth."

Clifford smiled, then glanced at Carolyn. "So you see, it scarcely takes any time at all."

"Not for a magician," Ella said, still annoyed that he'd tricked her.

"Or a skinwalker," Clifford said.

"Or a *hataalii*," Carolyn added with a wry smile.

"True," he conceded.

Ella glared at Carolyn. "A *hataalii*? That's below the belt."

"I wasn't suggesting your brother did this. But, without evidence, anything could be argued. One could say a medicine man's motive would be to give credence to the old values and push people into losing faith in the new. This may have nothing more to do with skinwalkers than it does with *hataaliis*. We don't even know for sure that any medicines were tainted."

"Point taken," Ella answered.

"I have to go tend to my family," Clifford said, heading out the door, Rose at his side.

Carolyn looked at Ella, her gaze unwavering. "Concentrate on the person who wants most to destroy me, not on phantoms. You'll have better luck with it that way."

"You think Yellowhair is behind what's happening?"

"He's the best candidate I can think of."

Ella heard the phone ringing and went to pick it up. Justine's voice was taut, so Ella steeled herself for bad news. "What is it?"

"One of the children who was inoculated died."

TWENTY-ONE
————— ✖ ✖ ✖ —————

Ella spoke to her assistant briefly, getting a full report, then went back into the kitchen to tell the others. It was odd how everyone always drifted into the kitchen here. It was definitely the heart of her mother's house.

"I have bad news. One of the children who was inoculated passed away."

"A reaction to the vaccine?" Carolyn's eyebrows arched.

"No, it was a severe bacterial infection. It looks like a strain of E. coli. The problem is the parents don't recall him eating any meat, much less undercooked hamburger or chicken. So the question is, where did he pick it up?"

"That couldn't have anything to do with the vaccine, or with the food served at the Chapter House. Hundreds of people ate that food."

"I know. I'll keep you posted." Ella grabbed her windbreaker from the hook at the back of the door. "I've got to get going. What are your plans for today?" she asked Carolyn.

"A car rental place in Farmington is going to give me a ride to get some wheels to use while my pickup is being repaired. They're expensive but give full service. Then I'm going to see about a new trailer. I asked your mother to go with me, but she said no. She's having her Plant Watchers group here today. Although she didn't say so, I think she's glad I won't be around."

Ella gave Carolyn a sympathetic smile, but said nothing. Her friend didn't need platitudes. She needed results. Ella decided right then to be at home when the Plant Watchers were there. Maybe she could learn something useful.

Ella was halfway to the police station when she received a call on her cellular. She was surprised when Jaime Beyale, the editor of the *Dineh Times*, identified herself.

"I'm sorry you were unhappy with our conversation yesterday," Jaime said.

"You were somewhat less than truthful," Ella snapped.

"We're all under pressure from someone. I didn't know how much information I should give you ahead of time."

"I suppose the rest of the story will be in tonight's paper."

"Yes, but I've got another headline that will bump the story about the M.E. onto page two. That's why I called you. I think you'll want to see it before it hits the stands."

"I've got a lot of things to handle this morning. Is it going to be worth my trip?"

"Yes. Trust me. You'll want to see this, particularly in view of the statement Dr. Roanhorse just made in response to the piece."

Ella cringed. She knew without being told, that Carolyn had once again opened her mouth and made things far worse. "I'll be there in thirty minutes."

It was nearly noon by the time she arrived at the paper. When Ella went into Jaime's office, the editor was eating a sandwich. "I got one for you, too," she said, gesturing to the paper plate at the end of her desk. "It's fried bologna. You used to like those back in school."

"Still do," Ella admitted, sitting down and picking up the sandwich. "What's up?" she asked, taking a bite. It wouldn't help if she stayed angry at Jaime, though now some of the trust she'd once had in the woman was gone.

Jaime slid an envelope over to her. "Don't worry about prints. Everyone has handled these, from the mail carriers to the people here in my office. The envelope arrived before I got here, and my staff was a bit overzealous."

Ella opened it and saw two grainy black-and-white photos of Senator Yellowhair. In one, he was being handed an envelope by a man in a wheelchair, whose face was nearly hidden in shadows. In the second, he was opening the envelope stuffed with bills. The background was so dark the surroundings couldn't be identified. "Do you know who the man with the senator is?" Ella asked.

"No, I don't. My staff called Senator Yellowhair and he insisted that we fax him the photo. We did, but he said he didn't recognize the man, and he just couldn't remember the incident. He urged us to investigate it, though. He says he doesn't want any allegations hanging over him when he's innocent of any wrongdoing."

"You said something about Carolyn making a statement?"

"We had called the M.E. to ask who she believed torched her home. She told us that the only real enemy she has is Senator Yellowhair. When we told her about the photos we'd received, she told us that she wouldn't be surprised to hear he was taking bribes, that crooked politicians usually do."

"You're not printing that, are you? It's nothing more than an opinion."

"We won't print it for now, but we are running these photos of the senator in the next issue. We also asked Senator Yellowhair to comment on the M.E.'s belief that he was behind the fire that claimed her home. He was outraged."

Ella stood up. "I need to take these photos in, you know that, right?"

"Yes, I've already had duplicates made." She slid a second envelope over to her. "And here's an extra set for you. Never let it be said we don't cooperate with the police."

Ella took the photos. "I'll get back to you if I find out who this Anglo is. Will you do the same for me?"

"No problem."

Ella walked out of the newspaper office with the envelope. She could imagine how Jaime's staff had reacted when they'd seen the photos and smelled a juicy story. The photos would be covered with prints, mostly from the newspaper staff, but she would still have Justine process them. Maybe a miracle would happen, and they'd find a clue that would lead them to whoever had sent them.

What bothered her most was the senator's reaction to the photos. It was simply too magnanimous of him to invite the staff at the paper to investigate. It made her believe that he knew precisely who the Anglo was, and was certain it would make him look really good when it all came out.

Ella met Justine at the lab a short while later. She handed her assistant the photos and explained. "I'll keep the duplicates for the time being. I want to show them to Blalock."

"We keep getting leads, but there's never enough time to process the new information before something else gets tossed at us."

"I know." Ella said, knowing how overworked they'd all been. "Anything else come up since we last spoke?"

"A few things. Another one of the kids who went to the inoculation clinic Dr. Roanhorse attended became sick. His parents finally took him to the Medical Center. The parents said that he hadn't been inoculated. They'd only been at the Chapter House for a few minutes. They'd stopped to pick up a sack of flour from another family there."

"Did he have any medication at all?"

"No, but his illness was caused by a similar strain of bacteria to the one that killed the other boy, only the infection wasn't as severe. He's going to be okay."

"Good. Keep on it. What else have you got?"

"The new truck driver who was recently hired at the mine, Joe Bragg, shot off his mouth again and Raymond Nez decided to shut it for him. Mine security guards were able to take care of things this time. They've been supplied with a particularly nasty spray similar to pepper gas and trained in how to use it effectively. The mine didn't press charges. I think they're hoping to minimize the incident by ignoring it."

"Get the driver's personnel files. I want to know more about him."

"I'll try. If I can't, I'll start a background check."

Ella led the way to her office, filling Justine in on what Rose had said about Angelina's boyfriend being married. "Has anything else on her boyfriend turned up yet?"

Justine shook her head. "The only lead we have is what you just told me."

"If the guy is married, that gives us a possible motive for murder, and also a possible lead to a suspect. If Angelina was pressing him to divorce his wife, for instance, he may have decided she was too much trouble to keep around. Or, the man's wife may have taken matters into her own hands. Some people say poison is a woman's weapon."

"Granted, but how are we going to follow up on this?"

"I want you to find out who, besides Bitah, was attending that Navajo Justice Church. Maybe one of the Navajo men attending was Angelina's boyfriend. The peyote had to come from somewhere. Get a court order to check all financial records with her name on them, too. I want everything that ties Angelina to her parents, the power plant, her boyfriend, and her friends."

"The senator is going to fight you tooth and nail on this."

"I know, so try to get the court order fast, before he knows what's happening."

"We haven't got a prayer of keeping it quiet for long. You realize that, right?"

"Yeah, that's why we've got to move quickly. While you're taking care of that, I'm going to try another avenue of information that may lead us to Angelina's boyfriend."

"What have you got in mind?"

"My mother reminded me that we've overlooked an important source—the women's groups. When they get together, they talk, and I'm ready to bet it's that talk that will lead us to the guy we need to find."

By the time Ella arrived home there were pickups parked all around the house, and two horses were grazing on the meager spring grasses.

Ella walked around the outside of the house and saw her

mother pointing out the different herbs in her garden to her guests, as another woman planted some seedlings. Ella waited, not wanting to interrupt.

The women were discussing the merits of salt brush to relieve fever and stomach pains when they became aware of Ella's presence. Mrs. Pioche, her mother's oldest friend, greeted her warmly.

"You should learn about these things, young lady." Mrs. Pioche gestured toward the plants with her cane. "The Plant People were put here for us to use as food and as medicine. Although Father Sky does the planting and brings us the clouds and the rains, there are fewer plants nowadays, so we have to cultivate them. Come, join us."

Ella went inside with the women and sat among them as they drank her mother's special herbal tea. As they spoke, she remembered the herbal remedies that had seen her through many childhood illnesses.

"The young don't see the importance of our ways anymore," Mrs. Pioche said sadly. "But maybe the terrible things that are happening now will help them find their way back."

"They don't respect our ways, so they bring on these terrible consequences," Lena Clani, an elderly woman said. "A long time ago we were told that the Holy People would become angry if we bothered the Sun or the Moon. They were lifted high by Wind and placed in the sky away from man, for a reason. Then men walked on the moon, and the Wind People got angry. We have more windstorms now, and more hurricanes and tornadoes. Still people don't listen."

"Our group is here to pass on knowledge, yet few want what we have to give," Mrs. Pioche complained. "We are the Plant Watchers and we have something important to share, but our young ones don't value it."

Ella listened for a long time before finally speaking. "I believe that a new time is coming when the knowledge you've protected will find its way to the right ears. But right now, we're facing danger from many sides. You hold the key to protecting us, though you don't know it."

"With our plants?" asked Mrs. Pioche.

"No, with another kind of knowledge, but it's just as crucial to the tribe. Will you help me stop the violence from escalating?"

"How can we help you?" Lena Clani asked.

"Women are the backbone of our tribe. That's the way it has always been. We talk, share our knowledge, and make things better for others. To break the cycle of violence I have to trace back certain events. What I need most right now, is the name of the senator's daughter's boyfriend."

"He was married," Mrs. Pioche said flatly. "That's why she kept him such a secret, even from her own family."

"I heard one of the women at the high school's parents group talking about that," Lena Clani said. "She won't talk to the police, I'm sure of that, but maybe I can talk to her for you. Nobody is threatened by a grandmother like me." She smiled.

Ella grinned. Lena was in her mid seventies, or maybe older. It was hard to tell sometimes, but her eyes were bright and alert. From what her mother had often told her about Lena, the woman still had the energy of a twenty-year-old.

"I'd appreciate the help. If you find it easier, tell my mother and she'll pass the information on to me."

"We will help you, but we want something in return," Lena said.

"All right," Ella conceded.

"We want you to learn all about our native plants. Open your mind to what we have to teach you."

Rose nodded. "Yes. The time will come when you will need that knowledge."

Ella felt a shudder travel up her spine. Her mother wasn't speaking idly. She could tell that from her tone. "What makes you say that?"

"The knowledge will benefit you," Rose repeated.

Ella didn't press. She knew that often her mother's predictions were based on feelings that were hard to explain. Having trusted her life to such inexplicable certainties many times in the past, Ella agreed. She could begin with her mother instructing her at home about what she grew in her garden. A little at a time was all she had room for in her life.

The women murmured together, obviously pleased by her response, and Rose looked relieved. Finished with the business she'd come to accomplish, Ella said good-bye to the group to return to work.

On her way back to the station, Ella decided it was time to pay Blalock a visit. She called him and arranged a meeting at his main office in Farmington.

Ella arrived at Blalock's office a short time later. His desk was all but buried beneath stacks of file folders.

"Come in. This is one helluva day. We had more cutbacks at the Bureau. My secretary's history, and I'm swamped with paperwork. Then again, maybe if I get behind enough, they'll see she wasn't a luxury, but a necessity, and let me rehire her. I've got a huge territory to cover."

Ella moved the papers stacked on the chair in front of his desk onto the floor, and sat down. "Have you turned up anything on The Brotherhood?"

"Nothing, and not for lack of trying. I've spoken to each and every Anglo at the mine more than once and run full background checks on all of them I could justify it for. The organization undoubtedly exists, but there's no paper trail to it, and nobody is talking."

"Well, I've got another lead I was hoping you could help me follow up. The newspaper got these photos anonymously," she said, handing them to him.

Blalock studied the photos. "Does Yellowhair know about this yet?"

"Yeah, he invited the papers to conduct a complete investigation. It's either a bluff, or he knows they'll find nothing but smoke."

"Any prints on the photos?"

"Justine's checking the original set. These are duplicates the paper gave me."

Blalock pulled a magnifying glass from his top drawer and studied details. "What's this little blob on the guy's lapel? The one in the wheelchair."

Ella took the magnifying glass from him. "Good eyes," she said. "Unfortunately, I have no idea what it could be."

"We may be able to blow up the print and get a clearer look."

"We'd have a larger view of it, but not necessarily clearer," she pointed out.

"It's worth a try. The images can be computer-enhanced to bring out details. There's a man in town who helps me with this sort of thing. He's as good as the FBI techs."

Ella rode with Blalock. It wasn't long before he parked in front of a large, Pueblo-style home just above the community college.

"This is it," Blalock announced.

Ella read the sign: JEFF RIVERS, PHOTOS FOR A LIFETIME OF MEMO-RIES. An arrow pointed to a windowless cottage at the back of the main house. Ella accompanied Blalock down the path.

A tall, brown-haired man with thick, tortoise-shell glasses looked up as they came into the small business office and display area. Architectural studies of businesses and homes filled one wall, another held landscapes from around the Southwest. Wooden shelves filled with photography books, cameras, and office supplies lined the third wall, framing a door.

Blalock explained what they needed and Ella noted the unmistakable eagerness on Rivers's face.

"I do love a challenge," he said. "Sit down. It won't take me too long."

Ella looked around the tiny office as the man disappeared through the far door into a back room. "He doesn't do a lot of commercial work, does he?" There were no family portraits or the usual school and yearbook gallery of shots that highlighted the walls of most area photo studios.

"He does work for *Architectural Quarterly* and for *Vistas Magazine,* as well as several other top-notch publications like those, but he doesn't have the personality or patience to attract the general public."

Jeff came out a short time later, and waved at them to come into what Ella had expected to be a darkroom. Instead, she found herself in a well-lighted workshop equipped with an expensive-looking computer, scanner, and several types of printers.

"I have a traditional darkroom, too, but photography is becoming highly technical nowadays, and a lot of advanced work is done with image processing on computers. This particular job is a perfect example of that. I scanned the photo, then ran the image through a program that brings out the details by stepping up the contrast in areas I select. Here's what I was able to come up with."

Jeff called her attention to a high quality image just coming out of a laser printer. "This is the best I could do, zeroing in on that pin."

Ella studied the shape. It reminded her of something, but she wasn't sure what.

Blalock stared at it for a long time, as if trying to force a memory.

"You guys don't recognize it, do you?" Jeff asked with a chuckle. "It's a service pin from a veterans group, guys. Jeez!" He walked to the outer office and returned with a small wooden box. "See?" He pulled a small lapel pin out. "This one belonged to my dad. I didn't get a lot from him after he died, but I did get this." He held it in his palm like it was the Hope diamond.

Ella looked at the pin, then back to the laser image. "Yes, the outline is the same, and the details seem to match up."

"That's what it is. I'm sure of it."

"Do you recognize the man in the photo?" Ella asked.

"No, but I don't belong to that organization myself."

After squaring the bill, Blalock and Ella returned to his car. Ella noticed Blalock's mood had darkened. "What's eating you?"

"That particular veteran's organization is highly respected, especially in this community. This doesn't look like a cover-up at all to me. In fact, I think the senator may be setting us all up to look like idiots."

"Yeah, I'm getting that feeling myself."

"You drive while I make a few calls, and see if I can get the address of their treasurer."

By the time they reached the end of the street, Blalock had

what he needed. He had Ella drive directly to a small office build-ing off Main Street. Before they went inside, he said, "Let me take the lead here."

"Why? You think you're more diplomatic?"

"I have jurisdiction, and in here we go by the book. The last thing I need is for a national organization like this one to file a complaint against me."

They found the treasurer, Henry Daniels, inside a small, two-room office. The sign at the front announced him as a CPA.

As they went inside and Blalock introduced himself and Ella, Daniels moved his wheelchair out from behind the desk and after a firm handshake, gestured for them to take a seat. "What can I do for you two officers?"

Ella looked at Blalock. Unless she missed her guess, this was the man in the photo.

Blalock passed the photo to him. "We're here on official busi-ness. What can you tell me about this?"

The man looked at the photo curiously. "What do you want to know? It was taken at our political rally last month."

"Rally?"

"We had a fund-raiser for the senator. He's been an absolute dynamo at the state legislature, lobbying for veterans' rights. We hosted a pancake breakfast fund-raiser for him, strictly working men and women at ten dollars a plate. That money came from the people who attended, and I had the honor of presenting it to him."

Daniels looked at her. "Is the tribe investigating this contri-bution? I assure you, I can get dozens of vets who'll be willing to testify that everything done there was above board and per-fectly legal. We even advertised on the radio."

"I don't doubt your word, Mr. Daniels," Ella assured the man, meeting his gaze. "I'm sorry for the bother, but we had to look into it. You see, someone sent copies of these photos to the tribal newspaper with the implication that something illegal was going on."

"Someone's obviously trying to make the senator look bad. This is an election year. I guess that explains why a reporter from the tribal paper called earlier and made an appointment to come see me."

At least they'd beaten the reporters to the answer, despite the fact that a newspaper employee had apparently managed to identify Daniels. "Thanks for your time."

"No problem, always glad to cooperate with law enforcement officers. Our organization thinks very highly of Senator Yellowhair. He's done a lot for us. He understands the nation owes its vets something for what they went through to protect our freedom."

Ella walked out with Blalock. "Senator Yellowhair engineered this; I'd bet the farm on it. Now, the next article that comes out about him will be nothing less than a glowing testimonial about how beloved he is."

After Blalock dropped her off by her Jeep, Ella thought about the photos a bit longer. It was amazing what photographs could do for an investigation. They could lead to answers, or lead down a false trail. Her thoughts drifted and circled. She was missing something. She could feel it. Slowly, a memory came unbidden into her thoughts.

Anderson had albums of snapshots taken at work, mostly of Navajo men, probably so he and The Brotherhood could identify "the enemy." She was trying to identify someone, too: Angelina's boyfriend. Furthermore, Angelina had been in the area near the mine when her car ran off the road. What if Angelina's boyfriend worked at the mine, and she had met him near there?

Ella picked up the phone and called Blalock. With the Bureau's juice, she could get a photo of every Navajo who'd ever punched a time clock at the power plant or mine in no time at all. With a full set to choose from, maybe the waitress at the country western bar would be able to ID Angelina's boyfriend.

When Ella arrived back at the station, Justine hurried to meet her. "I got the personnel file on the driver, Joe Bragg. There's nothing out of the ordinary about it. Everything checks."

Ella explained quickly about Blalock's efforts to get all available photos of the miners, then dropped down into her seat. "Any luck getting a court order for Angelina's bank records?"

"It's already been executed. Judge Goodluck is my grandfather," she smiled. "And I know for a fact he really dislikes Senator Yellowhair."

Ella smiled. "I knew you two were related, but I've never wanted to ask you to cut corners and go to him. Did we get a break?"

"Nothing more than we already knew." Justine grew somber. "Angelina's trust fund includes ownership of a company that has a lot of shares in the coal mine. Oh, and before I forget, you also had a call from Dr. Roanhorse."

"What's going on with her?" Ella asked.

"She's at your house right now, and said for you to call."

"Thanks." Ella picked up the telephone and dialed home. Her mother answered and handed the phone to Carolyn. "What's up?" Ella asked.

"I found a trailer in Farmington. They'll be setting it up next to where my old trailer stood. It'll be a fine home."

"I think it might be a bad idea right now for you to move anywhere that isolated. If you need to keep busy, focus on getting yourself a lawyer and forcing the hospital to reinstate you, rather than moving."

"I tried that," Carolyn answered, her voice suddenly weary. "But the tribal attorney I saw seems to be afraid of me, or maybe of our esteemed senator. I'm not sure which."

"Call Kevin Tolino. If I'm any judge of character, that guy won't back away. If anything, he'll thrive on the fight."

"I'll look into it," Carolyn said. "Your brother just came in. He wants to talk to you."

Clifford took the receiver from Carolyn. "Loretta and Julian are fine. I thought you'd want to know."

"Great! I'm really relieved to hear that! Would you mind if I stopped by your place and spoke to Loretta?"

"You can try, but she's still pretty angry. She thinks we all should have avoided the inoculation clinic."

Justine watched Ella, curiosity flickering in her gaze. "You think Loretta might know something?"

"I don't know, but she can be very observant. She thrives on details. You coming?"

"Sure."

Ella drove quickly, spurred by a feeling that she was finally getting close to some answers. "If we could only close one of these cases, I'd feel one hundred percent better. Of course, indications are that once we solve one, the others will break wide open, too."

"Do you think Senator Yellowhair is behind what's happening to Carolyn Roanhorse?" Justine asked.

"Not directly, no, but he's got his mitts in this somehow, I'll wager." Ella downshifted as they cut across country.

"Even Bitah's murder?"

"That I'm not so sure about, but who knows? If nothing else, I know the senator's holding back on us. When I can prove that, I'm going to come down on him like a ton of bricks, and see what shakes loose."

Thirty minutes later, Ella pulled up in front of her brother's home. Loretta was out front planting seeds in a redwood box.

"I'm glad to see that you're okay again," Ella said.

Loretta gave her a cold stare. "We wouldn't have been sick at all if we had stayed away from that blasted clinic. I trusted your judgment and look what it got me and my son!"

"How can you be sure your illness was connected to the clinic? You certainly didn't accept any medications from the medical staff, did you?"

"Of course not," she huffed.

"Then why are you convinced your illness started there? Did you or Julian eat anything while you were there?"

"No, we didn't."

"Then your accusation doesn't make sense. There couldn't have been anything contagious going around there, or more cases would have popped up."

"You're just defending your friend, the doctor."

"No, that's not true. I'm asking you to use your head."

Loretta stood up abruptly. "That's your problem. You're always analyzing! I don't know how or why we got sick, but we did, and it was awful. Poor Julian couldn't even keep juice down."

"So you caught a bug," Ella prodded, knowing she was incensing her sister-in-law, but also figuring that Loretta would try to justify her beliefs and perhaps then she'd get some information.

"You can be the most irritating person in the world. You know darned well my son and I are always healthy."

"Chance, then," Ella said with a shrug.

"Those medical people are around all kinds of sick people and are exposed to things they could easily pass on to someone else. And they're always so cold and impersonal! Well, all except that young man, Howard Lee. At least he acts human when he's dealing with The People."

Ella felt her heart start pounding. "The man is barely competent, and Carolyn says he's irresponsible." Ella suddenly remembered that Lee also worked as a medic at the mine, and felt a sudden chill.

"That woman is the cause of half her own problems. That assistant of hers was the best of the lot. He was trying hard to be nice. He took the time to talk to people, instead of treating them like sheep being dipped for insects. He even gave pieces of candy to some of the kids so they wouldn't be scared."

Ella scarcely breathed. She didn't want Loretta to stop and think, she was doing just fine angry. "I thought you never allowed Julian to have candy."

"I don't usually, but Julian had been so good! Even so, I didn't let him have the whole piece. It was too big, and I didn't want him to spoil his dinner. We each ate half. But that's what I meant about the young man trying to be nice—" Loretta's eyes grew wide. "Wait. You don't think that one tiny piece of candy was what made us both so sick?" she whispered.

"I don't know. But I'm going to find out," Ella said flatly.

TWENTY-TWO

— ✖ ✖ ✖ —

Loretta sat down on the ground. "You can't trust anyone or anything anymore. I should have known better."

"Quit blaming yourself. We don't know anything yet, for sure. Right now it's all speculation." Ella tried to think back to that day at the clinic. "I was there, but I don't remember Lee giving out candy. Was it in a dish somewhere?"

"No, he kept it in his jacket pocket. He said he couldn't afford to buy enough for everyone, so he only gave it to the people who looked like they could use a pick-me-up."

"How noble," Ella muttered.

"I can't believe that he'd do anything to hurt anyone, particularly the kids."

Ella nodded. Maybe she should have listened to Carolyn more when she'd spoken about Lee as being bad news. "Let me check things out. In the meantime, don't tell anyone what we discussed. We all know only too well how easy it is to ruin someone's reputation through innuendo."

Loretta nodded, but guilt clouded her eyes. "You'll let me know if it was him?"

"Of course," Ella said, then walked back to the Jeep with Justine.

"What now?" Justine asked.

"I want you to make some discreet inquiries about Howard Lee at the hospital as soon as you can. If he contaminated that candy, we need to know where he got the bacteria."

Justine shuddered. "Maybe from the dead bodies in the morgue?"

"I don't know, could be. I'll talk to Carolyn and see if she can come up with anything. I also want you to start working on putting together the evidence to support a request for a search warrant, but hold onto the paperwork for now. I want to look through his home, but we don't have probable cause yet."

Ella drove back to the station, adding a few more specific instructions as they went.

Justine nodded, jotting a note to herself to get the photo Ella had requested of Howard Lee from his personnel files. The one they had of him with a group of miners, via Anderson, was too small for easy identification.

As Justine got underway, Ella knocked on Big Ed's open office door and walked inside. "I think we have our first break on the case against the M.E. and, with luck, it may also crack open the one concerning Angelina Yellowhair." She filled him in on all the details.

He let out a whistle. "There's going to be all hell to pay if that med student used contaminants from the dead to create the problems we've been having. How are you going to go about getting evidence? If you spook him now, all he'll do is cover his tracks."

"Yeah, I think you're right about that. I'm going to talk to Carolyn and then play it by ear."

Ella met Carolyn at a diner in Farmington. It had taken some time to track her friend down, but she'd played a hunch that had paid off. Though Carolyn was suspended from work at the hospital, Ella had suspected Carolyn would still carry her pager. She had guessed right.

Carolyn was sitting in a booth facing the street when Ella arrived.

A moment later a young waitress brought them some iced tea,

took Ella's order, then left. "I've been shopping for new furniture," Carolyn said. "What's the emergency?"

"It isn't an emergency, but I do need to pick your brains." She told Carolyn what she'd learned about Lee.

"That little no good son of a—" Carolyn clutched her glass of iced tea as if she wanted to strangle something. "How dare he use my team as cover for something so vile! If I'd seen him, I'd have shoved that candy right up his nose." Anger blazed in her eyes.

"I don't have any real proof yet. It's still possible he's completely innocent. But I intend to check this lead out carefully. Can you think of a way he might have obtained the contaminants that were used? All the illnesses were caused by bacterial infections of one type or another."

"Lee's on staff at the hospital. He can go anywhere he wants to there, and has duty stations outside the hospital, too. You'd need the log of his daily activities to find out all the places he's been. It's on file somewhere, but I'll warn you, the center is really picky about giving out information from hospital or staff records."

"I could get a court order, but that will take time and some fast talking. I have nothing substantial to offer a judge yet, and if I'm wrong about Lee, a lot of people in and out of the police department will look bad."

"What's more important, the welfare of The People, or looking bad?" Carolyn asked.

"Lee isn't going to any more clinics, so the danger is far from imminent."

"There's one way to circumvent the problem you're facing. Go in and find a way to borrow the records."

"You mean just take them? In a hospital filled with people?" Ella shook her head. "Even if I managed to find any evidence that way, it wouldn't stand up in court, and I'd lose any case I had against him."

Carolyn stared at an indeterminate spot across the room, lost in thought. "I have a suggestion. Do you know Dr. Charlie, the center's toxicologist?"

"I've met her once or twice."

"Lee's always bugged the heck out of her. He worked in her lab last semester. One day she overheard him saying that middle-aged women were easy to get in the sack because they were always grateful when a man paid attention to them. She was never sure who he was referring to, but she gave him hell after that."

"I'll talk to Dr. Charlie, then."

"I think she'll help if you tell her the whole story. Lee, by the way, *is* afraid of her. He hated even taking autopsy samples to her."

Ella left Carolyn at the diner and drove directly to the Medical Center. The long drive tested her patience. Once there, Ella went straight to Toxicology. It was down the hall from the pharmacy, just one floor above the morgue. In the lab, she found a woman wearing a white lab coat staring into a microscope and taking notes.

"Excuse me, Dr. Charlie?"

The woman looked up, rubbed her eyes, and reached for her glasses. "Can I help you?"

Ella identified herself. "I'd like to talk to you in private, if you have a moment."

"There's nobody else here. This is as private as it gets. What can I do for you?"

"I need your help. Carolyn Roanhorse suggested you might be able to point me in the right direction on something."

Lea Charlie exhaled softly. "Poor Carolyn. Someone's setting her up, you know. That woman's heart is tied to her work and this center. She could no more jeopardize that than I could sprout wings and fly to the moon."

"I wish you'd call and tell her that. She would benefit from knowing that there are still a few people in her corner."

"I can't call her. Some jerk decided to burn down her trailer. I don't even know where she's at."

"She's staying at my mother's home for now. This is our number," Ella said, scribbling it down on the back of her card. "But I'm not sure how long she'll be our guest. She's already found a new trailer and is shopping for furniture."

"I'll give her a call later. Now tell me what can I do to help?"

Ella told her the whole story about Lee.

"So, you're looking for a source of bacteria that he might have tapped into, right?"

"That's it."

"I've seen him hanging around the microbiology lab quite a bit lately. I know he trained there for a semester, and that he likes lab work. When we had that outbreak of meningitis, Dr. Murphy was swamped and I believe Lee volunteered to help him out."

Ella felt her body thrumming with tension. "Is Dr. Murphy around?"

"Yeah, I'm sure he is, but his lab is way at the other end of the building. He deals with a lot of strains of bacteria that are really nasty, so you can't just walk in there and talk to him. I could page him, but that's not going to put him in a good mood. These days he's been working harder than any two of us here."

"Can you get him on the phone, and at least verify that Howard Lee worked with him there recently?"

"I'll try." Dr. Charlie disappeared into an adjoining office.

It took several minutes but finally she returned. "He was defensive about it when I asked. He thought I was complaining about the help Lee gave him."

"Did you tell him why you were asking?"

"I just said that I was hoping to get someone to help out here, and I wanted to find out how it had worked out for him, particularly during a crisis."

"What did he say?"

"He gave Lee glowing praise. He said he'd never seen a harder-working student. He said if it hadn't been for Lee and the other staff members who came by and volunteered to help, he wouldn't have been able to keep up with the workload, identifying the type of bacteria causing illnesses, confirming viruses, and maintaining safety protocols for biohazards."

"Did he mention the names of any of the others who helped?"

Dr. Charlie rattled off the names of several doctors and medical students, none of whom were familiar to Ella, then added, "He said Nelson Yellowhair, an orderly, spent hours there running errands for him, and some of the day shift nurses helped. He was very proud that Judy Lujan was one of those who showed up, since she'd had both a patient and a friend pass away recently."

The addition of the senator's brother and Bitah's girlfriend to the list gave her a bad feeling. The center was short on staff, so helping out during an emergency wasn't unheard of, but it still made her uneasy to have so many of her possible suspects turn up in such a sensitive area.

"Is it busy enough at this lab that someone could have taken samples of some strains from there without being detected?"

"I'd say so."

Ella considered things. One lead at a time. "Where's Lee now? Do you happen to know?"

"Since Carolyn was suspended the morgue is being staffed on a rotation basis. Coverage there could fall to any doctor. Lee isn't assigned there right now because he has to have a full-time supervising physician with him and there isn't one available there currently. Do you want me to try to find him?"

Ella shook her head. "No. In fact, I'd appreciate it if you didn't even mention that I've been here asking about him."

"No problem."

Ella was in her Jeep, driving back to the station when Justine called her on the cellular. "I've got some news you're not going to like."

"Howard Lee wasn't Angelina's boyfriend?"

"I don't know about that yet. I haven't managed to catch up to that waitress. She's due in for work at eight. I'll try to meet with her then. I called because Blalock has a situation on his hands. He found out that we were doing a check on Joe Bragg, and asked me to back off."

"Why would he care?" Ella spoke the thought out loud, then shook her head. "No, don't bother. I can guess."

"He wants to meet at the Totah Café. All three of us."

"How soon?"

"He can get there in thirty minutes."

"Can you meet me there in ten? We should talk first."

Justine agreed.

By the time Ella arrived, Justine was already there, nursing a glass of iced tea, looking restless.

Ella sat down facing the room. "We don't have much time, so listen up. I don't want Blalock to know that we tried to get our own informant, but never got anywhere."

Justine's eyes narrowed. "You had someone you were trying to cultivate on your own, didn't you?"

"Yes, but his use to us was limited," Ella said obliquely. "What I don't want is for Blalock to know that he managed something neither of us were able to do."

Justine nodded slowly. "Yeah, he'd never let us forget it, would he?"

"You can bet on it." The door opened and Blalock came in. FB-Eyes was early. "Follow my lead, but don't volunteer information. I can't seem to let this pass without appearing angry, or he'll smell a rat."

"Detectives," Blalock greeted congenially.

"Since when do you tell my people to stop investigating?" Ella demanded.

"Calm down. That's why I asked both of you here. I've got good news for you."

"It better be great news," Ella mumbled.

"Joe Bragg is working for me. He's a former cop who agreed to help out."

"But his references checked out, and there was no mention of police experience. I went over his employment record myself," Justine protested. "Was this guy a cop in a previous lifetime?"

"I arranged for all the references to be verifiable as part of his cover. That's how I found out you were checking up on him. People called me after you called them."

"And you got the mine's head honcho to agree to this undercover operation?" Ella asked.

"Bureau credentials open doors. Some people still trust us," he said. "But the reason I'm here is that we just got a big break. Joe was approached to join The Brotherhood."

"So you now know who some of the members are?" Ella asked, leaning forward.

"No. He was approached in writing. I ran that note through every test we've got, but there's nothing we can follow up on. It was handwritten on school notebook paper, and there's nothing special about the ink. And before you ask, no, it doesn't resemble the writing in the notes you've been getting," he said in a quiet voice. "It was block-lettered, all caps."

"When is your man going to meet with The Brotherhood?"

"I don't know. There's a fly in that ointment. There's a chance he's been made, but he wants to let it play out a little longer."

"So, what do you need from us?"

"Backup, tonight when I meet with him to get his report and give him some equipment he'll need for his meeting with The Brotherhood. I need you to observe from a distance and make sure my man wasn't followed. The standard routine."

"When's the meet?" Ella asked.

"At eight, north of Shiprock and off the Cortez Highway near Blue Hill, right where a dirt road passes under the second transmission line coming from the San Juan Power Plant. I picked the spot because its on the reservation and can be easily located on a topographic map. Bragg can find it, but is less likely to be noticed by The Brotherhood this far off their 'turf.'"

"If I remember the area, that's a good spot and a bad spot. There's not a lot of places for anyone to hide—including you two and us."

"We'll stay low profile, no radios or wires. I have my misgivings, but Bragg insisted. He's worried about scanners. Just make sure nobody comes to blow us to kingdom come."

"All right. We'll be there. But let me fill you in on what we've learned about a med student named Howard Lee."

Back at the office, Ella and Justine brought out a detailed topographic map of the area where the meet was to take place. "I've only seen this area from the highway," Justine said. "What do you know about it?"

"Not much. There's a bunch of gas wells to the east. It's only about four and a half miles from the Colorado state line. There's a mesa to the west, but it's a bit far for us to maintain visual contact. We could always climb partway up Blue Hill. We used to go up there to have parties back when I was in high school. I understand the kids now don't use it though. Too lazy to drive that far."

"Sounds perfect. I'll pick us up some good binoculars for tonight, and some scope-equipped rifles in case we need them," Justine said, helpfully.

"I remember a nondirect way up to that hill. Though it'll take us about twice the travel time going directly there would, it's worth it."

Ella went through her phone messages, then checked the computer for interdepartmental memos and E-mail. Finding nothing that was urgent, she stood and went to the door. She wanted Howard Lee's personnel records from the hospital as well as Judy Lujan's and Nelson Yellowhair's, but she also wanted to avoid trying to get a court order. She needed to keep this facet of the investigation under wraps, for now.

She mulled the situation over, considering her options, and came up with a plan. She'd go to the one person guaranteed to want to avoid negative publicity—hospital administrator, Andrew Slowman.

When Ella arrived at the hospital, she made her way quickly to the administration offices. The fewer people who knew about this visit, the better. The last thing she wanted to do was tip-off Howard Lee before she was ready to make her move.

Slowman stood up and regarded her warily as she came in through the door. "Is there a problem, Special Investigator Clah?"

Ella shook her head. "Believe it or not, we're on the same side," she answered with a smile.

"Maybe, but I represent the interests of this medical center and, to me, that precludes knuckling under to abusive police officers."

She watched him for a moment, then decided that her best

chance lay in playing it straight with him. Asking that he agree to keep their conversation confidential, she told him what she'd managed to discover about Howard Lee, and confided her suspicions about Nelson Yellowhair and Judy Lujan. "I can get their records with a court order, but we both know that will take time and could leak to the press. If you cooperate, things will move faster, and fewer people would know. That works to the advantage of this center, as well as my investigation."

"So our interests coincide." He nodded slowly. "Okay. I'll pull their files."

Slowman walked out of the office, then returned a short time later. "Here they are. Anything else?"

Ella smiled slowly. "There is one thing. Could you check and see if anyone has been brought in suffering from a drug overdose, specifically hallucinogenic drugs, within the last three months?"

He gave her a wary look. "Patient records are strictly confidential. I could lose my job if I give you that."

"I don't need a patient's name. Just tell me if anyone has been brought in. If you don't, I'll have to ask the ER nurses, and that's guaranteed to start some bad rumors. The press would also eventually want to know why I was asking, and they'd likely start an investigation on their own, which could end up on page one. With your help, we could avoid all that."

"That's blackmail."

"Sort of, but at least you're getting to make a choice." She shrugged. "What option will you choose?"

"I'll get the information for you."

While she was waiting, Ella studied Lee's records and those of the other two; but there was nothing exceptional or noteworthy about any of them. She was about to give up and consider the trip wasted, when Slowman came back to the office.

"One girl was admitted suffering from an overdose of psilocybin, a mushroom that causes hallucinations."

"Okay. Can you tell me who signed her admittance papers?"

"That I can do. It was Angelina Yellowhair."

Ella sat upright. "And the name of the patient and attending hospital staff?" she prodded.

"Sorry. I can only give you the names of our people, not the patient. And if you try to interview our staff nurses while they're on hospital time, I'll have you removed by our security."

"Understood."

Ella wrote down the names of the hospital personnel who had treated the girl, then left the center, pleased she had managed to get as much as she had. Now the drug connection seemed clearer, and pointed toward Howard Lee. Who better to know about herbs, dosages, and drugs in general than a medical professional?

Bitah had worked at the mine, so Howard Lee could have easily known him, and even belonged to the Navajo Justice Church. Bitah and Angelina had both taken peyote. If Lee turned out to be Angelina's boyfriend, it was possible Bitah had supplied the man with drugs for his girlfriend.

Ella got Justine on the cell phone. "If the waitress IDs Lee later tonight, run that photo by Judy Lujan, Bitah's old girlfriend tomorrow. She might remember if Bitah and Lee associated with each other."

"You're hoping to cement that drug connection?" Justine speculated.

"Yeah."

The next step would be talking to Wilson Joe about student absences. The thought of seeing him left her feeling empty inside.

Telling herself sternly that self pity didn't become her, Ella drove to the college. By the time she arrived, Ella had gotten her feelings under control. She was determined to put up a good front. There was no way she would let her friend see how she felt: That much she could do for herself as well as for him.

Ella found Wilson entering grades at his computer terminal. "Hey, Professor. How about helping a cop do her job?"

Wilson looked up and smiled. "You know I'm always willing to help the law, particularly when they ask nicely."

Ella sat across from his desk and declined the can of soda he offered. "I need you to check which one of Angelina's friends showed the most absences this past semester. Also, if there's a record of any of them missing class with a medical excuse, like hospitalization."

"I'll look into it. How soon do you need the information?"

"Yesterday?" she answered with a sheepish smile.

"I'll see what I can do, and give you a call as soon as I have something." He was about to say more when a petite Navajo woman came into the office, distracting him. She glanced at Ella, then beamed Wilson an affectionate smile. "Hello, Husband-to-be."

The soft words hurt Ella much more than a yellow jacket's sting, but she kept it hidden.

Wilson looked completely happy as he took his fiancée's hand affectionately. "Ella, this is Lisa," Wilson introduced.

The pretty young woman smiled at Ella coldly. "I've heard a lot about you, Ella, and how dedicated you are to your job."

"It's my first and best love," Ella admitted. It was at that moment that she realized what she was mourning. Wilson was building a future, while her whole life had been dedicated to safeguarding the present so that others could see their futures unfold. She knew she was doing precisely what she was meant to do, yet she envied her friend his happiness and peace.

Noting it was time to get ready to backup Agent Blalock, Ella excused herself quietly and left the building. She found herself looking forward to the rugged climb that would keep them concealed from anyone tailing Bragg.

Restless, Ella fingered the badger fetish around her neck wondering about this meeting tonight. She took a deep breath and let it out slowly. There was no sense in making too many plans now. She'd have to take things as they came.

Ella met Justine at the station. Hard plastic rifle cases and two pairs of powerful-looking binoculars lay on top of Ella's desk.

"The rifles have night-vision scopes," Justine said, "and it took some wrangling to get them. They're extras from SWAT, and are sighted in to be dead-on at two hundred yards. Ammunition is in each case. We also have low-light binoculars, since it'll be more comfortable looking through those than trying to survey the area with a rifle."

The way she felt now, Ella knew she was going to be using the rifle scope most of the time. There was going to be trouble tonight. She could feel it as clearly as she could the blast of air from the fan that cooled her office.

"You want to ride together, I assume?" Justine asked.

"Yes. The fewer vehicles, the better. We're going to have to be extremely careful. The weather's been dry, and that makes for highly visible dust trails."

"We better take your Jeep then. It's better suited to the terrain than my sedan," she said.

"My Jeep it is."

Ella drove out to the site, choosing a roundabout approach from the north that would make it difficult for anyone to follow. It made the most out of the sparse cover the land provided them.

On the way, they speculated about Howard Lee and his possible involvement in their investigations. Although they reached no conclusions, it was clear they were in agreement about one thing—the medical student merited a much closer check.

After twenty-five miles of driving, the last five cross country, they approached the site. Blue Hill stood as a silent sentinel overlooking the surrounding arid terrain. Further south was another sentinel, White Hill, and to the northwest a long mesa faded into the twilight. Ella glanced around, trying to find a suitable place to leave the Jeep before darkness arrived. It wouldn't make it up the steep, rocky sides of the hill.

"What about that arroyo?" Justine suggested, pointing by pursing her lips, Navajo style. "You could drive the Jeep down inside and we could break up its silhouette with some brush."

"Good idea. Once we get it covered we can hike up to our observation point."

Finding thick enough brush for the purpose wasn't easy but, fortunately, the Jeep was almost hidden by the arroyo itself. In an hour, when it was completely dark, it wouldn't be noticeable at all.

After unpacking their gear and loading the rifles, Ella led the way slowly up the hill, cautioning her assistant to avoid presenting herself as a target against the horizon. About halfway up, they crouched low and circled around to a point to their right where they could look south. Finding a good spot, they sank to the ground and waited.

"I told you we could see the entire area from here," Ella said. "I remember some fun parties here. We could keep a lookout for any parents wanting to crash the scene."

"I didn't think you had such a wild past," Justine said with a trace of a smile.

"I didn't. And don't get me wrong, I would have liked one, but my brother never let me get away with anything. Believe me, there's nothing more humiliating to a teenager than having a big brother show up and spoil the fun." Ella shrugged, then smiled. "Nowadays he doesn't bug me. He knows I can arrest him," she added with a chuckle.

"Now I know the real reason you got into law enforcement."

"We all have our secrets." Ella laughed.

As darkness descended, shrouding the land, Ella surveyed the junction of the power line and the dirt road through the scope of her rifle. "There are two vehicles coming up. The first one's Blalock. My guess is the second, about a hundred yards behind him, is probably his contact."

"Looks like we have one car too many," Justine warned, looking through her binoculars. "There's a pickup approaching slowly from the south, driving on the access road parallel to the power line."

TWENTY-THREE

———— ✖ ✖ ✖ ————

Using the rifle scope, Ella zeroed in on the third vehicle, which had stopped. "Neither your binoculars nor this rifle scope is powerful enough to give me a clear look at that driver. With everything tinted green on this scope, it's hard to make out details."

"How do you want to play this?"

"We wait for Blalock to meet his contact. You watch them, and in the meantime, I'll keep my rifle trained on the guy who took the back way in. He may only be there to eavesdrop." Ella watched the third driver get out of his truck and head up the line of transmission poles. "He's got at least two hundred yards between him and Blalock, but he's narrowing the gap fast. And forget the eavesdrop theory. He's carrying either a rifle or shotgun. There's no scope."

"Blalock's just met Joe Bragg," Justine confirmed.

"I wish I knew who this third guy is. He's staying low and he keeps his face and silhouette in the shadows of the poles, like a pro," Ella said. "I should have pressured Dwayne to carry his radio anyway."

"Blalock is staying near his vehicle. Good move. Now if he can just keep his man from walking out into the open between the vehicles."

"We've got trouble," Ella said. "My man just stopped by a pole and is using it to support his rifle. He's going to go for it." Ella took aim. "I have to take him out."

"It's well over two hundred yards, and he's halfway behind that pole. Maybe you should fire into the air. That'll warn Blalock."

"No. The sniper could still take his shot." Ella focused on the shadowy figure. As the man's head lowered so he could sight down the barrel, Ella squeezed the trigger.

The crack of her rifle shattered the stillness. Ella saw the man drop like a sack of flour as the bullet sliced through him. Quickly glancing over at Blalock and Bragg, she saw that they'd hit the dirt and taken cover. "He's down and our guys are safe. Here are my keys. Go get the Jeep and call it in. I'm going over on foot."

Ella half slid down the hill, then jogged toward the power line. As she approached the sniper's position, she stopped behind a pole, waiting for Justine. Her assistant drove up five minutes later, illuminating the scene with the Jeep's headlights. "I'm covering you," Justine shouted, and Ella could see her behind the Jeep's door, pistol ready.

As Ella moved forward, the figure bathed in blood remained motionless on the ground. Kneeling down by his side, she felt for the pulse point at his neck. "He's dead."

She rolled the man over and recognized Truman. "I'm not surprised," she whispered, then moved away.

Blalock pulled to a stop in his own vehicle, showering the area with dust which drifted across the headlight beams like mist in a horror movie. "You fired, so I assume he was about to take one of us out?"

"Yes."

He studied the body. "Truman, you should have stayed in jail where you belonged. Where were you, Ella?"

Ella pointed to the hill.

Blalock's eyebrows rose. "That must be three hundred yards." Ella said nothing.

"Wish you'd have clipped him in the shoulder. We could have questioned him then."

Ella glared at FB-Eyes.

"Don't get hostile. It's just an observation."

"Next time I see someone aiming at you, I'll just pop a paper bag to shake him up. Who knows? He might miss."

"Point taken," Blalock said, standing up.

"Where'd your informant go?"

"Away. He's from out of state and he thought now would be the perfect time to head home. He told me that he'd just found out they'd made him for sure. That was before either of us knew about the sniper."

"And The Brotherhood?"

"Remains unidentified, except for Truman, of course. You might have better luck finding a Navajo informer."

Ella shook her head. "It's not that simple. People are not only scared of the other side, they're afraid of one another. The atmosphere is poisoned by mistrust."

Blalock bagged the sniper's weapon. "The stock on this rifle is brand new, and looks hand-carved and fitted. From the yellow-gold finish, I'd say its French Walnut. Wasn't that the same wood used to bash in Bitah's skull?"

Ella's eyebrows rose. "It was."

"He's Anglo, so I'll do the follow-up on the weapon, and also have our lab try to match the wood with those splinters Dr. Roanhorse collected. Truman might turn out to be Bitah's killer."

"That would be a break."

Ella waited with Justine until a coroner's van came from Farmington to recover the body. Since the reservation morgue was no longer fully operable, and because Truman was not a member of the tribe, his body would be taken off the reservation and turned over to the county.

Ella finished signing the papers releasing the body to the county authorities as Justine came up to her. She'd been in the Jeep working on her report.

"Are you going to be okay?" Justine asked as they walked back to the Jeep.

"Yeah, unfortunately this isn't the first time I've had to shoot to kill," Ella said quietly.

"Does experience make it any easier to handle?"

Ella sighed softly. "No, not really. There's always a sense of failure that goes hand in hand with it, and lots of second-guessing on how you might have handled it differently and avoided taking a life."

"Do you want to go straight home? I can get a patrol to give me a ride back to the station."

"No, you still have a waitress to see about a boyfriend. I can handle this. Let's go back to the station."

Ella concentrated on the driving, and her assistant said nothing for a long time. Finally Justine spoke again. "I'll give you a call if your hunch plays out."

Ella arrived home tired and depressed. In trying to take a life, Truman had forfeited his own. She had nothing to feel guilty or sorry about. It could have just as easily been Blalock's body or Joe Bragg's they'd zipped up in the bag tonight.

As she walked into the kitchen, she saw Kevin Tolino seated there along with her mother. Ella paused, surprised to see him.

"He came to visit," Rose said, obviously sensing her reaction.

Tolino stood up and came toward her. "You've had a long, tiring day. It's in your eyes. Perhaps my visit is ill-timed."

"Not at all," Ella said, wondering how much he knew. "Was there a specific reason you came?"

"I thought you'd like to know I've accepted the doctor's case. I'm forcing a hearing at the hospital. I'll have her reinstated soon. They don't have a leg to stand on."

"I'm glad to hear that." Ella studied the man before her. He was undeniably handsome, but a pretty face didn't say much about the person inside. Still, he had helped her escape the harassment of the van the other day, and he was preparing to defend her friend Carolyn, despite the doctor's current controversial position. That said something about his character.

"Take a walk with me?"

Ella hesitated, wondering what he had in mind. Then she glanced at her mother, who was busy cooking. If Tolino was going to create any problems, then it was best she find that out away from her mom.

"Sure. Let's go."

Ella matched his pace, trying to figure out from his body language what he wanted with her. As before, he didn't give much away.

"I heard what happened to you today."

"What are you referring to? Many things happened today," Ella answered.

"The shooting tonight."

"How could you know about that? It wasn't reported on the radio. The press doesn't know about it yet."

"I'm a lawyer for the tribe. Many trust me, even a few police officers. My clan also has considerable influence. That's why Billy Pete asked you to meet him on my property. He knew danger wouldn't follow him there, at least not from Navajos. Because of that, I believe the person in the van was an Anglo."

Ella stopped and turned to face Kevin. "Are you saying you're part of the Fierce Ones?"

He shook his head. "You misunderstood me. I have neither the time nor the desire to get involved with pressure groups like that. But knowing about them is another matter."

"Do you know who the members of The Brotherhood are? Perhaps the name of the person who was driving that van that almost ran me down?"

Kevin shook his head. "No."

Ella met his gaze with an unwavering one of her own. "Instinct tells me that you're a man of many secrets."

"I have as many secrets as you, I'd be willing to bet. That makes for balance," Kevin answered with a half smile. "I will tell you this. If you come to me for help, you'll get it, and there won't be any strings attached. Except, of course, next time we chase someone cross country, *you* drive."

He smiled, then said good-night. In seconds, he had disappeared into the darkness.

As Ella walked back into the house, her mother came out of the kitchen. "What's wrong? What happened to you today? And don't tell me nothing. It was written all over your face when you came home." She studied her daughter's expression and smiled. "But it seems your new friend has managed to get your mind focused on something else."

"Not again," Ella snapped, and went to her room.

Without turning on the lights she sat on the window seat, staring outside. The single light in the distance probably came from Tolino's home. She stared at it for a long while. He was close by, but he was a dangerous ally. Too many emotions came into play when she was around him.

Turning away from the window, she went to the computer and switched it on. Routines were good, and she needed them now. As her people said, in everything there was a pattern, and in discerning it, one found harmony.

Ella woke up later than usual, but, judging from the fact that her phone hadn't rung, she figured Justine had struck out the night before. Still reluctant to disbelieve her instincts, Ella decided that not identifying Lee as Angelina's boyfriend could simply be a mistake on the waitresses's part. Photo IDs weren't infallible.

As she finished getting dressed, she heard Wilson Joe's voice out in the living room. Curious, she hurried out to meet him. Ella glanced at her mother, then at Wilson. "What's going on?"

"I wouldn't let anyone wake you," Rose said adamantly. "You're always working late, then getting up early. Everyone can wait for once!" she said, then strode out of the room.

Ella glanced at Wilson and shrugged. "Sorry about that. She gets protective every once in a while."

"She has a right to be," he said quietly.

Ella met his gaze, trying to figure out whether he was referring to the shooting incident. It was amazing how quickly news spread on the reservation. It was worse than any small town.

"I heard rumors about a shooting, but there hasn't been anything on the radio. You wouldn't happen to know anything about that, would you?"

"I can't discuss it. I'm sorry," Ella said. "But it wasn't one of our people, I'll tell you that much."

He nodded and didn't press. "I found out what you needed. It wasn't easy, though. The senator's daughter had few scholars for friends. They all cut classes regularly. I kept digging, though. Finally, one of the professors I spoke to remembered hearing that one of his students, Ruby Atso, had spent some time in the hospital, something to do with drugs."

Ella remembered the young girl she'd dubbed Diamond Nose. It fit somehow. "I can't thank you enough. I really needed this piece of information."

"When you can, will you tell me the whole story?"

"You've got it. How are the wedding plans coming?" Ella forced herself to ask, walking with him to the door.

"We'll have a small ceremony. Nontraditional. It's what she wants, and it's okay by me. I'll talk to you there."

Ella nodded in agreement. After saying good-bye, she watched him drive off. Rose came to join her. "Regrets?" she asked.

"No, not anymore. Wilson wasn't for me. He needs more than I could have given him."

Rose placed a hand on her daughter's arm. "There could be another for you."

Ella looked hard at her mother, her eyes narrowing. "Don't you dare start playing matchmaker."

"I don't think I'll have to," she said, then walked back into the kitchen.

Ella groaned. There was no way she'd ask her mother to elaborate. Some things were better left alone.

"I'm going now," Ella yelled out, grabbing her jacket from the hook on the wall.

"No breakfast?" Rose asked, coming back out of the kitchen.

"No, I'm already running late. I'll grab something later."

Ella hurried out to the Jeep. She wasn't hungry. It was a symptom she recognized from the aftermath of the shooting in the L.A. diner so long ago. As she traveled down the highway, images of the men she'd killed merged in her mind until her body began to shake.

Ella slowed down, pulled over, and stopped the Jeep. Her

hands gripped the wheel hard as she fought to push back the emotions that threatened to overwhelm her. No. She wouldn't give in to this. She had other responsibilities now. Unless she remained clear and focused, the department would place her on mandatory leave. Officers were watched carefully after a shooting.

Slowly the shudders eased, and Ella pulled back onto the road. She'd done her job, that was all she could ask of herself. Gathering her courage, she drove to the station.

Reaching her office, she practically smashed into Justine coming out as Ella came in.

"Oops," Justine said, stopping abruptly to avoid colliding with her. "I have sorta good news. The waitress *thinks* Howard Lee is Angelina Yellowhair's boyfriend. And you might be interested to know that Judy Lujan said Bitah not only knew Howard, they attended the Navajo Justice Church together. It was too late to call you last night by the time I finished all the paperwork. I just left copies of my reports, including the one on last night's incident, on your desk."

"I better go talk to Big Ed. At least I'll finally have some promising leads to give him.

"I'll save you a trip to my office, Shorty," Big Ed said, rounding the corner and blocking the hall with his barrel-chested body. "FB-Eyes just called me. He suggested we give you a commendation. I've read your assistant's report, and I tend to agree."

Ella forced herself not to cringe. "Please, Chief, can I pass on this? I just reacted to the situation like I'd been trained to do."

His gaze was sharp, searching for dangerous nuances in her behavior. "You okay with what went down? There are people you can talk to who can help you get through this."

"Not necessary, Chief. I'm handling it."

"All right," Big Ed said after a long pause. "According to Officer Goodluck, we may be able to link Truman to Bitah's death with that unique gun stock of his. You'd think he'd have burned the wood up instead of carving it into a rifle stock," Big Ed said.

"Maybe he wanted it as a reminder of his victory over an

enemy. Kind of a gruesome trophy, but Truman seems the type," Ella suggested. "Or maybe it was too expensive to throw away."

"We'll just have to see if FB-Eyes can link that wood to the fragments from the victim's skull. So, what's new on the senator's daughter?"

Ella filled him in on their progress regarding Howard Lee. As she did, she saw a flicker of understanding and more, perhaps excitement in his eyes. "I'm going to go track down Ruby Atso. She may be more open to us now that we already know who Angelina's boyfriend was. Maybe we can finally learn why someone thought Angelina had to die."

"Are we close to the important answers?" the chief prodded.

She knew he was asking her to use her almost legendary intuition. "Yes, I think so."

"But you're not sure."

"I think we're still missing something significant. I know it's there, but I still can't see it clearly," Ella tried explaining, then shook her head. "I follow my intuition, Chief, it's not something I lead with. Do you understand?"

He shrugged. "Keep me current."

As the chief left, her phone rang. Ella picked it up, and heard Blalock's voice at the other end.

"I tracked the rifle our sniper was using," he said. "The French walnut stock *was* custom-made and added by Truman, replacing the original. The hand-rubbed finish is still curing. He bought the rough-cut stock blank three weeks ago from a mail order place in California. The serial number of the action, however, is the same as a rifle stolen from a Farmington resident who's a member of my gun club, but not an employee of the mine. I'm checking him out anyway, just in case The Brotherhood has members not connected to the mine."

"Thanks for letting me know. I'm going to check on Ruby Atso," Ella said, filling him in, as promised, on her end of their joint investigations.

"Let me know what you turn up."

Ella hung up and took the note Justine handed her.

"It's Ruby's address. She's a tough cookie. I don't think she'll give us any more information that she already has, despite the fact that we now know about Howard Lee."

Ella considered it. "Then let's rattle her a bit. Pick her up and bring her in. Maybe we'll get a better response from her once she's one room away from a cell."

Ruby sat in the barren room used for questioning, looking as if she wished she were anywhere but there.

Ella watched her through the two-way glass, waiting. Ruby was so nervous she couldn't keep still for even a minute.

"How long are you going to let her stew in there?"

Ella had deliberately kept the young girl waiting for over twenty minutes. "Let's go in now. I want her scared, not angry."

Ella walked in slowly, then sat across the table from Ruby. "We know you've been playing games with us."

"That's not true. I told you what I knew about Angelina."

"How long had you all been experimenting with drugs?" Ella asked pointedly. "The mescaline, peyote, maybe a little of something else?"

Ruby looked ashen. "I don't know what you mean."

"Angelina took you to the emergency room here in Shiprock. She signed the admission papers herself. Start telling the truth, Ruby, we know enough to catch any lies."

"Okay, okay. Yeah, we bought some mushrooms and peyote from someone, I don't remember who. We thought it would be a kick. They're not like cocaine or anything. You don't become an addict. The Native American Church, for example, uses peyote for enlightenment and stuff."

"It's a sacrament for them, not something to be done for a lark, and using peyote is only part of their beliefs."

"Yeah, well, it seemed like a good idea at the time. Angelina had found some tunnels that she swore had been used by skinwalkers once, so we went there. We knew we'd be okay, because we were with a guy who knew first aid."

Ella looked directly at the girl. "We know about Howard Lee, Angelina's boyfriend. That's old news now. What happened next?"

Ruby's eyes widened, then she sighed. Relief, or defeat, finally showed on her face. "Sooner or later, I knew you'd figure out who he was. Well, he handed out small amounts of the ground-up mushrooms and, though we all took that, none of us had any peyote. The only reason I got sick is because I insisted on taking an extra portion of the ground-up mushroom."

"Why?"

She shrugged. "I figured if Howard could do it, so could I."

"Why did Howard take extra; was it his greater body size?" Ella held her breath, grateful that Ruby had confirmed their ID work.

"No, he said that as a medical professional, he knew exactly what the danger signs were, and he could handle the effects better. I thought that was bull and said so. But he didn't end up in the hospital, and I did. So maybe he was right."

"How long had Angelina been dating Howard?" Justine asked.

"Several months, but, with his wife and all, they were very careful. Angelina was protective of him, too. She was afraid that Howard would get in trouble and that his medical career would be ruined, so she made us all promise that we never would tell about the drugs, or about them being together. Now that she's dead and I'm in trouble about it, that promise doesn't matter as much to me."

"How often did you guys meet to experiment with the drugs?"

Ruby looked around nervously before answering. "Just a few times at the tunnels. Then we started meeting in different places, wherever it suited us. Sometimes, if he had some, we would take peyote along with the mushrooms. But when things started getting crazy, we stopped."

"Crazy how?"

"Howard started talking about skinwalkers, and about how wonderful your dead father-in-law was."

"What?" Ella was unable to avoid her surprise.

"Oh, yeah. He was totally obsessed with him. He thought old Police Chief Clah was guiding him, and that maybe they were linked." Ruby tapped her head with one finger. "I'm telling you, he sounded nuts. It even scared Angelina."

"What did she do?" Ella prodded.

Ruby regarded her with a worried frown. "Look, I'm telling you a lot here. I want to make sure you won't throw me in jail until my hair turns gray, okay?"

"I'm investigating a murder. The only way I'll throw the book at you is if you withhold any more of the information I need. Understood?"

Ruby nodded.

"Okay, now tell me about Angelina."

"When she heard Howard say that Randall Clah was guiding him, she got really upset. She told him that they shouldn't take any more peyote buttons, that the stuff was dangerous. Howard calmed her down, and promised that he would stop 'kidding' her about skinwalkers. He was really good getting her to do or believe whatever he wanted, you know."

"Was he angry at her for spoiling his fun, angry enough to kill her?"

Ruby shook her head. "No way. He knew Angelina was crazy about him, and he loved knowing he could control her. I always thought that the real reason he didn't leave his wife was that he used his marriage as a tool to make Angelina want him more."

"Did Angelina ever ask him to leave his wife?" Justine asked.

"Oh, yes! And he'd said that he would, but I knew it would never happen. He had Angelina under his thumb. He even convinced her to start taking peyote with him again, just the two of them, after he got off work on the weekends."

"Did anyone else know about this?"

"Sure. All of us did. The other girls may not tell you though, not matter how much you pressure them. We loved Angelina. She was wild, but she was also a lot of fun and she was a good friend."

"One more question, Ruby. Where did Howard get the peyote? Think hard. I know he's too busy with work at the hospital and the mine to go out into the desert to collect his own." Ella waited. This was a critical detail. If she could track down

Howard's dealer, she might learn who had contaminated the peyote buttons with jimsonweed.

"Angelina told us Howard was bringing it back from his new church, the Navajo Justice one. He'd do a little magic trick he learned. He'd pretend to put the buttons in his mouth, but palm them instead, then pretend to chew. He'd get two or three each service that way and bring them back to Angelina, and for a while, us, too; if he could get enough. Angelina wanted to go to the church herself, but she was afraid her father would find out."

Ruby fidgeted in her chair. "Look, I really have told you all I know. Can I go home now?"

"Sure," Ella answered, "once you sign a statement for our records."

As Justine escorted Ruby out to make her statement, Ella rested her back against the cold wall. She had a good suspicion where the notes she'd received from Randall Clah had come from now. Howard Lee was good at deception, almost as good as Randall himself had been.

An hour later, Justine joined Ella in her office. "Ruby Atso's statement is logged and I've finished the checks on Nelson Yellowhair and Judy Lujan. Both are well liked, and seemingly law-abiding. Neither has a record."

Ella sat still, thinking. "Nelson Yellowhair had access to the same source of bacterial cultures as Howard Lee. He could be responsible for the illnesses and deaths at the inoculation sites, or be an accomplice. I don't think Judy Lujan is a player, though."

"Should I keep digging into Nelson's past? I really don't think we'll find anything there, except for his link with a certain senator."

"You may be right, but let's not remove him from the list of suspects. We may be jumping to conclusions if we assume Howard Lee has been solely responsible for everything that has happened."

"Why do you think Lee is so enthralled with our old police chief?"

"I don't know, but I'm going to find out. Until we have an answer, though, put a close tail on Howard Lee, but not close enough for him to suspect he's being followed."

"You think it would do us any good to haul Howard in about the notes?"

"No, he's been pretty good at lying to protect himself. But let's check the handwriting on the notes against Howard's. Also see if anyone knows of a connection between Nelson Yellowhair and Howard, besides work. Then I want you to ask Judy Lujan if Bitah ever suspected that Lee was skimming peyote buttons for his own use. Bitah doesn't sound like someone who would let something like that go unpunished."

"Got it."

"And leave me Howard Lee's photo, the big one. I'm going to try tracking things from another angle."

After Justine left, Ella stood up slowly. Her mother would be an excellent source of information. She knew practically everyone on the Rez. Ella left her office and drove to her home. She found Rose in the open-air porch, knitting.

Rose glanced up, surprised. "What are you doing home this time of day?"

"I'm trying to track down some information, and I'm hoping you can help," she said, explaining.

Rose took a deep breath and let it out again. "I can't help you with that, but there is one person who might know. The problem is, she scarcely speaks to anyone since your father-in-law died."

"Who is it?"

"Your father-in-law's aunt."

Ella stared at the floor, lost in thought. She remembered hearing about Jane Clah but, to the best of her recollection, she'd never actually met the woman. "I don't remember ever seeing her."

"She came to your wedding, but didn't stay long. She was always nervous around your father-in-law. At the time, I thought it was because he was a policeman."

"Will you come with me to see her? She may speak more freely to you."

Rose shook her head. "No, she and I were never friends. I always had the impression she hated our entire family."

"Where does she live? Do you know?"

"After the news of your father-in-law's death, and his secret life, she moved out somewhere west of Bisti, just south of one of those big microwave towers. She doesn't come to town anymore, so nobody has seen her for a long time. I'm not even sure if she's still alive."

"Is there someone else I can speak to?"

"Someone who would know who your father-in-law associated with? No. The others I can think of are all either dead or hiding somewhere from the law." Rose grew somber. "If your father-in-law's aunt chooses to talk to you, she could probably tell you a lot. She lived next door to him most of his adult life."

Ella checked a map for more detailed directions on how to find the woman she needed, then began the long drive. The paved road gave out about six miles west of highway 666, and the dirt track after that had obviously suffered badly over the last winter. As the miles stretched out, Ella wondered if the trip would be fruitful, or turn out to be just another waste of time.

Almost sixty minutes of washer-board road later, Ella arrived at a log and mud hogan in the middle of an open stretch of beautiful, barren desert right out of a John Wayne western. The rundown corrals were empty, an open gate swaying in the breeze. Wondering if the woman she sought had indeed passed on, Ella waited in the Jeep, glancing around for signs of life. Minutes stretched out into eternities as the sun pounded on the Jeep. When the heat became intolerable, Ella stepped out of the Jeep and leaned against the side door, waiting.

Ella wasn't sure why, but she felt certain that she should wait.

She followed her intuition.

Finally, an elderly woman leaning on a cane appeared at the entrance of the hogan, brushing the faded blanket aside. Her face was a patchwork of deep, intricate lines, like the spiderweb of roads Ella had just traversed. She waved at Ella to come in. "You're persistent," Jane Clah said, sitting down on the ground.

"Why are you here? I am *xa'asti*, and too tired to deal with visitors."

Ella understood the word for extremely old, but the term also contained another warning. According to the Navajo Way, the elderly were believed to be spiritually strong, and their power for evil worthy of being feared.

"I need your help, Aunt," Ella said, telling her who she was.

"I've known who you were all along. I remember when you married my kin. But why do you come to me now?"

"Do you know of the recent trouble on the reservation?" Someone had to be bringing the old woman food and supplies, and news of the meningitis threat had been widely disseminated.

Jane nodded slowly. "But you have no reason to worry. My nephew is gone now. He can't harm you or anyone else anymore. You can't blame him for this."

"There is a young man who claims to be, well, connected or linked to him. I wondered if my father-in-law sought the friendship of some young people after his son was gone."

The woman stared at the ground, drawing patterns in the soft earth with her long, twisted index finger.

Ella waited, knowing she could not interrupt or push for faster answers, no matter how much she might want to.

Finally, Jane looked up. "My nephew hurt many people, even his son. Why should I help you hurt others who are not to blame?"

"This young man who claims a link to my father-in-law might be at the center of some serious troubles facing our people," Ella said, and went on to explain about the meningitis outbreak and the sudden illnesses experienced by the children at the clinics.

The woman exhaled softly. "I don't know about friendships, but your father-in-law had another family that only a few knew about. He had other sons."

Ella felt her body grow cold. For a moment, she could almost feel her father-in-law's presence reaching from the grave. She pulled out Howard Lee's photo. "Is this one of his sons?"

"Yes." The woman looked away quickly after viewing the image.

Ella fought a crazy sense of vertigo as she struggled to remain cool. There was no entry in Lee's hospital records naming his parents. Both had been listed as deceased. "Where can I find Howard's brothers and how many are there?"

Jane Clah shook her head. "They are all trying to forget. I won't betray them. You can't blame them for the actions of their father. They pose no threat to you or anyone else."

"But—"

"You got what you came for. Now go."

"Did my father-in-law love them?" Ella asked as she stood.

The elderly woman nodded. "They were a part of him."

Ella now knew how Howard had been able to forge Randall Clah's writing, and how he'd known so much about the man— his father. But the certainty that there were others in that family was like a needle piercing her to the marrow. She was certain that someday, one or more of them would also come after her. Yet, until they did, there was nothing she could do except wait.

Howard Lee was another story.

TWENTY-FOUR
———— ✖ ✖ ✖ ————

As Ella drove back to the station, a plan formed in her mind. She dialed her brother's number, and filled him in about Howard Lee. "If he's really trying to act in his father's behalf and assume the skinwalkers' ways, can we use something traditional to rattle him? I need a weakness."

"There are ways to reveal a Navajo witch. But, to expel the evil from one contaminated with the *chindi* it's necessary to do a Sing and other complicated rituals."

"What I want is something that will lead Lee to think he's been exposed and weakened somehow. I need to undermine his confidence."

"Let me think about this. I'm on my way to the hospital to see a patient of mine who's there for breathing treatments. Why don't you meet me there?" Clifford asked.

"Sure. I was on my way there anyway. I've decided to pick up Howard for questioning," Ella answered.

After saying good-bye to her brother, Ella contacted Justine and asked her to go ahead with the request for a search warrant for Lee's home. "I'm going to pick up Lee and bring him in. Get word to the officer tailing him to not let the man out of his sight until I arrive. I may need backup if Lee resists."

"Ten-four."

When Ella arrived at the hospital a short time later, she found Clifford waiting inside, near the front entrance.

The expression on her brother's face chilled her. "What's wrong?"

"I passed by our enemy," he said, knowing there was no need for him to specify. "He was very agitated and wasn't able to hide his true nature like he had done earlier at the inoculation clinic. There *is* much of the father in him."

"Yeah, he has managed to fool us all up to now. He certainly has the deceptive powers of a skinwalker."

Clifford shook his head. "There's more to this. I actually felt our old adversary. The father and the son are one, at least in his heart. The hatred was there, filling the space between us. The intensity, the power in him, felt familiar. I'm glad my family isn't at this hospital."

Ella remembered when Loretta had given birth. Someone had sneaked into the nursery and placed a possession of Randall's on Julian.

"Flint protects against the *chindi*," Clifford said thoughtfully. "I suggest you have some with you when you approach your quarry."

"You think it'll give me an advantage?"

"It will give you *protection*," he said sternly, handing her a small stone.

Ella took the piece of gray flint Clifford offered and put it in her pocket, then she watched him walk down the hall. She could understand her brother's concern for his family. They'd been targeted before. The ritual in the nursery had been meant to harm his baby by infusing Randall's *chindi* into the child. But her brother had done a Sing and protected his son, not only from the dangers the skinwalker ritual had posed, but from the burden of carrying that stigma for the rest of his life. If Howard had been the one who'd tried to harm the child once before, would he do so again?

Following a hunch, Ella went to the maternity ward, walked up to the nurses' station, and identified herself.

The nurse looked at her calmly. "Yes, I remember you from when your brother's child was born."

"Do you remember the incident with the baby?"

"The watch chain that was found inside the incubator? Every nurse on the ward was looking over her shoulder for weeks after that. We can't have people threatening the babies under our care."

"Do you know Howard Lee?"

"The med student? Sure. He's worked with us here."

"Could he have been in the nursery the day the chain was placed on my brother's child?"

The nurse thought about it. "He could have been, I suppose. He was assigned here around that time."

"Thank you, Nurse."

Ella hurried to the elevator and went down to the first floor. As the doors slid open, she saw Justine. "What brings you here?"

"Our officer lost track of Lee half an hour ago. He left the hospital in his car, then whipped around in the new housing area and dropped out of sight. He apparently noticed we'd put a tail on him."

"Where's the officer now?"

"Still out on the highway, searching. A motorist said he saw Lee's car heading west. The officer tried to call in several times, but was in a canyon area that blocked the transmission. We finally got enough of his report to get a handle on the situation, and that's why I'm here. From where he lost him, the officer thinks Lee is taking the back way to your brother's home."

"Did you send someone to cover Clifford's home?"

"Yes, one car was already in the area. We've sent other units, but I doubt they'll get there before Lee does."

Ella jogged down the hall, Justine keeping pace by her side. "I'm going there myself. Clifford is here visiting one of his patients. Find him and let him know what's going on. He needs to be with his family now. As a *hataalii*, he can protect them from someone like Howard Lee. What's with the search warrant?"

"It's in the works. I can't push it past my relative this time; he's gone fishing over at Bluewater Lake. I have another piece of news. According to Judy Lujan, Bitah had suspected Lee was

336 * AIMÉE & DAVID THURLO

keeping his peyote buttons instead of consuming them during the rituals. He was angry and determined to teach him a lesson."

"What kind of lesson?" Ella already knew the answer. Bitah had placed the jimsonweed in the buttons handed to Lee, intending to punish his sacrilege with death—only Angelina had received a fatal dose instead.

"Judy didn't know what Bitah had planned," Justine said, then nodded, understanding the look on Ella's face. "I guess we know how Angelina was killed."

"Howard Lee was a victim of his own manipulations, and killed his girlfriend accidentally. But that doesn't excuse what he's tried to do to Carolyn and to the innocent people who went to the inoculation clinics. Now Lee's going after my brother's family, and he'll come for me next." She ran across the parking lot, heading toward the Jeep.

"But why would he try to kill our M.E? That doesn't fit."

"Yes, it does. He tried to kill Carolyn because she discovered Angelina had been poisoned," Ella continued. "He knew the trail would lead back to him eventually and destroy him, unless he destroyed her first. He's after my family now because the net is closing in on him. He's lost the game, so he'll strike out at those who were responsible for the death of his father."

Ella slipped behind the wheel. "Once you find my brother and warn him, come out and meet me at his home. Then call Neskahi and tell him to stay by my mother's side, and keep Carolyn safe, too, if she's there. Lastly, get word to Wilson Joe. Tell him that Howard Lee is out to get those responsible for killing Randall. He should be on his guard."

Ella switched on the sirens and sped down the highway, weaving past the slower-moving vehicles in her way with ease. As she reached the narrow, two-lane stretch of old highway, she glanced in her rearview mirror and saw a big, six-wheeled pickup right behind her. It seemed determined to stay with her, and that meant he had to be traveling at least twenty miles over the speed limit. Then the truck began to gain ground. Ella picked up the radio, but the canyon and mesa terrain filled the transmission with static. She could barely make out the dispatchers 10-1, asking her to repeat.

Knowing from experience the cellular phone was spotty in that area, too, Ella tried the radio again. It was no use. Almost as if sensing his advantage, the large four-seater pickup pulled up alongside her Jeep as if to pass, then eased over into her lane, trying to force her off the road. Ella accelerated, trying to pull away, her hands gripping the wheel tightly. Suddenly she felt the jarring impact as the large vehicle slammed against the back end of her Jeep, metal screeching against metal. The sturdy Jeep remained under control, but barely.

Fear twisted through her. She didn't recognize the two Anglo men in the truck. This attack wasn't connected to Howard Lee. Had she chased the wrong criminal, giving a more dangerous enemy the chance to move in on her?

The terrain flew past her. She was traveling close to eighty miles an hour on a road designed for fifty-five; and the road was so narrow, if a vehicle met them head on, surely someone would die.

Seconds later, still racing neck and neck with the truck, Ella approached a bridge that traversed a forty-foot-deep canyon. The truck swerved again and slammed into her Jeep, hurling her vehicle against the guardrail. She jerked on the steering wheel, and bounced back onto the road, wrenching herself painfully from side to side against the seat belt. If she could only make it past the bridge, she would have a better chance, particularly if her vehicle went off the road. Here, she faced certain death. Elsewhere, it was a matter of surviving a rough trip up or down a hillside.

As she got to the end of the bridge, she let off the gas and touched the brake hard, realizing she'd never be able to outrun her pursuers, yet unwilling to give up without a fight. As her Jeep suddenly fell back, the truck swerved again, clipping the left front fender. The steering wheel jerked erratically, as if with a life of its own. Her teeth clacked together and the pain that exploded down her jaw made her wonder if that would be the first of her bones to be broken in the assault.

Before she could regain control of her vehicle, the truck cut right in front of her and braked hard. The Jeep hit the heavy metal truck bumper, throwing Ella against the seat belt harness and inflating the air bag with a frightening whoosh.

Ella was blinded and helpless as the Jeep left the road and continued its acceleration wildly up the side of a hill. As it neared the top, Ella managed to bring the Jeep to an abrupt stop, but the soft sand of the hillside gave way beneath her, and the Jeep toppled over onto the driver's side. Ella's head was snapped sideways, and she banged against the side glass hard enough to stun her. The Jeep slowly slid downhill, metal screeching. After what seemed like forever, it came to rest.

Ella pushed away the half-collapsed airbag and groped for the seat belt release, but her fingers were clumsy, her ears were ringing, and her eyes refused to focus. Finding the button finally, Ella stood on her door and reached up, moving the lever to open the passenger door like the main hatch on a submarine. Looking around for her attackers, she cautiously climbed up onto the side of the Jeep. Before she could really orient herself, both men suddenly sprang up from where they'd been crouched beside the Jeep, and pulled her off the car onto the ground.

Ella rolled away quickly and reached for her gun. Her knees were still wobbly as she struggled to stand and face her adversaries.

A stocky Anglo she'd never seen before kicked the pistol out of her grasp just as it cleared her holster. "You're going to lose this fight, squaw," he laughed. "Your good luck has just run out."

Ella ignored the pain shooting through her body, using adrenaline to stay alert and evaluate her situation. The second man, almost a head taller than the first, held a lug wrench in his hand like a club. It was obvious they intended to finish her off. "Who are you and what do you want?"

"Decent, hard-working white men are suffering because of your racist laws. You're working to take away their jobs. It's time you had a fatal car crash."

As the stocky man grabbed at her, Ella jumped to one side. Every muscle in her body screamed, but by the time she scrambled to her feet, her backup pistol was out of her boot and in her hand. She fired two shots at her closest attacker, the shorter man, and he went down hard with two hits in his chest.

"You only have two shots in that little derringer, Indian. Your luck just ran out," the other spat out, waving the lug wrench back and forth to taunt her.

Ella knew her chances were slim, but maybe she'd still be able to pull off a miracle. She certainly couldn't afford to give up. Ella fell to her knees as if exhausted, clutching her head with one hand and groaning. It wasn't much of an acting job. As her adversary moved in confidently for the kill, she threw a fistful of sand into his face.

He staggered back, covering his eyes, and Ella scrambled to her feet and kicked him in the groin. When he doubled over, dropping the wrench, she clasped her hands and delivered a blow to the back of his neck.

The man fell to the ground, stunned, but not unconscious. Ella quickly grabbed her fallen pistol, then dragged her adversary over to the Jeep, handcuffing one hand to the frame. Moving back, she tried to clear her thoughts. Glancing over at the man she had shot, she saw he hadn't moved. Blood covered his chest and she knew he was dead or dying.

The other man tugged at the handcuffs, struggling to free himself. "This vehicle's dripping gasoline. Can't you smell it?" He glanced down. "It's running onto my shoes and pants. We've got to get away from here."

"*I* intend to get away. You, I'm not worried about. Let your Brotherhood buddies bail you out of this one." She wouldn't let him die here, but it wouldn't hurt to let him think so. Fear could expedite the kind of deal she'd never get from him otherwise. "Like they say, what have you done for me lately?"

"You can't leave me here. You're a cop," he added, his voice rising.

"Yeah, one very pissed-off cop. I've got more important things to do than worry about what happens to slime like you," she shouted, climbing down the hill slowly, looking for an approaching car.

"Come back! I can help you neutralize The Brotherhood. I know the leader, Anderson. I'll also identify the man who killed Bitah. It was Truman. I was there when he hit him with that gun-stock. And Anderson hired us to kill you. We were waiting at the highway junction, knowing you had to pass by sooner or later. A while ago we spotted you up on the way to the hospital. We were supposed to run you off the road, making it look like what happened to the senator's daughter. If you survived the wreck, we were to finish the job, then set the Jeep on fire to destroy your body."

Ella knew she had his attention now. The threat of being burned to death could soften the hardest criminal. She stopped to listen, but still looked back and forth down the road, not moving toward him at all.

"Why did Anderson want me dead?" she asked.

"He hates your guts, trust me. And he wanted to kill you to prove how much power we have. You've managed to survive everything he's thrown at you, even the bomb in the van. If we could take you out, others would have been very reluctant to fight us." He glanced down at the pool of gasoline around his feet. "I've answered you. Now get me away from here!"

Ella turned around slowly. "You're willing to testify in a court of law?"

"I know enough to convict Anderson. That's my deal. I give you the testimony you need, you get me the hell away from here."

"That's almost enough to save your life. What else have you got?" she pushed, pretending to be trying to make up her mind.

The man tugged at his handcuffs, almost in a panic. "Come on, let me loose. I won't try to run."

"Keep talking. Oh, and by the way, if you keep moving around like that, you might cause a spark with those metal cuffs," Ella cautioned.

"Okay, okay." He grew still. "Noah Charley was taking money from The Brotherhood for keeping us informed about the Fierce Ones. Charley told Anderson that Bitah was planning to sabotage the heavy cranes and drag lines to shut down the mine.

But it turns out Charley was lying about that. We grabbed Bitah, and once we found out the sabotage idea was crap, we decided to work him over just to make a point. Bitah fought pretty well, but he was outnumbered. Finally, Truman nailed him, and that was it."

"Then Noah Charley took off," she said, remembering the tracks that had been left at the scene.

"Yes, yes. He suddenly realized he was the only witness who wasn't one of us. Nobody has seen him since. We never could figure out who paid Charley to tell us about the phoney sabotage, and why he was so willing to deliver Bitah to us." He glanced at the ever-widening pool of gasoline around him, fear in his eyes. "That's all I know. Now you've got to get me away from this death trap! Please?"

Ella nodded. She couldn't prove it unless they found Noah Charley and persuaded him to talk, but she was suddenly certain Howard Lee had used The Brotherhood to keep Bitah from exposing his theft of the peyote buttons. Lee had committed murder all right, but it was Bitah's, not Angelina's, death he'd engineered.

Ella got the cellular telephone unit from her Jeep, and her shotgun, then unhooked her prisoner, cuffed his hands behind his back, and, at gunpoint, forced him to climb uphill with her. He was so relieved to still be alive he was almost eager to cooperate. After making him lay facedown, she managed to get a call through to Justine.

"Where have you been?" Justine demanded. "All hell has been breaking loose out here."

"No time to explain now," Ella replied wearily. "What's going on?" She looked over at the man she had shot. His eyes were open and expressionless.

"When Phillip Cloud arrived, he found the officer assigned to follow Lee lying there, wounded but conscious, about fifty yards from your brother's house. Lee had ambushed him, armed with a pistol. Your brother and I came out and drove Lee away. After making sure Loretta and the baby were alright and that help had been called for the wounded officer, we left Cloud to watch over Clifford's family, and went after Lee. We lost the trail in the area of scrub oak and piñon west of your brother's home. We're about to head down to the road to see if we can pick up the trail again."

"I'll rendezvous with Clifford at the road. You go back to the house and get a car. I need you to pick up a prisoner for me. I'll leave him handcuffed to the bridge. Get him to the station and have him write out a statement. He's going to blow The Brotherhood wide open for us. There's another one of them here, too, but he's dead."

Once assured that Justine was on the way, she walked her prisoner back down to the road, handcuffed the man to a sturdy portion of the bridge railing, and reached for his truck keys.

"Someone will come along soon to collect you," she said, climbing into the man's truck.

She was relieved to hear the rumble of the big V-8 engine. The truck was still in good condition, except for the passenger's side exterior and a dent in the rear bumper.

Ella sped down the highway, glad for the first time that her new transportation had such a powerful engine. With the exception of some sheep, however, there were no signs of life along this stretch of road. As she cleared the next rise, she spotted a figure at the bottom of the hill waving his arms, trying to flag her down. There was another person on the ground at his feet. As she drew near, she recognized Clifford as the man standing.

Ella pulled to a screeching stop. She didn't recognize the wounded man, but she did recognize the uniform shirt. He was a school bus driver. His shirt had been torn at the shoulder, and herbs had been placed over the wound there to staunch the flow of blood.

"I followed our enemy," Clifford said as she came up, "but he reached the road long before I could. Apparently, he laid down in the middle of the highway, and this poor man stopped to help him. When he left the bus to see what was wrong, our enemy shot him with a pistol, and then took the bus. There are eleven second- and third-grade children on board."

The bus driver's voice was fierce with concern. "I shouldn't have stopped, but I thought the man needed immediate help. He was flailing his arms but couldn't seem to get up. I know it's my fault, but you've got to do something to get those kids back safely."

Ella rushed back to the truck for her cell phone, and called Justine, asking her to relay the message to the station. "They say we have no more units in the immediate area, but one way or another, I'll find backup for you," Justine said, her voice fading in and out.

"Forget backup. Get people looking for the bus!" Ella ordered as Clifford and the driver came up. "You two stay here. I'm going after Lee."

"He's not alone. There is another," Clifford warned.

"No, there was only one man," the driver argued.

Clifford shook his head. "You'll need me with you, little sister. Your quarry has help from someone even stronger than him. I sensed it, and you will, too, when you reach him. You can't go into this alone."

"If you're talking about Randall's *chindi,* you're wasting your time," Ella said, starting the engine. "I'm not worried about anything that's not flesh and blood."

"Then worry now. There's another powerful skinwalker working with him, *not* a spirit. I'm right about this, trust me. I sensed the second person's presence."

Ella knew the value of intuition. It was all too often based on information processed by the subconscious and as valuable a tool for survival as anything could be. "You'll have to stay here. We can't both leave the driver."

"I'll go with you. I'm not staying out here alone with a skinwalker on the loose." Before Ella could stop the driver, he climbed onto the back seat, sinking into the cushion with a groan.

"I don't have time to argue with you two," she said. "Get in, big brother. We're going."

Ella floored the accelerator, holding the wheel with both hands. Trucks were not known for handling ease at high speeds, but this big baby held the road pretty well. She'd already experienced that fact earlier, the hard way.

Three minutes later, at a speed near ninety, she saw the bus about a mile ahead. "I've got you now," she muttered through clenched teeth. "You can't outrun me and get away, so all I have to do is wait until you run out of gas. I'll be right on your tail the whole time."

Despite her bold words, Ella felt a tingling at the back of her neck. There was going to be trouble. She glanced at her brother. His eyes were narrowed, and he was Singing softly under his breath. He looked a million miles away, his forehead furrowed deep in concentration. Yet she knew he was aware of every detail of what was happening.

Ella slowed down to fifty, following her intuition. Suddenly the brakes of the bus squealed, and the massive vehicle turned in a tight circle, the driver's side tires leaving the road. For a hair-raising moment, she thought the bus was going to tip over.

As it finished the loop, the bus began accelerating toward them down the middle of the road, on a collision course.

Ella stared at the vehicle, her hands tight around the wheel. He was trying to force her to give way so he could make his escape. "Hang on and make sure you're buckled up!" she managed through clenched teeth, slowing the truck to under thirty-five.

"Move to the shoulder," the bus driver yelled.

"No. Not yet," she whispered. A warm, feverish glow spread over her as she listened to her inner voice.

"Swerve!" the bus driver yelled again.

Ella held the truck steady, playing the crazy game of chicken. "No. He'll turn into us. He wants us dead, and is perfectly willing to die along with us to get his way."

The bus was so close she could see Howard Lee's face clearly. His expression was one of rapt concentration. Heeding her inner voice, Ella suddenly threw the stick shift into low, stomped on the gas, and swerved sharply to the left, fishtailing up the hillside adjacent to the road. The bus would not be able to follow them there.

Glancing in her rearview mirror, Ella saw Lee try to follow. Before he could get far, the bus bogged down in the soft sand. Ella braked hard to a sliding stop and jumped out of the vehicle, shotgun in hand. As she moved down toward the bus, she saw Lee forcing the children across the road. A short distance away on that side was a steep drop-off to a deep canyon.

Ella tried to angle for a clear shot, but there were too many children and, in a panic, their movements were erratic at best. Clifford had followed, and she handed him the shotgun. "Stay here," she ordered. "I'm going around."

Ella hurried toward Lee, crossing the road quickly and taking cover in the junipers. The children were nearly at the edge of the cliff, which jutted out over the sandstone-lined canyon. The young hostages were almost all crying, too frightened to do anything except obey Lee's orders.

Ella knew Lee hadn't seen her yet. She glanced around, discovering a small shelflike ledge below the top of the cliff. It was about ten feet down and ran around to an area she could approach without being seen. There would probably be enough handholds and footholds to get to the top after that. Most important of all, the element of surprise would work for her. He'd never expect her to come at him by climbing straight up the cliff face.

Ella successfully made it to the ledge undiscovered, then inched her way around. As she reached up to start the vertical climb, she suddenly felt dizzy and sick. She gasped, trying to draw in a breath. The air around her seemed to grow thick, weighing her down.

Ella sensed someone's gaze on her. Hearing the children crying, she glanced up. Lee was staring right down at her. He'd herded all the kids to the edge and seen her when he looked down.

"I'll throw them off this mesa two at a time if you come any closer," he yelled, waving a revolver at her. He fired four times in rapid succession and she ducked, praying he'd somehow miss. None of the bullets came close. Howard was obviously no marksman.

As the children screamed at the frightening noise, anger

swept over her, mingling with frustration. Just then, she caught a flicker of movement out of the corner of her eye. It was only for an instant, but she knew Clifford was drawing near along the canyon top, hidden from Lee's view.

Suddenly the wind rose, and the junipers shook with a loud hissing sound that drew Lee's attention to where Clifford was located.

Ella saw her brother freeze as Lee stared into the trees, searching. Taking advantage of her enemy's distraction, Ella resumed her climb.

Then, over the desperate cries of the children, she heard her brother's Song. It seemed mournful and terrible all at once. Goosebumps broke out over her flesh. Ella fervently hoped the sound would rattle Lee all the way down to his socks.

Ella was halfway up when a cloud of dust rose high in the air, blasting against her, making it impossible to see more than a few feet ahead. The children started crying again, and in the next instant, she heard them running downhill toward the bus. Lee yelled frantically for them to stop. The clicking of his revolver told her Howard was out of ammo.

If her vision was hampered, then so was Lee's. Ella scrambled to the summit, the wind at her back spurring her forward.

As she reached the top, and crouched low behind a rock, the windstorm abruptly ceased. She could see the children running madly across the road along with her brother, who was urging them back onto the bus. She had only a moment to savor the sight.

Lee lunged at Ella from behind a juniper, knocking her to the hard sandstone. She rolled to one side, avoiding a punch that would have broken her nose, had it connected. Lee's fist hit solid rock, and he screamed from the pain.

"It's over for me, but I'm taking you down with me," he vowed.

Unable to reach for her pistol, Ella fought hard, delivering several blows to his face and head that would have incapacitated most attackers. But Lee's rage gave him strength and endurance. They rolled around on the ground, each trying to pin the other down. Lee's struggles were deadly as he pulled her closer to the edge of the cliff. Something hard scraped across her ribs, and she vaguely noted the massive silver buckle on Lee's new leather belt. Ella saw the danger and tried to twist free. She grabbed for her pistol, but fueled by desperation, Lee's strength grew. In the distance she heard her brother's Song. Each syllable seemed to resonate, filled with the power that came from The People's history of survival.

Then another Song rose, an evil, harsh sound from a new direction, and Ella felt the earth slipping away beneath them. They were too close to the edge! "Let go. We'll both die. The edge is about to collapse."

"Then so be it!" Lee raged.

Ella felt the deadly grip of Lee's fingers as they clenched around her hair. Suddenly the rock they were on tipped over, and Lee slid over the edge, pulling her with him. Lee released his hold on her as he grabbed in vain for a bush growing out from between the rocks.

Ella, who was second to go over, had a heartbeat longer to reach out for the same bush. As her fingers coiled around it, her descent stopped abruptly and her body slammed against the hard-packed cliff face. As Ella struggled to catch her breath, Lee's final scream of rage surrounded her, drowning out the evil Song that had helped send them both over the edge.

In the silence that followed her enemy's fall, Ella forced herself to remain calm. Somehow, she had to climb back up. She reached upward trying to find another hold. Suddenly she felt a hand around her leg, pulling her down. With a cry, she wedged her fingers between rocks and glanced down. Nobody was there. Her adversary was gone, his broken body lay sprawled on the rocks below. Was another evil, the source of the second Song, working against her now?

She'd never been prone to hysterics, though if ever there had been a time when they would have been justified, this was it. It was her imagination, it had to be. She forced herself to ignore the downward pressure on the lower half of her body. It was an illusion created by the steep drop beneath her and her uncertain footing.

As the ground crumbled beneath her one remaining foothold, she was left dangling. She struggled desperately to find a new toehold without success.

Then she heard her brother's voice from up above. "I'm here, little sister, but you need to come up to the next ledge before I can reach you. Keep going. You can do it."

Ella's hands were raw and bloody as she dug her fingers into what seemed impossibly tiny crevices in the crumbling sandstone. The pressure dragging her down increased, as did the temptation to stop fighting. Pain racked her body. Finally she found a solid place to plant her right foot.

"Keep trying!" Her brother's voice cracked through the air like a whip, encouraging her with his power.

Ella looked up. She was twenty feet or more from the top. She'd never make it. She searched for a higher handhold, but there were none. Tears of outrage and frustration poured down her face. Her body refused to fight past the pain.

"Don't give up!" her brother ordered, his will becoming part of hers.

As Ella tried to find a way to dig her fingers into the unyielding side of the cliff, she kept her body pressed to the wall of sandstone. The badger fetish around her neck dug into her skin, hard, yet warm with the blood and sweat that poured off her body.

Ella thought of the badger and its strength. She focused on the indomitable will that had always been a part of her.

As she sucked in a ragged breath, the downward pressure abruptly disappeared, and Ella felt a surge of energy washing through her. She couldn't give up. She'd come too far for that.

Ella forced herself not to look down as she pulled herself toward the ledge she knew was just above. Finally, she felt her brother's strong hands grasping her forearms.

"You're safe now," he said, pulling her the rest of the way to the top. "You've defeated the evil pulling you down."

Ella sat on the ground, relief flooding over her. Hearing rushing footsteps, she looked over her brother's shoulder. Help had finally arrived. She could see Sergeant Hobson and the children safely on the bus, and Justine was running up the hill toward her.

Justine reached them a moment later. She went to Ella's side, and helped her stand up. "Congratulations. The case has broken wide open. A warrant has been issued for Anderson's arrest. Your canary has begun to sing."

"Anderson won't worm out of this one," Ella said, walking back downhill toward the road with Justine and her brother.

As Justine took a statement from Clifford, Ella walked to the truck. When she reached the edge of the road, she saw Carolyn taking care of the wounded bus driver. "What on earth are you doing here?"

"I was at the station going over the independent lab's report with Big Ed when your report came in, so I caught a ride with Justine and Hobson when they headed out here. They didn't want to bring me, but I wouldn't take no for an answer. As the M.E., I *am* part of the police department."

"Have you been reinstated?"

"You bet. Tolino backed the hospital board to the wall and forced them to do what was right. Your hunch about him was right on target."

Ella leaned against the truck wearily as Justine came up. "It's all wrapped up now," her assistant said. "This case is in the hands of the courts."

"Not quite," Ella said. "We know a few of The Brotherhood's key players, but only time will tell if we've dealt that organization a death blow; and I'm afraid we haven't heard the last of the Fierce Ones either."

"Do cops ever win a complete victory?" Carolyn sighed.

Ella smiled at Clifford as he approached and joined them. "Evil always exists. It's part of the balance, and only by accepting that, can we walk in beauty."

Clifford smiled. "There's hope for you yet."

As a police van pulled up, Clifford and Carolyn, went to help Sergeant Hobson calm down the children.

Over the excited voices of the young, the distant howl of a

coyote rose, making her flesh crawl. Ella's hand closed over her badger fetish. The sun was sinking fast behind Beautiful Mountain. Ella looked around, studying the adjacent ridges. In the fading light, she thought she glimpsed an old woman with a cane on the opposite side of the canyon, making her way into the concealing shadows. But then she blinked, and the woman was gone, making her wonder if she'd really seen anyone there.

"The chief wants you back at the station," Justine said, interrupting her thoughts.

"On my way." Ella glanced around one last time, trying to push aside her uncertainties. It was time to let go, at least for now, and wait for fate to make its next move.

MEET THE AUTHORS

——— ✖ ✖ ✖ ———

Aimée and David Thurlo are the authors of two other Ella Clah novels, *Blackening Song* and *Death Walker.* Aimée is a native of Havana, Cuba. David grew up on the Navajo Reservation in Shiprock, New Mexico. The Thurlos have been married for more than twenty years and have been writing together for nearly that long. To date, they have published thirty-seven novels. Some of their recent works are *Cisco's Woman, Fatal Charm,* and *Her Destiny,* the first book in the Four Winds trilogy.

Aimée and David Thurlo live in Corrales, New Mexico, with a varied and ever-changing menagerie. They are a vital presence on the Internet, and can be contacted at their home page at http://www.comet.net/writersm/thurlo/home.htm. or via E-mail at 72640.2437@compuserve.com.